PENGUIN BOO

THE SECOND WIFE

Praise for Elizabeth Buchan

'Gorgeously well-written – funny, sad, sophisticated' *Independent*

'Deliciously told, with characters you warm to at once, and I loved every page' *Daily Mail*

'What a good writer Buchan is' *Daily Telegraph*

'This perceptive, beautifully written book brings fresh perspective to an age-old situation . . . For women of all ages, a poignant, unforgettable novel' *You*

'A finely written, highly intelligent romance, without any of the slushiness usually associated with the genre' *Mail on Sunday*

'Wise, melancholy, funny and sophisticated, Buchan's new novel is more satisfying than a romance' *The Times*

'Buchan deftly juggles multiple characters and plots in a perceptive analysis of contemporary life' *Independent on Sunday*

The Second Wife

ELIZABETH BUCHAN

PENGUIN BOOKS

PENGUIN BOOKS

Published by the Penguin Group
Penguin Books Ltd, 80 Strand, London WC2R ORL, England
Penguin Group (USA) Inc., 375 Hudson Street, New York, New York 10014, USA
Penguin Group (Canada), 90 Eglinton Avenue East, Suite 700, Toronto, Ontario, Canada M4P 2Y3
(a division of Pearson Penguin Canada Inc.)
Penguin Ireland, 25 St Stephen's Green, Dublin 2, Ireland (a division of Penguin Books Ltd)
Penguin Group (Australia), 250 Camberwell Road, Camberwell, Victoria 3124, Australia
(a division of Pearson Australia Group Pty Ltd)
Penguin Books India Pvt Ltd, 11 Community Centre, Panchsheel Park, New Delhi – 110 017, India
Penguin Group (NZ), 67 Apollo Drive, Rosedale, North Shore 0632, New Zealand
(a division of Pearson New Zealand Ltd)
Penguin Books (South Africa) (Pty) Ltd, 24 Sturdee Avenue, Rosebank, Johannesburg 2196, South Africa

Penguin Books Ltd, Registered Offices: 80 Strand, London WC2R ORL, England

www.penguin.com

First published by Michael Joseph 2006
Published in Penguin Books 2007
2

Typeset by Palimpsest Book Production Limited, Grangemouth, Stirlingshire
Printed in England by Clays Ltd, St Ives plc

ISBN: 978-0-141-01988-8

For Marika

'We will now discuss in a little more detail the
struggle for existence'
Charles Darwin, *The Origin of Species*

Acknowledgements

I owe many people for generously giving me their time and expertise. In particular I owe a huge debt of gratitude to Clive Sydall, Antony Mair and Sebastian Leathlean. Any mistakes are mine. I would also like to thank Janet Buck, Lucy Floyd, William Gill, Ann MacDonald, Pamela Norris, Belinda Taylor and many other friends who, as ever, gave rock-like support. To my editor, Louise Moore, and the team at Michael Joseph and Penguin, Hazel Orme, Mark Lucas, my agent, and lastly my husband and children, a big thank-you.

How It Began

On my wedding day, I got dressed in a red silk full skirt, to hide my ten-weeks pregnant figure, and a black jacket. For a considerable time I hovered in front of the mirror in the cramped bedroom of my flat, fiddling with the lie of the skirt, adjusting my makeup and wishing I could wear high heels, but pregnancy made my feet hurt. I think I was trying to persuade myself of my imminent new status: 'Mrs Lloyd'. The mirror reflected my lips shaping the words – but, of course, what I saw was the distortion. What I really saw in the mirror was 'the second Mrs Lloyd'.

Nathan hailed a taxi and we sailed off to the register office. He had worn his dark grey office suit, and had cut his hair rather short, which I disliked. It made him appear unfinished, not the worldly, sophisticated man I rated, and, since he had lost weight, underfed. He did not seem particularly happy.

'You could look a *little* pleased,' I remarked, from my side of the taxi.

His face cleared. 'Sorry, darling, I was thinking of something else.'

I watched a cyclist weave suicidally in and out of the traffic. 'We're on our way to our wedding and you're thinking of something else?'

'Hey.' Nathan reached over and captured one of my hands, which were permanently hot – another little pregnancy joke. 'There's no need to worry, I promise.'

I believed him but I wanted to drive the point home. 'This is our special day.'

He gave me one of his strong-man smiles. 'Everything's fine. And I promise I'm thinking of you.'

I nipped the flesh of his palm between my fingers. 'Well, here's a shock. The bridegroom's thinking about the bride.'

Nathan had specified 'casual' to the guests, who were eight. No fuss, he had said. No fireworks. He had been anxious not to make a big deal of the day. 'You *do* understand?' he asked, more than once, which irritated me but, pregnant and jobless, my negotiating position was limited.

When we arrived, Nathan seemed transfixed by the ugly stone office block. Inside, there was an anteroom adorned with fake panelling, crude gilding and a stand of plastic flowers in hideous pinks and blues that no one had dusted.

As we filed in, Paige rushed up behind us. She was still working at the bank, and wore a beige suit with a white blouse. There was a lick of grime on the lapel. 'You look great, Minty.' She hefted a briefcase, which bulged with papers, from one hand to the other. 'You did say not to dress up and I've just dashed out of a meeting.'

'Yes . . .'

She peered at me. 'Oh, my God, you wanted me to dress up.'

I could only stare at her, mute and uncomprehending. For, so help me, I did. I wanted Paige to be in her best Alexander McQueen and a hat that shrieked 'occasion'. After all, and after everything, I craved silk and tulle, a flash of diamonds in the ear, the hiss of champagne, the scent of expensive flowers and the welling up of emotion and excitement – the kind that stirs the guests to stand on metaphorical tiptoe, united for a moment by unselfish kindness and by the yearning to start all over again themselves.

Paige frowned. 'Where's your flowers, Minty?'

'I don't have any.'

'Right,' said Paige, and you could not fault her. 'Hold on.' She thrust her briefcase into my hand and disappeared.

Nathan beckoned me to a group in which his eldest children, Poppy and Sam, and their spouses, Richard and Jilly, were talking to Peter and Carolyne Shaker. Poppy was in black and Jilly was markedly pregnant in a denim smock that needed pressing. Only Carolyne had made an effort in a glaringly bright red dress and a white jacket.

Sam did not quite meet my eye. 'Hello, Minty.'

Jilly made more of an effort and pecked my cheek. Her long, silky hair brushed against my cheek; it smelt of shampoo and wholesome things. 'How are you feeling?' she whispered meaningfully, one pregnant woman to another.

'Fine. Very little different – apart from very hot hands, and feet that hurt.'

Her eyes raked over me. 'You hardly show, you lucky thing.'

Jilly meant the opposite. Every line of her body, with out-thrust belly, proclaimed her delight in being so obviously fecund. She leant against Sam. 'You wait. Sore feet is only the start,' she said contentedly.

Paige burst back into the room. 'Here's your bouquet, Minty. It's terrible, but it'll have to do.' She thrust into my hand a bunch of red roses, the kind that were sold at street corners by oppressed immigrant workers. They were tightly furled and only half alive.

The registrar cleared his throat. 'Are we ready?'

'The Cellophane,' Paige hissed.

I ripped it off, squashed it into a ball and left it on the table.

'Oh, Minty,' Nathan said. 'I forgot you should have flowers.'

In the restaurant afterwards, where Nathan had booked lunch, we were joined by Aunt Ann, Nathan's last remaining relative, and there was a great deal of fussing and rearranging of chairs to accommodate her wheelchair.

I observed the guests at the table. Mostly, their expressions were fixed, as if they were struggling collectively to find a way through the experience. Jilly drank ostentatiously from a glass of water, Sam's arm draped round his wife. Poppy chattered and fluttered, her Thai silk scarf round her shoulders flashing scarlet and gold. Every so often, she touched Richard's shoulder or his arm. Once, she pressed her lips to his cheek. Not once did any of them look in my direction. There was comment about my first name being Susan, a fact revealed by the registrar. For most of my life I had hated it and had refused to use it since I was fifteen, but now I went to its defence. 'What's so funny about Susan?'

Jilly and Poppy put their heads on one side. 'It's just that you're so *Minty*,' Jilly explained.

'I'm sorry you haven't got any family here,' Sam remarked, as we ate Dover sole and scallops.

'My father vanished when I was small, my mother's dead and I don't have any siblings or cousins.'

'I'm sorry.'

'I don't miss what I've never had,' I said, then added stubbornly, insistently, 'It's not so terrible.'

Sam might have said, 'We're your family now.' But he didn't.

At the end of the meal, I watched Nathan proffer his platinum credit card to pay the bill, and thought, with relief, that I wouldn't have to worry about money any more. Then I went to say goodbye to Aunt Ann. I stooped over the wheelchair, inhaling face powder and dust from her hat with its black feather. 'Goodbye. Thank you so much for coming.'

She raised a startlingly thin liver-spotted hand, on which rattled a platinum wedding ring and diamond solitaire, to touch my cheek. 'So nice,' she murmured, and I felt a rush of unexpected tears. They say cynics are the only true romantics. I was marrying Nathan without any of the true and proper feelings, only non-feelings, but I was doing it all the same. And Aunt Ann's touch was worth more than it was possible to describe.

Poppy was hovering. 'Aunt Ann, we must take you home. I promised I wouldn't let you overdo things.'

Her exhaustion and confusion obvious, Aunt Ann groped for words: 'Goodbye, Rose,' she said.

I

I have found that, for me, it is wise to have a few rules tucked inside my head and the ones currently governing my life are these.

Rule One: there is no justice.

Rule Two: contrary to a husband's hopes, a second wife does not have the *Kama Sutra* nestling in her handbag. It is more likely to be aspirin.

Rule Three: never complain, particularly if you have been instrumental in demonstrating Rule One. Which I have.

Rule Four: never serve liver or tofu. It is not clever.

Nathan and I were wrestling over the guest list for the dinner party.

'Why do we need to give one?' he demanded, from the sofa. It was a Sunday afternoon in early November, and he was sleepy after roast chicken with tarragon. Newspapers paved the floor and the room was stuffy with winter and central-heating. In their bedroom directly above the sitting room, the twins played at airports, taking off and landing with excruciating thumps.

I informed Nathan that it was necessary for his position at Vistemax to *keep going*, that I had already compiled a list of key Vistemax couples, and that it would be smart to mix them with friends.

Nathan leant his head against the back of the sofa, closed his eyes and contemplated the manoeuvres necessary to keep a career afloat. 'Been there, Minty.'

He meant with Rose.

There it was. Despite having left his first wife, Rose, for me, Nathan still measured his life with regard to that first marriage. Holidays, house decoration, even the choice of a new jumper were accomplished beneath the arid rain shadow of the past. Worse, he punished himself for what he perceived as his and my transgressions. It was a bad habit, and I had failed to nip it in the bud. In this marriage, the quality of mercy had been in short supply, and during our years together, it had been thinned, strained and darkened, like the varnish on an old painting.

My gaze drifted past the figure on the sofa to the perfectly normal London view outside seven Lakey Street. The trees seemed weighed down with grime, and the pile of rubbish outside Mrs Austen's flat opposite more than usually noxious. This type of exchange between Nathan and me had become commonplace and held no surprises. What kept me in a state of perpetual astonishment, bewilderment, even, was my miscalculation in having got myself into this position in the first place.

Never complain. 'What about the Frosts?'

Sue and Jack were Nathan's very special friends. They were also Rose's special friends but they were *not* my special friends. The reverse, in fact, for I was – Sue had been heard to say – a husband-snatcher and a home-breaker.

I couldn't deny either.

As a result, Nathan was frequently invited to their house a couple of streets away for cosy evenings but I never set foot over their threshold. What they talked about I don't know, and I never asked. (Sometimes I amused myself by imagining the conversational hole around which these special friends tiptoed.) Was Nathan disloyal? No, he needed to see his old friends – but nobody, *nobody*, appeared to note the irony in the situation: both Frosts were on their second marriage.

'Would they come, do you think?'

The hissing noise, which meant 'I don't think so', issued from Nathan, and his eyes flicked to the painting above the mantelpiece. It was of Priac Bay in Cornwall, by a Scottish artist, and rather dull. But Nathan liked it and, frequently, I caught him peering into the turquoise-paint depths of the sea at the base of the cliffs.

'No,' he said.

The outlook on the friends front was grim. 'What about the Lockharts?' They were also friends of Nathan and Rose.

Nathan sprang to his feet and removed a fleck of something from the bottom right-hand corner of the painting. 'Minty, it's no use flogging dead horses. They feel strongly . . .' He did not have to finish the sentence.

I glanced down at the list of guests, which, so far,

included only work colleagues. 'Did I mention that I met Sue Frost the other day in the supermarket and I tried to sort things out?'

'Actually, she told me,' Nathan confessed, 'but she didn't go into detail.'

I found myself inscribing two heavy underlinings on the list. 'Well, I will. I asked her why, since she and Jack were both on their second marriages, I'm banished from their court. What makes me different from them?'

Sue Frost had tapped her pink suede loafer on the ground and peered over a trolley stacked with vegetables and cleaning aids. Her cheeks had flamed in her pretty but obstinate face as she replied, 'I would have thought it obvious. I'm not the one who left my first husband. I wasn't the party who broke up a marriage.'

'So . . .' Nathan shoved his hands into his trouser pockets. He put on the face he used for tricky business meetings: unreadable. 'What did you say?'

'I said I wanted to get the situation as she saw it absolutely straight. As a second wife, Sue was OK because her first husband had had the mid-life crisis and left, while I, as the second wife and the object of the mid-life crisis, was not. I wanted to know what the position would have been if she had *driven* her first husband away.'

That amused him. He stopped looking haunted and relaxed back into the kind, clever man he was – the man who beat his chest and produced gorilla noises to make the twins laugh, and the man who had recently persuaded the Vistemax board to rethink their position on the future of newspapers. As an able man he could do both.

'And?'

'She vanished into the frozen-fish section.'

Nathan uttered a short, barking laugh. 'You won that round, Minty.'

'What I really wanted to ask her was why I'm a home-breaker and you aren't.'

Nathan met my eyes steadily. In his lay the detritus of painful history. 'I'm blamed too, Minty.'

'No, you're not. That's the point.'

His gaze drifted towards the painting, as if he were seeking reassurance in the shimmer of water, rock and cliff.

'In Sue's eyes you're still married to Rose. There's nothing I can do about that. In the complicated hier-archies of marital morality, Sue gets a tick, Rose gets sainthood, and I get the cross.'

Any trace of amusement had been wiped off Nathan's features. 'Would you prefer it if I didn't see the Frosts any more?'

In *Successful Relationships*, a manual that, in the past, I had studied diligently, it says that to bind a partner you must release them. I'm a great believer in self-help manuals – although, lately, I have found myself won-dering if they only add to the confusion by suggesting problems you didn't know you had. However, mindful of *Successful Relationships*'s teachings, I said, 'Nathan, I insist you see Sue and Jack Frost.'

I offered him the unfinished guest list – Nathan's boss

and his wife, Roger and Gisela Gard, and my boss and his wife, Barry and Lucy Helm. 'We haven't got very far.'

Before I married Nathan, I'd pictured my life so differently. Who didn't dream of a fine, harmonious household in which friends and family gathered? 'It's no use asking Poppy and Richard, I suppose? And Sam and Jilly are too far away.'

As always, Nathan brightened at the mention of his elder children. 'Poppy *is* very busy,' he said carefully, 'and I don't think Sam's due up in town for some time. And he'd probably go and see . . . his mother.'

If I had to choose one overarching objective in my marriage it would be 'get rid of Rose'. Scrape her away from the surfaces of this house, then dig deep, as she had once dug the garden, to exhume the Rose roots that throttled Nathan and me. She was everywhere, I was in no doubt of that, and her power lay in my victory and her suffering.

'Minty.' Nathan disliked it when I ignored him, which was one of my weapons. 'I'm still here.'

I turned my head. 'Don't mention Rose, then. Don't. *Don't.*'

He came over and hauled me to my feet. 'I wasn't thinking.' He placed his hands on my shoulders and looked into my eyes.

'We have to try,' I murmured. Automatically.

'Course we do.'

He smelt of vetiver and – faintly – of tarragon and garlic. Whatever went on in Nathan's head was only half my business, but there were times when I couldn't face even a tiny percentage of the mixture of disappointment and fatigue that I suspected churned within him. I craned my head back and took a good look at him. It struck me that he was very pale. Nothing a useful dinner party wouldn't put right. I reached for another of my weapons and slid my arms round his neck. 'Come here.'

After a while Nathan saw the point, which I had known he would. 'Sometimes, Minty,' he played with my fingers, 'you can be so sweet. And sometimes . . .'

'And sometimes?'

'Not.'

He wanted to say more, but he would never get it out in a month of Sundays, and there was no point in wasting more time. I placed a finger on his lips. 'Hush.'

I returned to the guest list and to my private thoughts, which were many and various – not least why it was that in such an apparently godless world, when anything went and everything possible was done, I was the object of such censure.

Later, getting ready for bed, I discovered a yellow Post-it note stuck to the back of my hairbrush. On it, Nathan had written 'sorry'.

At seven fifteen a.m. on the day of the dinner party, I picked up the phone to Five-star Caterers: 'Just checking that everything's OK for this evening.'

A voice reeled off, 'Ten twice-baked cheese soufflés, chicken with ginger in soy and sherry sauce. Bitter cherries in maraschino served with a frangipane and *pâte sable* tart.'

I had toyed with having menus printed because I relished the names of the dishes, but Paige had put her foot down. 'Nope. Not the thing.'

'Not the thing' was annoying, but I bit my lip. Paige was a neighbour and also a good friend. She had never met Rose so her relationship with me held the extra sweetness of the untainted. Paige knew what was what, and during her years as an international investment banker, she had been on the receiving end of many dinners like this one. I needed guidance through the pitfalls. Paige provided it. Enough said.

Paige had also given the thumbs-down to sticking taffeta bows on the chair backs, which, I reckoned, would be the finishing touch. 'Finish the guests off, more like.' She hooted with amusement. 'For goodness' sake, you're not a brothel.'

Yes. Someone had to tell me what was what. I knew that much.

I'm a fast learner but, as the taffeta-bows incident indicated, there were gaps in what I knew, and what I understood – puzzling, slippery points of taste and appropriateness.

Knives, forks, wine glasses . . . I checked the place settings on the dining-table, which I had laid at six thirty that morning – i.e., before the twins were up. Only the flowers were missing and I had ordered an exact match of an arrangement I had seen in *Vogue*. Hovering in the doorway, I gave the *mise-en-scène* a final sweep, and concluded that there was nothing to embarrass Nathan, and everything to enhance his reputation.

I nipped back to the table and adjusted the angle of a knife.

My watch said 7.20 a.m. Say goodbye to twins, race to hairdresser, then on to work.

Eve – twenty-two, Romanian, not a threat – was bathing the boys when I arrived home at six fifteen.

As I let myself in, the draught made the cat-flap in the back door – long since disused – open and shut with a bang. For the hundredth time, I cursed it.

'It's Mum!' Lucas's high-pitched voice. I stopped and waited.

Sure enough, Felix echoed, 'It's Mum.' I hadn't clocked in until I heard the echo, which meant everything was fine.

Upstairs, I snatched up my bath hat and put it on. I hadn't spent all that money at the hairdresser's to have the results ruined by steam.

Eve raised a moist face. She was kneeling beside the bath. 'They have so much energy, Minty.' Her eyes ranged disapprovingly over the bath hat – which I didn't mind. As long as Eve did her job, she could think of me as she liked. 'Lucas fell down this afternoon,' she said, in her awkward English.

On cue, Lucas shot a grimy knee out of the water for me to inspect. The graze had puckered at the edges, and was pretty businesslike. 'I was braver than Superman, Mum.'

'I'm sure you were, Lucas.'

At the plug end, Felix scowled. 'Lucas cried a lot.'

'Eve, did you disinfect it?'

The briskness of Eve's nod made it clear she considered the question redundant. She knew her job. Lucas was always knocking himself about. He hurled himself at life as if its obstacles – stairs, kerbs, walls – were there to be conquered. Felix was different: he watched, waited, then made his move.

The slippery bodies heaved in the scummy water. They chattered away, releasing snippets of their day.

'You look so funny, Mum.' Lucas poked Felix's leg with a foot. 'Funny, funny.'

'Out,' I ordered. 'Eve's waiting.'

Eve sat on the stool with the cork seat and Lucas clambered on to the towel spread in her lap. Felix was instantly riveted by his red plastic boat. He did not look at me. Reluctantly, I reached for a second towel and spread it over my Nicole Farhi trousers. 'OK, Felix.' A wave of water hit the sides as he ejected himself, bullet-like from bath. 'Careful.'

He paid no attention and buried his head in my shoulder, nuzzling and whinnying like the ponies he loved to read about. 'I've got Mum.'

Instantly, Lucas abandoned Eve and forced his way on to my lap too. 'Get *off*,' he ordered his brother.

Eve was watching. She liked to ticket and docket my behaviour and imagined I didn't notice. It gave her material to share with her friends, and she liked it best when I failed to rise to her strict notions of good mothering because then she had plenty to discuss.

What did Eve know?

Nathan and I had created the squirming bodies competing for space on my lap . . . the skinny limbs, the raucous bellows of laughter or distress, the endless craving for warmth and reassurance. They had been a logical consequence of my longing for that fine, harmonious household.

Yet even Eve could sense that the story required fleshing out. She knew that when I was tired or low I recoiled from the twins' *urgency*. I found it impossible to reconcile myself with their kidnapping of time and energy, their need to creep inside my mind. Then I was back in the box from which there was no exit. *Then* I took refuge in imposing strict routines, making lists, striving for perfection.

In the peace of my own bedroom, I removed the bath hat and inspected my face and hair in the mirror – the daily patrol along the border between, to quote Paige, the wife and mother who was still 'pretty sexy' and the woman who 'looked good for her age'. There was a difference.

I ran a bath. One of my first acts after the twins were born was to insist we built a separate bathroom for Nathan and me, which entailed Nathan sacrificing his wardrobe and knocking a hole in the wall.

Nathan had been appalled. 'We can't,' he said.

'Why not? Are walls sacred?' It was five thirty in the morning and the twins hadn't slept much. 'We must have somewhere to make ourselves smell nice.'

Nathan sat up in bed with Felix over his shoulder. 'We always managed before.'

We. I ignored the small word that carried such weight. I leant over and kissed Felix, then Nathan. The gesture pleased him. 'OK,' he conceded. 'New bathroom it is.'

If he was truthful, Nathan loved it – the marble, the honey travertine tiles, the glint of mirror and stainless steel, his separate basin. 'See?' I teased him.

'I take pleasure in small things.' He was smiling.

'In that case, I'll give you plenty of small things in which to take pleasure. Carpets, curtains . . .'

But I had gone too far, too fast, and the smile was quenched. 'We must be careful, Minty. Things are a bit tight.'

I kissed his mouth lingeringly. A Judas kiss. 'I promise.'

It had taken me four years, inch by inch, stealthy infiltration by sly addition, to redecorate the house – a bedroom painted in pretty yellow here, a chair re-covered there – to achieve the transformation of Nathan and Rose's house into Nathan and Minty's house.

In the days when Rose and I had been friends, when she was my boss – editor of the books section of the *Weekend Digest* – and I was her deputy, she beguiled me with her domestic tales. I can see her now: head bent over a book, or a piece of copy, hugging a mug of coffee to her chest, dropping those details into an atmosphere that snapped and crackled with other considerations. *Parsley caught a mouse. Nathan bought me a white penstemon and I planted it by the lavender. The washing-machine flooded.* I pictured the grey scum running over the kitchen floor, the scrabble to mop it up, the penstemons nodding in the breeze. I eavesdropped on the family exchanges, with all their coded allusions and easy shorthand. Poppy's challenge to her brother: 'When were you born, then?' And clever Sam's riposte: 'Before you, you dag.'

Rose's family portrait was chocolate box, framed by comfortable, warm words. Then it had been foreign to me, that pretty picture. I don't have a family and it doesn't bother me, I'd told Rose. Nor did I want children. Why hang a millstone round your neck?

Looking back, I should have insisted that she told me what she had left out. But when I asked, Rose laughed, all apology and sweetness. 'There's nothing to leave out.'

How would she couch her reply today?

I'll never know. Never again will I hustle her into a coffee shop, or accompany her on the walks she liked so much. Or pick up the phone and demand, 'What do you think?' Never again will I observe her huddled over a pile of books, sifting through them with the greed of a child let loose in the pick 'n' mix.

Between us lies the deepest and darkest of silences, sinister in its composition of pain and betrayal. And absolutely appropriate.

2

Dinner was going well. (The timetable was stuck to the fridge: '8.15 – guests arrive, 9.00 – serve . . .' A schedule was crucial to my peace of mind.)

We were ten in all, a number that ensured separate conversations could be conducted and, thus, mask any awkward little silences. The final guest list was mostly Vistemax but, in view of my *keep going* philosophy, not wasted.

The Hurleys arrived at eleven minutes past eight precisely. When I opened the front door, Martin pushed Paige, nearly seven months pregnant and large, into the hall. 'Thought you could do with some early back-up,' he murmured, as Nathan unwrapped Paige from her coat. 'And Paige wanted to check out what you were wearing.'

I flushed. 'Will I do?'

Martin studied my green, wraparound dress approvingly. 'Sure. You look great.' He touched my arm in a gesture of support and I felt as if I'd been given a million dollars.

But a little later, with the Shakers and Barry and Lucy still to arrive, Paige lumbered over and hissed, 'The dress is too tight.'

I pushed a plate of miniature blinis and caviar in the

direction of her bump. 'Yours is just as bad. Besides, your husband approves.'

'My husband wouldn't recognize taste if it sat in his lap.' She flicked a glance in his direction, and it was not an affectionate one. 'Look, you fool, this evening depends on the wives, not the husbands. You're thinking like a singleton. The wives will have taken stock of that dress. It outlines your nipples and shows you're wearing stockings.' She lifted a finger and waggled it at her temple. 'They'll be thinking, This woman's planning to sleep with my husband. In the car on the way home, the assaults will begin. Remember, husbands listen to their wives, even if they hate them.'

'I wouldn't touch any of the men with a bargepole.'

'Try telling the wives that.'

Every so often I glanced at Nathan from my end of the table. These days, candlelight suited him. It lent his eyes a sparkle and disguised his frequent pallor. I liked that. And myself in the candlelight? A woman in a green dress (hastily loosened over the bust), a trifle anxious but concealing it competently. Granted there was a string of fatigue behind my eyes and, every so often, an unseen hand tugged at it. I raised my wine glass and willed Nathan to look at me across the silver and crystal. I wanted him to register pleasure in the scene, and to know that he was pleased with my creation.

Gisela Gard sat on his right. Married to Roger, chairman of Vistemax, her little black dress, Chanel corsage and hefty sprinkling of Grade E diamonds advertised his status. Roger was sixty-five to Gisela's forty-three and gossip reported that his money had lured her into his den. 'Of course, it was his money,' Gisela was also reported to have said. 'What else? But, in return, I look after him beautifully.'

Carolyne Shaker on Nathan's left, married to his colleague Peter. She had chosen a royal blue dress – a mistake however you looked at it – and bright gold earrings, and was listening to Gisela and Nathan. Generally, Carolyne left conversation to others, and wore her silence with an expression that suggested she knew her limitations. Not by so much as a flicker did she suggest she minded that she didn't shine on these occasions. Carolyne knew where her strengths lay – in the home – and I had learnt from her too: it helps to know thyself.

Nathan said something to Gisela and turned, courteously, to Carolyne, who seemed a bit sleepy. He whispered in her ear, which made her laugh.

On Gisela's right, Peter Shaker was talking to Barry's wife, Lucy. When she arrived Lucy, who was in a complicated Boho outfit, had seemed nervous and I'd whisked her over to reliable, kind Carolyne. The latter had obviously done the trick because Lucy was responding animatedly.

'The cherries are good.' Beside me, Roger dipped his spoon into the bittersweet juice. 'I like tough skins.'

On the other side of me, Barry nodded. He had been pleased, as I had calculated, to dine with a man as powerful as Roger, and Barry's pleasure took the form of agreeing with everything Roger said. A dedicated foodie ('You should hear the fuss if I don't buy Hunza dried apricots for his cereal,' Gisela had told me), Roger had kept up the food bulletins throughout the meal. Did I know that the best cherries came from a valley in Burgundy? Or, now that they were eating more meat, the Japanese were growing taller? So practised was his conversation that it could almost have been dubbed automatic, but Roger was too clever to let that happen. His party trick was to gaze directly at whomever he was speaking to, and the listener enjoyed the illusion that they were the only person in the world. The magic was working beautifully until he let fall, 'I remember the best salmon was at Zeffano's. It was when Nathan was still married to Rose . . .'

There followed a tiny pause. My smile did not waver. 'Yes, Roger?'

Barry's radar locked on to the tell-tale flicker of tension. 'And?' he encouraged Roger.

'It was years ago, but I remember that salmon so well.' Roger steered past the minefield. 'Nathan was less enthusiastic . . . but we won him round.'

Reminded of my place, my pleasure in the evening was now spiked with resentment. Rose sat at the end of the polished, laden table, not I. Rose had chosen the flower centrepiece from *Vogue* and brought these people together. Rose's ability to soothe, her love and concern, were what the majority of the guests at my table remembered.

In such a situation, it's no use looking hopeless or weighed down by the burden of being wife number two. The best thing, I find, is to trade on through, thus emphasize how sensible and mature everyone involved is being. I maintained my shiny smile. 'Isn't it wonderful how Rose's career as a travel writer has taken off?'

'Yes,' agreed Roger. 'I saw a very good article she'd written on China – in the *Financial Times*, I think it was.'

Barry was amused. I could sense him piecing together a history – first wife, a minx, old dogs, new tricks, etc., etc. – and making such a thorough job of it that there was a good chance he would think it correct. He muttered, 'You're Nathan's second wife?'

'Yes, aren't I lucky? Not the first, but definitely the last.' The words tripped off my tongue and I made sure I included Barry in my next remark to Roger: 'Nathan and I must visit the cherry valley. I'll make him take me.'

Roger tapped a cigarette packet. 'Is it permitted?' He exhaled a plume of smoke. 'You must be the only person in the world who can make Nathan do anything. We have to work hard to convince him sometimes to come on board. It's one of his strengths.'

Suddenly, shockingly, I scented danger. 'Vistemax have had an exceptional year,' I explained to Barry. 'They've wiped the floor with the opposition.' I pushed an ashtray in Roger's direction. 'You must be so pleased. Nathan is.'

Before Roger could respond, we were interrupted by a cry from the doorway. It was Lucas, in his teddy-bear pyjamas, hopping from one foot to the other. 'I can't sleep.'

The red mark on his cheek suggested otherwise. Nathan turned round. 'Lukey!' He smiled and Lucas tumbled towards him, arms outstretched. Nathan pushed back his chair, scooped him up and settled him on his lap. 'What are you doing up, you naughty boy?'

'Naughty boy,' Lucas agreed, and settled himself against his father's shoulder for the duration. He reckoned he was in with a chance and, judging by the way Nathan was holding him, he was right.

The clatter of forks and spoons acted as a counter-point to Lucas's high voice and Nathan's deep one. This had not been included on the timetable stuck to the fridge. My gaze slid to Roger, who was observing the tender little scene with an expression that did not necessarily bode well for Nathan. This is the way the wind blows, he was thinking. This is why a man loses his sharpness, his edge.

Gisela touched the red patch on Lucas's cheek. 'Wide awake, eh?'

Lucas grinned at her, and I rose to my feet. 'Come on, Lucas.'

But Lucas had no intention of budging. I bent down and scooped him up. 'No bed, no bed,' he wailed.

I whispered in his ear and Lucas screeched, 'Mummy, don't smack me.'

'Minty!' Nathan threw down his napkin, shot to his feet and wrested Lucas away. 'I'll deal.'

He and Lucas vanished upstairs, and we heard Lucas's chuckle. My cheeks flamed, and Roger and I exchanged a long, measured look. 'Nathan's quite a hands-on father,' he commented.

'Oh, not really,' I said. 'An on-and-off sort of father,

depending on how available he is.' I switched subjects. 'Are you planning more changes this year? A new launch?'

'Sadly, even if I was, I couldn't tell you, Minty.'

Roger enjoyed his business secrets. And why not? 'Of course, Roger.' Instead I urged Barry to elaborate on one of Paradox Productions' more recent successes. When a somewhat tousled Nathan returned, I rose (NB 10.45: serve coffee) and suggested we adjourned to the sitting room.

Paige grimaced. She and I had debated whether to have coffee at the table or in the sitting room. I was never *quite* sure. Paige maintained it gave you an escape route if you'd been bored, and I said stiffly that I wasn't planning on anyone being bored. '*Ayez pitié de moi*,' begged Paige, who sometimes fell back on her international past. 'I can't move. In my present condition I'd rather be bored silly than have to move. Anyway, with my legs under the table no one can spot my varicose veins.'

I sacrificed Paige.

I showed Gisela upstairs to the guests' bathroom, a haven of brilliant white towels, Jo Malone essences and French soap in the shape of a mermaid.

'The house looks very nice.' Gisela bent forward to peer into the mirror. Her voice was warm and pleasant, and I had a feeling that she had marked me out for more serious acquaintanceship.

I adjusted the angle of a towel. 'It took a bit of time and persuasion. Nathan isn't exactly receptive to change.' It struck me that that was not a sensible remark to make to the wife of your husband's boss and I added, 'Over matters of paint.'

'Men!' Gisela smoothed back her hair. She didn't mean it – she was undoubtedly too intelligent to fall into a gender trap. 'Nathan's a tiny bit haggard.' The manicured fingers continued to pat and adjust. 'Is he quite well?'

'He caught a bug from the twins. It was a women-have-colds-men-have-flu sort of thing.'

She turned her head to check her profile. 'Even so, he's looking a little worn.'

Once upon a time I had been twenty-nine, slender, glossy. I had celebrated this condition by dressing in tight tops and pink-leather kitten heels. I squinted down at my chest to check the neckline of my dress. 'Don't we all?'

Gisela picked up the soap mermaid. 'Charming.' She returned it to its dish. 'Carolyne really shouldn't wear velvet hairbands. And Minty . . . it's a lovely dress, but I wonder if blue isn't more your colour?' The charm and lightness of Gisela's smile neutralized the criticism. She put her head on one side and exhaled thoughtfully. 'It isn't easy being the second wife . . . or the third.'

'Was it awful?'

Gisela searched for her lipstick from her tiny evening bag and applied it. 'Nicholas was very old, and I had to do a lot of nursing. It was lonely, and the children hated me. Richmond wasn't quite so old, and his children not quite so bad. In fact, we liked each other . . . until Richmond died.' She pursed her lips and the colour stained them. 'All hell broke loose over the will. We lived in Savannah in the family house, so I came over here and met Roger and, *poof*, everything was fine.' She made it sound easy, but I dare swear it was anything but. 'Don't get me wrong, Minty. I chose to do what I did.'

I ran a rapid life review through the internal projector. The resulting picture wasn't romantic, being more practical and calculating, but that was life. 'So did I.'

As we went downstairs, Gisela surprised me by saying. 'Don't you think we're realists?'

'Do you mean that we look after ourselves?'

She tucked a hand under my elbow. 'That's exactly what I mean.'

I carried the coffee into the sitting room and Martin helped me to set it down on the side table. 'We'll be off in a minute,' he said. 'Paige needs her sleep.' He was fair-haired with strongly marked dark eyebrows that gave him a permanently questioning look. If he was the slightest bit cross, they snapped together and suggested a thunderous temper, which must have helped him as deputy chairman of the bank where he had met Paige.

'You're sweet to her. Are you ready for the new arrival?'

'Paige is,' he replied. 'She's got it organized down to the last contraction.'

I gave Roger his coffee and he took a sip. 'Very good.' He replaced the cup on the saucer and his eye fell on Barry, who had cornered Gisela. 'Did Nathan protest when you returned to work after the twins?'

This wasn't a conversation that I wished to conduct at this moment for I had been thinking about changes. 'But the twins were three, and it's only part time . . . at the moment. No, not at all.'

'Of course not,' said Roger. 'He made that mistake with Rose.'

I slept badly. The cold had crept into me, and I searched my mind for sources of warmth. I pictured myself as a void filled with echoes that made no sense. I did not mind very much how others judged me, but I needed to make some connection, somewhere, somehow.

Beside me, Nathan was breathing deeply, a little laboriously, the price of a rich meal and good wine. I stroked his cheek, a gossamer touch. He stirred and moved away. My hand fell back to my side.

Around four thirty, I slipped out of bed, went down to the kitchen and made myself a mug of mint tea. When I returned upstairs, I poked my head round the door of the twins' bedroom. Felix was flat on his back, making puppyish, whiffling noises. Lucas was curled into a ball and I could just make out the outline of his spine. This was sweet, innocent sleep, such as I could never have.

Cradling the tea, I took myself up a further flight of stairs. The twins now occupied the original spare room, and its replacement, next door to Eve's bedroom, was much smaller with sloping eaves. There was scarcely room in it for one person, which suited me as I didn't wish to encourage guests.

The bed was slotted under the eave, with a painting of white roses in a pewter vase above it. Nathan was especially fond of it but, like the Cornish picture, I couldn't see much in it. I didn't come up here very often, but since we had had the new bathroom, Nathan had used the cupboard to store his clothes. A pile of his ironed shirts lay folded on the bed. I lifted them and stowed them on a shelf. As I did so, my fingers encountered a hard object amid the pile. It was a notebook, black and bound in hardboard, held shut by an elastic band now slack with use and age. I slid it off, and opened the book. Inside ruled pages were filled with the distinctive slope of Nathan's left-handed writing. Notes for the office? Financial plans? Nathan was careful with his money. Private things?

Of course they were private. I got into the bed, and cradled the mug and felt its heat trickle into my cold joints. I drank the tea before I picked up the notebook and began to read it. It was some sort of diary, and began shortly after we had married.

'5 January. Minty angry . . .' The scope for my anger was as great as anyone's, and its sources just as forgettable. What had I been angry about? True, the list of things had been accumulating. Married things. Nathan's habit of leaving cufflinks in his dirty shirts. Small change dropped from his trousers, which clogged the Hoover. His inability to tell me what he wanted for Christmas or birthdays.

I leafed back through time. '17 March: Felix and Lucas arrived. They are beautiful. Minty took it well . . .'

Did I? I hated pregnancy. I hated labour. 'Look at your babies,' cooed the midwife, and invited me to peer through a plastic incubator at two tiny frogs. I remember being surprised at the precision of my response. I had expected to tip into a maelstrom of passionate feeling, only to experience nothing, *absolutely nothing*, like that, only the sharp pain of my Caesarean scar.

'20 July: Twins thriving. Exhausted. What can I do to make Minty's life easier?'

If Nathan had asked me, I would have told him. He could have helped me search for the tenderness, the physical desire for my babies that eluded me. That would have made my life easier.

I leafed forward. '6 June [two years ago]: I would give almost anything to be walking the path above Priac, smelling the salt and feeling the wind in my face. A healing solitude.'

Then I read. '21 February [of this year]: Disappointment with oneself is a fact of life. It is something one must try to come to terms with.'

I looked up from the notebook and through the window where the darkness was just lifting over the city. How was I going to deal with this discovery? I was conscious of irritation at the revelation of Nathan's hidden inner life, and the forensic manner in which he was analysing us. I was aware that I should consider how to square this circle, and puzzle away at Nathan's mindset in order to *understand* him, but I only possessed so much energy.

'30 October [this year]: I read somewhere that most people have a secret grief, and that seems correct.'

And yet I minded about Nathan's secret grief. Its existence, its confirmation in writing, pointed to a wound, and a failure. The words spelt out the ridiculousness of our ambition to be happy, and its defeat.

31

Here was the deal. I had seen Nathan and taken him. He had talked a lot about 'new beginnings', 'freedom', 'climbing out of a box', and that had made it all very exciting. Rose had wept and grieved and gone away, leaving me to run her house and produce more children for Nathan. Before I knew it, that had constituted the main business between Nathan and me. Bringing up the children and running the house – or was it the other way round? Nathan had made a terrible miscalculation. He may have climbed out of his box, but he had jumped straight into another.

I made to shut the notebook. As I did so, I noticed the document tucked into the pouch at the back and pulled it out. It was a professional drawing of a small garden – ten metres by fifteen, according to the plan – and a compass indicated that it was south-west facing. An arrow pointed to a line of trees that bisected the space: 'pleached olive'. Other arrows pointed to plants: *humulus*, *ficus*, verbena . . . Typed at the bottom of the diagram were the words: 'Height. Route. Rest.' At the top was scribbled: 'This is it. What do you think? Why don't you talk it over with Minty?'

The handwriting was Rose's.

Downstairs, Nathan was sleeping on his back. He murmured as I got back into the bed and took him in my arms. 'Wake up, Nathan.'

After a second or two, his protests died, and I helped myself to my husband's body, as angry with him as I had ever been, as angry as he was riddled with secret grief.

3

At nine fifteen precisely, hair brushing cleanly across my cheeks and smelling of almond shampoo, I walked up Shepherds Bush Road, past two pubs – hitherto unreconstructed and raucous – that had catered for the Irish and were now undergoing rebirth as gastropubs, then past the recently repaved green. 'The Bush is the new Gate,' read the graffito on a brick wall.

Once upon a time the old United Kingdom Provincial Insurance building had been what its name suggested. These days, United Kingdom Provincial Insurance operated entirely from Bombay and the building was home to seven start-up enterprises. They shared a reception desk, coffee facilities and conversations, conducted on the stairwells, which centred chiefly on the inequities of the rent.

Some things are eternal but not, as I have discovered, the obvious candidates. The stained nylon carpets and the smell of plastic and paper in offices never change. Yet I had never been so glad to inhale a deep, plastic-filled breath as I was when I returned to work after three years at home with the twins. It notched up my pulse rate from lacklustre to viable. Nathan's response to my exhilaration, I remember, had been a little sour. The office – he stabbed the air to emphasize the point – isn't all it's cracked up to be. For all the fuss he made, you might have concluded that I, not he, worked from eight until eight five days a week, rather than the three days on which I had compromised.

Paradox Pictures was one of the numerous small independent television production companies clustering in Shepherds Bush. 'Dirt cheap rents and easy access to the Beeb and Channel 4,' confided Barry, chief executive and executive producer, when he interviewed me over lunch at Balzac's. (In the letter that accompanied my CV, I pointed out that we had both taken degrees at Leeds University, a sliver of research that had probably earned me the interview.) He cast an eye round the crowded restaurant. 'I'd say most of the Beeb are here at the trough right now. I got the sack for being a naughty boy.' His lived-in features slackened with nostalgia. 'She was *very* beautiful. Anyway, Auntie and the then Mrs Helm took a dim view, and I had to take off to the States for a time where I made *Spouse Exchange*. When I came back there had been the Thatcherite decree that the BBC was to use independents. I met Lucy. So here we are.' He held up both hands, palms towards me. 'No longer a naughty boy.'

There was a pause while we drank the wine and mourned the death of naughty boys and, by implication, naughty girls. Then Barry came to the point. 'I need ideas. The more bizarre the better. We need to reach into a younger audience. We need to think *interactive*. I need someone who knows people, who has a hinterland.'

I liked the idea that I might possess a fertile hinterland. 'My husband,' I told him, 'is chief executive of Vistemax. We entertain all the time.'

That did the trick too.

So, three days a week, I schmoozed with journalists, authors and agents, kept tabs on anniversaries and big public events. I watched television, listened to radio, read books, magazines and newspapers. I learnt rapidly that, far from being scarce, ideas were ten a penny but their implementation was a different matter. Ideas fluttered round the office but few, so few, soared.

Now, when anyone asked what I did, I replied, 'I'm a deputy development producer with Paradox Pictures,' which took a little time to articulate but was all the better for that. Certainly, it took longer to say than 'I'm at home with twins.'

'Morning,' said Syriol, the receptionist, who spoke four languages and was studiedly casual in Sass & Bide jeans with striped plimsolls. She was eating a bowl of granola with one hand and sorting the post with other. The script she was trying to write in her spare time was flickering on her screen. Thriftily, she had based it on life in a television company.

'Morning,' I echoed, picked up the stack of newspapers and headed for my office where I dumped them to read later.

On Friday we had the weekly ideas meeting and, armed with a file, I took myself off to the meeting room. It was an oblong box, with natural light and a coffee-machine. It emitted a smell that scraped the back of my throat. Barry was already *in situ* wearing a white linen suit with a black shirt, which suggested he was in an executive frame of mind. Deb, the current development producer, in combat trousers and a denim jacket, was logging his every move.

'You seem a bit pale.' Barry had looked up from the enormous Filofax he preferred to an electronic diary. He complained that it was so heavy it gave him tennis elbow, but he couldn't help it if he was an old-fashioned bloke at heart.

I took the chair next to Deb. 'It's the excitement.'

Barry grinned at me over Deb's head. As a boss, he was tough but nice, the sort of person who did not allow everyday exasperations to get to him. 'She gives a cracking dinner party. She's a wife and mother. She looks good. For God's sake, she *reads*.'

From this I deduced that Barry had gained something at our table. Yet there was the tiniest suggestion of a bared fang buried in the praise. Barry expected his employees to give their pound of flesh.

'Easy when you know how, Barry. Ask Lucy,' I said, cucumber cool.

The first idea came from a book, *Vanishing Rural Crafts*. 'It would make a series.' (Plus point: more money could be squeezed out of the television companies for a series than a one-off.) 'It would be a valuable social document with archive footage.' (Minus point: if it includes black and white film, it's likely to end up in a late-night slot.) I cited an example of a rush-basket business on the Somerset Levels. For generations the Bruton family had passed on their expertise from son to son (NB no daughters). A Bruton basket lasted a lifetime, which might have been a self-limiting market but for the success of their increasingly popular willow coffins. The quote from John Bruton was lovely: 'My job is my life. The two are bound together. Like this landscape, and the water that makes the willows grow.' I had scribbled in the margin a potential title: *From the Cradle to the Grave*.

Barry did not take the bait. 'Sounds a bit regional-telly. You might get some local funding but no foreign deals. Pass. Anything else?'

'*Women Between the Wars: A Lost Generation*'. The homework had produced: 'In 1921, there were 19,803,022 females in England and Wales, 9.5 million of child-bearing age. There were 18,082,220 men, of whom fewer than 8.5 million were of marrying age. Thus, the women were not so much lost as surplus to require-ments, which resulted in depression, low self-esteem, poverty and emigration.' I looked at Barry. 'It was a terrible collective experience of loss. Loss of expecta-tion and ideals, not to mention a comfortable future.'

Barry shrugged. 'Maybe. Who are you targeting?'

'Ben Pryce at History is planning a two-week season around the First World War. He says he's run out of Nazi stories and needs material. But the main target must be Channel 4.'

Barry gestured at Deb. 'Pour us a coffee.'

I knew then that it was a non-runner, but I ploughed on: 'One of these women, a Maud Watson, set up the Feline Rescue Association.' I read out a quote from Maud:

'"I was an old maid and a useless one for I could never have been a doctor or a lawyer. Men were stupid enough to kill themselves on the battlefield and I couldn't stop them, but I could save cats . . ."' Mistake. I should have been talking about a signature director, foreign sales and hourly rates. I should have been talking lunch.

Barry stirred the tar-like coffee. 'Half of today's audience won't have heard of the First World War.' He exchanged a glance with Deb, which excluded me.

Barry's assistant, Gabrielle, appeared in the doorway. Her Lycra top strained over her breasts and the waistband of her jeans marched across the dangerous area between her belly button and her groin. 'Barry, chop-chop.'

Gabrielle bit a glossy lip, her teeth nesting on the pink platform, and looked important. 'The meeting,' she explained, to the now five-year-old Barry. 'With Controller Two. You're due at the restaurant in five minutes.'

'I'd forgotten.' Barry jack-knifed to his feet. 'Deb, I'll hear what you have to say this afternoon.'

And that was that.

Deb swept up the plastic cups, dumped them in the bin and rubbed a tissue over the table top. 'No green lights today. We'd better have a chat, Minty. Tomorrow.' She checked herself. 'Oh, but you're not here tomorrow, are you? You won't be in till next week.' Her expression was quite nasty and she had scrubbed so hard that the table was dotted with balls of wet tissue.

*

'So . . .' Gisela arched her eyebrows '. . . Rose and Nathan are in touch.' She was giving me lunch at the Café Noir as a thank-you for dinner. We had talked long and hard, which had given birth to confidences I had not intended: I had found myself explaining to Gisela how I had discovered that Rose and Nathan were in contact. Gisela's eyes sparkled. 'Did you read the diary?'

I owed Nathan some loyalty. 'No.'

Gisela did not believe me. 'Have you talked to him about Rose?'

It had been a relief to confide in her. 'No, but I will.' I reached for my water, so stuffed with ice that I had difficulty drinking it. 'It's complicated. Nathan and I haven't got to the stage where we're each other's best friend. Perhaps that's where Rose fits in.'

'Perhaps not.' Gisela had sounded a warning note. 'Perhaps not, Minty.'

The ice clinked against my teeth and sent an unpleasant frisson through the enamel. 'Technically, can you commit adultery with an ex-spouse?'

'You think it's like that?'

'No,' I said quickly. I changed the subject: 'I'm thinking of going back to work full-time.' I recollected Deb's nasty look. 'There are tensions when you work part-time, and I never feel I'm giving it my full attention.'

'I admire you for working in an office. I could never do it – have never done it.'

'You entertain, run the houses. Not hard work? I think it is.'

Gisela spread out her hand, nails sculpted and polished, skin creamed. 'Remember, I have time to concentrate on one thing. I don't have children or a job, so I can give my all to the husband of the day. Nice. And simple.' She closed her eyes briefly. 'But tiring, from time to time.'

Her mobile shrilled. Gisela gestured towards it apologetically. 'Do you mind? It'll be Roger. He likes to check up on arrangements at about this time.' No one could accuse Gisela of shirking her duties as she ran through Roger's schedule. 'Meeting at two thirty tomorrow. Three thirty-five, you're seeing Mr Evans in Harley Street. Remember Annabel's birthday . . . And, Roger, the guests are arriving at seven o'clock sharp.' There was more in this vein, so much so that I had finished my apricot and arugula salad by the end of the call. 'Minty, I'm sorry. Such bad manners, but if I'm not on tap for Roger he gets into a state.' She did not, I noticed, turn off the phone.

I twirled my water glass. 'Can I ask you something? How did you cope with Richmond's first wife?'

'Ah.' Gisela tapped my hand. 'I didn't think about her. That was the trick. There's no safety in thinking. If one harps on about all the questionable things that one does, and I acknowledge that I do them, then one's at a disadvantage. Her name was Myra and she rescued Richmond when he was down on his luck, and they built up the business together. But she made a mistake. She forgot to treat him as a husband. So . . .' Gisela looked thoughtful '. . . it was simple for me.' After a moment, she added, 'Richmond wanted me, elderly as he was. So you see –'

The phone rang again. Gisela answered it. 'Roger,' she sounded sharp, 'I *am* having lunch.' To my astonishment, colour flamed into her cheeks. 'Marcus? Where are you? No. Not tonight. I'm entertaining.' She swivelled away from me. 'I'm having lunch with a friend. No. Yes. Soon.'

Now she did switch off the phone. 'Would you like some coffee?' The colour still danced in her cheeks and she made a show of dabbing her mouth with her napkin, then an eye. 'Mascara,' she declared, and consulted her handbag mirror.

'Is everything all right?' I watched her smooth a tiny line at the corner of her eye. 'Is Marcus one of the hostile family?'

'Marcus . . .' Gisela dropped the mirror back into her bag. She fixed her eyes on me, evidently making some kind of calculation. 'I've known Marcus all my life. He sort of . . . fits in between my marriages. Some people do, you know. You can't get rid of them.'

'*Between* marriages? Are you . . . ?'

She played with the diamond on her left hand. 'No. But there's work and there's play. Tonight at the dinner Roger and I will give, there's a good chance that I'll be a little bored by the person sitting next to me. But I will not suggest it by so much as a flicker, and I will make that person feel good about themselves, and it will benefit Roger.' The coffee had arrived and she glanced down at it. 'I never confuse work and play.'

41

Gisela had been exceptionally indiscreet and I was curious to know why. Across the table, I observed the expertly tinted lids mask the knowing eyes and the equation was solved. It was simple, even for one whose mathematical skill was limited. Gisela knew perfectly well that her secret was safe with me because her husband was my husband's boss.

By mutual consent we moved on to safer subjects – the Gard house in France, Roger's clutch of directorships and the rumour that Vistemax was being eyed by a German conglomerate. The Chelsea house was in the process of redecoration, and Gisela was fretting over the colour schemes. 'Did I tell you that Maddy Kington, who's advising me, has run off with the builder on the last house she worked on? She's now living in a bungalow in Reading. A case of *l'amour du cottage*. What do you think the *cottage* is like?'

I returned to the office knowing that, under Gisela's Chloé suit and the matching Bulgari jewellery, the woman had worked out to the last flutter of those mascaraed eyelashes what was necessary for her survival.

I let myself in at the front door of number seven and braced myself.

Sure enough, Lucas appeared at the top of the stairs, half in and half out of his trousers. I put down my bag, and went up as he launched himself at me. I picked him up and carried him into the bedroom where Eve was battling for supremacy with Felix. Lucas nuzzled my neck, damp little lips nibbling. Then he wriggled down and dived towards Eve, who seized the moment to haul off his trousers.

A fully dressed Felix was standing by the window that overlooked the street. He turned round. 'Mummy, there's a poor cat out there. I think he wants a home.'

I went over to inspect the scene. 'That's not a poor cat, Felix. That's Tigger. He belongs to the Blakes, you know that.'

'But he *looks* lost.' For some time now, Felix had been begging for a kitten. 'If he was lost and came here, Mum, he'd sit on your knee. You'd like that and he could go out of his special door.'

I stroked the thin little shoulders. 'I don't like cats, Felix.'

He fixed a bright blue gaze on me. 'Daddy says we can have one.'

'Did he? When?'

'Last night.'

'You were asleep when Daddy came home last night.'

Felix discovered that discretion was the better part of valour. He dropped his trousers and stepped out of them. 'It *seemed* like last night.'

I sighed.

Half an hour later, they were settled on either side of me as I read their bedtime story. '"Once upon a time, there was a big jungle where it was very hot . . ."' Felix's thumb had sneaked into his mouth and I removed it. The illustrator had gone to town. There were scarlet and blue parrots, and pale beige monkeys in the trees. On the ground, he had drawn in a scurry of ants, an anteater with a long, businesslike snout and, tucked into the left-hand corner, the sinister coils of a boa constrictor.

Lucas pointed to a monkey. 'His eyes are as big as yours, Mummy.'

'"The ants were very good at keeping house,"' I read. '"But along came the anteater and ate them all up."' The illustrator provided graphic detail and the boys shrieked. '"Afterwards he became very sleepy, and forgot to look round."'

'Ohhhh . . .' said Felix. 'The snake's squeezing him.'

Downstairs the front door opened and shut. Nathan's briefcase hit the hall floor with a clunk. Eve ran up to her bedroom and, presently, the sound of rock music floated down.

On the final page, there was a swoop of striped fur and a glint of bared fangs as the tiger leapt on to the snake.

'Mummy,' asked Felix, 'does everybody always eat everybody else?'

'Yes.' Lucas bared his teeth. 'Like this.' He sank his teeth into his brother's arm.

Nathan arrived in the mêlée and roared for order. I fled downstairs where I took a ready-made dish of chicken breasts and mushrooms from the fridge, shoved it into the oven and set the timer. Eve had done the laundry so I picked up the basket and took it upstairs to the landing where I had set up the ironing-board.

Unless Eve stepped in, Nathan did his own shirts

and was frequently sighted on the landing. He had burnt himself once, come to find me and held out a hand on which a red strip glowed. 'What do I do?'

I held his hand under cold water, made him a cup of tea and asked every hour or so if he was feeling better. For days afterwards, I caught him examining it, and eavesdropped on his phone conversation to Poppy: 'It could have been very nasty.' In due course, the scab fell away leaving a scimitar-shaped scar. 'Poppy tells me,' Nathan was pleased with the information, 'that this kind of burn is listed in medical textbooks as "Housewife's Syndrome".'

I scrutinized my unscarred wrists. 'What does that make you, Nathan?'

'Experienced at ironing,' he replied evenly.

I returned downstairs. Nathan was not in the study, so I went into the sitting room. He had drawn up a chair by the french windows and was staring out into the darkness towards the lilac tree. He was quite, quite still.

The hairs on the back of my neck prickled. In the kitchen, the timer shrilled. I took a step into the room. 'Nathan?'

He sighed, stirred. 'Yes?' He looked at me. 'What do you want?'

After supper Nathan rolled up his shirtsleeves and tackled the glasses that were too delicate for the dishwasher. It was late, the heating had gone off and gooseflesh colonized my arms.

Nathan worked in his usual methodical way, running fresh hot water into each glass and setting it on the draining-board. I tipped the hot water into the sink, rubbed them with a cloth and placed them on a tray.

'Nathan, what would you say if I went back to work full-time?'

'That again,' said Nathan.

'That again,' I echoed.

Years ago Timon, my boss, had called me into his office at Vistemax. On the door, a plaque read Editor, *Weekend Digest*. I remember in particular the emphatic curve of the 'D'. Timon, who modelled himself on Gordon Gekko, was in a pinstriped suit and braces. 'Look, we want you to take over from Rose.' He had never bothered much with preliminaries.

My skirt was short, the skin of my legs was buffed and polished. My heels were high, my hair lustrous with youth. With the aid of kohl and grey eye-shadow, my eyes were darkly inviting. I had dreams of domination – not the sexual kind, but of being able to manage my life effortlessly. 'Are you sacking Rose, Timon?'

He sent me his best Gekko look. 'You know perfectly well that that's what you've been angling for.'

The previous evening, Nathan had slipped into my bed, shuddering with emotion. He had left Rose. At that point he had had no intention of marrying me, but he craved the transcendence of the love affair. He gazed so deeply into my eyes that he was in danger of X-raying my skull, and I grew uncomfortable with the intensity. Nathan was funny, tender and much more

46

polite than I had been used to in my lovers. 'Do you mind?' 'May I?' As we moved this way and that on my cheap, inadequate double bed, sealing his arrival, I told myself that Rose had not deserved to keep him.

Timon drew a perfect circle on his notepad. 'Six months' probation. Yes or no?'

'Yes.'

I quit his office high-wired with nerves and exhilaration. Abraham Maslow had been correct when he drew up his pyramid and formulated an individual's hierarchy of need: when food, warmth, safety and sex had been seen to, it was vital to have the respect of colleagues. And respect for oneself, of course.

Six months later, I received one of those letters: 'Your probationary period has now run to its close. While we have appreciated your efforts on the Books Pages, we have decided not to appoint you. Perhaps you will consider the alternatives . . . etc.'

This time Timon didn't bother to call me into the office.

It took me a while to decide where to file this record of my failure. Eventually, I slotted it into 'Family History' in Nathan's immaculate files, fitting it between – chronologically – the photographs of Poppy's surprise wedding in Thailand, and the christening of Jilly and Sam's Frieda. Nathan demanded to know why I had put it there, and I told him there was no point in not facing up to the fact that I'd been sacked. He lost his temper, cursed Vistemax and raged round the room. I watched him, my heart galloping under my pregnant bump. For

Nathan, life was no longer obedient and tidy, and his family had lost its shape. I knew then that his regrets were for the loss of symmetry as much as his guilt at having cut it into bits.

Nathan placed the penultimate glass on the draining-board. Foam flecked his forearms, and his fingers were rosy. 'Your timing, Minty. It's late.' Pause. 'Why?'

Again, I recollected Deb's nasty expression. 'I don't think part-time works.'

He pulled out the plug. The greasy water churned away. 'I know it doesn't, but the boys need you. It seems to me that you have a good balance with what you've got.'

'I *need* to work and I think I'd do better at Paradox if I was full-time.'

He nodded, and wiped down the draining-board with a cloth. 'You see that as your priority?'

'I do. It'll be OK, Nathan, I promise. It's not so difficult. Hundreds of women do it.' I slid my arms round his waist and made him turn to face me. 'Surely you're not surprised?'

'No.' He moved out of my reach. 'I had an idea you might be thinking along those lines.'

Why hadn't he *said* something? 'Don't make me sound like a monster who abandons her children. I need to do something properly. You do see?' I thought of the ideas landing in my lap. I would nurture them, make them grow and watch them fly.

'Don't you put your heart and soul into your sons?' Nathan gave me a long, slow appraisal, in which all our differences were reflected. 'I'm tired.' He rubbed his eyes. 'Let's go to bed.'

I tried to read beyond the set look on his face. What could I say to dissolve them? Somewhere – and I could put my finger on it – I had lost my hold on the essential Nathan, the one who had tumbled so willingly into my grasp.

I turned off the lights one by one, and the kitchen slid into darkness. 'I've decided, Nathan.'

'Well, then,' he said, from the doorway, 'you've decided.'

'Oh, for God's sake!' I said. '*Don't* make it sound as if I plan to murder you all.'

With that he swung back to me. 'And you,' his anger broke through the fatigue, 'are never satisfied.' He checked himself and when he spoke again it was with a low, wooing voice. 'Minty, why can't you just get on with what we've got? It's good enough, isn't it?' He pulled me to him and buried his face in my hair. 'Let's not quarrel over this.'

Quarrelling spelt another sleepless night. It meant what the self-help manuals called 'a session to settle the issues'. It meant the whole question of my work spiralling from a minor problem into a nuclear disaster. I kissed Nathan's cheek. 'Let's not.'

4

Last night Rose was on television. Granted, it was one of the lesser-known digital channels, but still . . .

Nathan was at a Vistemax dinner, one of the many in the run-up to Christmas. On those occasions, he rolled home smelling of cigars and brandy, often with a chocolate mint in his pocket. 'Mints for Minty.' Tender, and pleased with himself, he would urge me to eat this fruit that had fallen from the tree of corporate life.

In the interim, I sat on the sofa with a tray in my lap and the opening credits of *Rose Lloyd's Wonders of the World* for company. The twins were asleep and Eve had gone out.

I had known about the programme. Poppy had made a point of telling me about it when she phoned to ask us to Sunday lunch. 'It's so exciting. Mum put up this idea of presenting her Seven Wonders of the World, and they let her have more or less free rein.' With my experience of television production companies I knew this was an exaggeration, but you could never accuse Poppy of forgetting whose side she was on. 'She's been all over. It's amazing.'

There was a pause and I said, 'That's wonderful.'

Poppy weighed my sincerity, evidently found it acceptable, and rattled on: 'Lunch, then. It's our anniversary so we thought . . . It's great being married, isn't it?' Having fallen into the verbal equivalent of a quicksand, she had changed the subject and inquired about Felix's recent stomach upset. She ended the conversation by saying, 'One o'clock. But, Minty, if you feel you want some time to yourself, which I'm sure you do, just send Dad and the twins over.'

I hadn't intended to watch Rose's programme. No, really. But here I was, eyeing the opening credits over a plate of grated carrot, sliced tomato and ultra low-fat salad-dressing.

How long was it since I had seen Rose? Two, three years? No matter, for in my case, *seeing* was irrelevant. You don't have to see someone to know they're there, and Rose and her shadow were sewn to me as securely as Peter Pan's had been to him.

Unable to make up my mind if I wished her withered and bony, which would have added to my guilt, or flourishing, as she appeared now, I scrutinized every inch of her. Rose looked wonderful, like a woman in charge of her life and unencumbered, which, if irritating to anyone struggling with encumbrances, let me off the hook. If Rose could look *that* good, she wasn't suffering and – perhaps – the balance had evened out a little. On the other hand, I reminded myself, this was the woman who had been discussing garden plans with her ex-husband, who happened to be married to me.

Rose's first wonder turned out to be hidden in a Polish salt mine. In combat trousers and a thick jacket, she led the viewer down a tunnel and, every so often, the camera panned over the figures and animals carved by the miners into the walls. 'This unicorn is fourteenth century,' she said, in voiceover. 'And this is a bas-relief of a church, and was probably done as a record during a period when churches were being destroyed. In making these carvings, the miners found relief from boredom and fear. They also gave themselves something beautiful to look at.' She went on to describe that they had worked by lamplight with the crudest of tools. Apparently, the rock crystal possessed special molecular qualities that helped to preserve the carvings, and each had accrued its own set of stories and myths. The camera settled on a figure in a long coat and hood. 'This is the butcher of Kransk who lured maidens into his shop.' The focus switched to a man on a horse. 'This is the knight who reputedly haunts the local forest and whose horn is heard on summer evenings.'

Rose had always preferred fiction to non-fiction. 'Novels contain the real truths,' she had once argued, in the calm way that had annoyed me because it was so *settled*. I could never budge her from that position – and now? Now I never will. For myself, I stick to the self-help and makeover manuals – which, when I first met him, Nathan said was *so touching*. He couldn't be doing with fiction either. I don't think he has read a novel for, oh, at least fifteen years.

I pushed aside the tray, took off my shoes and tucked my feet under me.

The camera focused on Rose's face, now fretworked by shadows. But she still looked wonderful. 'The real treasure of the salt mine, the one I have come for, lies further down this corridor . . .' I followed her progress along the passage and into a vault whose walls blazed with pinpricks of light. 'Here,' her excitement infected even me, 'is the Madonna of the Salt. Work began on her in the fifteenth century, and legend has it that she was based on a nun from the convent of St Caterina who died after experiencing visions of Mary, the Mother of Christ. Each year, the community celebrates the statue's reputation for protecting mothers with an underground candlelit procession and women, who are not normally allowed inside the mine, come with their babies to be blessed . . .' She gestured with her right hand, and the large gold ring she wore slipped down her finger. 'The Madonna of the Salt may be out of sight but she is very much a presence in the town. She is referred to as the "hidden mother". Incidentally, the phrase "hidden mother" is also used for brides. For obvious reasons, no one may touch the Madonna but, as I stand here in front of her, I'm finding it difficult not to reach out as she's so lifelike . . .'

That was enough. More than enough. I reached for the remote and switched Rose off.

That Poppy had never accepted me, and doubtless never would, bothered me not a jot. Well, not much. That she had only to pout her red lips and Nathan went running did. 'She's a good girl,' he had told me, more than once. 'Her heart is absolutely right.'

Nathan did not tolerate criticism of his children. Not

one word – however tactfully I went about it – which I considered misguided. We could all do with a little, especially children, but when it came to Poppy and Sam, Nathan retreated to a locked, soundproof chamber and no amount of knocking would make him open the door.

Poppy's heart might have been made of the best-tempered Toledo steel, but she was often *wrong*. For instance, it had been unkind to wear black at our wedding, and to persist in making her feelings about me so clear even now was divisive. When Nathan left Rose for me, Poppy spat defiance at her father: 'I never want to see you – or that woman – again. *Ever.*' Floating on a tide of moral certainty, she had reduced him to shivering and weeping. 'She called me an old goat,' he confessed to me. 'An *old goat.*'

Poppy and Richard had made the transition from flat to large house in a disgustingly short period of time. Richard had made a lot of money in 'strategy' and Poppy spent it. The house was Edwardian, spacious and newly refurbished. The windows and paintwork were pristine. The front garden had been designed by a professional. It featured box and carefully graded grey stone. An olive tree in a blue ceramic pot stood in the centre.

The door was flung open and there was Poppy. 'Dad!' she cried, interposing herself between Nathan and me. 'How lovely.'

Father and daughter were very alike. They had the same colouring, and facial structure. Naturally Poppy was modelled more delicately – her waist was tiny, and

I found myself pulling my pink cardigan edged with ribbon down over my hips. Underneath I wore a lacy half-cup bra that was digging into my flesh. Before the twins, a half-cup bra fitted like a second skin but, these days, I was bothered by its secret chafe. No longer the student, Poppy was groomed, highlighted and wore contact lenses, never glasses. Yet she had never lost her short-sighted habit of peering at you, or her quickness, or her tendency to outbursts. She grabbed her father's hand and carried it to her cheek. 'It's been ages. I've missed you, Dad.'

Nathan put his arm round his daughter and glowed.

'Hallo, Minty,' Poppy said, at last. Her gaze veered past my shoulder. She broke into a huge smile and opened her arms. 'Twins! I've been counting the minutes.' She swooped down and drew them close to her.

'I've got red socks on,' Lucas informed his half-sister.

'And I've got blue ones.' Felix brought up the rear.

'I'm wearing socks too,' Poppy hoicked up her trouser leg, 'with spots on. Now, boys, I have an important question to ask you.'

Felix knew exactly what was coming. 'No,' he said. 'I haven't.'

Poppy held them tight and pushed her head between theirs. 'How naughty have you been? Tell me everything.'

There was much whispering and muttering, and Poppy giggled and said, 'Felix, you're tickling my ear.'

Eventually she pronounced, 'Is that all?' Then she said gravely, 'I can be *much* naughtier than that.'

Lunch was a gigot of lamb cooked with flageolet beans and garlic. NB Flageolet beans are a useful, sophisticated vegetable. Half-way through, I glanced at Nathan. He was talking about oil prices, but there was an abstraction about him, a suggestion of discomfort, because every so often his eyes squeezed shut.

Did Poppy notice? While she talked, she fiddled with her expensive crystal necklace – the leather thongs, feathers and beads she had loved to wear when I first met her had been long banished. It was beautiful and she caressed it reverently. When she thought no one was watching, her gaze rested on her husband and there was no doubt of her adoration.

Richard appeared unconscious of his wife. He had settled in to enjoy himself – which he showed every indication of doing. He and Nathan had moved on to detailed discussion of hedge funds, the twins were concentrating on their ice-cream and I was behaving myself.

Poppy seemed restless and had disappeared more than once into the kitchen. She jumped up again, this time to refill my water glass. 'Daddy and Richard are boring for England.' Her eyes rested indulgently on them as she cast around for some point of contact with me. 'How are your friends, Minty?'

'Oh, Paige is fine. About to have her third baby.'

Poppy put down the jug on its mat and wiped away a minute spot of water from the table. 'She gave up her very high-powered job, didn't she, to be with the children?'

'She made the sacrifice.' I spoke lightly.

Poppy's long eyelashes beat down over the short-sighted eyes. 'Women just don't know which way to go.'

'Isn't that sloppy thinking? All we have to do is choose.'

'But it's so *complicated*.'

True, but I was reluctant to yield a point to Poppy. Furthermore, she was spoiling for confrontation. Nathan was watching me. Please, he begged silently. No arguments. Why Poppy should escape censure for some of her sillier statements, I would never fathom, but I did the right thing and, conversationally, ducked. 'How are things at work?'

Poppy used to work in publishing but recently she had astonished her family by taking a job in a firm that imported exotic candles from China and sold them through upmarket shops. 'Fine, fine, fine. The mad Christmas push is still going on. So mad, sometimes, I have to help with the packing.' She sketched an imaginary box with her hands. 'I like that. I like physically handling something, and the colours and scents are exquisite.' She added, 'As a culture, we're not hands-on enough. We don't like to get our hands dirty.'

Richard had been conscripted into telling the twins a story. Lucas was snorting with laughter, but Felix was puzzled, I could tell. His expression meant that he was questioning what he was hearing. 'The big brown bear,' said Richard, crooking his fingers and placing them at either side of his head, 'gobbled up the wizard.'

'Wizards don't get gobbled,' said Felix, flatly, and I rejoiced in his capacity not to be taken in.

Richard lowered his hands. 'I can't make you believe me.'

Lucas shouted, 'I believe you! I believe you, don't I, Mummy?'

I was about to reply, 'Of course you do,' when I met Felix's anxious eyes, and saw that he was terrified of being shown up. Nathan sent me the tiniest shake of his head. 'You can believe what you wish, both of you,' I said.

'Of course you can,' said Richard, all good humour, but with the unease of someone who was not truly at home with children.

Felix slid down from his chair and hurled himself at me. I ran my fingers through his hair, relishing the texture of his tufty curls. His breath was scented with garlic, his body pressing mine. Whether I liked it or not, the connection between him and me flowed up through my fingers.

After a few seconds, Lucas climbed down from his chair and leant against Nathan in imitation of his brother.

'Twins,' Poppy reproved them. 'We haven't quite finished.'

'Leave them,' said their indulgent father.

'But you mustn't let them be spoilt.' Poppy laid a hand on her father's shoulder. 'Not even a teeny bit.' She shook her head and the crystal necklace glinted very satisfactorily indeed. 'You mustn't spoil them, Dad.'

'They're *not* spoilt,' I said crossly. 'Far from it.'

For a second or two conversation was suspended. Richard threw in a diversionary tactic. 'Are you going on holiday this year?' He managed to sound so interested that the tension was broken.

Grateful to him, I sipped my wine and assessed the room. To her credit, Poppy had got it right. A striped wallpaper in old rose and gold, comfortable chairs, flowers. The effect was simple and muted, and I wondered if I had overdone the dining room at home. Was the effect too crowded? Had I tried too hard? I decided that the Chinese figurines should go.

Later, I went up the freshly painted and carpeted staircase to the bathroom, past a shelf of photographs, all framed in the same way. And there was Rose – *of course* – in shorts and strappy sandals, sitting at a café table in what seemed to be a Mediterranean port. The sun was shining, and the scene exuded a shimmering iridescence. Leaning back in the chair, she was inclining her face to the camera, a mark of trust, and a smile played on her lips. One hand held a coffee cup, the other rested in her lap. Tenderness was apparent in the composition of the photograph by the unseen eye. From the bottom of my heart, I envied Rose her ease, and the sensation of hot sun on her arms and legs.

Coming up behind me, Poppy said, 'That one of Mum was taken last year on Paxos.'

'I saw the programme the other night. It was very good.'

'Yes, Mum's brilliant.' Poppy was poised between challenge and the good manners she imposed on herself as hostess. The latter got the better of her. 'Which bathroom do you want to use?'

I murmured that I didn't mind. As she led me to the second guest bathroom, we passed a small room in which a computer terminal was switched on. The screen-saver showed brightly coloured fish darting about. When I returned from the bathroom, the screen read, 'Poker On Line. Game Five.' Someone had been in there.

Before we left, I sought out Poppy, who was stacking china in the kitchen. 'Thank you so much for lunch,' I said and, then, surprising myself, 'Is everything all right?'

She cast a glance at the crockery, and her lips tightened. We didn't say a word but she knew I'd seen the on-line poker. Then she fixed me with defiant eyes. 'Absolutely,' she said. 'Couldn't be better.'

As we drove home in the late afternoon, Nathan touched my thigh. 'I know you've tried with Poppy.' I must have started because he added, 'Am I such a pig? Do you think I don't notice?'

'You're not a pig.' I looked out of the window, unsure how to respond. I had grown used to saying nothing. Anyway, the silences that characterized Nathan's and my life together were deceptive: they were noisy with the unsaid. The London streets rolled past, revealing their Sunday aspect – serviceable acres of Tarmac and city trees that struggled to survive.

The interior of the 4 x 4 required cleaning, and smelt of the cranberry juice that one of the boys had spilt in the back. NB Put on the list for Eve. I searched my bag for a tissue. 'Poppy and I rub along.'

Nathan's hand tightened on my thigh. 'I wasn't thinking about Poppy when I married you.'

It was a small concession, but I felt a sudden comfort and pleasure in his ratification of my place in his hierarchy. In my handbag, my fingers encountered a sucked boiled sweet that Felix had discarded and I had rescued from the car seat. The stickiness, and the fact that it was in my bag, which I liked to keep immaculate, instantly banished the feel-good factor and I said, more sharply than I'd intended, 'You married me because you thought I'd make you happy. I don't think you are happy. And I don't know what I can do about it.'

Nathan stared straight ahead. 'You read my notebook, didn't you?'

'Yes.'

'You shouldn't have.'

'Perhaps not.' I could hear the sound of many doors banging shut in Nathan's head. 'Nathan, we should make time for a discussion.' I can't pretend that I said this with urgency and conviction, but I thought I should try.

'Not here.' He jerked his head at the back, where the twins were making their favourite aircraft noises.

'Of course not. What do you take me for?'

We halted at traffic-lights, and the occupant of a small Fiat shook his fist and pointed to the poster on his back windscreen: '4 x 4? Y?' The lights changed. Nathan drove into Lakey Street and parked. 'Minty, the note-book was private.' He rubbed his forehead. All the same, I detected a frisson of . . . relief? 'I can't trust you not to pry.'

'What, Mummy?' interrupted Lucas. '*What*, Mummy?'

'Maybe you can't.' I left it like that, swung out of the car, released the twins from captivity, and exhumed spare clothes, toys and the books without which Felix never went anywhere. Thus burdened, I walked up the path behind my husband and sons.

A little later, Nathan said, 'I need some exercise.' He had changed into a pair of worn corduroys and a checked shirt with frayed cuffs.

I was unpacking the twins' toys and working out what to give them for supper. 'A walk? Take the boys, will you?'

'I think I'll have a go at digging the garden.'

'Digging the garden?' Wooden engine in hand, I whirled round. 'You haven't done that for years.'

'All the same,' Nathan stuck his hands into his pockets, 'I think I will.'

The twins' football sessions had turned the lawn into a Slough of Despond. I watched Nathan pick his way across it and haul a fork out of the garden shed. From the set of his shoulders, he was perfectly happy, and it was a fair bet that he was whistling. He began to dig under the lilac tree and, after a while, earth was piled beside him.

Half an hour later, I took him a mug of tea. The

dark was galloping in, it was chilly and Nathan's shirt was damp with sweat under the arms. He wiped his hands on his trousers. 'Good girl.'

'Why the interest in the garden all of a sudden?' The question was redundant because I already knew the answer.

He drank some tea. 'It used to be beautiful.'

'You've been thinking of Rose,' I accused him, 'haven't you? You've been talking to her. That diagram I found in your diary. Was it for this garden?' I gestured at the broken fence, the tangle of grass, the leafless lilac. '"Height. Route. Rest." Was it for here?'

'*Don't*, Minty,' Nathan said heavily. 'We don't discuss Rose. Remember?'

'About the diary –'

'Forget it. It's mine. *Private*.' His brows twitched together.

'Are you all right?'

'Fine.' His finger beat a tattoo on his chest. 'Bit of a pain. I ate too much.'

In chapter three of *Coping with Life Strategies* (currently beside my bed), the author recommends cognitive behavioural therapy for tricky problems. If a bad thought recurs to the point of damaging one's well-being, it's best to avoid it, using thought-evasion techniques. Weary to the bone with marriage, I bent down and plucked a trailing white root from the pile of earth, and let it dangle from my fingers.

I thought hard of Paradox's Monday agenda. I conjured up the Chinese figurines, whose days were numbered in the dining room. I thought about the fish pie I had taken out of the freezer for the twins' supper.

Failure.

I turned back to Nathan. 'Why on earth did I believe you when you said you came to me with the sheet wiped clean?'

I should have kissed him, and prevented him answering. Regrets are a waste of energy, I should have pointed out, stopping his mouth with that ungiven kiss. I should have talked about anything but this.

Nathan wiped his upper lip with the back of his hand, leaving an earth moustache. 'There's no point in fighting over something you can do nothing about, Minty.'

I gave up. Memories do not obey commands. You cannot pronounce that the past is in the past. It is in the present with you, dug in.

I left him to it.

I went inside, fed the children and put them to bed. Then I gathered together my notes and files and went up too. On the kitchen table I left a Post-it note: 'Get your own supper.'

5

'Hey, Minty.' Barry's summons was issued via the internal phone. 'We need you.'

I was flicking through the daily papers, the phone between shoulder and neck, a pose I found useful for suggesting that I was engaged on top-whack activity. Lately I had noticed that my shoulder and upper arm were stiff and ached. Nathan laughed when I explained why and murmured that he'd missed a trick.

'Can you wait while I answer this call, Barry?'

'No,' he said. 'OK.'

The message was unmistakable. When I arrived at his office, Gabrielle and Deb were ensconced on the super-sized sofa, wedged so far back that their feet were barely touching the floor. From his desk, Barry loomed a telling couple of feet over them. He was in a leather blouson jacket and chinos. A white silk evening scarf was draped round his neck, and when he raised his arm, a red Kabbalah wristband was prominent. His eyes were sharp and intelligent. He held up a green plastic enve-lope and kicked off: 'There's a mass of stuff in here about middle age. What is it? Who is it? The *girls* agree that it's worth a look, but will it pull together?' Without a mitigating shred of irony, he handed the dossier to me. 'The consensus, Minty, is that this one's yours.'

Gabrielle and Deb exchanged a look. 'Gabrielle and I don't feel we know enough,' Deb pointed out.

A small but significant note sounded in my head. 'And I do?'

I could choose any number of metaphors to explain the transition from imagining you're one of the girls to knowing you're not. Depending on my mood, they would make me laugh or weep. In this case I would decide which later.

Deb shook back her long, wavy hair – very North London, Pre-Raphaelite hair – and the gesture suggested (it was intended to) unfettered vision and youthful bold-ness that knew *exactly* where it was heading. Gabrielle focused on Barry, who, as usual, was pretending not to notice.

'I sense possibilities here.' Barry was passing me the baton. 'I think you could deal nicely, Minty.'

I skimmed the first paragraph of an article from the *New Statesman*. 'The social and cultural emphasis of youth has resulted in a neglect of the middle years. We have more than sufficient cultural and financial data on youth and, to an extent, on the old. But what do we know about the important phase between the two?'

An urgent phone call took Gabrielle out of the room, which released Barry for proper thought and the 'creative' discussion that followed. Was middle age defined by behavioural habits? (Avoiding danger? Inability to sleep in? Caffeine intolerance? Regular checking of the bank balance?)

Deb tapped a Biro on her clipboard. 'I wouldn't know.'

Barry dropped a small rocket. 'Or is it when people discover, or rediscover, faith?'

'Good heavens!' She sounded appalled. 'Really?'

Barry retracted. 'Perhaps not. Maybe middle age is defined financially, when the mortgage is paid off.'

Deb swept back her hair and anchored it with a hand, exposing her smooth, unlined forehead. 'Middle age is forty?'

'Fifty.' Barry was firm.

'Oh? OK.' She sounded now as though she'd never heard of fifty. 'You think?'

Not once during this exchange did either Barry or Deb look fully at me.

'Minty, have a word with your friends.' Barry closed the meeting. 'People who know. What do they think about middle age?'

'I've hunted out a few statistics that might help,' Deb said kindly. She handed me a sheaf of papers, her hair mimicking the pliant, supple movements of her body. 'Maybe you could go through them during your days at home.'

The following morning, I came in early, when I knew Barry would be in the office, and presented him with a memo detailing why Paradox Productions would benefit from hiring me full-time. I had dressed carefully in linen trousers, a camisole that exposed a hint of cleavage and a tight denim jacket.

At home, his wife's thank-you postcard of a Matisse silhouette in brilliant blue was still pinned to the kitchen noticeboard – 'Barry and I thought the dinner excellent . . . PS Could I have the recipe for the chicken?'

Barry listened to what I had to say. Then he tapped his finger on his Filofax and spoke pleasantly and reasonably: 'Not sure, Minty.'

Any minute now the phones would go mad, and Barry's focus would switch. I had always believed in being straight. 'I have everything you need.'

'Ye-es . . .' Barry was still reasonable. 'Don't take this the wrong way, darling, and I'd like to help, truly I would.' To show willing he skimmed the main points of the memo. 'You do have a lot on your plate.'

'I know.'

'There are plenty of smart women like you . . . and unencumbered, if you see what I mean.' This was thin ice, and he switched tack. 'I have to consider the dynamics. It would put Deb's nose out of joint.' He added, with ironic inflection, 'Budgets, you know.'

Under the camisole, the half-cup bra itched. 'At least consider my suggestion.'

Barry's smile was cat-like. He would so much rather not have to deal with my request. 'I'll do that. We'll talk after Christmas. OK?'

He didn't so much as glance at my cleavage.

At the end of the day, mindful of Barry's warning about Deb, I went to find her. 'Have you got a moment?'

She was gathering her stuff into a leopard-print tote bag. She worked efficiently, handling the papers with a kind of reverence. She listened without comment to the outline of my plans and I made sure she understood that I posed no threat to her position. Eventually, without a mirror, she dabbed on some lip gloss. 'It really doesn't matter one way or the other, Minty. We take it as it comes.' Mobile phone in hand, she hovered in the doorway. 'You're not in tomorrow, are you? See you the day after.'

'So?' Paige manoeuvred herself into the car seat, like a ship's container into its berth. The baby was due late January, but during this final trimester, she was finding it difficult to walk and I was ferrying her to the shops to do some Christmas shopping. 'Why do we *need* categories of age or behaviour?'

'We don't. Or, rather, sensible people don't. It's business and marketing that require them.'

Paige considered. 'You'd better watch that Deborah. Take it from me.' This was not light advice. Paige knew whereof she talked. She had survived coups and counter-coups. 'By the time she got home after you talked to her, she would have worked out several scenarios as to why no one else was needed full-time at Paradox, all of which spell bad news for your plans, especially when Barry consults her – which he will.'

I absorbed the advice. 'After Nathan left Rose, and she was sacked, I wrote to her saying it was my turn now.'

'You didn't?'

'I did. I regret it. And I can't believe I actually did it. At the time I wanted to explain. To show why things had turned out as they had.'

After a moment, Paige said, 'Some going.'

I eyed her bulk. 'How *is* it going?'

'*It*'s fine.'

This was not the former Paige – all hustle, smartness and gloss – who had featured in the photographs that adorned the Hurley household. That Paige had been a top banker. No, Paige had given it all up when Jackson, now eight, and Lara, six, arrived. She had had no choice, I'd overheard her telling Nathan – who'd lapped it up. Children cannot flourish at home without a mother. *Period.*

This Paige was deeply fatigued in her third pregnancy. Her lipstick had been carelessly applied, leaving a rim round the pale interior of her stubborn lower lip, while a smudge of mascara adorned the papery skin under her left eye.

'You look tired.'

'So?' She shrugged, and still managed to convey . . . excitement and commitment. 'You know, even though I feel like the largest sack of potatoes on the planet, I wish I'd started earlier.'

'Your energy is ferocious. You should be working in a bank.'

'Ha.'

We drove past the common. Paige eased herself back in the seat and gazed hungrily out of the window. 'Do I look like a prisoner offered an hour's exercise in the yard?'

'The sacking smock gives you away.'

The dog-walkers were out in force, some struggling

70

with as many as six or eight charges. 'Look at them.' Paige sighed. 'That's how I feel.'

Winter had snapped its jaws shut. The trees were stripped bare and, since the autumn, the grass had returned to its proper colour. The shops were bright with Christmas lights. Suddenly Paige asked, 'What if I die with this one? Women do sometimes.'

I was startled. 'You won't.'

'If I do, will you insist that I have "mother" somewhere on my headstone?' Paige laughed as she spoke, but it was not a happy sound.

'Don't you mean "wife and mother"?'

She shook her head, and I saw the suggestion of new flesh settling under her chin. 'Sort of surplus, don't you think?'

'Paige, what's going on?' In my book, Paige and Martin were a *happy* couple. They represented all that was stalwart in the battle to preserve family values. All of a sudden, I experienced a disconcerting flash that I had been looking at the wrong picture.

'Nothing, sweetie. Nothing at all. Husbands are tiring.' There was a pause. 'Hey, did I tell you about Lara? I've got her into Partington's, the ballet school. She's been aching to go and the list was this long . . .' Paige sketched a gesture that fishermen frequently employ when discussing a catch. 'Anyway, I collared Mary Streatham at the book club. She's a governor, and we understand each other, and she said she'd see what she could do. No favours, mind. Martin isn't so pleased with his bit . . . Apparently a donation to the new studio fund would not go unnoticed – and no favours, mind.'

I snorted. 'I smell a similarity to Nathan taking paper suppliers to Paris for a long weekend of cultural adventure.'

'Whatever you say.' You could have cut Paige's smugness with a knife.

Back in Paige's kitchen – complete with a pink Aga and a copper *batterie de cuisine* – I unpacked and hid various items while Paige instructed me from a chair into which she had lowered herself with a groan. The table had already been laid for supper by Linda, the au pair, with a full complement of china, glasses and napkins. One of Paige's nostrums, one of the many to which I had helped myself, was that children should be made to eat properly at table with adults.

'Does Martin get home in time?' I asked.

Paige sighed. 'What do you think?

Jackson, a big blond child, bounded into the kitchen. 'Mum, where have you been?'

Paige jerked out of her torpor, as if an electric switch had been tripped. 'Darling. How was your day? Say hello to Mrs Lloyd.'

Jackson was full of his news. 'Guess, Mummy!' But he couldn't wait for Paige to run through the options. 'I came second in the spelling test.'

Even I knew my duty. 'That's wonderful, Jackson.'

Paige cupped her son's chin in her hand. 'Only second, darling?' So gentle she sounded, yet so inexorable. 'What went wrong?'

*

I drove home from Paige's, parked and let myself into the house. All over the country parents were hurrying home to scoop up their offspring. Parents who, laden with briefcases and last-minute shopping, kicked open the front door and cried, 'I'm home.' That species of parent sank gratefully into a welter of warmth and children's muddle, ambition laid aside in embraces.

According to the list in the kitchen, the twins were at Millie Rowe's for tea. I checked the post, which included a volume of poems by the feminist poet Ellen Black, whom I had schmoozed at a party. It was entitled *Origin of a New Species*.

One of Lucas's red socks lay on the stairs. I picked it up and smoothed it absently. It was very small with the suggestion of a hole in the toe. Soon I would have to think about supper and endless more meals. Then there was the twins' Christmas party. I had made a list: sausages, pizzas, crisps, jelly in the shape of a cat, pirate hats. I knew that for days afterwards I would be picking up bits of sausage and crisps that had been trodden into the floors and carpets.

The front door opened and the boys did their windmill act – arms outstretched and flailing towards me. 'Here's Mummy!' Lucas's cry rang with a note of pure joy. His shirt was hanging out of his trousers and encrusted with Bourbon biscuits. Felix had a green paint splodge on one cheek. Laden with their stuff, Eve brought up the rear.

Felix tugged at my hand. 'You are my real mummy, aren't you?'

'Of course I am.'

He looked important. 'Lucas says Eve's our real mummy.'

'*Lucas!*' I shot a glance at Eve, who shook her head.

Lucas seemed shifty. 'Millie says her nanny's her real mummy . . .'

Millie was a recently acquired friend, the only child of divorced parents, and spent her life shuttling between two tight-lipped adults. She had the bewilderment – and malice – of a child at sea. The boys needed reassurance, and I thought rapidly, inventively. 'Why don't we invite Millie to tea, and she can see who the real mummy is?'

Nathan arrived home, pale and shivering, and I ordered him to bed. Later I took him a tray of scrambled egg, smoked salmon and cranberry juice. 'You've been overdoing the parties.' I pummelled his pillows, patted the duvet straight and checked that the bedroom was in apple-pie order.

'There's a bad flu going round.' He placed a finger on his pulse, and squinted up at me with a grin. 'It's galloping.'

I grinned back. 'Probably terminal.'

I sat down at the end of the bed and studied him. True, Nathan was not in the pink, but his hair was thick, in good condition and attractively grey-streaked. Thank goodness, he wasn't coarse, lumpy or hairy. He hadn't run to fat either, and the veins in his hands were still decently buried beneath his skin. Thank goodness, too, he was not the sort of man who smelt, a roaring masculine presence whose limbs and noise invaded every space. Instead there was delicacy and proportion about his appearance. '*Should* you have a check-up?'

He ate some egg. 'I might.'

'I insist.'

'Bully,' he said, without rancour. 'I'd prefer a holiday in Cornwall. How about it, Minty?' The old spark flickered in his eyes. 'It would be fun. The boys would love it. It would do us all good – it'd be like old times.'

Outside, a car door slammed and rain spattered the window, but in the bedroom it was warm and peaceful.

I sidestepped Cornwall. 'Talking of the boys . . . About the Nativity play.'

'What about it?'

'Mrs Jenkins promised that Lucas could be a Wise Man.' Nathan raised a questioning eyebrow. 'I'm afraid, she said Felix could be a sheep.'

'What?' Nathan pulled himself upright. 'And you didn't *do* anything?'

'There was nothing I *could* do.' I rescued the tray and set it down on the chest-of-drawers. 'There's no need for drama, I'm sure that next year Felix will be a Wise Man.' I cast around wildly. '*Joseph*, even.'

'Minty, come here.' I obeyed and he caught my hand in a grip so fierce that I cried out. 'Don't you understand anything about your sons? Can't you remember anything of what it's like to be a child? Don't you *see* how Felix will mind? How that fragile little bit of confidence, which is all he has, will be shot to pieces? God knows, we have to learn about suffering and exclusion and mistakes, but not yet for our two. Not yet – if I have anything to do with it.'

I stared down at the figure in the bed. The warm, peaceful atmosphere had dissipated. 'You're hurting me, Nathan.' He released my hand. 'Don't you think Felix should learn that the world isn't fair?'

'At *five*, Minty. Are you totally without mercy?'

'Almost six,' I heard myself say.

Felix was the younger by ten minutes. It was nothing and everything. Ten minutes had given Lucas the greater percentage of confidence and attention.

'So, what do you want to do, Nathan? Tell Lucas he can't be a Wise Man?'

'If I ever see that woman, I'll wring her neck.'

'Why? She's only doing her job.'

There was a long silence, and Nathan whistled under his breath. 'Well, the boys can count on their mother.'

That hurt. 'I see things differently, Nathan.' I picked up the tray and prepared to leave the room. 'While we're on the subject of loyalty and support, are you coming to see them in the play?'

Nathan rubbed his earlobe, and I glimpsed a bone-deep weariness that frightened me a little. He was only fifty-five. 'As it happens the fifth is a bad day – big meeting scheduled – but I'll talk to Roger.'

I had a lightning change of heart. 'Actually, Nathan, I'm not sure that's a good idea. Don't mention it to Roger. Trust me. Just *don't.*'

'Do you know something?' he asked sharply.

'No, just instinct.'

'Hum,' he said. 'Your instincts are usually sound.' He moved restlessly and the once neat bed was a muddle. 'You think I'm not up to it any more?'

'I didn't say that.'

'But you think it.'

The question went through my mind: how would Rose have handled this? Nathan's flash of neediness left me cold and unsympathetic – and I knew I was failing to grapple with the uncertainties and strains of his life. Instead I asked, 'Nathan, do you want some coffee or tea?'

'Can't drink coffee in the evening any more.' He pushed the tray aside. 'Come back, Minty.'

Something of the old, decisive Nathan made me melt, and I knelt beside the bed, and laid my head on his chest. He stroked my hair. In our story, there had been no time or room for gradual wooing. No leisurely drinks or dinners. No trips to the zoo or meanders in the park. I had sent the message '*I would like you*.' Nathan had received it, turned up at my flat and come straight to the point. 'I want to sleep with you.' He was trembling, and I was struck by the gap between the man I observed at his work and the manner of this request. It touched me, and filled me with exhilaration.

Sleeping with Nathan had been the easy part. It was the rest that had been difficult.

'How do we manage to misunderstand each other?' he asked.

His fingers moved to my face, stroking my neck and cheek. Between us there was a cessation of darkness and hostility. Instead, there was warmth, communion and peace.

I willed those precious moments to expand, cradle and buoy us up for the hours, days and years ahead.

The Nativity play had come and gone, and by the time Christmas arrived, I had overdosed on lists. There was one for presents, another for food and menus, yet another for events.

Initially, 'Events' had read 'Sam and Jilly to us?' That had been crossed out and 'Sunday before Christmas to Sam and Jilly' substituted. When I had rung Jilly to ask them to come to us on Christmas Day, she said she was frightfully sorry but they had already arranged to be in Bath. When I suggested that we joined them, Jilly had been acutely embarrassed: 'It's not that you're not welcome, Minty – *of course* you are – but we're pretty booked up. Poppy and Richard are coming, my parents and . . . Rose, actually.'

We agreed that Nathan, the boys and I would drive down to Bath on the Sunday before Christmas and arrange a separate meeting with Poppy and Richard. Into this settled plan, Poppy inserted a spoke: 'Could you come over to us on the Sunday before Christmas? Otherwise we won't have a chance to see Dad and the boys because Richard and I are nipping off to Verbier on Boxing Day.' I explained that we were going to Bath. 'Oh, well,' said Poppy, with only faint regret. 'We'll pop in to you on Christmas Eve on the way down to Sam's.'

We drove to Sam and Jilly's through lashing rain and

arrived on the dot of one o'clock. Jilly greeted us at the front door in a pair of old jeans and a baggy sweater. This put us all on the back foot. Nathan was in his suit and I was in my best green dress and high-heeled boots. Furthermore I had insisted that Nathan stopped at the service station before we left the motorway and the boys were spruce to a fault, with washed faces and brushed hair.

'Goodness!' said Jilly. 'Don't you all look smart!' She led us into the kitchen where Sam was sitting in muddy gardening clothes with his feet on the table. 'Here they are,' she sang, and a look passed between husband and wife: a slight widening of the eyes, which indicated, 'We've been caught out.'

Lunch had been hamburgers for the children and stew for the adults. 'I meant,' Jilly said, as she dished up the latter – with another silent exchange between her and Sam – 'to cook something special. But getting ready for Christmas takes up so much time. You know how it is?'

No, I don't, I wanted to say, outraged by the lack of ceremony. I thought of the goose stuffed with raisins that I would have bought in, the crackers in their box, the silver candles and gauze ribbon that would have adorned my table.

Nathan reached over and picked up a fork that Frieda had dropped on to the floor. 'This is lovely,' he said quietly. 'No need for a fuss.'

Jilly sat down and gazed at her stew. 'The important thing is that we've all met.'

'Absolutely,' said Sam.

On the way back in the car, I said to Nathan, 'They didn't go to much trouble.'

Nathan was paying keen attention to his driving. 'No fatted calf, certainly,' he said lightly, but his lips tightened.

On Christmas Eve, Poppy and Richard arrived in a rush, their car stacked with luggage and presents. It was raining hard and Poppy stood in the hallway, shaking her wet hair, and demanded, 'Where's the Christmas tree? It's always in the hall.' I explained that this year, for a change, it was in the sitting room. 'Oh, what a pity.' She flung her coat on a chair and swept past me. 'Dad? Where are you?' She hugged Nathan. 'Haven't seen you for ages. How are you?' Then she rushed round to kiss Felix. 'Have you been a good boy? No? I thought not. No pressie for you.' Felix raised stricken eyes, and Poppy sank to her knees beside him. 'Darling Felix, don't look like that. Of course I've got you a present. A *big* one.'

'How big?' Felix was – rightly – suspicious.

Poppy sketched an air-square. 'That big.' Felix was marginally reassured and went off to tell his brother. Poppy got gracefully to her feet. 'Sweet.' She turned to Nathan. 'We can only stay for half an hour. Otherwise we won't get to Sam's in time for dinner.'

'Oh, no,' said Nathan. 'I thought you'd be with us for a bit.'

'We'd better eat,' I said.

In the dining room, I had laid the table with a dazzling

white cloth, and set out on it a plate of cucumber sandwiches. (*Tip*: boil half a cup of water with brown sugar, add cider vinegar and soak the slices of cucumber in it for a couple of hours.) There were also tiny sausages roasted in honey and mustard, slices of pizza for the boys and a Christmas cake (thank you, Selfridges) with a tiny skiing scene on it, including a twinkly ski lift.

I made to light the candles and Poppy exclaimed, 'Don't on our account. We'll have to go any minute.' She surveyed the laden table. 'Goodness, you have gone to a lot of bother.' Nathan offered her a sandwich. 'I'm not that hungry, Daddy, and I don't want to spoil dinner.'

Richard was kinder, accepted two sandwiches and ate them. Lucas climbed on to a chair and strained for the nearest cracker. Nathan picked him up and settled him on his lap. 'Hang on, young man. We'll pull them in a minute.'

Poppy addressed me in a low voice: 'Jilly told me how smart you all were when you went down to see them. She was a little worried that you might have been offended because they were so disorganized. I said *of course* you wouldn't. You knew perfectly well that she had to concentrate on Christmas Day.' She stopped, eyes on the empty plate in front of her and, as a great concession, said, 'Maybe I will have *one* sandwich. Actually, Jilly doesn't need to worry. Mum will take over cooking the lunch. She does it so brilliantly.'

I sneaked a glance at Nathan. He was still cuddling Lucas, and talking to Richard but I detected a wary, whipped look in his eye. There were not many

6

On the way to work, I met Martin Hurley. It was Monday, January, very cold, and I was still recovering from Christmas. Unusually for Martin, he was mooching along, weighed down by his briefcase. We stopped to chat outside Mrs Austen's front garden where frost smeared the jumble of flowerpots and yoghurt cartons that, typically, lurked on the windowsill. Mrs Austen was a fanatical gardener, but as she lived in the first-floor flat of the multi-occupied house, she had no proper space to indulge her passion. It was lack in a life such as Mrs Austen's that turned a man or a woman sharp-tongued, nosy and tart as a lemon, and on cue, she appeared at the window.

'Not your usual style, is it?' I said. I normally saw Martin stepping into a chauffeur-driven car.

'Broken down.' He made a mischievous face. 'Actually, I feel as if I've been let off school. Big meeting today and I wouldn't mind escaping. I keep thinking I could go AWOL travelling the District Line.'

I smiled. We both knew that Martin wouldn't miss the meeting for the world. His meetings, as with so many people who worked, ratified his professional existence. 'I doubt if you'd think Ealing or Hainault a destination resort, and after two seconds on the Tube, you'll be begging for a fleet of cars. Trust me.'

'I do trust you,' he said, which was nice, and also unexpected. It would have been wrong to dismiss Martin as a one-dimensional man, focused only on meetings. He was discriminating, and generous with many things. Even money. Also, he was nice about his wife, which not every husband was. From time to time, when Nathan and I were *chez* Hurley, I caught Martin observing Paige carefully. It was a version of paying attention to the fine detail, which had made him such a success at work.

Snooping from the window was not yielding enough rewards and Mrs Austen emerged on to the front step to edge closer to this interesting street theatre. I waved at her. 'Paige OK?' I asked Martin.

'So-so. Pregnancy is an exclusive business. Unlike conception.'

'Are you looking forward to number three?'

Martin didn't reply immediately, and when he did he sounded a little troubled. 'It's very crowded – life, I mean.'

That worried me a little. 'Too cryptic for this time of the morning, Martin.'

'I feel cryptic, Minty. Never mind. Now for the meeting.' He dropped a kiss on my cheek. 'See you.' He raised his briefcase in salute to the watchful Mrs Austen, and we went our separate ways.

Sandwiched between bodies on a packed train, I began to wonder in earnest about Paige and Martin. 'I'm practically the only mother in the world prepared to put her children first,' Paige had maintained, and she wasn't entirely joking. 'It's lonely. If we go on like this, there'll be no population in the West. Look at Italy.

Look at Germany. Child-free countries.' Paige's zeal was both heartbreaking and infuriating: a missionary among the heathens. Yet there was something reassuring about her straightforward outlook, which did not involve any of the ifs and buts that draw the sting of rules and regulations.

Barry sauntered into my office, but his greeting was sharp. 'What kept you?'

I cursed inwardly and flushed: I was twenty minutes late. 'Sorry, Barry. The Tube.'

He glanced at his Rolex. 'You can make it up later.'

He threw himself into a chair. 'I've got a tricky day. We need the green light for the Aids film, so say your prayers.' He was dressed in a dark Armani suit and red tie, which meant Big Meeting and probably explained the sharpness. He smelt of aftershave, and a hint of claret from the night before.

Again he checked his watch. 'Five minutes before the off, and I'm going to waste them with you.'

What's up with Gabrielle? hovered on the tip of my tongue, but I resisted. On closer inspection, Barry's collar points were not quite adjusted. Then I understand that he did not, at this moment, require the diversion of a superb body and a sexy giggle. What Barry needed was an adult, sensible, grounding conversation before he went into a Big Meeting. As we talked, I was unsure whether to cry because I no longer occupied the pretty-and-diverting category, or laugh because I had been elevated to 'serious'.

Barry departed, and I was left to beat the working day

into shape. I went through my in-tray and sorted it into 'urgent' and 'pending'. Rose had taught me the tricks and procedures of an office, and the lessons remained with me. Funny, that: she had handed me profession-alism and her husband on a plate. I wrote a report, made phone calls. I read scripts until my eyes blurred.

Eventually I pulled the file marked 'Middle Age' towards me. I had been avoiding it. Definitely. I opened my notebook and wrote: (1) *What* is the story? (2) *Why* are we proposing it? (3) *Who* will make it? (4) Likely costs?

What was there to say? Wasn't middle age a furtive, secretive stage? When I'd bought my first bra, there was no one I didn't buttonhole with the news. Ask the spirit of my dead, unsympathetic mother. But I'd rather die than reveal the existence of a varicose vein in my leg. (Thank you, twins.) I had no desire to discuss my body's slippage. The first blows of age. It was akin to tourists tramping round a ruin. And which of us would volun-teer to examine the mistakes, guilt, regret or banalities of working, nurturing and fretting? Who wished to acknowledge the loneliness of growing older?

'When middle age creeps up on a woman, she discovers that younger women are just as much wolves as men,' a newspaper pundit stated in one of the cuttings that Deb had handed over. On that point, I conceded, I was the expert.

I remembered playing the wolf . . .

Nathan had tracked me down in Bonne Tartine. He must have followed me from the Vistemax offices. He slid into the opposite seat, then nodded at my coffee and the plate on which sat a tiny, untouched croissant. He seemed inordinately pleased with himself, his expression absurdly young and his hair ruffled. 'Is that just there for temptation?'

'How did you know I was here?'

'I watched and waited.'

I swallowed the uneven lump of excitement and apprehension: now that I had got to this point, questions needed to be asked. 'What about Rose?'

Carefully, Nathan cut the croissant into pieces. 'Rose is busy with her own life.' He paused. 'All things considered, I don't think she'd mind. I've never been her first concern . . .' He leant forward and began to feed me the croissant. Its sweet, crumbling texture dissolved in my mouth, and I thought, Rose must be mad or stupid to be so blind.

'Why did you do it?' asked the forty-two-year-old Rose, after I had taken Nathan. 'We were friends.'

Yes, we had been friends. Sweet, sweet friends . . .

'You look stuck in.' Deb sashayed into my office. 'Anything I should know about?' Uninvited, she perched on the edge of my desk, and I suppressed the desire to push her off.

'OK.' I sat back. 'Do women feel middle age more acutely than men?'

'God, I don't know.' Deb gave an exaggerated shudder. 'Isn't it all over for the middle-aged, whichever sex?' Her eyes drifted past me towards Reception in case anyone useful was waiting.

'I think my husband feels it.'

Deb transferred her attention back to me. 'Barry says you're a second wife. Is he a lot older? Is he nice?'

'He's very nice,' I said flatly. 'That's why I married him.'

'How much older?'

'Twenty years.'

The corners of Deb's mouth went down, registering distaste. 'How . . . very brave,' she said, after a few awkward seconds. Then she said. 'I wish . . .'

'You wish?' She might have been wishing for a new body or a new life. Or maybe she was just wishing she could fall in love, in which case I might warn her off it. Apart from anything else, love is ageing. You fetch up with twins, varicose veins and being hated by a clan.

'Did I tell you I'm going mad in my flat? It's above a curry restaurant and it reeks – *I* reek – of curry. The landlord won't do anything about the ventilation and is threatening to put up the rent.' She spread her hands. 'I long to live in a clean white palace high above the trees. I long to be different. But at the moment the future doesn't look bright.' She paused. 'Did you know that Barry's taking on another producer? . . . You *didn't*? He's brilliant apparently.'

Annoyance with Barry clocked in. No doubt he'd had his reasons for not mentioning it when I talked to him earlier, which showed that one should never forget the boss always has a hidden agenda. I closed my notebook with a snap. Perhaps things were not going to work out with Paradox. I experienced mild regret at the thought, but there were other production companies and I would allow Nathan an I-told-you-so conversation.

Deb stood up and stretched. The junction between her cargos and T-shirt revealed gooseflesh. I nearly said, *I so nearly said*, 'You'll catch cold if you're not careful.'

I returned home in good time to take over from Eve, who was going out. 'Thanks, Minty.' A rare, pale smile stretched her lips. 'This is big night.'

Best not to ask. From the window of the boys' bedroom, I watched her clatter down the street in a cheap pair of high heels. She looked released, happy, her hair loosened from its customary prison wardress's clamp, and I reminded myself I must never forget that Eve was entitled to an off-duty life.

'You are a busy mummy.' Lucas's fair hair, which was beginning to darken, was tumbled and mussed, and he was the image of his father.

The *Thomas the Tank Engine* clock clicked on the chest-of-drawers. Two pairs of socks, two T-shirts and two pairs of underpants dripped off a chair that was stencilled with dragons. Under their duvets, I could see that the boys had a long way to grow before they reached the end of the bed. It would take years and years, in fact.

'Never too busy for you two.' I tried to remember which bed I had sat on the previous evening and chose the opposite. Felix smiled shyly, his gaze flicking to a point above the bed where he had stuck a drawing on the wall. I was about to expostulate, *Felix, the wallpaper*, when it dawned on me that Felix's drawing was of a large cat with black and white stripes. Underneath it he had written 'My Lost Cat' in blue crayon.

When they were asleep – Felix curled up on his right

side, Lucas spreadeagled over the bed – I turned on the nightlight and left them to dream.

Then I found myself slipping upstairs to the spare room where the white roses in the painting appeared to leap out of their dark background. I searched through Nathan's shirts for his notebook.

On 21 January, three days ago, he had written, 'Is it better not to care?' and yesterday, 'I feel that I don't really exist. I look in the mirror and I am not sure who I am looking at.'

I closed the notebook, and only then saw the yellow Post-it note stuck to the front. 'Private,' it said, in Nathan's handwriting.

That made me smile. If the notebook was private, why did he not hide it more securely? Answer: he wished me to read it. It was a challenge and I took it up. I went downstairs, found a pen and wrote underneath: 'Talk to me, Nathan?'

The candles I had placed on the table guttered. Nathan ate the organic fillet steak slowly. 'Not bad.'

Not bad? Every mouthful had cost a fortune. I swallowed the final piece as if it was gold dust and said, 'One day I'll learn to cook.'

Nathan uttered a snort midway between laughter and derision. 'It's not you, Minty.'

Upstairs, there was an eruption. Despite the direst warnings, the twins were swapping beds, as they did most nights. Nathan cocked an ear. 'It's fine,' I reassured him. 'Tell me what's happening at Vistemax. I talked to

Gisela yesterday and she said Roger's ultra-preoccupied. I thought you'd had a good year?'

Nathan pushed away his plate. 'A big libel suit,' he confessed. 'It was an article in *Weekend Digest* about bungs for football managers. It's likely to cost Vistemax, and it happened on my watch.'

'But not your fault.'

'Not directly. My responsibility, though.'

'You should have told me.' The kitchen was quiet. 'Journalists,' I murmured. Since leaving Vistemax, I had lost track of what went on in the company. Nathan, however, swam with ease though the numbers and strategy. 'You should have said something,' I repeated.

Nathan shrugged.

The silence had become that of two people who were not communicating on the same level. On this point *Successful Relationships* was firm and clear: it was a situation that should be sorted.

'I've bought you these,' I heard myself say, and handed him the bottle of multi-vitamins I had picked up in my lunch hour.

He tossed the bottle from one hand to the other. 'Thank you, Mother Minty.'

He changed into an old shirt in a washed-out blue that he had had since the dawn of time and refused to throw away. In the candlelight, the colour deepened. My skirt, a deep black, now gleamed bluish. One of the candles flickered and went out. Nathan leant forward, nipped the wick between his fingers and said, with regret, 'Minty, you shouldn't be spending your life watching me.'

'It *has* been a bad day.'

He blew on smoked fingers. 'Yes, it has.'

'Nathan . . .' The words trembled on my tongue. What is your *'secret grief'*? But I already knew the answer. Nathan's secret grief was Rose and the past . . . and so was mine.

'Take one of those vitamins.' I reached for the bottle and unscrewed the lid. 'I'll take one too.' I held a pill between my thumb and finger. 'Be a good boy.'

Nathan observed it for a second or two. 'Later,' he said.

I should have pressed on: *Let's discuss your diary.* Let us, together, sort out what is making you unhappy. But the expression that had settled on his face meant that my words aborted. It was not so much impatience and distaste, although those were mirrored in his face – and I was unsure whether they were directed at himself or at me – it was his obvious, disturbing, detachment. Nathan had removed himself from the kitchen, and I had no idea where to.

I tried again: 'Nathan, I know I shouldn't have read what you wrote, but we must talk about it.'

'What?' With effort, Nathan refocused on me. 'Actually . . .' He stopped.

'Nathan, I want to talk to you about . . . the diary. About what I read.'

'No,' Nathan cut me off. 'I don't want to discuss it. It's silly, and very private.'

'But . . .' The obvious question was, why did you leave it for me to read? However, I had learnt that most things in our relationship were not straightforward and I had to pick my way through the maze.

'I said I didn't want to discuss it.'

'If you feel like that.' Suddenly I had lost interest in exploring my husband's psyche. I shoved back my chair and got to my feet. If I'd had three magic wishes all three would have gone on summoning back the old Nathan. I could never have the young one, but I would dearly have liked to reclaim the version who had swash-buckled into my life and said, 'Let's escape.'

'Nathan, can you pass me that saucepan?' I busied myself running hot water and swishing in washing-up liquid.

'Sure.' If he was surprised at my change of mood, he was not going to remark on it. 'But there is something . . .'

The sound of the doorbell shot through the house. Nathan started. 'This is what I should have mentioned.'

I stiffened, but said coolly enough, 'You'd better go and answer the door, then. Hope it hasn't woken the boys.'

'But . . .' Nathan was alight with an excitement and dread I couldn't place. Then he shrugged. 'OK.'

He went into the hall, and I heard voices, then the front door closing.

Nathan led the visitor into the sitting room and I wiped my hands, tucked my hair behind my ears and went to see who it was. Nathan whipped round as I walked in, a curious smile hovering at the corners of his mouth. 'Look who's here.'

But a sixth sense had already told me.

Rose.

This was the encounter that provided material for any late-night demons, any restless dreams, for the chill of a dawn catechism when I asked myself what I had done in taking Nathan. My first impulse was to laugh: it was ridiculous that Rose should be standing there. Then my knees drained of strength.

'Rose.' I held the back of a chair for support.

'Hello, Minty.' She held out a hand. 'You're looking well.'

She was dressed simply but expensively in jeans and a tweed jacket nipped in at the waist – slimmer than she appeared on television. She was tanned and her hair was glorious: long, highlighted and silky. She was barely recognizable as the woman I had known in the office, wearing a grey skirt and black jumper that bagged in all the wrong places. 'Literature, Minty,' I pictured her saying, as she did in those days, 'is full of stories about tension between servant and master.' Her hair would have been bundled up any-old-how, and her lipstick was always too pink. 'There's a short story about a pair of sisters who were so in awe of Cook that they never dared go into their own kitchen. They spent most of their lives fearful and thirsty.'

Then, Rose had hovered between wryness and laughter. This Rose did too. There was no hint of bitterness, only a polite interest as she took in the changes to the sitting room.

Terrific, I thought. We end up where we began. Where once I had observed this room through Rose's eyes –

painted a pale dove grey, the sofa and chairs arranged close to the window – Rose was observing it through mine: a cream-yellow paint wash, the sofa and chairs pulled closer to the fireplace. She was probably concluding, as I had done: That woman does not *understand* this room.

'What are you doing here, Rose?'

Her gaze swung between me and Nathan. 'Didn't Nathan tell you?' Her eyes gleamed. 'Nathan, you didn't *tell* Minty. That's bad of you. I wanted to talk to Nathan and he suggested that I drop in since I was going to be in the area. We'd have had to meet sooner or later though, wouldn't we, Minty? Is it OK?'

'I didn't know,' I said. 'I'm not prepared.'

Rose could have said, 'Nothing prepared me for you to take Nathan.' She considered. 'I don't think either of us has anything to be afraid of. Not any more.'

I missed her – I mean, I missed the kind, soft Rose, the wife to Nathan who had brimmed with the desire to help and who said things like 'Tell me what's wrong, Minty', or 'You're *not* to worry.' Unsurprisingly, that Rose had vanished from my life.

She shifted a bag, with fashionable buckles and straps, from one shoulder to the other. Her love of handbags hadn't changed. The smile she directed at Nathan was friendly and well disposed, and I swear he winced. 'Nathan, about Sam . . .'

I raised an eyebrow at Nathan, who looked utterly helpless. He ran his hand through his hair. 'Sam has a problem and Rose wanted to discuss it.'

'Ah,' I said. I didn't add, *Why didn't you tell me?*

'Dad!' There was a cry from the top of the stairs.

Nathan went out of the room and hissed, 'Get back into bed, Lukey. Now.'

'I'm really sorry, Minty,' Rose said. 'I wouldn't have come if I'd known Nathan hadn't cleared it with you. I should have realized he'd duck it.' I gave a little laugh, and she added, 'I remember your laugh. It's distinctive and I could always tell where you were.'

For some reason, that made me both angry and sad. 'Do you still see Hal?' I asked. 'How is he?'

Her eyes narrowed, but she answered politely: 'We still see each other, of course. Quite a lot. It's great . . . A great friendship. I'm lucky in that.'

'I've always wondered.'

Nathan returned and pressed on Rose a drink, coffee, whatever she would like. 'Some wine,' she conceded.

'I'll check on the twins,' I said. 'You'd better get on with your conversation. Don't mind me.'

Nathan sent me a look that meant, Please don't be like that. I sent him one back: Give me a good reason why I shouldn't.

'The twins? How are they? I hear a lot about them.' Rose could only summon a polite interest in two children she'd never seen. 'I gather Frieda – Sam's Frieda – gets on well with them.'

'I know who Frieda is, Rose.'

'Minty . . .' Nathan intervened, with a note of warning.

Rose merely replied, 'How stupid of me. Of course you do.' She turned back to Nathan. 'As for our son . . .'

'Our'. It dropped from Rose's mouth with all her rights to its usage.

I fled the room and ran upstairs. Lucas had settled and both boys were sleeping calmly enough – in the wrong beds. Felix was hunched under his duvet. Lucas had thrown his off, and I tucked it over him, adjusted the night-light and found myself by the ironing-board on the landing.

Downstairs the voices murmured. I heard Nathan laugh and say 'No . . .' in the way he did when he was particularly amused. The construction and timbre of that word seemed expressly designed to exclude me.

I snatched up one of his ironed shirts and began to fold it this way and that. In the perfect syllogism, the logic flows without a hitch from proposition A to proposition B, which results in the only possible conclusion. For example: husband leaves first wife because he is unhappy; he marries second wife who he 'knows' will make him happy; she believes him; they are happy.

Perfect syllogism. Imperfect world.

I was clutching Nathan's shirt so tightly that my hands hurt. I dropped it on the floor, stepped over it and crept downstairs, like the thief I was.

Light spilled into the hall from the sitting room. The door was half closed, but sufficiently open to allow me to watch the scene inside.

7

Nathan and Rose were ensconced on the sofa. Rose was toying with her glass, fingers curling and uncurling round its stem. The big gold ring she wore on her right hand caught my eye, so bright it hurt. Nathan was leaning back against the cushions, one hand spread along the top of the sofa. It was a pose suggesting relaxation and ease. Every so often, his gaze settled on his first wife like that of a starving dog on a bone.

'They never last,' Rose was saying, all indulgence and affection, which meant she could only be talking about her daughter. 'How many times, Nathan, have we seen that?' Nathan hung on her every syllable. 'All the same, I'm a little worried about Poppy. I detect a certain, well . . . restlessness. I asked if she and Richard were getting on all right, and she said she'd never been happier. But you know how it is, Nathan – you can sense that some-thing's not quite right.'

Nathan lifted the hand that lay on the back of the sofa in agreement. 'Can't be money, surely.'

Rose said affectionately, 'No, Nathan. It's not money. At least, I don't think so. It can't be. Richard earns such a lot.'

'Someone has to think about money.' He smiled at her, complicit and gentle in a way he never was with me.

I could have enlightened them as to what Poppy hadn't told her mother. Almost certainly it was to do with the on-line poker. I could have said to them, 'Do you realize that Poppy's probably gambling and losing? And the more she loses, the more she'll play. It's the nature of the beast.' They could have seized the chance to act in concert, and asked, 'How much and how deep?' They could have gone in tandem to have it out with Poppy. *You can tell us. We're your parents. We love you.* But, yes, I held my silence. I didn't hold any brief for Poppy, but what was her business was her business.

Nathan put his elbows on his knees and leant forward. It was a pose he adopted frequently, which emulated Rodin's *The Thinker*. 'About Sam, is Jilly happy for him to take the job?'

Rose tucked a leg under her. 'That's what I wanted to discuss. Jilly's furious at the idea of leaving Winchcombe. Apparently she's threatening to stay behind. She says she *hates* America, Texas in particular.'

'She's never been to Texas, and she won't stay behind. She's not that kind of woman. She knows it's a big step up for Sam, and that it's important.'

Rose clicked her tongue against her teeth, but it was not an impatient or angry sound. It was a marker that formed part of the discussion. It meant she was considering what she would say next and my husband, my foolish husband, waited, a smile on his lips, doting to the point of being offensive. 'Difficult, Nathan. Jilly's very settled in the village. Parish council, book club, and the school is perfect.' Rose turned to Nathan and her

99

hair tumbled over her shoulders. Nathan . . . Nathan reached over and tucked a tendril behind her ear.

'It's uncanny,' he said, in a low voice. 'Frieda looks more like you each day.'

Rose ignored the gesture, but she was pleased. 'Do you think? She's very special. Has she told you about the pink bike? Last time I went down, she and I conducted a ballet class. We leapt off armchairs and pointed our toes.' She drank some wine.

'Savour the merlot,' he said, in a Russian accent, which made Rose laugh.

'Don't remind me of *him*,' she said, and I had no idea who she meant. She tapped the glass. 'This is nice, though. Did you buy it at the usual place?'

I had an impression that I was gazing into one of those fairground mirrors, which, by their curvature, invert what they reflect. In theory, it should have been me sitting on the sofa, all cosy and intimate, Nathan's hand resting behind my shoulder, and Rose should have been peering through the door like a prize snooper.

I must have moved for they swung round. Immediately Nathan looked tense and reared back against the sofa, but Rose stayed where she was. I advanced into the room. 'Since you ask, darling, the twins are fine.' I sat down in the chair opposite them. 'Have you sorted out whatever it was?'

Rose got to her feet and smoothed her jacket. 'Yes and no. I'm sure Nathan will tell you about it.'

The 'tell you about it' was irritating but, under the circumstances, I had to let it pass. 'I enjoyed the television programme, Rose. It was very good.'

'Yes,' she replied simply. 'It was, wasn't it? We had a lot of fun making it. It came about by serendipity. I was mulling over the idea and Hal introduced me to a producer. It took a lot of haggling, and I had to persuade them I was the right person to front it, but we got there.' She made a rueful *moue*, which invited me to enter into a solidarity with her. 'Camera adds ten pounds, though. Not that one should mind.'

I was trying not to stare at her too obviously. But I couldn't avoid the conclusion that the woman standing before me was the model I had taken a lot of trouble to copy. Rose had worked through the messy bits of her life, and there she was, furnished and burnished with an electricity I was supposed to possess. Yet here I was, weighed down by minutiae, my lists, my children . . . and my husband. Then it occurred to me that hundreds of thousands of second wives had been faced with encounters such as this one, only to realize that what they had suspected was true: they had volunteered for the predicament of the younger sibling, who would never, ever catch up with the dazzling elder.

'There might be a follow-up series,' she was saying. 'I had no idea . . . until . . .' There was a frozen little silence. 'Until I . . . I mean I've only just discovered how vast, diverse and wonderful the world is.'

Nathan pulled himself to his feet and moved a fraction closer to Rose. 'Don't feel you have to go.'

Rose knew Nathan. I knew Nathan. We both knew he was making a bad job of concealing that he ached with regret. If I had truly loved Nathan . . . if I *had* . . . this imperfect, humiliating pretence would have cut my heart in two.

'Let us know,' I said. 'We'll make a point of watching.'

Rose picked up the fashionable handbag and searched inside it. 'Did I leave the keys in my coat? I shouldn't do that – they're always falling out. No, here they are.' She managed to convey a sense of charming disorder that, nevertheless, would not inconvenience anyone.

Nathan was completely taken and gazed, spellbound, down at her. 'I'll ring Sam tomorrow,' he touched her arm, 'and find out if he's serious about this Texan job.'

'I'm going to Italy tomorrow. Last minute, spur of the moment. Long weekend. Then I have a couple of pieces to write, which will take lots of research but they should be fun.'

There was so much more about Rose that she could have told us. She had walked into number seven with a new history about which Nathan and I were largely ignorant. She could have told us about her intriguing new life. *I live here. I work there. I had dinner with so-and-so.* If I had been prepared, I could have dealt with it. I would even have wanted to hear it because I would have been able to make realistic comparisons, instead of the reverse.

She placed her hands on Nathan's shoulders and kissed his cheek lightly. 'I'll give you a ring next week. And, Nathan, about that other idea . . .' the light caught the gloss on her hair and the sheen of her jacket '. . . let's talk about that too.'

Nathan's hands clenched. 'Yup.' He stuffed his hands into his pockets and rocked back on his heels. Suddenly I glimpsed the younger Nathan – the one who had swept the young Rose up from her disaster with Hal Thorne, married her, given her children and a domain she had guarded until I came along.

The light in the sitting room was flattering – which it should have been for I had gone to a lot of trouble to make it so. Rose seemed so fresh, so mysterious in her intentions and busyness – but mysterious with what? I struggled to understand precisely what I was up against.

The answer seemed to be that Rose had become powerful because it was impossible any longer to pin her down.

Nathan led Rose into the hall: there had been a further conversation lasting five minutes or so, and I heard him say, 'Tell Frieda I'll be looking out for her pointy toes when I come down.'

The front door closed, and he came into the kitchen to face the inevitable scene.

I had taken refuge in checking the store-cupboard in readiness for Eve's weekly shopping trip. It was lucky I had: it was practically bare.

He was braced for a major explosion and knocked his clenched fist on the table. Deliberately, I kept my back to him. 'I'm sure you didn't mean to make me feel uncomfortable or humiliate me, Nathan.' I kept my anger in check and turned round. 'Why would you wish to do that?'

He was shocked, and took a step towards me. 'Of course I didn't want to humiliate you. Of course not. Rose was going to be in the area and she wanted to talk to me.'

'It might have suited Rose, Nathan, but was it the best thing for us?' I strove to keep calm.

'Oh, come on,' he said, but he was on the defensive. Of course.

'Look at us both,' I pointed out. 'All churned up.'

Nathan fished the whisky bottle out of the cupboard and poured himself a slug. 'It's not much to ask – can't you be a little flexible and civilized about it?'

My anger escaped the leash. 'Were you civilized when you left Rose? I think not. I don't hold with this be-nice-at-any-price thing, Nathan. Even if she doesn't show it, Rose hates me, and rightly so. I hate her.'

'Why? She's done nothing to you.'

We glared at each other. The adrenaline pumped through me, drained away and left me weakened. Of their own volition, my hands continued to rifle through the contents of the store-cupboard. 'If you don't understand, I can't explain.' My fingers encountered a stray pasta shell, and I knew – I knew – that I was walking into a darkness of the spirit, that I was about to say things I would regret. 'It's not rational, certainly not civilized, what I feel about Rose. I hate her because . . . I've wronged her. Can't you see that, you stupid man? It's to do with the battle for possession – but I don't think you wish to see it, let alone acknowledge it. And you want it both ways.' I emptied the remainder of a rice packet (wild) into a glass jar. 'You want to have me and see Rose. You want us all to be friends.'

Nathan sat down at the kitchen table and put his head into his hands. 'Wouldn't you like to be friends with her? You were once.'

I kept myself busy with the rice because I couldn't bear to see his unhappiness. 'You can't have two faces looking opposite ways. As a matter of fact, you can't have two wives. Not in this country, at least.'

I heard him swallow some whisky. 'I can't talk to you about this, Minty. It's like trying to have a conversation in a foreign language or with a total stranger.'

That was more than enough. It was far too much. 'OK, Nathan, let's talk plain English. I think you're hiding behind the let's-be-nice mask because what you really want is to see Rose without feeling guilty.'

He made an indeterminate gesture with his hands, which, if I'd needed it, would have provided proof. 'It's meant nothing, has it?' I threw at him. 'And I've tried with you, and your family who loathe me. If you remember, you were the one who felt imprisoned in your marriage with Rose. *You* said, not me, that it was dull and void. That was why you left her. You convinced me, and I believed you.'

Nathan went white, presumably with fury, for I had pricked his vulnerable area: he didn't like to be thought of badly. 'Could I point out that you fell over yourself to believe me? You couldn't get enough of how Rose had failed.'

'Times change, don't they? For two pins you'd go back to her. If it wasn't for the children –'

'*Someone* has to put their interests first!' he cried.

A long, dangerous silence ensued. 'I'll forget you said that, Nathan.'

Another mouthful of whisky went down.

'Don't,' I said sharply, alarmed at his pallor. 'It's not good for you.'

'Shut up.'

'Look at me, Nathan.' Reluctantly, he did so. 'Tell me the truth. You want to see Rose. You miss her. You find this marriage less than satisfactory. Disappointing. Is that plain enough for you?'

'Stop it.'

'Rose is more your age, Nathan.'

'*Stop* it.'

'Coward.'

Nathan snatched up his glass and left the kitchen. The study door banged shut.

'Rice', I wrote on Eve's list. 'Spaghetti shapes'.

I crept up to the boys' bedroom, and peered through the door. There was a pillow on the floor, and Lucas had flung his teddy bear to the other side of the room. The shade on the nightlight had been knocked askew. My fingers twitched to put everything in order.

I leant against the door jamb, closed my eyes and imagined a future that featured hundreds of objects to pick up. And hundreds of shopping expeditions: tins of soup, cartons of orange juice.

Every year I would have to buy larger clothes for the twins. They would demand to play cricket and football. *Football!* Maybe Felix would prefer to learn the violin or the piano. That would cost money. Where would it come from? Barely a week went by without Nathan saying, 'We have to be careful. Our funds aren't limitless.' What he meant was that he was still paying Rose for her share of our home. Nathan might get ill. He was at the age when the body began to slow down. He would demand more peace and quiet. Where was *that* to come from?

That night, I slept in the spare room. Rattled and miserable, I dipped into the poems in *Origin of a New Species*, which Ellen had sent me. The publisher had been generous – or rash – and bound them in stiff board with facsimiles of her writing on the endpapers. The titles ranged from the epic 'Men's Lament' to the domestic 'The Object in the Fridge', and the eponymous 'Origin of a New Species'.

At forty-seven, I have reached the age of reason
No longer female, but no man either
Triumph?

Two pieces of news here. The narrator had a decade on me, and the outlook was not all bad. Throughout, the language was littered with references to 'banging', 'clacking', 'clashing' and 'the rush of dark tides' – enough to keep a small orchestra busy – and its noise permeated my sleep.

Some time during the night, one of the boys cried out and I heard Nathan moving around their bedroom, his voice low and hushed, soothing whoever it was.

In the early morning, Nathan slid into the bed, dragging me up from the long, slow depths. He was cold and needy. He spooned himself round me, and placed his mouth on my bare shoulder. 'Why didn't you come back? You should have come back, Minty. We shouldn't have slept on our anger.'

'Because . . .' I murmured, '. . . officially I hate you.'

'I was wrong, Minty, not to say anything. OK?'

I felt the bitter chill of not getting anywhere much and the sadness that descends after a major quarrel. 'OK.'

He smelt of sleep, his breath of whisky. 'What happens today, Minty?'

Ellen's poems were still racketing around my head. 'I don't know what happens today.' Then I remembered. 'It's Parents' Evening at school. Are you coming?'

'Yes.' His reply was barely audible. 'But probably late.'

I was suddenly alert. 'Do you need to tell Roger?'

Nathan chuckled in my ear. 'Roger's not my keeper. But if he asks I'm seeing the lawyer.' Nathan's fingers walked across my shoulder. 'I don't like lying. Much. But I have an idea you may be right.'

They were not our best sheets as they had too high a percentage of man-made fibre in the cotton but, for that reason, they were ideal for guests. 'You and I "worked late" most evenings. Remember?'

Nathan pressed the nervy point between my shoulder-blade and my spine. 'I didn't feel I was lying then. Isn't that strange?'

Those days had been made up of . . . what? Episodes that featured the pitching stomach, unreliable knees and fast-beating heart of the clichés? Yes and no. Certainly I had been dazzled and mesmerized by my own power. 'Get over it, Nathan. Most working mothers lie every day,' I said, then added, 'A check-up is a *good* idea.' His body was warming up. 'Are you feeling OK?'

'Fine. Don't fuss.'

If I had been more collected, I might have pointed out that I was only fussing because lately he had been behaving like a man of a hundred and ten. Furthermore, I reckoned we could alter our routines a little bit, do things in a different way, exercise more. The twins would love him to take them bowling. Or to play football on the common.

'As a matter of interest, have you ever considered that Roger is nearing retirement? Well, if you haven't, and I bet you have, why don't you think about his successor? They might get rid of Roger sooner rather than later.'

Nathan poked my hip. 'A little tasteless?'

'Yes – and?'

He changed the subject. 'Has Barry said any more about you going full-time?'

'He's still thinking about it.'

There was a small silence.

'About Rose, Minty.'

The sigh came from a black and bitter place. I was heartily sick of Rose. 'What about her?'

'Why don't you remember sometimes that you were friends? Good friends.'

Mornings in the Vistemax office that smelt of bad coffee and photocopying and Rose saying, 'Here, take these,' and passing over several dozen manuals on low-fat/no-fat/Outer Mongolian cuisine, or Five Hundred Ways to Thinner Thighs. 'You deal.' Coming in once, and finding her weeping, her too-pink lipstick smudged and the ends of her hair damp with rain. 'It's Sam,' she confessed. 'He's having a hard time with his girlfriend, and I can't bear it.' I had put my arm round her and kissed her cheek.

'Nathan. Please shut up.'

Their shared history, their shared children, their past – all mixed up together. 'Nathan, Rose said there was something else you had to discuss . . .'

'Nothing,' he said. 'It was nothing.'

'What was it?'

There was a pause. 'Nothing worth bothering about.'

You know what they say? When the mistress marries her lover, a vacancy is created.

He moved even closer and his hand snaked between my thighs. His stubble was grazing my skin. 'Minty, about what we said last night . . .'

Nathan probed even further and I bit my lip. He was hot now, and urgent. In our bedroom downstairs, my skirt and jacket were waiting on a chair. I had sufficient change in my purse for the morning's journey and a cappuccino. The bag containing my documents was zipped and ready to go. By my reckoning, I had precisely an hour to get the twins and myself up, breakfasted and ready to go.

So much in life is about timing. Truly it is.

His voice echoed in my ear: 'About last night . . .' And then I realized what Nathan was doing.

'Oh, my God, Nathan . . .'

His fingers dug into the soft part of my arm. 'Minty . . . I'm sorry about not warning you. She looked good, didn't she? Rose seemed in charge. Happy. That's good, isn't it? I'd never seen her hair that long before . . .'

He turned his face to me, and his eyes burnt with a fever that was not of my making.

With all my strength, I pushed him away. 'I'm not . . . Rose. Do you understand? I'm not Rose.'

8

The following week Barry called me into the office. 'Hey,' he said, 'I'm sorry I've taken so long to get back to you about the job.'

How lucky that I'd made an effort that morning and dressed up – floaty floral skirt and belted black jacket.

Barry eyed me with detachment, and apprehension flickered in me. Maybe things wouldn't go to plan. 'You know the Aids series has been green lit?'

'Yes. Congratulations.'

'Charles at Channel 4 is very excited about it.' Barry ticked off the points. 'Big money. Big foreign sales. And Kevin Stone to direct. Fantastic package.' Again the speculative appraisal. 'You know, Minty, you started me thinking.'

Generally when bosses think, it's bad for someone.

'I reckon this is how it is for Paradox. I've been looking to expand the output and I need plenty of ideas. You can come full-time on a probationary basis. Six months. Then I'll take a raincheck, see what's working and what isn't. We'll discuss money, et cetera, et cetera, later.'

I noted that Barry was not keen to go over the 'et cetera'. 'I'm delighted. Thank you.'

He leant forward. 'No problems with childcare?' I

raised an eyebrow and he added hastily, 'I'm asking as a friend.'

'All taken care of.'

'Six months, then.'

The joke that had darted like marsh gas through the offices when I left Vistemax had been quite funny. At other times, I would have savoured and dissected its delicious taste of *schadenfreude*. Which board director uniquely has two wives sacked from the same job? Answer: Nathan Lloyd. 'What a sap that makes me,' Nathan had pointed out. *Was he blaming me for my failure?* 'And what a fool me,' I had flashed back.

'Fine.'

Barry tipped back his chair. 'Also . . .' the word was elongated, '. . . Chris Sharp will be joining Paradox as producer. He used to work for me at the BBC. Bright. Sharp as his name. You'll be working together. He doesn't suffer fools.'

I smelt gladiatorial combat but I snapped my fingers in a bullish manner. 'So he'll thrive here, won't he?'

We were introduced to Chris Sharp at the Friday meeting. He turned out to be slight, brown-haired, hazel eyes, dressed entirely in black Armani. All the same, he was not that noticeable. Barry ushered him into the room. 'Say hello, girls.' Deb and I obediently smiled a welcome.

Chris raised a finger in greeting and sat down. Deb presented a proposal for a six-part series on gardening, *Dig for Victory*. 'Each programme will be fronted by a different celebrity gardener and deal with a different topic. The format of each programme will be a general overview and two related features. In the cities edition, we'll discuss a couple of city gardens, one established, one in makeover, then a feature on window-boxes – the pensioner window-box, the window-box for children –'

'Won't you need to put in something like the bachelor's window-box?' Chris interjected. 'Otherwise . . . a little unbalanced?' His confident gaze shifted round the table, tabulating and assessing. A feline quality was evident, a subtle and determined sniffing out of motive and opportunity. 'And should you stick to UK gardens if we want to sell in Europe?'

Her certainty punctured, Deb pushed back her North London hair. 'Sure,' she said. She retrieved the initiative. 'I would have come to that.'

Barry muttered about costs and Chris totted up a column of figures. 'You might have to increase the unit cost initially, but with anticipated wider subsidiary sales your margins are better.'

Barry looked pleased. 'Nice.'

Next up was *Middle Age: End of the Beginning*? NB ran the memo to myself: assurance and fluidity. 'I see this as a two-parter. One, defining what middle age is. Two, following a selected group and showing how it affects them. The conclusion being, it is a desirable phase of one's life.' I went on to show how the programmes would touch on affluence, diet, exercise, plastic surgery and spiritual regrowth. My commentary flowed over the rocks and pools of statistics and attitude, consumer practices and personal histories. Barry pressed his Biro up and down between his fingers. Chris cupped his chin in one hand, observed me carefully and took notes.

Deb got up and poured the coffee. She slid a cup in my direction and Barry's hand hovered over the biscuit plate. 'I shouldn't. I shouldn't.' The hand dived towards the Jammie Dodger. 'Middle age sounds like a destination resort,' he commented, without irony. A spray of crumbs accompanied the remark and Deb got a tissue out of her bag and gave the table a furtive wipe.

'We should emphasize to the controllers the spending power of this group,' I continued, 'which is underestimated, according to some experts. The grey pound is huge and middle-aged people will want to watch this programme. Particularly if we show them positive things.'

Chris scribbled away.

Barry ate a second biscuit and reflected.

Chris looked up from his notes. 'It's an interesting subject, but it's lacking . . .' the cat's eyes closed briefly '. . . sharper orientation. Shouldn't we be asking, "Are you, the thirty- or forty-something, irrelevant because you're middle-aged?'

Paige's eyebrows climbed Everest, then did so again. I enjoyed the effect.

'Rose just turned up out of the blue? Outrageous!' Propped up on some uncomfortable-looking pillows with her knitting, she begged for every detail. It sounded simple – Rose came, she and Nathan talked, I snooped, Rose went – but it wasn't.

After a couple of false alarms, Paige had been admitted to the People's Hospital and I had dropped in to see her on the way home from Paradox. The People's Hospital was the size of an airport and had been billed as the latest and finest, state-of-the-art. State-of-the-art or not, someone had failed to grapple with temperature control and it was far too hot. Also it had taken the entire reservoir of my patience to find the Nelson Mandela Maternity Unit.

Paige listened, her needles clicking. When I had finished, she said, 'You mustn't read too much into it.' Then she laughed. 'You've just described the perfect triangle.' She finished the row with a flourish. 'And Rose is at the top.'

'I've realized that Nathan didn't leave Rose because he was tired of her. He left her because he was tired of himself.'

'Maybe so.' She began a new row.

Paige's one-woman craft industry was a revelation. 'I didn't know you could knit.'

The crying of newborns punctuated our conversation. Reedy little sounds from lungs that were still learning how to function.

'There's nothing I won't do for my babies.' Paige counted stitches. 'I like to think of them wrapped tight and warm in something I've made.'

'You could buy a shawl.'

'Not the point. Putting myself out for them is . . . Ten . . . twelve . . . fourteen.'

A woman with long fair hair shuffled past the bed,

hoicking a drip after her with one hand, the other clasping her stomach. Flesh bulged on either side of her fingers.

Now I had embarked on the subject, it was difficult to stop. 'Perhaps she'd been thinking about Nathan and the old days. Perhaps she was missing him. I don't know. They seemed so cosy together, Paige. It was as if the conversation between them had continued all these years.'

Paige was not a natural knitter and she had trouble looping a stitch back on to the needle. 'Think yourself lucky it's just an occasional encounter. In the old stories, Rose would have died of grief, or killed herself, and returned to haunt you.'

'She does that without having gone to the bother of dying.'

'What a pity you don't write or paint. It's a good subject and your experience *is* first hand.' Paige put her needles together, wrapped the work-in-progress round them, and stowed it in a bag.

'Ah!' I cried. 'That's the trouble.' The too-well-remembered sounds of the new babies in their plastic cots provided a counterpoint to my cry. 'That's the point. Everything I do is second – second-hand. Nathan set up home before. He had children before. He had friends before . . .' The frosty Frosts, the disapproving Lockharts. 'A whole raft of them. Lined up in rows. And Nathan has family – boy, does he have family – which was set in stone before I arrived and has no intention of unsetting itself.' I paused. 'And then there is Rose.'

That blew the lid off the jar of maggots in my brain and they were crawling everywhere. Soon I must catch them and put them back. I contemplated my hands. 'I'm not complaining or anything,' I said. 'Just telling.'

'Well, you are complaining,' Paige pointed out. 'But that's fine. You can complain to me. And I can tell you that Rose is nothing. You've built her up into something for no good reason.'

'I'm sorry,' I said. 'I didn't mean to give you an earful. We should be discussing your bump.'

'Aren't you forgetting one thing?' Paige placed a hand on her abdomen. 'No one else had the twins, did they? That's not second-hand. Or am I missing something? And, by the way, you're godmother to the new arrival.'

'Oh!' Godmother meant acceptance. Godmother meant a settled role, a place in the hierarchy. 'Thank you, Paige.'

When Sam and Jilly's Frieda was born, Nathan went around in a grandfatherly glow. He wanted to know her weight, how well she fed and slept, was she wearing the Babygro he had chosen?

Pregnant myself, I listened to this with only half an ear. I had never reckoned on Nathan being thrown into such a fuss, but he was and that was that. However, there was no fuss over the seating arrangements at Frieda's christening, and that was that too.

'I'm sorry, darling,' Nathan apologized. He was awkward and out of his depth. 'Sam and Jilly feel it would be best if you didn't sit with the family.'

It did not take two wits to picture the kind of conversation that had taken place behind my back.

I grabbed his wrist. 'Did you stick up for me, Nathan? Did you fight at all?'

He hunkered down beside the chair I was sitting in. 'Of course I did, Minty. I'd fight a lion for you. But it's a difficult situation.'

Not that difficult. Divorce and remarriage were not unknown. 'Are you ashamed of me?' The words issued from between my clenched teeth.

'No. *No.*'

But I knew the question struck a note of truth and, what was more, Nathan was ashamed of himself.

'Where will you be sitting?'

'At the front.'

'With Rose, you mean.'

'She is the grandmother,' he said stiffly.

There are not many good things about being pregnant. In fact, there is nothing good about being pregnant – except one thing. If you're disposed to weep, and I was, it could be employed to advantage. I turned to him as tears drifted down my cheeks, and whispered, 'I know your family *hates* me.'

Deposited by Nathan on a back pew in Winchcombe's village church near Bath, and given a couple of cushions to prop me up, I knew I was the focus of many eyes – some of whose owners longed for me to fall to my knees (impossible at thirty weeks) and declare, *'I beg pardon for my sins.'* Everyone would have felt much better, including any sinners.

But I was tempted to rise to my feet and declare instead, in ringing tones, *'Nathan was not happy with Rose. He told me, again and again. Listen! I rescued him.'*

My reflections were interrupted. 'Minty.' Poppy's Richard edged past me and sat down on the empty seat on my left. 'Nathan thought you might like company, and I'd like to provide it.'

There was sufficient flirtatiousness in his manner to cheer me up. I smiled at him. 'That was nice of you.'

He smiled back, sympathetic and not unfriendly. 'Confession time. Being married to a Lloyd is rather exhausting, don't you think?'

After the main bit of the ceremony was over, and Frieda had shrieked in the approved manner, Nathan came back down the aisle. What it cost him, I dared not reckon. But that was the bargain I struck with my tears. He slid into the seat on my right and took my hand. 'Hi,' he said.

At the point of doing – such as stealing a husband who belongs to a woman you rather love (but not enough) – the exhilaration of the doing and taking is what matters. Only afterwards, during cold, reflective nights, does the enormity of what had happened assume its true shape.

Nathan stuck the photographs of Frieda's christening into the album covered with red leather he had bought specially. Photograph number one showed Jilly, Sam, and Frieda in a lace gown that had serviced several generations of Lloyds. Frieda's mouth had dropped open and there was a milk blister on her upper lip.

Photograph number two featured Nathan and Rose. Dressed in her favourite olive, a proud Rose was holding Frieda in an irritatingly competent way, and Frieda's tiny fingers curled round one of hers. But there was a clue to how she had been feeling: she had inclined her head to the left. 'Left is my best profile,' she had told me once. Nathan had his arms by his sides, but in a way that suggested he had wished to put one round Rose. Photograph number three was the formal group. In an old-fashioned hat, Jilly stood in the centre with the baby, Sam protectively beside her. Nathan, Rose and Jilly's parents, plus godparents, siblings and cousins, fanned out from this nexus.

I was not in the photograph. Nor did I speak to Rose during the whole affair. But I caught her looking at me. Many times. I knew this because I had been looking at her . . .

I seized Paige's hand, which was slick with sweat. 'How can I kill Rose off? In my mind, I mean. How can I stop her menacing my marriage?'

She sent me a look filled with pity. 'I'm surprised at you. It's simple. Just think of your children.'

I dug in my bag for the magazines I'd brought for her and handed them over. 'Is there anything I can do?'

'Linda's in charge, and Martin takes over in the evening.' Paige frowned. 'I have a funny feeling that Linda's thinking of quitting, which she absolutely cannot do.' She bared her teeth. 'If she does, I'll throw the book at her. Being here is a big nuisance. I wanted to be at Jackson's form play. I'd planned a huge tea-party, with all the works, and invited his teachers. This baby isn't scheduled to arrive for two weeks. I've been telling it off very severely, and it's not listening to me.' Filaments of knitting wool clung to the front of her nightdress. I picked them off and threw them away. 'Thanks.' She raised herself gingerly up the pillows and settled back with a tiny shriek. 'Ouch! That's my sciatic nerve. Martin's temper hasn't improved. He didn't really want this one. He says we won't have time to breathe.' She raised her eyes to mine. 'Did I mention I tricked him into it? It wasn't pretty, but it was the only way –' She stopped mid-sentence. 'It's acting up again.' She patted her stomach. 'Stop it.'

'Paige, I'll call at your house and check things for you. Is there anything you'd like?'

'Actually, yes. A huge bloody steak with a plate of chips.'

A group of male and female nurses were conferring by the nurses' station. One of the men, in a pretty blue uniform, headed for Paige's bed. 'Hi, I'm Mike. Just making sure you're not worried about anything, Mrs Hurley.'

'Nothing at all, except the small matter of heaving a huge baby into the world.'

He patted the bedclothes. 'You've done it before.'

'Precisely, Mike,' said Paige.

He consulted his clipboard. 'I thought we'd run over a few things with you, give you a timetable to work with. At midnight tonight, we'll give you . . .'

Unwilling to listen to these intimacies, I moved away,

only to be confronted by more intense ones: mothers feeding, changing their babies, groaning as they shifted in their beds. Some seemed bewildered, an emotion I recollected perfectly. There was an almost sinister quality to the hopefulness of others and their visitors who clustered round the cots. Each time a baby was placed in one, it was assumed that a good, successful, loving life lay in store.

I glanced at Paige. Mike was writing on his clipboard, and Paige was talking at him, arguing in a decided way. I found myself smiling. How very like Paige to try to organize the ultimately unorganizable such as birth or, for that matter, death.

Mike bustled away and Paige beckoned me back. 'I rather like being asked by nice men if there's anything I'm worried about.'

The drugs trolley was progressing down the ward as I bent over to kiss her goodbye. 'I must go – it'll take me *hours* to find my way out of here.' There was an unmistakable smell coming from Paige, the milky odour of giving birth. 'What made you decide your children should come before your career?'

Not an iota of doubt clouded Paige's serenity. 'Simple. When Jackson was a baby, he cried at night and I was the only person who could shut him up. He needed me, and only me.'

Nathan was already at home when I got back, reading to the twins who were tucked up beside him. Number seven was warm and hushed. Eve had put a stew into the oven, Nathan, Felix and Lucas presented a tangled, contented tableau, and I halted in the doorway to savour the moment.

I inspected the boys. Damp, soap-smelling and tousled. 'Lucas, have you put on your cream?'

He had a rash, but resisted every attempt to make it better. Beneath his father's arm, he shook his head. I fetched the tube. 'Come on.' Reluctantly, he tilted his head, and I dabbed cream on the red patches by his ears. Beneath my fingers, his skin was both dry and soft, softer than anything else I had known.

Nathan rubbed his knee. 'That's sore.' He spoke lightly. 'Falling apart.'

'Poor you.' I sat on the bed, buttoned Felix's pyjama jacket and smoothed his hair. 'Maybe you need some exercise.'

'Too tired for that.'

I glanced up as a spasm darkened Nathan's expression and I knew what my husband was thinking. If I had been Rose, I would have gone upstairs, searched out embrocation and insisted on rubbing it into his stiffening muscles.

Secret grief.

I could picture this intimacy – the collusion – to the last detail. No, I could *feel* it: a warm cosiness, with no spectre of the past to cast a chill. Nathan and Rose had acted in tandem. Which school for the children? Did the hall require painting? Hey! They had talked to each other over breakfast, after a night of sex that had left them with burning eyes and aching flesh. We can take it.

Was Rose aware of how lucky she had been? She had helped herself to the young, strong Nathan, the one who had carried a laden breakfast tray up to her in bed as if it had been thistledown, the one who had balanced job, wife and children in his palm with the skill of the juggler. *Look, I'm not tired. Look, I cannot fail.*

I switched off the light and we stood in the doorway as the twins settled under their duvets.

'What are you thinking?' I asked.

Nathan slipped his arm round my shoulders and kissed the top of my head. 'Nothing very much,' he said.

9

Early the next morning – shrieks of protest from the twins, abandoned bowls of corn flakes, mad hunts for school reading books, a flustered Eve, a preoccupied Nathan – the phone rang. It was Martin.

'Minty! We have another son. He arrived late last night. Isn't that great? He's big, he's beautiful – he's perfect! He's even textbook weight.'

'Oh, that's lovely. Congratulations.' I cocked an eye at Nathan, who was departing. 'We're thrilled.' Nathan sent me a thumbs-up and disappeared.

Tiny baby in cot. All limbs and digits accounted for. Clean and sweet after the trauma of its arrival.

A good, happy, successful life.

There was traffic noise in the background of this phone conversation. Martin was clearly on his way to work. 'Did you get any sleep? Shouldn't you take the morning off?'

'I had more sleep than I bargained for.'

'Oh, was it that fast?'

'Ask the mother. Paige kicked me out at the final stages. She said it was her business, not mine.' Martin's tone altered to convey a touch of anger and disappointment. 'But both are doing well.' After a pause, he added, 'I'm told.'

I cast around for a safe comment. 'Did Paige manage to finish her shawl before it all happened?'

Martin was at his very, very driest. 'Paige finished her shawl. She put the final touches to it during the second stage.'

'Good grief. She's made of iron.'

'That's a rather apt description,' he said, anger again creeping into his tone.

'I'll see her over the weekend. From next week I'm working full-time.'

'I know,' he said. 'She disapproves. She thinks it's frivolous to work full-time when you don't have to.'

Paige's disapproval hung over me as I organized a delivery of organic yoghurt and fruit for her, and settled down to making final arrangements: preparing to go back to full-time work was full-time work. Nathan had had fun teasing me about it: 'You're not going to war, you know.' Then, a little later: 'How's the supply train?' Or 'Do remember that the general requires a slap-up meal?' The joke ran and ran.

I pinned Eve's reconfigured timetable to the kitchen noticeboard, and considered the logistics of provisioning, school runs, recorder lessons and swimming practice, and felt a sneaky but shameful admiration for Mussolini: he had made Italian trains run on time.

I ran my finger over the blocks marking off days and hours. There was no going back. Come to that, there was a theory that the First World War had happened not because of the shots at Sarejevo – an archduke or two were expendable – but because the Russians had mobilized the trains. Once that had happened, it was impossible to cry halt.

Eve had walked the twins to school and, to my astonishment, had volunteered to take them for a session in the park afterwards. Already I felt differently: I had waved them off, pleased that all concerned in this household had reached another milestone. Again, I ran over my timetable. It was impressively severe in its just-in-time scheduling, with no margin for slack.

I ploughed on. Wardrobe checks. Nathan required new socks, and the twins had grown out of their dungarees. Equipment: 'Frying-pan,' I jotted on the shopping list. 'Food: Menus for the next two weeks.'

The phone rang. 'Minty.' Poppy dispensed with preliminaries. 'Can I ask you something? Do you think you could speak to Jilly?'

This was entirely unexpected. 'Why on earth?'

Poppy was full of importance. 'I don't know if Dad mentioned it but she's refusing to go to the States with Sam, who's been offered this fantastic job. Well, you know what that means. Sam will be the target of every predatory female in the state. And did you know that he bumped into Alice? His girlfriend before he married Jilly? She was very cut-up when he went off with Jilly. Personally, I think Alice manoeuvred it. She's never got over losing him. Anyway, he talked about her last time I saw him, and it set alarm bells ringing.' I knew Poppy well enough to grasp that it would be a short wait before all became clear. 'Minty, I'm sorry, but there's no two ways to put it and I'll have to be rude. Could you talk to Jilly and explain how the Other Woman seizes her chance? I shouldn't put it like that, but if Sam goes off by himself, then . . . who knows what damage Alice will do? Or someone like Alice. She'll believe it if *you* talk to her –'

My gasp brought Poppy to a halt. I didn't waste time saying things like 'Sam would never do that.' I didn't point out that it was hardly likely Jilly would appreciate anything I had to say and there was a good chance that she would be very angry. Or I might be very angry. Or that I had no wish to interfere. Or, even, it might be Jilly who found someone else. Instead, in simple acknowledgement of my Other-Womanness, I said, 'I'll see what I can do.'

'Would you? *Would you?*' Poppy was surprised by her own success. 'You don't mind?' She rattled on: 'I know it's a long shot but I couldn't think of anyone else. Or, rather, you seemed the best person . . . and everything seems a bit *muddled* at the moment.'

There was sufficient upset in Poppy's voice for me to take a risk. I took a deep breath. 'How's the poker?' I asked. 'Are you winning?'

'What are you talking about?' Then she fell silent. Finally she said, haltingly, 'Does Dad know?'

'No,' I said. 'I've said nothing. It isn't my business. But he and your mother are worried about you.'

Poppy began to cry and I couldn't make out what she was saying. Eventually, I heard, 'I'm going to have to ask Dad for money. I've had a bit of a bad patch . . .'

'No, you're not,' I flashed back. 'He has worries

enough about money as it is. You know he does. Can't you ask Richard?'

'No.' Poppy sounded terrified. 'I can't.'

'I won't let you bother your father.'

Poppy stopped crying and her voice was icy cold as she said, 'As you said, this is none of your business.'

'Maybe.' I rolled Poppy's dislike round my head. 'But it doesn't alter the situation.'

We said goodbye, more or less politely, and almost immediately Deb was on the line. 'Deb, you sound very cheerful. Have you won an Oscar or something?'

The words almost choked Deb, so anxious was she to spill them. 'Actually, I spent the evening hooked up with Chris Sharp. Quite by chance. He's fascinating. Done lots of things.'

I supposed – correctly – that this information was the real point of Deb's call. 'Chris is your new best friend.' I tried to make it sound like a question, not a statement.

'My new best . . . yes, friend. What I was calling about is *Middle Age.*' Deb's incredulous lilt underlined how remote it was from her own situation. 'There's a whole new lot of stats come in, one of which gives a rather shocking percentage of widows living below the bread-line. Might be something you should build in?'

'Sure. Thanks.'

'By the way,' Deb added, 'does the name Rose Lloyd register with you?'

'No,' I said. *No, no, no.* 'I mean, yes. She's my husband's first wife.'

There was a small silence. When it was clear I was not going to elaborate further, Deb said, 'Someone mentioned her as a possible presenter for my city-gardens edition. I'm having trouble finding anyone and apparently she's considered good news. I think I might pursue it.'

'I thought Barry wasn't keen on the idea?'

'*I*'m not giving up on it,' Deb said stubbornly.

When the phone rang yet again, about one o'clock, I pushed aside my notes with resignation.

'This is Sam.'

'And what can I do for you, Sam?' If my voice was a trifle hysterical, it was to be expected.

He was taken aback. 'Are you all right? You sound a bit odd. Is Dad home? I'm trying to track him down and the office said he was on a personal lunch but his mobile's turned off.'

'He isn't here,' I said, cheerfully enough, but unease and suspicion were running invasive fingers down my spine.

'Oh, well, not to worry. He'll be somewhere.' Sam sounded positive. 'Did he tell you about my new job? It's a big leap but I have an idea it'll work out. Jilly isn't so happy but I reckon, if I can get her out there, she'll settle. If not, we'll just have to improvise . . . or maybe Jilly can come out every six months. We'll miss each other, of course.'

'Sam . . . do you think that's wise?'

His tone cooled. 'We'll manage, but thanks for your concern. Are you sure you don't know where Dad is?'

But I was no longer listening. As soon as I could, I terminated the conversation. I was aware, of course, that old habits died hard. That's how addiction clinics make most of their profits. On the warm summer evening when Rose had brought me to number seven to meet Nathan for the first time, the three of us had discussed loyalty and Nathan had said, 'You end up being loyal simply because you've known someone a long time.'

Rose and Nathan had known each other for ever and there was nothing I could do about it.

I really imagined I'd cracked the problem of the future when I offered Nathan the alternatives to habit of a glossy body, hot blood, excitement, a – to quote Rose – 'comforting gaze'. I pictured our life together like postcards: a firelit winter scene with snow outside; sunny uplands, with hay baled in neat lines. I had imagined, too, that tenderness and laughter lasted.

I snatched up my bag and keys and found myself in the car, driving down the street, telling myself I had no idea where I was heading.

I lied.

As I approached the river, I lowered the window and smelt the sludge of low water. The city unravelled before me: dirty, assured and industrious, new buildings springing up like dragon's teeth in every empty inch. This was the city I admired, and melted into. It hustled and bustled: unsentimental, indifferent, surviving the knocks. It did not crave love.

There was a space outside Rose's flat, and I slid the

car into it. I turned off the engine and dropped my head into my hands. I considered what I was doing. I considered switching the engine back on and driving away. I considered how badly spies were rated in the food chain.

After a while I raised my head. The building on which I focused was a tiny, pretty, flat-fronted Georgian house with large clean windows.

And there was Rose. She was sitting in what appeared to be the bedroom of her ground-floor flat talking to someone out of sight. She was dressed to go somewhere smart, in a black linen skirt and tiny jacket to which was attached a fake camellia corsage.

She picked up her brush, ran it through her hair and the sun caught a glint of diamonds in her earlobe. Then she shook her head in an impatient gesture, ran her fingers through her hair. She looked grave – the exchange between her and the unseen person appeared to be intense.

Just discernible in the corner of the window, the bed was covered with a blue and white vintage quilt. Very pretty, very Rose. Rose sat down on it.

Had Nathan occupied that bed? Had he sneaked away from the office with a bottle of champagne? Had he drawn his first wife down on to the blue and white expanse and placed his lips on her bare shoulder as he had on mine? Had he propped himself up on his elbow and asked 'Can you forgive me, Rose, for what I did to you?' Or, had he murmured, 'I can't live without you'?

Was he sitting there now, out of sight?

I turned my head away, so sharply that my neck protested. Rose might have been beaten by the circumstances of her life but, plain as day, she had not. I don't know quite what I had envisaged – that she should live out her life on some prison ship with hard labour? And I have no idea why I thought that someone to whom I had done such wrong should suffer more. But I did.

I could taste my hatred and despair, and I could smell the musky odour of sweat springing under my arms in the heated car. I turned back to look through Rose's sparkling windows, and I was peering into my mind's secret mirror, with its reflected darkness and turbulence.

A man bearing a bouquet of spring flowers – meltingly beautiful, whites, yellows and pale greens, crossed the road and let himself into Rose's front garden. He was tall, with sun-bleached hair, wearing scruffy old trousers and a brown jacket with leather patches at the elbows. I knew him well from the photographs.

He rang the bell. It took Rose a minute or so to open the door. A minute when she would have said to the hidden Nathan, 'What's your story?' And Nathan would reply, 'There's no point in hiding it any longer.'

Rose appeared on the doorstep. 'Hal,' I heard her say. 'Oh, good. Oh, *good*.' She reached up and kissed him, and his arm snaked round her. Then I drew a sharp breath as Rose called over her shoulder, 'Mazarine, he's here,' and a smartly dressed woman came out.

The three chatted for a while. Mazarine was a small woman, with carefully dyed hair, who gesticulated a lot. Hal was less vocal, but amused, his arm round Rose's shoulders. When he smiled the lines on his face were etched deep. And Rose? She was radiant, her happiness almost palpable and living – something she woke up to each day, which defined the seconds and minutes as they slipped past.

Those time-tested loyalties stretched between the three. Even had I not known who they were, it was clear that they were old friends. But I did know who they were: years ago, Rose and I had sat over salad lunches and discussed most things, including their friendship.

Nose buried in the flowers, Rose went inside, then came out again to lock the door. Hal linked arms with both women and they walked on to the street. They were too busy talking to notice me. As they passed, I heard Rose's friend say, '*C'est la bêtise, Rose. Tu sais.* Hal is impossible . . .' Rose turned her head and looked at him.

Together they turned in the opposite direction and disappeared.

When I got home, I went up to the spare room and searched for Nathan's notebook. It was no longer there. Up on the wall, the painting of the white roses presented its challenge. The bruised, dying petals scattered at the base of the vase sent a mocking message. *It was all so brief.*

Downstairs in Nathan's study, my shameful search continued. I scanned the bookshelf, opened drawers, rifled through the filing trays.

Nothing.

Was I going mad with suspicion and supposition? Possibly. I glanced up and caught a blurred reflection of myself in the window. There was a woman in danger of being suffocated by hatred and guilt.

After a while, I had to accept defeat. Nathan had withdrawn from the conversation I had tried to hold. He was covering his tracks, and denying me the tiny glimpse he had given me of himself.

Perhaps, if I had remained silent, in the true, repressed English way, it would have been different. Perhaps if he had known that I knew but had not tried to turn it into words, he would have been satisfied. NB No marks here to *Successful Relationships*.

A scarlet woman possessed the virtue, at least, of being useful. We need sinners in order to feel superior. To be the other woman, as Poppy had indicated, also had its uses. The role of second wife trailed way behind in interest and excitement. But that was what I was left with. No doubt the moralists would rejoice, and I was prepared to allow it – after I had insisted on having my say. *Nathan had been unhappy with Rose.*

Downstairs, in Nathan's study, I picked up the Post-it pad, and scrawled on the top one: 'Don't go.'

I stuck it on the filing cabinet.

Nathan never mentioned whether or not he found the Post-it.

I did not refer to it either. But I did say, in passing, 'You're not letting things slip at Vistemax?'

Nathan had never been a fool. 'Do you know something?'

A nerve flickered in my cheek. 'I don't *know* anything. But it's a jungle out there and you have to keep up.'

'Has Gisela said something?'

'No, but I don't trust Roger.'

'Shall I tell you something? Neither do I.' He placed a finger on my shoulder and pressed down. 'Let's hope nothing happens. Otherwise . . . Well, a lot of things, but money will be a problem.'

His finger hurt. I thought of Nathan steering a path through the rough jungle. He would need all the help possible. I gave him what I had. 'Gisela has a lover, Nathan.'

Nathan went very still. 'Why are you telling me?'

'I promised I wouldn't, but I thought you should know. It might help. You're my husband and we share things and I know whose side I'm on. He, the lover, wants Gisela to leave. But I don't think she will.'

Nathan removed his finger. 'You never know what people are capable of doing.'

No. One was never sure. 'Really?' I replied, but what I really meant to say was: 'Will you being seeing Rose again?'

Gisela rang me in the office. 'How's the new routine?'

I told her that, two weeks in, it was going fine, and she asked if we could have lunch. 'I know it's last minute,' she said, 'but I do have something to discuss.'

I scribbled 'Dance? Series?' on the article I was reading about ballerinas in *Harper's* magazine, and we agreed that she'd pick me up at twelve forty-five.

She was in Roger's Vistemax company car. The interior had been sprayed with a manufactured flower scent that made me long for the smell of Tarmac – or manure, even, anything normal. The comfort of the leather upholstery provided insulation from the real world – which, presumably, was why a company executive had favoured it.

My head was full of ideas, the ones that ached to take flight. 'What do you think about a television series on modern dance? Salsa, tango . . .' I rattled on until I noticed that Gisela was not paying attention. 'What do you want to talk to me about?'

'Several things,' she replied enigmatically. 'Vistemax for one. But let's enjoy ourselves first.'

'How's Roger?'

'A bit gloomy. A lot of boardroom activity . . . There's talk of selling off the *Digest,* and of launching a free newspaper. Apparently the younger generation doesn't read newspapers and the advertisers have spotted this. But Roger's capable of dealing . . .' Gisela checked herself and pointed out of the car window. 'Did you see those shoes?'

I pictured the scene. Nathan and Roger in shirtsleeves at the gleaming boardroom table, mineral water, crystal glasses, biscuits and a plate of fruit – exotic stuff like paw-paw or star fruit, the chef's fantasy, which no red-blooded male would dream of eating.

Gisela said dreamily, 'Roger gives me a nice life, you know. And he's promised me a merry widowhood. Don't look shocked, Minty. Roger and I have discussed it many times.'

The car slid along Piccadilly and turned left, then into one of the small streets off Bond Street and stopped in front of a gallery with a bow window and discreet gold lettering, that read 'Shipley Fine Art'.

Gisela swung gracefully out of the car, thanked the driver and instructed him to return in a couple of hours. She was wrapped in a leather jacket, so supple it was like silk, so well cut that not one wrinkle marred the line across the shoulders. 'Come.'

The gallery was a rectangular room, painted cream with antique-stained floorboards. At one end there was a desk with a flower arrangement in pink and white and a couple of spindly chairs. There was no evidence to suggest that money changed hands, no paperwork, only a stack of catalogues.

Two men stood by a large painting at the far end of

the room. It depicted three boxes of differing sizes suspended in a night sky dotted with stars and planets. The boxes looked as though they should fit into each other, but on each an attachment made it impossible. The first, painted red, had a chain looping over the sides from which hung a ball inscribed 'Poverty'. Dozens of naked babies clung to the sides of the second, so numerous that – shockingly – a couple had let go and were falling through space. A tree grew out of the third, a pretty arching shape with withered leaves. The painting was entitled *Slow Apocalypse*.

'So good,' Gisela breathed in my ear.

'*Is* it?'

She smiled. 'We shall have to educate your eye.'

No doubt this was an oblique – and unflattering – reference to Nathan's taste in Cornish pictures. Gisela's eyes widened a little, but even if I had been in complete sympathy with her I could not have dropped Nathan into the black hole of flawed taste.

She smoothed the sleeve of her jacket, and my un-educated eye immediately noted that her hands were trembling. 'That's Marcus.' She indicated the taller of the two men.

Everything fell into place. My main reaction was surprise. This was the man with whom Gisela had a special friendship, whom she probably loved, and there was nothing out of the ordinary to single him out. Marcus wore a linen suit, rather rumpled, with a gold watch-chain. He had thick, unruly hair, smallish but nice eyes and a pleasant expression. He gestured a lot and talked fluently. 'Simple to ship . . . a couple of weeks. Insurance . . .' He acknowledged our presence by raising a hand.

'OK.' The client was American, expensively dressed. 'I'll phone you the details.'

Politely, Marcus ushered him out of the gallery and whipped round. 'Hello.' He touched Gisela's shoulder. 'This must be Minty.' We shook hands. 'Forgive me, I was finalizing a sale that had been a long time cooking.' The pleasure of the sale shone in his eyes, and his voice was surprisingly deep. 'Good, eh? I've only just opened here, and the rent has to be paid.' He lifted his shoulders in a gesture designed to include me in his despair at the iniquity of landlords. 'Shiftaka is an extraordinary painter. I hope you'll take a look at the rest of the exhibition.'

There was sufficient suggestion that I was extraneous, and I took the hint and moved away. But not before I saw Marcus draw Gisela close.

For a second or two, Gisela relaxed against him. 'How are you, Marcus?'

'You know *exactly* how I am.'

'I wouldn't have come if I'd known you were going to be difficult.'

'Don't bother with games, Gisela.'

And Gisela – cool, determined Gisela – still trembled. 'Sorry.'

In the back room, I studied an oblong painting, *Submission*. It featured a series of broad horizontal stripes running through the red palette, from brick to palest pink. The eye longed to remain anchored to the red at the top of the canvas, and it took a conscious effort to pull it down through the spectrum, which, I suppose, was the point. It was only after I had examined the bottom section of the picture that I realized the pale pink contained a misty outline of Africa. The link between the pretty pink and the implication that Africa had been bled dry was intended to shock, and it did.

In the other room, the murmur of voices was punctuated by Marcus raising his. 'Haven't we muddled around for too long?'

Gisela said something unintelligible, and Marcus added, 'End of the road, Gisela.'

I edged back into the main gallery. Marcus was leaning against the desk, inspecting his shoes. Gisela was flushed and upset, fingering the necklace of Persian coral round her neck.

'I think I should go,' I told them.

'I'm coming, too.' Gisela grabbed her bag.

Marcus rolled his eyes, and levered himself upright. 'OK.'

Gisela snapped open her bag, got out a mirror and, in a now familiar gesture, dabbed at the area below her eyes. 'Give me a minute.'

I turned to Marcus. 'The artist? Tell me about him.'

Without a blink, Marcus shifted into another gear. 'Abandoned on the streets of Kyoto, he was fostered by a retired geisha. He's a political painter . . .'

His gaze slid past my shoulder, and rested angrily on Gisela.

As we left, Marcus placed his hand under Gisela's chin and forced her to look at him. 'Dinner tomorrow. You owe me that.'

Yearning was printed all over her porcelain perfection. She seemed docile, obedient, even. 'Tomorrow, then.'

But outside in the street she slid back into her normal self. 'Did you like him?'

'Very much. But, forgive me, he doesn't seem your type.'

She tucked a hand under my elbow. 'He isn't. That's the point. Isn't life funny?'

We skirted a pile of rubbish spilling out of a black plastic bag, and stepped into the road. 'Surely Roger knows,' I said. 'How do you get to see Marcus?'

'Oh, details.' Gisela was impatient. 'One can always arrange them. How did you get to see Nathan? But Roger doesn't know, and he never will. OK?' She squeezed my elbow. 'OK?'

I crossed my fingers. 'OK.'

We reached the opposite side of the street, and Gisela said, 'I met Marcus when I was eighteen and already married to Nicholas, who was my godfather. Nicholas was fifty, but well-off, concerned, generous. Marcus came to catalogue his paintings and he's been in and out of my life ever since.'

'Why didn't you marry him after Nicholas died?'

Gisela swivelled to a halt, and flicked her finger in the direction of the Hermès shop window on the corner of the street. Reverently framed in it, on a bed of flowing silk, was a beige Birkin bag. 'You get used to certain things, and Marcus was very poor in those days. He says I'm a gold-digger. He's right. I am.'

We continued our progress towards the restaurant where Gisela was taking me for lunch, traffic wailing, shop windows crammed with desirable objects. 'Marcus and I would have worn each other out,' she said at last. 'I didn't want that, Minty.' She pushed me towards a door that looked expensive. 'I want to give you a good lunch.'

As I was being helped off with my coat in the hushed restaurant, my mobile rang. 'Yes?' I answered.

'Minty.' I felt the hairs rise on my arms. 'It's Rose.'

Maybe Rose had seen me outside her flat after all and she was ringing to say, 'Please don't do that again'. Or, 'What do you think you're playing at?'

I stiffened with dismay. 'Rose, this isn't a good moment. Can I call you back?'

Rose's voice veered uncharacteristically from its normal modulations. She sucked in her breath, with evident effort. 'Minty, is anyone with you? . . . I'm afraid . . . you must prepare yourself. Minty . . . Minty . . . Nathan.' She collected herself. 'Minty, I think you must come at once. Nathan isn't very well, and it would be best if you came –'

'Where?' I said. Alarmed by my tone, Gisela laid a hand on my arm. '*Where* should I come?'

'My flat. As soon as you can.'

Gisela asked almost shrilly, 'What's happened?'

'It's Nathan. Something's wrong. That was Rose. He's at her flat.'

'Oh, my God – I hadn't imagined –' She checked herself. 'Right. I'll cancel the car. It will be quicker to get a taxi and I'm coming with you.'

'What's he doing with her? Gisela, what can have happened?'

'Let's get the taxi.' She pulled out her mobile and called the Vistemax driver, spoke briefly and disconnected.

I can't remember much about what happened next, apart from staring hard at a set of traffic-lights. Then there was the motorcyclist who edged so close to us that the driver shouted at him.

'You shouldn't have come,' I said to Gisela. 'There's no need.'

Gisela was matter-of-fact. 'It did sound urgent but it's probably nothing. Anyway, I'd like to meet the famous Rose.'

'Gisela,' I repeated, 'what is Nathan doing at Rose's?'

She did not meet my eye. 'There's probably a very good reason.'

I stared out of the window. *Nathan and Rose. Old times.*

Keeping one hand on my leg to anchor me, Gisela hunched forward on the seat and issued instructions to the driver. Once, she asked me for more precise details and I heard myself giving them: 'It's left at the bottom of the street, then right . . .'

Was Nathan really ill? He had rung me that morning on my way to work. It had been a relaxed, easy conversation, almost intimate.

'Lost my glasses.'

'I saw you put them in your briefcase.'

'Ah.'

'What have you got on today?'

'Roger wants to see me about something. Probably to do with the supplement on Africa we're planning for the autumn. How we can help it without inflicting Western values at the expense of indigenous ones, that sort of stuff. Doesn't stand a prayer of enlightening anyone because it'll be so politically correct it'll be utter rubbish.'

I had laughed and now, in the speeding taxi, with anxiety beating a rising crescendo in my ears, I wondered if he'd heard that laugh.

Surely there could be nothing wrong with Nathan. But perhaps there was. Perhaps Nathan so missed the nice, loving things that happy couples say to each other that he had gone to Rose and said, 'Let's go back to where we were,' and the effort had made him ill.

He had been pale lately.

When we arrived at Rose's gleaming-windowed flat, Gisela gathered up her handbag and I searched in mine for the fare. 'I think I should stay with you, Minty. It might be that Nathan's had a shock.'

My eyes narrowed. 'Gisela, what do *you* know?'

She pushed aside the notes in my hand. 'I'll pay.'

The front door to the flat appeared to open of its own volition and Rose was on the doorstep. She was white – whiter than a clown. I had never seen anyone quite so drained of colour, and there were black streaks on her cheeks. She looked from Gisela to me, and back to Gisela. 'You'd better bring Minty in.'

I stepped into a small hallway painted mushroom and white, with sanded floorboards. It flashed through my mind that this was a place I would like to be.

'I have something to tell you,' said Rose, directing a warning look at Gisela. She took both my hands in hers. Her touch burned. 'Minty, will you come and sit down in the kitchen? Please?'

I was silent. 'Where's Nathan?' Rose snatched my hands away, and my anxiety changed to fear. 'What's he doing here?'

'Please, Minty,' said Rose. 'C-come and sit down.' Awkward and stammering, she seemed completely at a loss. Then she pulled herself together. 'Come into the kitchen.' Again, she looked at Gisela. 'Could you help me, please?'

I cried out sharply, 'Has Nathan gone? Is that it? Tell me.'

Rose shivered. 'I'm trying to explain to you, Minty, and I'm not sure how to do it.'

'Something *has* happened to him.'

'Yes,' she said, and again she took possession of my hand. Her fingers pressed into mine. 'Yes, yes, it has.'

'But *what*?'

'Has Nathan complained of feeling ill lately?'

'No . . . Yes. I've been a bit worried.'

Rose was drawing me towards the kitchen. 'I must talk to you before . . . anything . . .' She glanced at Gisela, as if for help. 'I'm afraid I don't know your name, but could you persuade Minty to come and sit down?'

147

I dug my heels in. 'Just say whatever it is, Rose. Have you got something to confess?' I paused, and threw out the first thing in my head even though I knew it would not delay whatever was making her so clown-white and shaky. 'What are you two up to?' I turned towards a door opening off the hall. 'Is he in there? Nathan!' I called. 'Nathan, are you there?'

'Don't . . . don't go in. Not yet.' Rose placed her two hands on my shoulders. 'Minty, you must prepare yourself.'

Various explanations presented themsevles. *Nathan had left me. A doctor had given him bad news. Nathan had gone back to Rose.* 'You and Nathan *are* cooking something up.' I was frightened – and angry that my husband should have shared the news with Rose. I tried to push past her, but she caught my arm – so hard that I winced.

'Minty, listen – *listen* to me. I'm sorry, but Nathan is dead.'

Gisela gasped. Dazed, confused, I shook my head and did not reply. Eventually, my head cleared and I said, 'Don't be silly,' in a conversational tone. Extraordinarily, I appeared to have this reply quite pat. 'I was talking to him earlier. He wanted to know where his glasses were. He couldn't find them . . .' Gisela's hand was at the small of my back, propping me up. The words slithered into silence, and I thought, *The boys.*

I was not prepared. It was not as though Nathan and I had had a long run in to this moment. I hadn't written a list. *Get used to idea. Read manual on bereavement . . .* There had been no doctor saying, 'I'm so sorry, but . . .' No Nathan saying, 'Minty, we have to face it . . .'

Painting and literature were stuffed with farewell scenes. Wives knelt beside the bed – not always weeping. Children were generally at the foot and wept enough for the wives. Black-clad relatives waited outside death chambers. This primary rite of passage, this moment when the strings were so tightly drawn that the merest touch would produce a note of exquisite beauty and sadness, had been rehearsed down the ages and everyone in these scenes knew their role.

An arm went round my shoulders, and I was enveloped in jasmine scent. Rose's. But the arm was awkward. I muttered, 'This isn't a joke, is it, Rose?'

'A *joke?*'

I disengaged myself so abruptly that Gisela reached out to steady me. 'When?'

'An hour ago. I don't know. It was . . . quick. Very quick. One minute Nathan was here. The next he wasn't. He gave a little sigh. That was all.'

I examined my hands in detail. Snagged cuticle on fourth left finger and a thumbnail that required filing.

Shocked and clearly agitated, Gisela asked, 'What can I do, Minty? Tell me.'

'Go,' I replied. 'It's best.'

Gisela shrugged the leather jacket closer round her shoulders. 'Of course.' The front door clicked shut.

I raised my head from the detailed observation of my hands. 'I need to sit down.'

I allowed myself to be led into the kitchen and put

into a chair. 'You must take your time.' Rose was so gentle, oh-so-gentle. She placed a glass of water in front of me and I stared at it. *Nathan is dead.*

After a while, I asked, 'Can I see him?'

'Of course. They haven't moved him. It was too late by the time the ambulance came. He hasn't been disturbed. There is nothing to be frightened of, Minty, I promise you.' Rose's voice beat on my eardrums. 'The doctor will be here in a minute. Death certificate. I'm afraid it's necessary.'

'Yes.' I managed a sip of water – its no-taste on my tongue the accompaniment to my slide from wife to widow. I buried my face in my hands. How was I going to tell the boys? Lucas had felt sick this morning. Had he been sick? 'Rose, I must phone home.'

'I'll do that for you,' said Rose. 'I'll explain that you'll be home later, but I won't go into detail.' She bent over me. 'Is that best? I think so.'

After I had drunk a glass of water, Rose helped me upright and led me to the door of the sitting room. She stepped back. 'He's in there.'

11

The room had magnolia walls, a chair by an open window upholstered in faded china blue, several pictures and a photo on the small table by the sofa.

The air coming through the window was cool and damp – the type that frizzes the hair. It held a promise, though, of spring, for it brought with it the tiniest drift of flower scent from the shrub blooming beneath the window.

And sitting in the blue chair? I took a snapshot look – and concentrated on a cushion. This was made from mushroom shot silk, looked old and there was a surprising variety of texture and colour.

My feet did not appear to be connecting with the floor and a pulse thudded in my ear. The detail of the room accumulated a dossier. If I had been cross-examined in court, I could have told you everything about it. *How useful she is*, the judge might think. *How indispensable.*

I turned back to the blue chair.

We're planning a supplement on Africa in the autumn, I heard Nathan say. *Shouldn't you have kept Lucas at home?*

He was sitting well back in it, his body folded in a natural position, his face turned towards the door as if he was listening for something, someone. A lock of his hair, tinged with grey, had fallen over his forehead. His mouth was slightly open. Had he been speaking to Rose when his heart shuddered, jumped and declared, 'Enough'? His left arm was tucked by his side, palm up, fingers curled a fraction.

He was still Nathan – that was evident in the bone structure, the angle of the chin, the width of his fore-head. Yet he had become remote. Between one heartbeat and the non-arrival of the next, he had weighed anchor and rowed far away. He had sped past his children, past his life with me towards a horizon of which I had no knowledge.

'Nathan . . .' I reached over and smoothed back the lock of hair. Tidying him as I knew he liked. His skin held scintillas of warmth, and hope flared that I could run from the room, shouting, 'He's not dead, only asleep.'

I touched one of the fingers, willing it to curl round mine. What was there left to read in his face, with the blind, closed eyes? There was no distress as far as I could make out, only surprise and a suggestion of . . . release?

In the other room, I could hear the murmur of Rose's voice.

Had she traced the line from nose to chin, as I did in the gentlest gesture? Had she bent over to be quite, quite sure that no rogue breath soughed from his mouth, as I was doing? Had she sunk to her knees and whispered, 'I don't believe you're dead, Nathan,' as I was now doing?

I shed no tears. No easy relief, then. Again I searched Nathan's face for clues. 'Why did you not call me, Nathan?' I begged the still figure, as I knelt in front of him like a penitent. I knew – I feared – that Nathan had struggled on feeling ill and alone. 'You should have called me. I would have come. Of course I would.'

How *was* I going to tell his . . . our . . . children?

Which would be the right words? My toes cramped, but I welcomed the discomfort.

In the end the pain was too acute. I got to my feet and went in search of Rose. She was in the kitchen, sitting at the table with her head in her hands. At my entrance, she looked up. 'Are you all right?'

'What do you think?'

'I don't think anything, Minty.'

I pushed myself into a chair. 'I was thinking how unfair it was on Nathan. He didn't *deserve* this.'

Rose got up and went to a cupboard, took out a bottle and presented me with a full glass. 'Brandy. We'd better have some.'

The glass was heavy, with a pattern incised into it. It felt expensive and weighty. I recognized it. We had two exactly the same in Lakey Street. 'We divided things,' Nathan reported, when he and Rose divorced. 'Straight down the line. I owed her half of everything.' He had been so pleased with his fairness and generosity that I had snapped shut my lips and had forborne to point out that two matching glasses out of four were not *that* useful and half a set of silver-plated cutlery limited one's options.

Obediently I drank. Rose asked, 'Were there any clues that Nathan's heart was giving him problems?'

'No. But, then, I hadn't been looking for any.'

She accepted this. 'I was concerned about him. Don't ask me why, as I hadn't seen much of him. But even so . . .' she was too upset to bother with tact '. . . there was always the connection between us and I felt . . . Well, I knew when things weren't right. I did try to ask him about his health, but you know Nathan . . .' She arranged both hands round her glass and lifted it to her lips. 'How like him. How very like Nathan to say nothing.'

I couldn't face talking about his death. The subject and the situation were too big and unknown, too fearsome and desperate. 'Did you talk to Eve?'

'Yes. She'll manage, so you're not to worry. I talked to her very carefully.'

Before I could stop myself, I lashed out. 'Did you talk to Nathan very carefully?'

'Stop it, Minty.' Rose raised a white face. 'Don't.'

I did stop it. Instead I groped for clues to the puzzle. 'I think he saw a doctor a couple of months ago. There were episodes when he said he was feeling really tired. But that was it.'

There elapsed another of those pauses that were impossible to describe, only endure. I gulped the brandy as if it were orange juice. They say men wounded in battle do not, at first, feel anything. Then they do. The brandy was a precaution.

Nathan had not often mentioned death. Not to me, anyway. We were too busy negotiating life. When he did talk about death, it was to wag a metaphorical finger: 'As long as it doesn't come too soon.'

What had Nathan been doing in Rose's flat?

I felt cold and faint. I struggled to reach past myself, to think of Felix and Lucas. They wouldn't understand, perhaps not for a long time. I tried, too, to consider Sam and Poppy.

And Rose.

And, yet, out of all the suppositions and shocks, the one question that forced itself past my lips was, 'Rose, what was Nathan doing here?' I stared at the brandy in the glass and waited for the answer. 'I must know.'

Rose positioned her glass on the table and got to her feet. Slowly, deliberately, she walked round to where I sat, bent down and wrapped her arms round me. It was a gesture we both suffered and endured. Rose needed to make it because it was in her nature. I had to accept it because I craved the comfort of contact, even from her. She gave a jagged sigh. 'Poor Minty, what you must think.'

'Yes,' I echoed bitterly. 'What I must think.'

Her soft cheek was against mine. 'Nathan was here for a reason. Had he told you what happened?'

It was pitiful to lie with Nathan dead in the next room – especially, if you're a person who prefers to call a spade a spade. But 'Yes' slipped through my lips. I didn't know what she was talking about but hated to admit it.

'Then you will know that Vistemax . . .' Rose's face was close to mine, her arms a circle in which I was trapped.

'Yes . . .'

My mendacity had a false, brassy note but I clung to it. A tap dripped and the fridge emitted a muted electrical choke. We both knew that I was not telling the truth, and Rose was debating how to handle my ignorance of something that was clearly important.

Rose released me. 'That's why.'

Wasn't death supposed to be a cleansing agent? A blow so huge and pulverizing that all the petty emotions, subterfuges and secrets were smashed? It certainly drew a line.

'Oh, for goodness' sake.' I braced myself. 'I *don't* know, Rose. Tell me.'

But the phone rang and Rose answered it. She said, 'Yes, his wife is here. Yes, we're waiting.' She was cool and in control, the sort of person who was practised at formalities and procedures. 'That was the doctor.' She kept her hand clamped round the receiver. 'He'll be here any minute.'

Impatient to know, I laid my hands flat on the table. 'What's happened? And why did Nathan come to . . . you?' My knuckles whitened with the pressure. 'Why here?'

Still clutching the phone, Rose told me the truth: 'Roger sacked him this morning.'

'Sacked!' The news was brutal enough to bring the blood rushing into my face. I pressed my hands to my cheeks. 'Poor Nathan.' Rose put down the phone. 'So they got him in the end,' I said. 'They always do.'

'Vistemax is hardly the gulag.' Rose leant against the sink. 'And Nathan had a good life with them.'

'You always did see the best in things and people.' Still I clung to the inconsequential, and I was curious as to how Rose's givingness could survive just now. 'I often wondered if it was a strength or weakness.'

'I leave you to decide. I don't think Nathan expected it. Do you?'

'Nathan did not confide in me' would have been the truthful answer. 'He had been there a long time, and he knew the form.' But, clearly, he had neither known nor cared enough to guard himself against the consequences of Roger's cynical appraisals. 'He was in his fifties . . . and there is a sell-by date for all of us. There was probably somebody else coming up fast, and you know how they operate at Vistemax.'

'Yes,' answered Rose, flatly. 'Funnily enough, I do.'

'Roger would have dressed it up to Nathan. He would have said, "Change is happening faster than ever and we must harness our energies to keep up." As sacking formulas go, it does pretty well for most people.'

Rose completed the narrative: 'By the end of the session, Nathan would have been persuaded into thinking his was a necessary martyrdom. To be desired, even.'

Rose was talking about her own sacking, as I had been talking about mine. 'No,' I had to defend him here because I wanted to get it right. 'He wasn't that sentimental. He knew his worth. He would have fought. He would have been angry . . . very angry, so angry his heart couldn't stand it.'

Rose turned away.

My gaze alighted on objects around the kitchen. A white jug. A wicker shopping basket by the door into which plastic bags had been stuffed.

'Nathan had his vulnerabilities,' Rose offered. 'Everyone does. Roger would have known which button to press.'

The picture assembled of Nathan listening to the delicately phrased insults of the sacking. I knew, *I knew*, that Roger's careful cruelty would have smashed into his pride. It was then Nathan must have felt the first intimations that his heart was faltering. Did he register then the choke and stutter of his blood, the pain of the failing muscle, and refuse to call out? God help us, Nathan would rather have died (and did) than ask the man who had just sacked him for help.

'Peter Shaker's taking over,' Rose added.

'Well, that would have killed Nathan if nothing else.'

Rose's lips curved in wry amusement. 'Yes, it probably did.'

Later, I told myself, I will force myself to believe that Roger chose Peter over Nathan for a *good* reason. After all his years at Vistemax, Nathan deserved that at the very least. Dull Peter and his good-hearted Carolyne in the navy blue suit and gold buttons – both of them, not so long ago, had eaten twice-baked cheese soufflé, then chicken in ginger and bitter cherries in maraschino at our table. On Nathan's behalf I felt a black killer rage dig in for the duration.

Rose choked, then made a sound like a small animal in distress. She heaved herself round, placed both hands on the edge of the sink and, retching, leant over it. I got up, filled a glass with water and handed it to her.

She wiped her mouth with the back of her hand. 'One should never drink brandy too fast.'

Now it was my turn to slide a hand round her shoulders and press her into a chair. 'Rose, are you getting drunk?'

A little colour crept back into her cheeks. 'Nathan had only been here fifteen minutes or so. He said he wanted to talk over what had happened, and how he was going to manage the changes. He wanted to sound me out.' She must have registered my instinctive flinch because she added, 'He would have talked to you, Minty.'

That was unanswerable and none of Rose's business. 'Don't say that.'

She was taken aback and struggled with her answer. 'After the doctor and the undertakers have been, you must go, Minty.'

'Undertakers?'

'Yes, I had to contact them. Nathan can't stay here.'

I left Rose in the kitchen, and fled back to the cold sitting room, the smell of spring and Nathan. 'Why didn't you ring me?' I demanded of the still figure.

'You married me because . . .' went the stupid, dangerous game we sometimes played in the early days and there was only one rule. All the answers were to be a tease. 'I married you, Nathan, because you drove a Lexus.'

'And? What else, Minty? My looks, my wit?'

'Naturally your serious bank account. And, Nathan, you married me because?'

'Oh, I married you, Minty, because you were pregnant.'

In his hour of need, Nathan had not defected to Rose because he wished to talk over his options or to block out a new future. He would have done that with me and I would have given him better advice. No. No, Nathan had turned to Rose because he craved her comfort, the long history, her sweetness in his hour of deepest trial, her reassurance.

Behind me, Rose entered the room and closed the window. She had got herself under control and spoke calmly. 'I opened it to allow his spirit to go. I think . . . I believe it's customary.' She clicked the catch into place, and I had an almost irresistible urge to laugh at the notion. Rose fiddled with the curtain – calico, thickly interlined and evidently expensive – and I imagined Nathan's spirit forcing his way past it and up into the dark somewhere.

'When the undertakers arrive, we shall have to take some decisions.' Rose nerved herself visibly because once this quiet interlude was over a process would begin. 'When I've spoken to Sam and Poppy.' She turned to me, as if appealing for help with such an appalling task, and I tasted fear at what lay ahead of me too. 'I dread that. They will be devastated.'

'Decisions?'

'All of us must decide what we want. We must try to think of what he would have wanted. Poppy and Sam will have views.'

'Rose. *My* decisions, I think.'

She shook her head, and a strand of hair worked loose. 'That can't be, Minty. We're all in this. We're his family.'

'And I'm his widow.'

'How will you tell Felix and Lucas? Will you need help?' Rose adopted the voice I had sometimes heard in the office when either Sam or Poppy rang up. It was ultra-soothing. I used to think it rather silly and false until, after I'd had the twins, I realized it was a means of staving off panic.

'No.' My rejection of the idea was instant. I did not want her softness and comfort stealing my children.

I glanced at my watch. Incredibly I had only been there three-quarters of an hour or so. I wondered who else knew and was, even now, telephoning others, or the florist to order flowers: *With deepest sympathy*. I wondered if the clocks would stop. Who would cry genuine tears and who would not. I wondered if Nathan had been a tiny bit ready, whether he had thought about his death at all. Or if he was circling up there, cursing.

'Why don't we sit with him?' Rose suggested. 'He won't be here for much longer.'

I chose a chair close to the body. Already Nathan was drawing further away, much as his body must have been stiffening. 'Your children had their childhood with him.' I was fierce with the unfairness for my boys. 'Mine won't.'

Rose sat on the sofa and her eyes met mine. 'Yes, Minty, there was that.'

After a moment or two, Rose began to talk about the old days when she was married to Nathan. Every year they had gone on holiday to Priac Bay in Cornwall, always to the same cottage. She described the slap of the water on the sides of the clinker fishing-boat, the hiss and heave of the sea, the oily smell and texture of mackerel.

'The thing I remember most is the rain. Sometimes it was hard and slanted in from the west. At others it was as soft as a caress, and seeped into your clothing. However carefully we put away the mackerel lines at home, they were always knotted when we got them out of the cupboard the next year. Nathan was impatient and demanded that we buy new ones, but I said, "No," and made it my business to make him laugh. It was an effort but I learnt the routines. I planned a good meal on the first night, and I bought a heater so that we weren't cold. By day two, he seemed always to breathe easier and he slept differently. Quieter. When he picked up the book I'd chosen for him, I knew the best part of the holiday was beginning. It was a sort of healing from the frazzle of the year. I don't think we would have survived so long without Cornwall.'

'I never let him go to Cornwall,' I said. 'What was the point? It was your territory. I thought it would be good for him to look at different things. I thought a little guaranteed Greek or Italian sun would work magic, but he never liked the heat. You knew that. And the boys were too young. The heat made them fretful and difficult to manage.'

'But I was tired, too, always so tired,' Rose said, 'until the children were older. I didn't realize, and it wasn't a question of accepting the tiredness. I just thought that was the way things were until I began to feel better. Really better. By then it was too late and Nathan had looked elsewhere.'

When the doctor arrived, he examined Nathan. 'It

looks very much as if it was a heart-attack,' he told us, writing notes, organizing paperwork. 'The post-mortem will confirm it.' He was a busy man, and overworked, and did not stay long.

The undertakers also arrived, three burly men, and the dimensions of the flat seemed to shrink.

Rose took Nathan's hand, kissed his cheek and stepped back.

'Please could I say goodbye privately?' I asked. Rose and the men shuffled away, leaving me with my husband. 'I'm sorry,' I whispered, bent over and adjusted his tie, and pulled his jacket straight. Just as he liked it. 'I'm so sorry.'

It seemed to me that the flesh was vanishing beneath my lips as I kissed him goodbye.

I retreated to the kitchen where Rose and I helped ourselves to more brandy.

Eventually there was a knock on the door, and one of the undertakers, an older man who introduced himself as Keith, addressed a series of questions to Rose. It was clear that he regarded her as the widow.

'Excuse me,' I interjected. 'I am the current Mrs Lloyd.'

Keith's gaze slid between us. There was a modicum of embarrassment but little surprise. 'I'll await your instructions, Mrs Lloyd. Your husband's body will have to go to the mortuary for the post-mortem, but after it is released we can discuss the details.'

I cast around in my mind. 'There's a church near us, I think. I'll find out who the vicar is –'

'Oh, no,' said Rose. 'Nathan would have wanted to be buried at Altringham, Minty. Where his parents are.'

'Altringham? That's too far away,' I cried.

Keith stepped delicately round this one. 'Perhaps it will be specified in the will. It always takes a little time to make these decisions. And we're at the end of a phone.'

Rose busied herself folding a tea-towel, first one way, then another. Finally she placed it on the table. 'Of course.'

They left, taking Nathan with them. The front door clicked shut, leaving a stony silence between us.

I broke it: 'I am his wife, Rose.'

Rose sighed. 'So am I. In a way.' She shrugged. 'So help me. In a strange way.'

'For God's sake . . .'

'It doesn't matter. Listen, Minty . . . listen to me, we *can't* leave him where no one will know about him. We can't leave him where he'll be alone.'

I hated myself for minding that Rose had got it right, and usually did. 'I will decide where Nathan is buried, Rose.'

She whirled round. 'Go, Minty.' She pushed me out of the kitchen and into the hall. 'I'll take you home in the taxi. Then I must – I want to see my children.' She turned an anguished face to mine. 'I *must* see them.'

As we left, Rose snatched up the briefcase in the hall and stuffed it into my hands. 'That's his. You must take it.'

12

The dark has never held any real terrors for me. It was the time in which hot, pleasurable things were accomplished. It was the moment to dream, to plan, to sleep: to touch a warm, sleeping body, and marvel at its beauty, or its power, or to realize that you hated it.

But I went to bed that night in fear.

There were scattered clues that I had come home and gone through the motions but I cannot remember much. A waterfall of socks, pants and trousers flowed out of the boys' linen basket. In the bathroom, my flannel was damp. In the bedroom, my shoes had been put away in the cupboard. In the kitchen, the dishwasher had been switched on and was ready to unload. A half-empty tin of tuna from the boys' supper was wedged between the cheese and the bacon in the fridge.

Eve and I had whispered to each other while the boys romped upstairs. 'So dreadful, Minty.' Her complexion combined an agitated red and white, and she had brushed her hair flat. 'Poor, poor Nathan.' She sketched the sign of the cross on her breast. Not once but twice, and I suppressed a hysterical desire to hiss, 'That won't help him now.'

'Eve, we won't tell the boys until tomorrow . . . after school.' She looked sceptical, and I summoned the energy to persuade her. 'It will be easier for me. It'll give me time to do some things before I concentrate on them. I can make arrangements . . .'

'OK.'

I knew I should be doing things – but what? There were procedures, but unknown ones. Then there were questions to be answered.

I rang Theo, Nathan's lawyer, and was forced to repeat that *Nathan is dead* because even *über*-professional Theo could not believe it. 'Will you help me?' I begged him. I was frightened that Vistemax would not honour Nathan's severance package.

'Don't worry.' Theo was swift with reassurance. He clicked his tongue. 'Hear that? That's the sound of the bit clinking into place between my teeth. They'll *pay*.'

I rang Barry to tell him. 'This is so awful.' His voice oozed genuine concern. 'Awful. You're not to think of setting foot in the office for the time being. We'll see to everything. I'll brief Chris.'

Chris would steal my ideas.

So be it.

But I had already forgotten Chris Sharp when I rang Paige. A similar species of words filtered down the telephone – it was the stockpile on which we drew in moments of blackness and emergency. 'So awful.' Paige was stuttering with shock. 'Terrible, Minty. Can you manage? I'm so sorry I can't help at the moment. Linda can come and take the boys.'

'I haven't told them yet. I'm waiting for the right moment.'

Paige could not, and did not, resist this challenge. 'Won't they guess something's up?'

'I'm good at pretending.'

There was a small silence. 'Yes, I suppose you are.'

Between these conversations, I did my best to make a list. But it proved beyond my powers. I struggled with words such as 'probate', 'death registration' and 'newspaper announcement', but they refused to slot into their hierarchy.

'Mum.' Lucas ran into the house and hurled himself at me. 'Mum, read me a story.' He was glowing with exercise, so winning and wholesome that any film director who happened to be passing would have scooped him up.

A hand slipped into mine. 'Hello, Mummy.' It was Felix. 'You look sad. Are you sad, Mummy?'

I bent down and pulled them into a hug. Their small hard heads butted into my chest. They were now my entire responsibility.

Nathan was with me throughout that fear-filled night. We were in the sitting room. The clock ticked on the half-moon table by the window and we were arguing about it. Nathan thought it would be safer on the mantelpiece. 'Please do as I wish, Minty.' I glanced up from a card of paint samples and heard myself say, 'Do you think Eastern Beige would look right in here?'

'Eastern Beige,' he retorted. 'Compost, more like.'

Nathan was in the garden, in his brown corduroys, favourite blue shirt and a pair of wellingtons, digging under the lilac tree. On the landing, I was struggling to iron a shirt, which, however I stroked and stretched it, would not lose its creases.

Nathan pushed the fork into the earth, reached into the ground with both hands and extracted a bundle wrapped in a white wool shawl. 'This is my secret grief, Minty,' I heard him say, in that restless, half-conscious interlude.

The bedroom was airless, and I alternated between sweating and shivering, which, I supposed, was shock. *Could I have done more? Yes, I could. Was Nathan so unhappy? Yes, he was* . . . I fled upstairs to the spare bedroom. The bed was not made up but I slipped on to the bare mattress, pulled the folded duvet over me and stared into the darkness.

I could not see the painting on the wall above me in the dark but, with an internal eye, I traced those roses. I calculated their dimensions, the arrangement of the shapes on the canvas. I struck up an intimate acquaintance with each shade and tint, ticking them off on my fingers: chalk white, clotted cream, weak tea, and the blood-brown of the darkening petals scattered at the base of the vase.

When I could bear it no longer, I slid out of bed, reached up and turned the painting to the wall.

There. They had gone.

A little later – how long? – I found myself in Nathan's study. I opened his filing cabinet to reveal the sections neatly labelled in black ink. 'Insurance', an orange file. 'House', blue. 'Lawyer', red. 'Health', yellow.

Why had he chosen yellow for health? It was not a

good colour. Yellow was dispiriting and suggested disease. Yellow fever. Dengue fever. Malaria. Jaundice. I flipped it open at the back, then rifled through the documents from the bottom up.

There were assorted letters from doctors with addresses in Harley Street. One reported the results of an eye test. Another a blood test. All routine, all normal, negative, non-threatening. The top letter on the pile was different. It read: 'Dear Mr Lloyd, As we agreed at our consultation, I have made arrangements for you to see my colleague, Mr Oxford, at the London Heart Hospital. I have explained my concerns – blood pressure, murmur, etc. – and he will proceed with the investigation. If you would kindly get in touch with him directly . . .'

The letter was dated six months ago.

I reread the polite sentences. Behind the bland 'concerns' by a professional's marker and coded allusion. Nathan, the consultant was suggesting, displayed a cluster of symptoms and was required to do something about it.

Nathan had failed to do so.

Angrily, I snatched up the letter. Why? And why had he not told me?

It would have been so easy to manage. We could have attended the appointment together. I would have sat meek as a mouse reading *Country Life* or dog-eared copies of *Hello!* in the waiting room while the highways and byways of his arteries and the chambers of his heart were flagged up on a screen elsewhere. As we listened to the verdict of what was wrong, I would have reached out and taken his hand.

He would only have had to say, 'I'm having problems with my heart,' for me to swing into action. It would have been a field day for lists. *Low-cholesterol spread, green vegetables, vitamins, an exercise bike.* And for timetables, which I was good at too. *Exercise, 7–7.30 a.m. Breakfast, 7.45 . . .*

The enormity of Nathan's silence was an excruciating reminder of how silent we had been during his life. I had failed to comfort him. I had not stroked his cheek. We had not waited stoically together in a consultant's anteroom.

Neither had my phone rung this morning, and I had not picked it up to hear him say, 'Minty, I've got something to tell you . . . It will be a shock.'

So he'd never heard my reply: 'Vistemax sucks. Have you rung the lawyer? Nathan, this isn't personal, you know . . .' And he never heard me say, 'Nathan, hold on. I'm coming over to get you and we'll talk this through.'

Nathan had chosen to bury his anguish in silence, and then to seek out Rose.

But Nathan was dead.

I fell to my knees by the filing cabinet, placed my hands on the open drawer, for it held the facts – the hard facts of which I was so fond – of Nathan's life.

I bowed my head and, finally, I wept.

It was three thirty in the morning on the first day of my widowhood.

*

At nine the following morning I sat at Nathan's desk in his study. The boys had gone to school, and Eve was vacuuming in the room next door.

The phone rang. 'I don't know what to say.'

'You don't have to say anything, Roger.'

'I assume it was his heart?'

I put down the phone. It rang again almost immediately. 'If there's anything we can do, it shall be done,' said Roger. 'Please will you let us know when the funeral is . . . Minty, I recognize that this is the most tragic, intolerable situation . . .'

Was this the moment to point out that Roger had made *such* a mistake in dismissing Nathan's accumulation of experience for the sake of change? Should I also mention that he had almost certainly driven Nathan to his death?

'I know you'll have mixed feelings –'

'No, Roger. Not *mixed* feelings. Very straightforward feelings.'

'We were doing what was best for Vistemax.'

'Peter Shaker? Really?'

There was nothing more to add. Roger was a businessman and I was a widow, and however much I might long to connect, there was no chance. Again, I terminated the conversation and took the phone off the hook. Not a moment too soon, for it was almost too much. And I could not let go. Not yet. Perhaps never.

The vacuuming drilled into my skull. I called, 'Eve, could you stop that?'

She appeared from the sitting room. 'You need clean house, Minty. People will come.'

Would they?

'You look bad. I get you cup of tea.'

I sat at Nathan's desk, holding the cup and wondering how long my fingers could stand the pain. That was easy to deal with – unlike the pain I must inflict on Lucas and Felix. An expert could tell me what to say. Experts had formulas at their fingertips. 'Daddy has gone on a long journey, and won't be coming back.' Would that do? Or . . . 'Daddy is watching over you, but he can't actually be here.'

The doorbell rang, and Eve clattered out into the hall.

It was Mrs Austen: crabby Mrs Austen. 'Eve. We've just heard. Here is soup. My tomatoes. Feed it to them.'

Ten minutes later, the doorbell sounded again. This time it was Kate Winsom from across the road. 'This is so awful,' I heard her say, as I cowered in the study. 'Look, I'm off to the supermarket. Can I do the shopping? Tell Minty I'll be in touch at a more – at a more appropriate time. Unfortunately, I have to fly now. The children . . .'

For the tenth time, I attempted to make a list. But what good was that?

The doorbell – oh, that doorbell – rang and I pressed my face hard into my fingers. Next thing, I felt a light touch on my hair. Gisela said, 'I came as soon as I could.'

I reared my head. 'You knew what Roger was going to do and you didn't tell me.'

'Would you have expected me to? Would you have done? But I was going to drop a hint at lunch.' She slid a finger on to my pulse and felt it. 'Have you slept? And when you did you last eat?'

My hair felt hot and heavy, and I pushed it back. 'Cup of tea. I don't know, Gisela.'

She bent over me and spoke with an urgency I had never heard before. 'You'll need your strength, Minty. You have the twins to think about. I'm going to get you some more tea and some toast.'

She led me into the sitting room, and eased me down on to the sofa. 'You will remain there until I come back.'

The morning light streaming into the room was so bright it hurt my eyes. I looked out of the french windows. The lilac tree was unfurling its first buds and, in the neighbouring garden to my right, a magnolia had unleashed tiers of porcelain-cup blossoms.

'Spring is cruel,' I said.

'Yes.' Gisela had returned with a tray. She put it down on the coffee-table, reached into her handbag and switched off her mobile.

'Goodness,' I said. 'It must be serious.'

The sun lit a patch of carpet that years of exposure had changed from dark grey to a lighter shade. I heard Nathan, so clearly: 'No, we can't afford a new carpet.'

'Minty . . .' Gisela picked up a finger of toast spread with butter and Marmite. 'Eat.'

'I never touch butter, Gisela. Waistline.'

'You do today.'

I took the toast from her and chewed. The tang of Marmite was not disagreeable, and the tea was hot and strong. Gisela sipped from a second mug. 'Terrible tea. What is it?'

'Ordinary stuff. I don't know.'

'Lapsang's better.'

Cross out 'ordinary stuff' on weekly shopping list and substitute 'Lapsang'.

From her vantage-point, Gisela appeared wise and Buddha-like. She was filled with substance and purpose while, overnight, I had shrunk into a depleted figure huddled on the sofa. 'Minty. About Rose.'

That piece of information was a gold mine for clacking tongues. *Do you know where he died? With his first wife.* It was unlikely to remain secret.

'Roger has talked to Rose. He rang her after he spoke to you. He's going to see her this afternoon.'

'But not coming here?'

'I'm here.' She reached over to put her mug on the tray. 'You know, cutting Roger off isn't going to raise Nathan from the dead.'

'No.' This exchange was superfluous because at that point Nathan did not seem to be dead. He was there, in the sitting room, because I could feel him very strongly.

Gisela continued, 'Let me advise you. Don't ignore Roger's offer of help. You'll need it.'

The remaining Marmite soldier sat an angle on the plate, so I adjusted it. 'Nathan was the reliable one. He was a man who tried to be the person who never left you in the lurch. But it was all too much for him. Leaving Rose. Marrying me. Vistemax. He couldn't keep the bandwagon rolling. His body protested.' I was feeling very odd behind my eyes. 'Am I making sense?'

Gisela was wearing one of her blindingly white blouses, with three-quarter-length sleeves and tucking across the breast. It was French, of an exquisite cut. A rope of large pearls circled her throat, with matching ones in her ears. She was hunched forward on the chair, her body language spelling pity, pity. 'I don't expect you to make sense.' She pulled a notebook out of her bag, wrote something and tore out the page. 'I can't do much for you, Minty, except help with the small things. Here's the name of a good florist. Just tell them what you want for Nathan and they'll understand.'

Florist? 'Thank you.' My lips were trembling. 'Did Roger say how Nathan was yesterday?' Gisela made a play of stowing the notebook in her bag. 'I'd like to know what he said, and how he looked.'

'All right.' She seemed almost to have been expecting my question. 'Roger was dreading the meeting. Nathan was a friend – no, don't look like that, Minty. You *know* it as well as I do. Roger told him straight. At first Nathan didn't say much.' Gisela paused. 'Roger said he walked over to the window and turned his back on him. It was a shock, he said, and he needed a minute or two. Then he went on to the attack. He told Roger the decision was crazy and wrong. Furthermore, Vistemax did not need destabilizing at the moment.'

'Nathan fought back.' To those who knew him intimately, the signs would have been readable. When he tightened his mouth, things were not good for the opposition. If he dug a hand into a trouser pocket, he had worked out the strategy.

'I have never seen Roger so sad, so rattled. At the prospect . . . of doing it,' Gisela offered. 'And Nathan gave him very hard time.'

'Gisela, Nathan was about to lose everything.'

'Not everything. He had you and the boys. Roger reckoned that he might quite glad of a period at home to see more of the twins.'

I stared at her, astonished. 'Nathan was sacked because Roger thought he'd make a good nanny?'

Gisela's lips barely moved. 'Nathan had had a good innings.'

'Let's hope Roger can be as philosophical when it's his turn to head back to the pavilion.'

With a touch of panic, Gisela said, 'There's no need, Minty –'

'Roger really concluded that Peter Shaker was a better man than Nathan?'

Gisela rearranged the cuff of her dazzling shirt. 'Is it the right time to discuss all this? It's impossible to be rational.'

'Oh, rationality,' I said. 'It's overrated.'

I got up and went to the half-moon table. I lifted the clock and placed it on the mantelpiece in the space Nathan had always intended for it.

Gisela picked up her bag. 'I must go. But remember,

Roger will help if he can. I'll do all I can with the arrangements. If you like.'

I heard myself cry, 'Why did Roger do it?'

Gisela put down her bag again, and looked deeply into my eyes. 'That's the way it is. Nathan did it to others, remember.'

'But it killed him.'

'No, it didn't. Nathan liked his whisky, he had a stressful job. He had a . . . busy home life. A large family. Those things contribute. It wasn't getting the sack, Minty. Nathan's *heart condition* killed him.'

The doorbell continued to ring, but I let Eve deal with it. Each time she returned bearing something. A bottle of wine with a label that read, 'Condolences.' A paperback entitled *Wills and Probate*. The cover was coffee-stained and many of the pages were dog-eared. In the section entitled '14.4.3, Fair Division Between Parties', someone had scribbled violently in the margin, 'I should be so lucky.' Who had sent it, I asked Eve, but she said she hadn't recognized the woman.

Wills and Probate lay on the kitchen table in front of me. I supposed the rest of the world was carrying on nicely without Nathan. Chris Sharp had probably enjoyed a good day. Peter Shaker's wouldn't have been too bad either, except for the odd jab of conscience. I felt sorry for Carolyne, who would be caught between loyalty to her husband and her strict notions of what was correct. Booting out Nathan in favour of Peter would not come under her heading of the latter.

Someone walked into the kitchen. 'Martin,' I said.

He placed a cling-wrapped Pyrex dish on the table and bent to kiss my cheek. 'I came as soon as I could and I've brought a macaroni cheese.'

I cast around for the polite response. *Any* response. 'Lucas loves macaroni cheese.'

He sat beside me and took both my hands in his. 'Paige asked Linda to make it.' There was a pause. 'This is terrible, Minty, but you'll survive. That's what I've come to tell you. It might seem that you won't, but you *will*.'

His grasp was cool and firm, and I was grateful for it. 'Keep telling me that, Martin.'

'I have every intention of doing so.'

The macaroni cheese had been made to perfection with a crisp cheese crust on top. 'I'm not sure what to do first.'

Martin let go of my hands, and took a piece of paper from his breast pocket. 'I've made a list,' he said, 'cobbled together from what I remember when my parents died. Funeral arrangements –'

'A list!' I exclaimed. 'You made a list when you have so many other things to do.'

'That's what friends are for.' Martin handed it over. 'It helps to have something concrete to think about.'

'How are Paige and the baby?'

He frowned a trifle. 'They're fine. I'm not sure how much rest Paige is getting.'

'Are the nights bad?'

'I'm in the spare room at the moment.'

It was getting dark, and the lights needed to be turned on, but I did nothing about it. Martin and I sat in the kitchen while dusk crept in, and I was grateful, oh, so grateful, for his presence.

'No story tonight,' I said to the boys. 'I want to talk you.' They were scrubbed, shining, hopeful. 'It's about Daddy.'

Two pairs of trusting eyes fixed on me. I patted Felix's bed. 'Come and sit beside me.'

Felix settled on my right, Lucas on my left. I put my arms round them and held on tight. Felix wriggled free, slid down and fetched *The Very Hungry Caterpillar*. He held it out to me with both hands. I shook my head. 'No story tonight, Felix . . . Daddy . . .' I faltered, and stopped. 'He . . .' I was searching for the words – the right words, the best possible ones. I was searching for control. That I *must* exert. I was searching to help them travel through a grief-stricken future.

'Daddy.' Lucas was confident and giggly. 'Our daddy?'

'Yes, your daddy.'

Felix picked up Blanky, hauled it up and climbed back into a position against me: a warm, surprisingly solid weight for his size.

'Daddy loved you very much,' I said, and pulled them closer, 'and he will always be with us, but I'm afraid something's happened to him . . .' I choked and struggled to continue. 'He got very ill, and his heart couldn't beat and he died. He's gone away and he won't be coming back.'

Lucas burst into tears. 'He promised to come to the football.'

I experienced an overwhelming sense of heaviness and defeat. 'Lucas, Daddy can't come to the football.' I took his little hand and stroked it. 'He would have come if he could.'

'Where's he gone *to*?' Lucas's sobs were panicky.

'He's gone up into the sky. He can probably see us, and he'll think about you all the time. I'm going to take care of you, and we shall be together. And we'll think about him a lot, won't we, boys?'

Felix wriggled out of my embrace and went to the window. '*Naughty* Daddy,' he said angrily.

'Daddy's not naughty, Felix,' I said. 'He couldn't help it.'

'Naughty, naughty.' Felix repeated. Then he said, 'There's Tigger in the street.'

'Come back, Felix.'

But he shook his head and remained stubbornly by the window. Lucas sighed and looked up at me. 'Does that mean we'll be a getting a new daddy to drive the car?'

13

Felix climbed into my bed and woke me. 'Mummy, where's Daddy?'

It was six o'clock and I had just fallen into a heavy sleep, but his question sent a shock through me. Through stiff lips, I murmured, 'Do you remember we talked about it last night, Felix? Daddy's gone away to where he's very happy and peaceful.'

The voice in my ear was insistent and anxious. 'Are you going away too?'

I wrapped him in my arms, and we ravelled into a knot of limbs under the duvet. 'No, I'm not.'

'Promise?' Felix wound his leg round my torso, and pressed his head into my chest. Bolted together in that innocent, sad embrace, I pictured the river of DNA that flowed through me into him. I was him. He was Nathan. He was me. Never before had I chosen my words with such care: 'I have no intention of going away, Felix. I've got you both to look after.'

Felix's grip loosened. 'Daddy's naughty to go away.'

Nathan had had no choice. He had not wanted to go. Either of those statements would have been true. Yet even a child could spot how hopeless and insecure they made the world appear, and the point of being a parent was to persuade your children that they were safe.

After a while, Felix relaxed. His body grew heavy and his breathing regular. I lay with my arms still round him as the sounds of the day outside multiplied and I knew I had to get up and face it.

The boys and I got dressed together. 'I bet I can put my trousers on quicker than you can put your socks on.' I held up a red pair and a blue one.

'Quick,' said Lucas, and hauled off his pyjamas. His bottom had a picture of a cat on it, drawn in black Biro.

'What on earth have you two been doing?'

At the breakfast table, I said, 'If you eat all your cereal, you can have ice-cream for supper and an extra long story at bedtime.'

In that way, with stops and starts, bribes and games, we got through that early morning and breakfast. That was how it would be for a good while: games, subterfuges and stratagems to make the days pass.

After Eve had taken them to school, I cleared the table and tidied the kitchen. I'm a widow, I thought, as I swished water round the sink.

As I went upstairs to make the beds, the letterbox in the front door rattled. The flap was lifted and an eye peered through. I recognized it, and opened the door. 'There's a perfectly good bell,' I said to Poppy's stooping figure.

'Minty.' Poppy levitated smartly. 'I wasn't sure about coming here but Mum sent me. There are things we need to go over.'

Clad from head to toe in black, her eyes red and sore,

she looked frail and devastated. Pity for her and Sam, pity for the boys, pity for myself swamped my tired mind. 'I don't know what to say, Poppy, except that I'm so sorry.'

'Sorry.' She experimented with the word. 'I didn't see him last week as usual. I cancelled because . . . well, because . . . something came up.' She grimaced. 'Isn't that typical of Fate – or whoever? Just so cruel.'

'Yes, it is.'

Richard had been parking the car and joined us. He was dressed for the office. He gave me a quick hug. 'Minty, are you all right?'

'You'd better both come in.' I stepped aside. Richard placed an arm round Poppy's waist and guided her into the house. Poppy's eye fell on Nathan's coat, which was hanging on its peg, and she stopped in her tracks. 'That's his. Oh, Dad.'

Richard manoeuvred Poppy past the coat and into the kitchen. 'Poppy hasn't been too well since she heard the news.' He eased her into a chair and brushed the hair off her forehead. 'Not surprisingly.' He turned to me. 'I hope someone's been looking after you, Minty.'

A hand squeezed my throat without compunction. The only person who was likely to take care of me was dead. 'Eve and the neighbours have been very good.'

Poppy's haunted gaze roved restlessly over the objects in the kitchen. 'Everything will change, won't it?' She glanced at Richard. 'I woke up this morning, and it seemed fine. Then it wasn't. Can you afford to stay here? You won't have to sell the house?'

'I don't know. I'll have to find out. I'm still trying to take everything in.'

'Sorry,' said Poppy. 'That was stupid of me. Unfeeling.' Her frailness was emphasized by the thin wrist she raised to her forehead. 'I'm sure Dad will have provided . . .' There was a tiny pause. '. . . for everyone.'

Very occasionally during the past few years, I had wondered if Poppy and I could skirt past Rose and become friends. Everyone benefited from an alliance within the family on which they could call at times when the chips were down. In this case, Poppy and I might have achieved something rather wonderful – a transformation where none had seemed possible.

But we had not.

'Where are the boys? How are they? I can't bear to think of them. At least . . . they're so young. Maybe it helps if you're that age. Maybe you don't feel . . . quite . . . in the same way, I mean.'

'It's a nice theory,' I said.

Richard positioned himself behind his wife, and laid a hand on her shoulder. 'It will take time,' he said, in his practical way, 'but they need normality, not you weeping over them.'

'That's not fair.' Poppy jerked away from him.

I seized on his lead. 'The boys are at school. They break up on Friday. We're trying to keep their routine as usual. They're bewildered, but OK. So far. I tried to tell them in the best way I could but they don't really understand. How could they? They're so little.'

Poppy made an inarticulate noise and covered her eyes with both hands. Richard cleared his throat, and said, very nicely, 'Would you like us to have them for a day or so? Poppy and I could take them for the weekend. Rose said she'd help.'

I had a sudden and terrible premonition of what life would be like without them. 'No, please, *no*!' I hadn't intended to be so confrontational but I couldn't bear the idea. 'They stay here. You mustn't steal them.'

'Minty,' Poppy sat up straight, 'we didn't want to steal them. We only wanted to help. We thought it might be best for them while you get on with arrangements.'

Richard was appalled. 'The offer wasn't meant in that way, Minty, believe me.'

I felt my way into a chair. 'I'm sorry. Of course, you didn't. Things are a bit odd at the moment, and I'm not sure what I'm saying.' Richard looked as though he might understand. 'It was kind of you, but I don't think they'd want to be taken away from home by strangers.'

'We're not strangers,' countered Poppy. 'I'm their half-sister.'

I licked my lips. 'Rose is a stranger.'

'OK. OK. We're not going to steal the twins, but the offer still stands, whenever you want to take it up.' Poppy pushed herself awkwardly to her feet. She hesitated. 'Was it . . . was it heart failure?'

'Probably. We won't know until after the post-mortem.'

'How typical!' Poppy let out a passionate wail. 'There was Dad just slogging on, providing for everyone. He must have been so worried, and he had no one to confide in.'

'Poppy!' Richard sounded a warning note. 'We don't know yet.'

She twitched a fold of her black skirt, which had caught on the chair, and said more quietly. 'Now we're all saying things we don't mean. Sorry. We're not ourselves.' She crossed to the wooden dresser ranged along the wall, and ran a finger along a shelf. 'He liked this, didn't he? And he loved this blue and white plate with cabbage roses. I was with him when he bought it.'

'Yes, he did.'

Richard interposed himself deftly between me and his wife. 'I want to reiterate that if you need help with anything, Minty, you have only to ask.' He shone with youth and affluence. The results of an organic diet and money were evident in his skin, the crocodile watch-strap and polished leather shoes. Once upon a time, Nathan would have shone with similar health and energy.

Poppy turned her attention to the back garden. 'Poor Mum,' she murmured. 'She's devastated.'

'Minty is too,' said Richard. If there was ever an order of honour for kind husbands with powers of restraint, Richard belonged at the head of it.

'The garden needs work.' Poppy shielded her eyes against the morning sun, which was sliding towards the lilac tree. 'I suppose if Dad's heart was playing up he didn't feel like gardening and, of course, he had no help.'

There was a clatter by the front door, the hissed admonition, 'That is not the action of a well-behaved person', and Paige shuffled bulkily into the kitchen holding Lara's hand and carrying the baby in a sling. 'Minty, I came as soon as I could.' She abandoned Lara. The baby bumped between us as Paige crushed her face to mine. 'What can I say?' Her cool flesh introduced a note of sanity, and I had never been so glad to see anyone in my life. 'I used my key to get in.' She held it up. 'But you have company. I can always come back.'

Dear Paige. It must have been such an effort for her to get over here. 'You remember Paige.' I made the introductions to Richard and Poppy. 'She's just had a baby. And this is Lara.'

Lara was wearing a smocked blue dress and woollen cardigan. She looked cross and uncomfortable. The baby snuffled. Paige cupped a hand over his head. 'Shush, Charlie,' she murmured. 'I'm so sorry about your father,' she said to Poppy. 'He was such a fine man. He'll be missed.'

'He was wonderful, wasn't he?' Poppy cried.

The grief in her outburst made us all wince. Richard put his arm round her. 'Perhaps we should go,' he said.

Poppy ignored him. 'Minty, we need to ask you something,' she shot a glance at Paige, 'but it's private. Family private. Some things need to be decided.'

Paige took the hint. 'Lara darling, why don't we find some of Lucas and Felix's toys for you to play with?' She cocked an eyebrow in my direction – which meant

'Call if you want reinforcements' – and disappeared. 'Come along, Lara,' we heard her say.

Poppy took a deep breath. 'About where Dad's buried. I . . . *we* feel strongly that he would wish to be at Altringham where he was bought up. He told Mum he would. He did. Ask her.'

All this was foreign territory, and Poppy's declaration knocked the wind out of my chest. 'He lived in London for most of his life, Poppy. And what about the boys? They'll want to visit his grave and it should be easy for them to do so.'

'You *can't* want him in some grim, municipal cemetery. All that disgusting soil and traffic. I know he lived here, but now he belongs where he was brought up. Everyone does. It's a sweet churchyard, all calm and peaceful.'

'No,' I said. '*No*. He must be near the boys.'

Poppy planted herself four-square in front of me. 'Please, Minty. I beg you. I know we don't see eye to eye, but we should be united on this.' She clasped her hands, and added what she obviously considered the clincher, 'It would help Mum.' Her chest heaved and the kitchen was filled with a cold, terrible sadness.

There was a movement behind me, and Paige came back into the kitchen. She had taken off the sling and draped a muslin square with the baby over her shoulder. 'Is it OK if Lara plays with . . . ?' She abandoned pretence. 'I couldn't help overhearing, and I know I'm interfering,' she said, 'but don't you think Minty has a point? It's important for Felix and Lucas.'

'Please,' Poppy sounded dangerously overwrought, 'I don't want to be rude to you. Please don't interfere.'

'The boys would want him here,' I repeated stubbornly. '*I* want him here, in London.'

Poppy's pupils enlarged so violently that I thought she was about to faint. 'You never did think of anyone except yourself.'

The baby shrieked. Paige ignored him and went into battle for me: 'As Nathan's wife Minty has every right to decide where he's buried. I'm sure that when you've thought about it you'll agree.' It was the calm, reasonable voice she had used for negotiations in the days when she had led the team.

My immediate concern was not to cry. I would have died rather than show my guilt and, yes, shame. Weakness too. Poppy's black skirt whipped round her legs as she turned to Richard. 'It's no use.'

Over the head of his wife, Richard sent me a look that suggested he would deal with Poppy in private.

'Richard,' I said, 'I'm not being difficult for the sake of it.'

'No wonder,' Poppy said slowly and quietly, 'Dad's heart wore out. It was worn out by *you*.'

'That is *outrageous*,' said Paige.

'I will forget you said that, Poppy.' To Richard, I added, 'But you must both go now.'

They left behind the bitter residue of what had been said and thought. Paige dumped the baby in my arms, and shuffled painfully round the kitchen – 'The episiotomy waltz, Minty' – and made yet another pot of tea. She wrapped my fingers round the mug and kissed me.

I held on to the baby, whose tiny face was crumpled with the effort of being alive. 'You know what I said about second-hand experience? Well, this isn't.'

'No,' said Paige. 'It can't be.' She sat down with a groan and reached for the baby. 'Sorry about butting in. I phoned and phoned, Minty, but you never answered.'

I passed a hand over my face. 'There were so many calls. I couldn't cope with them.'

'That's why I'm here to help.'

'That's nice, Paige.'

'How are you feeling?'

'My husband has died.'

'Not all bad, then,' escaped her, and was followed by, 'Sorry. *Unforgivable.*'

Thus it was that I found myself sitting at the kitchen table rocking with hysterical laughter at Paige's unforgivable joke. Charlie burped and regurgitated a stream of milk, and she dabbed at his mouth.

'My husband's for sale,' she remarked. 'Any offers?'

The post brought a copy of the post-mortem. I sat at the kitchen table and deciphered it word by word at the kitchen table, decoding the medical terminology to understand Nathan's heart, lungs and brain.

The brain was fine. I could have told them that. Any fool (which included Roger) knew that. Snap, snap. The messages in that brain zipped unerringly from synapse to synapse. One of those messages had been a simple one: I must provide for my family. Another: Let me get on with my job.

Nathan's lungs? For a man of his age, in excellent condition.

The arteries? They had been Nathan's Achilles' heel, if it could be put like that.

How often had I observed his outer casing? Hundreds of times. He was a man who looked good for his age. (NB A label that is quite different in meaning when applied to the male.) He looked right in his old blue shirt at home or on the beach, tousled and wind-blown. In his favourite grey office suit, he seemed substantial and capable of action. Yet, as it had turned out, that pleasing outer casing was host to those high-ways and by-ways that had hidden treacherous blockages.

Yet as I pondered and deciphered I saw so clearly that we are the architects of our own death. Nathan's brain and lungs belonged to the successful, upright man. But layers of his secret grief had been laid down in his arteries, and they had killed him.

I abandoned the post-mortem on the kitchen table, unlocked the door and went out into bright sunlight.

It was spring.

Early in our affair, during one of the lunchtime sessions at my flat, Nathan gave me a Valentine. It was large, vulgar, and had a padded pink satin heart at the centre – his idea of a joke. Inside he had written: 'In spring, thoughts turn to love.' 'Love,' he had said dreamily, propped on an elbow, 'I wish I could describe what it feels like . . .' With his other hand, he ran his fingers up and down my bare shoulder, a whisper caress. 'I had forgotten how perfect it is.'

Back in the office at Vistemax, a mini production crisis was brewing. While I was illicitly kissing her husband, Rose was snatching a sandwich at her desk and dealing with it.

'You will forgive me,' Nathan's finger rested on my breast, 'if I'm rusty on the subject.'

'Of course,' I answered. Now that the sex was over, I was impatient to be back in the office to see what was going on.

He lay back on the pillows. 'I feel you've rescued me, Minty. Given me back a sense of purpose.'

'Do you never talk to Rose about this sort of thing?'

He grimaced. 'It's easy to tell you've never been married.'

'You must have done once.'

'It gets buried, Minty, under the everyday.' He held up a hand and ticked off his fingers: 'Bills. Travelling to and from work. Endless discussions about the children. House maintenance.'

I remember feeling outraged on Rose's behalf. That was to my credit, at least. 'She only bore your children, kept house, warmed your bed and, no doubt, sorted your socks. All to make your life easy.'

'I can't deny it.' Nathan pushed me down, and kissed me, his mouth hot and lazy with spent passion.

Had he, when he was married to me, purchased a

bottle of good champagne and stolen a lunch-hour with Rose? Had he drawn her down on to the blue and white quilt, kissed *her* bare shoulders and, afterwards, propped himself up for the delights of Elbow Talk? Would he have confided to his ex-wife, 'Minty and I only discuss bills and house maintenance but you, Rose, offer me love more perfect than I imagined'?

I wish, I wish, I'd told Nathan then, over the padded satin heart, that I loved him, because it would have made him happy.

The lawn was ragged, and the boys had trampled the worm casts into the grass. Very soon I would have to think about mowing it, which I had never done. That had been Nathan's department. Felix's football had been abandoned by the door, and I picked it up. Flakes of dried mud dusted my fingers.

I was ravenous, but food made me nauseous. I choked when I bit into a piece of bread or tried to swallow a mouthful of soup. Yet hunger was making me shaky and weak. I held up my hands and examined them. The fingers were trembling. One of my thumbnails had torn on the lock, and a tiny pearl of blood was drying on the cuticle. I sucked at it. The metallic taste made me retch.

I halted by the lilac tree – such a perfect resting point in the route round the garden. (Rose knew that.) I looked up into it. A few leaves in a bright, trashy green had shaken themselves loose. The colours hurt my eyes; the sounds and scents of new growth were unbearable.

'The young and pretty,' one of Rose's friends had

comforted her when Nathan left her (and Poppy had told me), 'can be pretty wicked. But they only get away with it for a short time.'

'Nathan,' I murmured, into that sparkling morning, 'what would you want? Do you want to lie in a peaceful churchyard under the yews? Or would you rather be where you lived, fought, hustled and made your children?'

My eyes filled. I would definitely have to mow the lawn, and I hadn't a clue how to set about it. Yet mowing lawns couldn't be that difficult.

14

Rose telephoned as I was planning the order of service. She asked how I was, and had I managed to sleep, then went straight to the point. 'Minty, I'd like to give an address at the funeral.'

'Do wives give addresses?'

'I'm not his wife, remember. I'm a . . . well, friend-wife.'

'I thought only people who didn't care too much gave the address. Otherwise you break down.'

'It's my last gift to him. The children would like it.'

'*Your* children.'

'Nathan's children.' She sounded very far away.

'Where are you?'

'Romania. A trip that's been planned for months. I couldn't get out of it but I'm cutting it short. Is that agreed? Only five minutes, but I don't trust –'

'Trust,' my voice echoed feebly.

'Anyone else to give the real Nathan.'

Was the real Nathan the man who colour-coded his files? Who said, 'We have to be careful with money'? The man who had longed to put on a worn pair of jeans, battered boots and walk the cliffs above Priac Bay? Or was he the man who had propped himself on his elbow and searched unsuccessfully for the words to explain how happy he felt?

'Rose, I've made a decision. Nathan will be buried in Altringham. I thought it better he was somewhere where he'd been known. Where he won't be alone.'

'Oh, Minty.' Rose was almost inaudible. '*Thank* you.'

Barely half an hour later, Poppy was on the phone. She was hostile and cold, and I no less so. 'About the hymns, Minty. Dad's favourite was "Immortal, Invisible". We should start with that. He was very particular about hymns.'

'Was he?'

'You wouldn't know, perhaps. You didn't need hymns when he married you. And "Love Divine, All Loves Excelling" to finish with.'

I groped for a dim memory of various weddings I had attended with Nathan when those hymns had been sung. 'I don't think he liked either of them. He thought they were boring.'

But Poppy had appointed herself keeper of her father's flame, and in this matter she was not to be denied. Her voice trembled with anger. 'I think we're the ones to know what Dad liked or disliked.'

During the first verse of 'Immortal, Invisible', Sam bent his head and wept. Jilly slid her hand unobtrusively under his elbow and pressed closer. He edged away from her and blew his nose. Jilly dropped her hand and stared straight ahead.

Across the aisle, seated on either side of me, Felix

and Lucas shifted uneasily at the sight of their big brother's grief. For the hundredth time, I questioned if they should be at the service. Both had gone missing as we were due to leave Lakey Street and, after an increasingly tense search, Eve discovered them in Nathan's cupboard. I bribed them out with a bag of normally forbidden Tangfastics. As Felix got into the car, he asked, 'If we put Daddy in the ground does that mean he'll grow again?'

In the pew directly behind us, elegant and sombre in black, Gisela's voice was a pleasant alto, '. . . God only wise.' Beside her, Roger sang bass rather badly. Gisela had been as good as her word and had kept in constant touch. 'Ask me anything,' she said. 'I'm a professional widow. I know what to do.'

I held Felix and Lucas's hands in my gloved ones and sang the hymn chosen by Rose, Sam and Poppy. I rarely wore gloves, and the weather was warmer, but they seemed *necessary* at a funeral, as necessary as this rite of passage, and I longed for the funeral to arrive. 'The dead are always with us,' runs the truism. Everyone is accompanied by a crocodile of ghosts, trailing fore and aft. I sensed that Nathan was hovering over us now, seeking permission to leave.

The church at Altringham was as pretty and ancient as Poppy had vowed, and every pew was taken, which, considering Altringham was more than an hour's journey from London, was a tribute to Nathan. The nave was filled with the scent of the narcissi and lilies that had been placed in the window niches in huge bowls. More were massed on the altar and beside the coffin, which was made of bamboo – Nathan was going to his grave with impeccable green credentials. There were two flower arrangements on top. The first was a bouquet of pink and white camellias whose label read: 'Nathan and Daddy, with love'. The second, white roses woven with laurel leaves and ferns, read, 'From Rose, Sam and Poppy, with all our love'. The scent was dense, almost solid. I pressed my gloved fingers to my mouth. For ever after, I would associate this light, sweet, *unbearable* perfume with death.

Earlier, just after the coffin had been brought in and before the service, I had left the boys in Eve's charge and sneaked into the then empty church. The porch was cluttered with leaflets, service manuals and post-cards whose edges were curling. Have I got it right? I wanted to ask the presence in the coffin, which was not quite body and not quite spirit. Do you like the flowers? Gisela's florist had been more than helpful. 'Just leave it to me, Mrs Lloyd,' she said. 'I'll make sure I get what you and he would want.'

Would the wine, to be served at the funeral wake at the local hotel, be drinkable, the sandwiches accept-able? The rules of this ritual and how it should be conducted were as mysterious to me as those that had governed my faltering marriage. I had a nagging feeling that a good funeral lasted longer in the memory than a wedding. I owed Nathan so much, a debt I could never repay, and if nothing else, I could ensure that the reach of his memory stretched long.

Hymns . . . undertakers . . . tea for the twins . . . There was a hint of hysteria as I ticked off the mental list, walking down the aisle. There had been so many to work through, and so much advice of which, mostly, I couldn't remember a word – except what Mrs Jenkins had offered at school. Glasses positioned at the end of her nose, a gesture designed to ward off intimate contact, she had said that Felix and Lucas should go to their father's funeral because it offered 'closure'.

I approached the coffin, craving the moment of silence and calm in which I would try to talk to Nathan for the last time.

I planned to tell him again: *I am sorry.*

My heels clacked on the uneven tiles and a woman sitting in the front pew swivelled round. 'I thought it would be you,' said Rose. Her hair was twisted into a chignon, and she wore an exquisitely cut linen dress and jacket (French, no doubt). A bouquet of white roses lapped with laurel and ferns lay on her lap. She was pale but she had presented herself with distinction as the not-quite-but-almost-widow.

I slipped into the pew beside her, then gazed into the face that was bent towards me. Like my own skin and bone, Rose was impossible to eradicate. I could never scrape her away. Nathan had lived with her first, had had his first children with her, died with her. On that last day, stricken and beaten, he had fumbled his way . . . to Rose.

She was to blame for everything and nothing.

In the window embrasures, the bowls of flowers

seemed to float, poised on the boundaries of this world and some spectral realm. 'Do you think the flowers will do? The florist was uncanny. She seemed to know,' I said.

Rose hesitated. 'I hope you don't mind, but I had a word with her and told her what Nathan preferred.' She touched one of the roses in the bouquet on her lap. They were creamy white, on the edge of full bloom, perfect, as flowers chosen by Rose would be. 'I thought I wouldn't be treading on your toes. You'd want what Nathan liked?'

'You should have asked me.'

At that she coloured. 'Perhaps, but you were busy and I know you want to keep contact between us to a minimum. I thought you would agree that it was Nathan who was important.'

We looked at each other and, for the thousandth time, I asked myself why I had chosen to use Rose, of all people, in the way that I had.

She pointed to the bouquet. 'I'm going to put this on the coffin with your flowers. It's from us, the family.'

'Ah . . .' The sound slid away from me.

'You can't *possibly* say no.'

Anything was *possible*. 'Please,' I said, and gestured towards the coffin. But I had the curious sensation that my years with Nathan had disappeared, pulverized in the fierce, implacable determination of his first family.

Rose got to her feet and her linen dress fell into place as it should. The heavy gold ring gleamed on her finger.

She placed the flowers beside mine on the coffin and rested her hand briefly on it. 'For you, Nathan,' she said to the coffin. 'They're the best I could get.'

She turned round. 'Are the twins coming today?'

'Yes. I wasn't sure about subjecting them . . . But they're here.'

'There you are.' Poppy rustled up, pale and hollow-eyed. 'I got here early to help out.' She slipped a hand under her mother's elbow and peered into her face. 'Are you OK?' she inquired anxiously. 'Will you get through?' Poppy wanted – *needed* – Rose to be bowed down with grief. 'You're doing brilliantly, Mum. I'll look after you later.'

Mother and daughter exchanged a glance of perfect understanding. Without being told, Rose knew that Poppy was terrified yet elated by the drama of her sorrow and Poppy understood that her mother's courage was stretched taut.

'Minty, I'm glad you agreed to let Dad be buried here.' Poppy looked round the church. 'It would have been wrong to put him elsewhere. What made you change your mind?'

Rose stroked Poppy's hand. 'Shush. This isn't the time.'

In the organ loft, the organist unlocked his instrument and settled himself. The pipes released a series of groans and sighs, some distinctly digestive. My lips twitched.

Poppy hadn't finished with me. 'It would have been awful in the future if you'd met someone else and gone to live – oh, I don't know, Spain or somewhere, and he would have been alone in London.'

'Poppy.' Rose was sharp. 'Enough.'

At that moment, I admired Poppy for her truculence and rudeness, and her fine line in insult. 'Listen to me, I would *never* live in Marbella. Got it?'

Organ and congregation stumbled to the end of the hymn. Out of the corner of my eye, I caught the flutter of several white handkerchiefs. In a dark suit and black tie, Roger approached the lectern. He cleared his throat. At that moment, the sun came out and a multi-coloured refraction of light from the window spread over the floor of the nave. 'I knew Nathan for twenty years, many of them as a colleague,' he began. 'He was a company man, through and through. We fought many battles together, and rejoiced when we won.'

Had Nathan been a company man? I supposed so. Roger smiled, suggesting recollected joys of the companionship he had shared with Nathan in pursuit of the company's welfare. We live a life of false smiles. It is one of the prices we pay for civilization – bared teeth and stretched lips, unholy thoughts teeming behind them. I bet Roger couldn't remember anything *truly* significant about Nathan.

'Loyalty is what distinguished Nathan . . . He was loyal to colleagues, to his work, ultra-loyal to the company . . .'

I bit my lip and blanked out the rest of Roger's speech.

The service wore on. Richard read an extract from

Walt Whitman's *Leaves of Grass*. Afterwards, Rose took her place at the lectern. 'This may seem strange,' she addressed the congregation, 'but Nathan discussed his funeral with me more than once.'

She was disingenuous. There was nothing strange about people who had lived with each for a long time, and presumably loved each other, discussing their finale. It was those amid the intricacies of the second act who never got round to it. For the record, Nathan and I had never touched on the subject.

There was a rustle, part-embarrassment, part-anticipation. The light fell over Rose. She was past coltish prettiness, and she had never been sexy, but there was beauty. If a face truly mirrored the inner being, Rose was offering hers for inspection, boldly and without pretence.

Poppy's hand flew to her mouth. Roger stared straight ahead and Felix whimpered. I bent over him. 'Listen, Felix,' I whispered, 'it's about Daddy.'

Rose went on, 'Nathan loved his family. He loved pottering in boats, mackerel fishing . . .' She told her story, deconstructing the bland company man whom Roger had presented. Rose's Nathan was a man who strove to think and to feel.

She could have added, 'The Nathan who shouted out the answers to a radio quiz programme, who disliked broccoli, who sat utterly still when he was thinking.' She could have described Nathan cradling one or other of the twins and his struggle to find words . . .

'He loved the poem I'm about to read. It was one of John Donne's and Nathan felt . . . Nathan honoured humour. A man of strong feelings, he sometimes found it difficult to see the funny side of things. I know he wouldn't mind me saying that, and I know he'd want me to tell you that he admired people who could find humour in difficult moments.' She paused, and peered at the paper from which she was to read the poem. 'Print's a bit small,' she said, and elicited a laugh.

> 'Sweetest Love, I do not go
> For weariness of thee,
> Nor in hope the world can show
> A fitter Love for me:
> But since that I
> Must die at last, 'tis best
> To use myself in jest . . .'

She read it in a husky but unwavering voice. This, indeed, was her gift to Nathan, the husband who had left her for me.

Then we sang the hymn I was sure that Nathan had hated.

The sandwiches were excellent, and the wine – Sam's choice – was also good, a fact tacitly acknowledged by the guests who were swallowing it in large quantities.

My former colleagues from Vistemax clustered round me. Rose's former colleagues clustered round her. In between there was a no man's land of relatives and friends who were not quite sure to which camp they should be seen to belong. The twins veered between the two and I lost count of how many times someone reached out and, almost absently, placed a hand on one or other of their heads.

A combination of shock, grief, the excellent wine – you could take your pick – loosened tongues. I negotiated past Maeve Otley with a plate of sandwiches just as she was confiding, to Carolyne Shaker, 'Of course, he was a nice man but he wasn't *exactly* loyal to his family . . .'

Carolyne, dull, sweet Carolyne, trussed up in a too-tight navy blue suit, replied, 'Well, he was loyal in his way.'

Nathan's cousin Clive collared me. 'You must remember me. We met at Poppy and Richard's wedding party.'

'Clive, of course.' Clive-the-expert-on-wind-turbines, arguably the most boring subject on earth.

Clutching his wine, he edged closer and I noticed that his black tie was stained, his shirt fraying at the cuff. 'What did the old boy die of?' He seemed anxious and unsettled. 'He wasn't . . . you know . . .' Clive tapped his nose. 'Someone mentioned he was . . . er, in bed.'

There and then, I abandoned Clive and made my way over to Sam. Glass in hand, he searched for something to say. 'Minty . . . you've done this well.'

That was something. 'I want to say how sorry I am.' Emotions had never been Sam's strong point, and he looked uneasy. But I persisted: 'He talked about you a lot. I know he wanted to talk to you about America.'

Sam's grasp tightened on his glass. 'I've accepted the job, and I'm off to Austin in September.'

'And Jilly.'

'She hasn't made up her mind, but I'm hoping to persuade her.' His gaze shifted to his wife. Evidently some telepathy was working for Jilly turned, from a group that included Carolyne Shaker and Rose, to her husband and the exchange was neither sweet nor happy.

'I'll commute for the first few months,' he said, then added miserably, 'I'll miss Dad.'

Many of the guests did not stay long. Those who spoke to me edged over and proffered an excuse: a meeting, a train to catch *and you know what the trains are like*. Carolyne and Peter Shaker were among the first to go. Peter held out his hand. After a second or two, I decided to take it.

'This is difficult, I know,' said Peter, 'but, despite everything, Nathan was a friend.'

'Well, yes. A friend.' My inflection of 'friend' was intended to convey irony. 'No doubt you have a meeting to go to.'

'As a matter of fact, I do.'

'A meeting that Nathan might have attended if he hadn't been sacked?'

Carolyne flushed, and stuffed a hand under her husband's elbow. On closer inspection, there were signs that Peter's elevation had had an effect. Her hair had been cut expertly and the flashy gold earrings had been replaced with diamond studs. 'There's no need to be like that, Minty.'

The Shakers dematerialized as Martin came up. 'Must go. The car's waiting. But we'll be in touch, as you know, Minty.'

'There must be a fleet of company cars outside. Don't get into the wrong one.'

He smiled. 'It was a good service, Minty. Good for Nathan. I'll remember it.'

'That's what I wanted,' I said.

The room emptied, leaving a whiff of tobacco smoke from a rebel smoker, spilt wine, and egg-and-cress sandwiches squashed on to plates. Some time ago, Eve had borne away the protesting twins. They had gone back to London, which, I promised them, would be much nicer for them than being bored by all the grown-ups. Now only the family and Theo, the solicitor, remained. He gestured for us to gather round. 'Why don't you all sit down?' he suggested.

Theo leaned back against the table, on which were stacked the wine bottles and dirty glasses, and explained what was in Nathan's will. 'The estate is to be divided as follows. The arrangements are quite complicated, and involve the appointment of trustees. I'll come back to that in a minute. But, briefly, the arrangements cover, first, the house at Lakey Street and its contents, and, second, Nathan's investments and cash. Minty has a life interest in the house at Lakey Street, subject to her occupying it. If she chooses to live elsewhere, or if she dies, it is to be sold and the proceeds divided equally between the twins. If that happens before they are twenty-one, the trustees are to invest the money until they reach that age. The contents of the house are left to Minty absolutely, except a vase and two paintings, which Nathan specifically wanted to pass to Rose, Sam and Poppy, plus the dining-room table and chairs, and an inlaid half-moon table, which he particularly wished the twins to inherit, although Minty will have the right to look after them until the twins come of age. That leaves the investments and cash. Here, the trustees are instructed to realize everything and first to pay any money outstanding to Rose under the divorce arrangements, then a specified amount to Minty. The remainder is to be divided as follows: one third each is to go to Sam and Poppy, and one third to be divided between Lucas and Felix when they come of age. Until that time it will be invested by the trustees. Nathan's only other asset was his pension, and he had already made arrangements to the effect that, in the event of his death, Minty would be entitled to a widow's annuity. As you will appreciate, these are quite detailed arrangements, and Nathan appointed his financial adviser and me as trustees to ensure that his instructions would be carried out.'

My hands twisted in my lap. At least I would not be destitute. With the parcelling out of his capital, Nathan had ensured that I had to work. Just as I had wished.

'One final point . . .' Theo held up a hand. 'There is a codicil that Nathan added a couple of months ago. It concerns the guardianship of the twins. In the event of anything happening to him, and to Minty, while the twins are still under age, he wished Rose to be their guardian and hoped that Minty would agree.'

'Surely he meant us?' Poppy's surprised interjection sounded very loud in the astonished silence.

Jilly leant over and muttered in Sam's ear. 'That can't be right,' Sam said.

Theo shook his dark head. 'No mistake.'

Rose was deathly pale. 'Did you know about this?' I demanded.

'No. Yes. He asked me in a roundabout fashion. I said it wasn't possible, but he insisted.'

'Over my dead body.'

'Don't, Minty.'

'Nathan wouldn't do that.' I said.

But Nathan would do that. He *had* done that.

Theo took off his glasses. 'The fine details can wait for another day. If each of you would care to contact me, I will explain probate. Et cetera.'

'Mum . . .' Poppy rushed over to Rose. 'Let's not talk about anything now. Later, when we've all calmed down. When you feel better. Go and get your bag, and we'll take you home.' She pushed her mother towards the cloakroom and addressed me more or less politely. 'Thank you for . . .' she seemed near breaking point '. . . giving him a good funeral.'

Sam and Jilly were talking to Theo and comparing diaries. The waiters were moving round the room clearing up plates and teacups. An end had been reached, and an end was in sight. 'I wanted to do the best I could for your father.'

This provoked a strange reaction. Poppy narrowed her short-sighted eyes. 'I want you to know that your extravagance got to my father. It worried him sick.'

Her cruelty acted like a lash. 'Oh? And how would you know?'

'You stupid, stupid woman . . .' Poppy's self-control collapsed and she began to shake. 'He told me.'

But of course. I pictured him talking to his daughter, she listening with her chin resting on her hands. *Minty wants a new bathroom . . . carpet . . . but we can't afford it.*

Seasoned poker hands play aggressively when they reckon they hold options, and I wasn't going to let Poppy get away with it. 'Actually, he worried about you too.'

'Did he?'

'You know he did. I told him nothing, but I know he thought you were in some kind of trouble.' I laid a hand on Poppy's arm. 'Going off tilt? Isn't that the term for poker players when luck has packed its bag?'

Rose emerged from the cloakroom, and Poppy looked me in the eye. 'Thank God we don't have to see each other again,' she said.

'*Thank God*' hovered on my own lips. If uttered, there would be a sundering, a clean one, and it would suit both of us. But as the words formed, I remembered my boys. The casual manner in which Poppy was ready to abandon them was as wounding as anything I had ever felt. They *loved* their big half-sister. *Naughty, naughty Poppy.* She offered them laughter, fun, exoticism.

Poppy was their family. The family might be a nest

of vipers, but the vipers were their vipers, unlike the vipers elsewhere.

I swallowed, and felt exhaustion clamp down hard. 'Nathan would have wanted us to be polite, at least. And it would distress your mother.'

'My mother . . .' Rose was walking towards us. 'My mother is the best. *The best.*'

Theo packed his briefcase. I gestured to the half-empty plates of sandwiches, dirty glasses and empty bottles. 'We're the only ones left.'

Theo surveyed the empty room. 'Who's taking you back to London?'

My list hadn't specified that. I'd forgotten to think about it. 'I don't know.'

He glanced at his watch. 'I'll give you a lift.'

'Thank you.'

15

Instinct told me to dress smartly to go in to Paradox. It was an effort but I chose black trousers, a green cashmere sweater and Stephanie Kelian boots. I pulled my hair into a ponytail.

When I went in, Syriol jumped up. 'We didn't expect you. Should you be here, Minty?'

Her raised voice brought Deb into Reception. 'Minty? How . . .' Deb had cut her hair in a different way and looked radiant. 'How *are* you? We didn't think . . .'

Chris Sharp, in black, opened his office door and stuck out his head. 'Deb, when you have a moment.'

At her name, Deb gave a self-conscious little jerk of her head, which made her hair swing seductively. 'I'm just talking to Minty, Chris. Won't be a moment.'

'Oh, Minty.' Chris came up to me and held out his hand. 'I want to say how sorry I am. We're all deeply, deeply sorry.'

Deb was not to be outdone. 'We are all *so* upset,' she said, in a low voice. 'And those poor little boys.'

Chris raised an eyebrow. 'Isn't it a little soon to be in?'

I explained I wanted to talk to Barry and check up on my projects.

'You needn't worry about them,' Deb said quickly. 'We've got them under control.'

Barry was sombre but helpful. 'It was good of you, Minty, to come in. We appreciate it.'

I opened my diary and spread it in front of him. The pages were mostly clean and white. 'I plan to take the boys away for a short break, and then I need to sort out Nathan's affairs with the lawyer. If it's all right with you, I'll come back in three weeks.'

'Three weeks?' Barry twirled his mobile thoughtfully. 'Are you sure that's long enough for you to get back on your feet?'

'Best to hit the ground running.' Both of us were resorting to clichés, but I had noticed that at pivotal moments, such as the giving and receiving of bad news, or making sure that my career survived in the face of a stealthy takeover by predatory colleagues, they did the job.

Barry looked extra thoughtful. 'Let's tease this out, Minty. I assume you still want the full-time position, but I wondered, given your new circumstances, if you shouldn't be thinking part-time.'

This time my answer was certified cliché-free. 'I can think all I like about part-time, Barry, but it won't do any good. It has to be full-time.'

'If that's the case . . .'

'About my projects.'

Barry leant over and placed a hand on my arm. 'You're not to worry about them. Chris will take over. He knows your thinking. You must concentrate on getting yourself through.' His voice was rough with sympathy, and his genuine concern almost masked the fact that it made no difference to him whether I was in the office or not.

'I'm afraid there's gossip,' said Paige. 'There always is. But' – she straightened up from the laundry basket – 'you have to admit it's not entirely unjustified. Why *was* Nathan at Rose's flat? Gossip-wise, Minty, it's the equivalent of throwing a juicy Christian to the lions.'

To reward myself for battling with a morning of paperwork and Theo, I had dispatched the twins to the park with Eve and come over to Paige for lunch. We sat in her neat, clean-smelling kitchen with something delicious cooking in the pink Aga. The baby was sleeping upstairs. 'I think Nathan went to Rose out of a kind of loyalty.'

'Really?' Paige's eyes widened in disbelief.

I pressed my forefingers into the pressure points on my forehead. 'Nothing more than that.'

Paige looked sceptical. 'If you say so.' She folded the sleeves of a shirt across its breast, like a figure in a church brass. 'Linda should be doing this, but I've given her a day off. She doesn't know yet, but it's a bribe because I want her to help me out at the weekend. They work most effectively I find, when they are *post facto*. It's too late then.' She picked up a striped yellow and black Babygro and inspected a tiny sleeve. 'This makes Charlie look like a wasp. How is it at Lakey Street?'

'Deathly quiet.'

Nathan had been dead for two weeks and the doorbell no longer rang innumerable times every morning.

There were no more deliveries of flowers. The boys, Eve and I had worked our way through soups and other offerings in unfamiliar containers that, at one point, had clogged the fridge.

The boys' understanding of the situation fluctuated. 'Daddy's gone to a nice place,' Lucas announced to Eve. But every so often their grasp modified and slipped. Several times since Nathan's death, I had woken to discover a pair of unblinking eyes observing me and one or the other of them had burrowed like a velvety mole into the safety of my bed. They seesawed between understanding and bewilderment, and it made them ragged-tempered and uncertain.

'Where *is* Daddy?' Felix had demanded at breakfast.

Paige hefted the basket into the utility room and checked the oven. 'You could do with a good meal,' she said. 'How does fish stew grab you?'

I was half-way through a plateful when the storm hit me out of nowhere. I was chewing prawn when I felt sweat break out on the soles of my feet and the rush of rage. 'How dare Nathan die?' I dropped my fork, and pushed the plate to one side. 'I'm so *angry* with him for leaving us. What was he thinking of, not getting his heart seen to?'

'That's better,' said Paige. She wiped away a drop of stew by my plate. 'You have a good hate. I always tell the children it's best to get it out of their system.'

Paige always favoured that approach. In her book, 'a good hate' would evacuate the agony of losing Nathan, and the sorrow of the what will never be.

'He *must* have thought about Felix and Lucas, and what it would mean if he wasn't there. How will they manage without him?'

Yet if Nathan came whirling back out of the darkness, I would say to him, 'Nathan, I will never again ask for a new bathroom. I promise to work at loving you.' I would even promise I didn't mind that I would be damned for ever by his family, and friends like the Frosts and the Lockharts.

I would promise to wipe the slate clean and begin again.

I pulled a shred of prawn shell off my fork. 'How am I going to cope? The boys – how am I going to help them? Keep them? Maintain a house?'

'Much as you're coping now, I imagine. Adapt.'

'I had a dream, Paige. I'd been transformed into a wise, hands-on mother like you. The sort of mother who says on a rainy afternoon, "Let's make a dinosaur out of a cardboard box." Or "Hell, why don't we write a play about Daddy and I'll run up the costumes?" But it was only a dream.'

'Eat.' Paige dumped another spoonful of stew on my plate.

I stared at it. My anger had burnt out, leaving only sadness. 'Nathan wanted to humiliate me, Paige, by suggesting Rose became a guardian . . . if anything happened. How could he have done that? Gisela says he was thinking clearly. Rose is the only one with time, she's older, and she knows what she's doing. She would put the boys' interests first.'

Paige considered. 'Gisela's right. But it's not going to happen. You're in rude health. Maybe, Minty, he wanted to put things right between you.'

'Well, he hasn't.'

Paige ate what was on her plate with a rapidity that any new mother would recognize. 'Charlie will wake up in a minute.'

On cue, a noise like a small lawnmower struggling into life drifted from the baby alarm. Paige threw down her fork and her face lit up. 'I'll fetch him.'

She returned with a now roaring Charlie and sat down to feed him, supporting him with one hand. With the other, deploying an elaborate movement so that her fork did not pass over Charlie's head, she shovelled food from plate to mouth.

'How's Martin?'

'I barely see him. I booted him into the spare room, which means I have Charlie all to myself.' Paige smiled down at the baby. 'Don't I? And it's delicious, isn't it, my tiny tiger? We have a *lovely* time.'

'Don't you miss the bank?' I gestured at the sterilizer, the timetable pinned to the noticeboard, the copper *batterie de cuisine*. 'Figures used to be your life.'

'Oh, I miss them,' she said. 'I miss their purity, but they were only part of the deal. Most of my time was spent politicking, schmoozing clients and firefighting trouble or bad press. You could never get a run at the purity.'

Whenever Paige mentioned 'figures' or 'statistics', her face was suffused with longing, as it was now. If she had been a nun, she would have brought the same steely concentration and ferocious will to being the perfect Bride of Christ.

She shifted Charlie to the other breast, and returned to the original subject. 'You're going to have to sort yourself out about Rose. You mustn't let her become an obsession.' She caressed Charlie's head, bent over him and cooed, 'Who's my pretty boy? Who's my good boy?' She straightened up and asked, in a normal voice, 'You don't really think anything was going on between them, do you?'

The question nagged away before I fell asleep at night, and it was there when I woke, still fatigued. Its implications swirled in my brain. 'I don't know. All I know is that I don't want to have to think about her at the moment. And Nathan, with his ridiculous request, made sure that I have to.'

'People do strange things, Minty.'

I became aware of the pulse beating in my right wrist. 'Yes.'

'Look, it's not a problem at the moment. Don't think about it.'

The fingers of my left hand circled my wrist and pressed down on the pulse. 'Do you think history repeats itself?' In other words, had it been predetermined that Nathan would seek comfort and pleasure from the source he knew so well?

'You mustn't mind.' She threw a muslin square over her shoulder, draped Charlie over it, and eased herself to her feet, where she performed a circular rocking movement, like some tribal elder. 'Helps with the wind.' Charlie obliged and, one hand rubbing her own back, Paige gyrated in the opposite direction. 'I've sent a search party for my waist, and it's still out there.'

I laughed. 'Presumably all your check-ups have been OK.'

'Back's a bit dodgy. The ligaments had gone into permanent tension. And I'm not so good at sleeping now. But, then, I anticipated on not sleeping for a hundred years. Do you want to come upstairs while I change Charlie?'

Paige was a champion mother. She was also a champion housekeeper. Her store-cupboards were immaculate, and none of her spice jars ever overran their sell-by date. Each shelf in the linen cupboard corresponded to a room in the house, and the clothes in her wardrobe were colour-coded. You could hate Paige, unless you loved her.

I trailed up behind her, noting that every shelf was dust-free and the curtains in the children's bedrooms had strips of transparent film sewn along the bottom to preserve them. When I passed the spare room and glanced inside, though, I did a double-take. It was awash with discarded clothes, books, a pile of papers on the floor.

'You're looking at the mess? Martin said the deal was that if we had a third, which he didn't want, he'd grab a space where he could live like a pig.'

'Ah.'

Paige changed and washed Charlie. For all her talk,

she was clearly tired, so I gathered up the discarded baby things and wiped down the mat.

'You shouldn't do that,' she said. 'But I'm grateful.'

'Have you any idea how I crave to do something ordinary?' I chucked the cotton-wool into the bin.

Suddenly Paige sat down on the nursing chair. Her stomach bulged over her skirt, and her thighs had a flabby underdone look. 'What next, Minty? What are you going to do?'

'Go back to work full-time. Keep the boys and myself.'

'You wanted to go back.'

'I did.'

Paige pinched the flesh of one suety thigh and glared at it. 'Well, it's a beginning.'

A week later I packed shorts, T-shirts, sweaters, buckets, spades, baked beans, favourite cereals, teddy bears and alphabet spaghetti into the car, loaded Eve, a map and the boys into it and drove out of London.

We were heading for Priac Bay in Cornwall. To be more specific, we were going to the house where Nathan and Rose had holidayed every year. It had been neither an easy, nor a difficult decision to make because it had not been a decision in the formal sense. I had never been to Priac Bay – I distrusted the idea of it. 'For God's sake,' I had protested to Paige in the past, when Nathan had brought up the subject of going there. 'It was where he took his first family.'

Paige had been suitably shocked. 'Is he stupid? Or very limited in the imagination department?'

Yet I knew I had to take the boys and myself to a place where Nathan had been happy, so I had got on the phone and arranged it.

It was raining, a light spume, when three hundred or so murderous miles later the car jolted down the unmade road that led to the cottage. Stupefied and bored, Felix and Lucas were silent in the back.

The world was drenched. The horizon was wiped out by mist, and the sea roared with white crests. The slate tiles on the roof gleamed, there were damp patches sprouting on the grey walls and the plants in the garden dripped.

Eve drew the sleeves of her jersey further down her wrists. 'It's cold, Minty.'

I, too, was cold, with apprehension and worry. We felt worse when we discovered that two of the bedrooms were damp, the plumbing questionable and the nearest shops several miles away. Eve and I did our best. We made beds, unpacked, stacked the buckets and spades by the front door. We ate a scratch supper of beans and fried eggs, watched rain sweep across the grey sea and listened to the gulls.

'Daddy came here,' I told the boys. 'Lots. For his holidays.'

'Daddy,' said Felix, and his blue eyes darkened. 'Daddy.'

After a moment, Lucas asked, 'Am I sitting in Daddy's chair?'

'It's possible. It looks as though it's been here for a long time.'

Eve chased a bean round her plate.

In the morning Eve and I led the boys down the steep path to the tiny beach. After the rain, the mud was as sticky as toffee, and the boys squealed with joy. As we slid and slithered down, moisture from the thick clumps of vegetation seeped into our clothes. The air was heavy with salt. The leaves and branches as we brushed past smelt of it and left its residue on our lips.

Down on the beach, the tide was retreating, leaving dark patches on the stones. Gulls screamed overhead. The boys ran madly up and down, calling to each other. I sat on a rock and watched them.

My feet were wet and, under my jacket, I was shivering almost uncontrollably. Nathan had loved this place. That much I knew, but little else. I had never asked why, or which was his favourite spot, the best bay to swim. I had been silent. Metaphorically, I had turned my back. 'You know, Minty, you don't know me very well at all,' he had once accused me.

If only I had taken the time to answer him. If only I had sat down, there and then, and said, 'Let's talk, Nathan. *Tell me.*'

To find myself, so ordinarily materialistic and without grace, at the mercy of such pain, impotence and ugliness was bewildering – it was like being dashed this way and that in a tide as strong as the one peeling back the water from the sand.

Eve beckoned to Felix. 'Felix, come. There is something here.' They huddled together and inspected an object in the sand.

Lucas circled them. He was cross and sang very loudly, 'Look at me. Look at me.'

Long ago in the Vistemax office, before the sea-change had taken place in me, I had told Rose, 'I don't have a family. Who wants one? I don't have children. Why hang a millstone round your neck?' Now I had a family, and the intolerable weight of the millstone tugged and pulled at every bone and muscle.

'Mum!' White legs flashing under his green shorts, hair pushed off his forehead by the wind, Felix came over the shingle towards me with a goosefleshed arm outstretched. 'See what I've got.'

He unclasped his hand to reveal a perfect mermaid's purse.

After lunch of bread and cheese, the boys were chased upstairs and put to bed for a rest. I left Eve grimly washing up and complaining of the lack of hot water, got into the car and went to find provisions.

The nearest supermarket was on the outskirts of Penzance. It was busy and noisy. This was the beginning (as Paige would have it) of the new economy, a different fiscal regime. I chose cut-price jam and chicken breasts, the least expensive butter, and every own-brand that I could bear to buy.

I drove away, slightly nauseous. The wind had dropped, and warmth from the sun had crept into the still air. The sea had turned into a gentle wash. It was a beautiful day, and out at sea, boats of all sizes were scudding across the water.

When I got back, Eve had taken the boys down to

the beach, and I could hear their shouts. I unpacked slowly and awkwardly, unable to shake off an overpowering, almost frightening feeling that Nathan was in the cottage.

In the end, I snatched up my jacket and went outside. The coastal path passed directly in front of the cottage, and I headed towards the point. After a while, I increased my pace until I was almost running, my feet bouncing over the turf and stones. The sun was blinding, and the sea, shallow near the cliffs, a transparent turquoise. The seabirds wheeled and dived noisily to the rocks. As I rounded a corner, the wind hit me and I slithered to a halt.

I smelt sea and turf and the freshness of the air. I faced the bay, where water, rock and vegetation shimmered, a mysterious and beautiful trinity. I knew that Nathan had been there. Maybe he had stood exactly where I was now and my feet were planted in the ghostly imprint of his.

I stood and listened to the unfamiliar music made by the wind and the waves. Its chords beat in my ears and, unwillingly, suspiciously, then with relief, I gave myself up to its sensations.

I knew then why Nathan had come to Priac Bay. Why he had loved it so.

A week later, we returned to Lakey Street late in the evening, almost speechless and dirty from the journey, and fell into bed.

I woke to find Lucas on my bed, wrapped in his

duvet, which he must have dragged in. Reluctantly, I focused. 'Hello, sweetie. How long have you been there?'

'Ages and ages.' His treble voice piped in the silence. 'Why didn't you wake up, Mummy?'

'Because I was tired.'

'I wanted you to wake up.'

I knew Lucas was trying to ask me something, but I was unsure what it was. 'You'd better come in.' I lifted up the edge of the duvet and Lucas, importing the morning chill, climbed in. He snuggled into me, and I smelt sand, salt and seaweed.

I waited.

'Do you think Daddy can see us?' His voice wavered.

I squinted down at him. He stared back, trying so hard to be composed. 'Probably.' Then I collected my wits. He wanted certainties. 'Yes,' I said.

'I can't see him.' His fair, rather stubby eyebrows twitched into the frown that was becoming habitual.

I stroked the skin between his eyes until the frown was smoothed away. 'We have to believe he's there.'

Lucas edged closer to me, and I slipped my arm round him. 'Daddy was nice, wasn't he?'

'Very.'

'Millie says her daddy is bad. He went away too. Daddies shouldn't go away.'

'Sometimes they can't help it, Lukey.' *Lukey* . . . Nathan's name for him. 'Your daddy couldn't help it. You must remember that. It's different for Millie's daddy.'

225

Lucas considered. 'Millie's daddy said he couldn't help it.'

I pulled Lucas as close as I possibly could. 'Lukey, you must listen to what I say. Millie's daddy is different from yours. Yours would never have left you unless . . . unless he had no choice.'

I was thankful that neither Poppy nor Sam could hear me.

'Will I get a new daddy?' Lucas asked.

I spooned my body round him. He was tense, and there was a lick of sweat by his hairline. Every one of his bones was so fragile, and I was shaken by terror for his safety. 'No, sweetie-pie. You only have one daddy.'

Outside the bedroom, the sun made an appearance. Fastened on to me, Lucas relaxed, his breathing slowed and he tumbled into one of those instant childish sleeps.

Cautiously, I eased myself out of bed and went into the boys' room to check on Felix. He wasn't there.

Oh, my God, where was he?

Then I spotted him at the bottom of the stairs, which faced the front door, sitting bolt upright. He was dressed, sort of, in one blue sock, and a T-shirt squashed over his pyjama top. His treasured, tatty bit of blanket was scrunched between his knees, and he clasped his teddy bear to his chest.

He was sitting utterly still, with an air of saint-like patience and expectation, of *determination* far beyond his years.

I ran down the stairs, sat beside him, my heart fluttering with anxiety. 'What are you doing, Felix?' I pulled him close. 'You gave Mummy a fright. I didn't know where you were.'

At my touch, Felix stirred, and seemed to return from somewhere far away. His eyes were so blue, so trusting, so bright. 'I'm waiting for Daddy to show him my treasure,' he said, and opened his hand in which lay the mermaid's purse.

16

I drove myself into Nathan's study where a pile of letters had to be read and answered.

'Dear Minty,' wrote Jean, Nathan's secretary. 'The shock is considerable and I keep asking myself if I could have *done* something. He was so considerate and so kind to me . . .'

Charlie on Vistemax Reception wrote, 'Mr Lloyd was never too busy to say "hallo" unlike some. He always asked after Sheila and Jody . . .'

To my surprise, Roger had written: 'Thank you for the privilege of letting me speak at the funeral. I realize what a hard decision it must have been for you. I meant every word. Nathan was a Titan, big in vision and strong in execution. He was also delightful to know.'

Clive-of-the-wind-turbines chose a more direct approach: 'Jolly good send-off for the old boy. Very difficult for you. Nathan and I did not always see eye to eye as he was an obstinate old buzzard but we came from the same stock and that always sorts things out in the end . . .'

A couple more letters were so adulatory that they were in danger of suggesting that Nathan was one of the great businessmen of our time. Another, from an old schoolfriend, was more modest: 'He was a sweet boy . . .'

'Dear Minty,' said Sue Frost. 'This letter could not be more difficult to write. We do not know each other, and that was of my choosing. But I thought about it and I thought you would want to know that we loved Nathan dearly . . .'

To read these letters was to shuffle a pack of cards. Nathan the businessman. Nathan the friend. Nathan the father.

Each one must be kept. I would buy a scrapbook and paste them in, and one day I would it give to the boys. Perhaps we would read them together. 'This letter is from Daddy's boss . . . This one is from the lady Daddy worked with.'

To my surprise, Jilly had written, 'Dear Minty. Nathan's funeral went off very well, and I know that Sam was comforted by it. Sam was going to write but he is so busy getting ready to go the States. Frieda is flourishing, and I hope the boys are not bad. Maybe we should hook up for Christmas . . .'

I must have moved awkwardly, for my elbow caught the pile and caused the letters to rain on to the floor. I bent over and picked up the one written in black ink on expensive white paper. 'Dear Minty . . .' The sharp strokes of her *t*s and *l*s cut into the paper, and the rounded *d*s and *n*s cradled the letters.

I am writing this after the funeral because I am at a loss. I know you will be too. You will be indescribably busy and tired at the moment, and perhaps the shock hasn't really registered. Please take care of yourself. It is important. I also want to say that, sometimes, you can be very angry with a person who dies. I was when, like Nathan, my father died unexpectedly. Actually, more than angry, I was outraged. But I wanted to say, anger will weaken you, Minty, as it weakened me when Nathan decided our marriage was over. I suspect you might be thinking, How dare Nathan leave it all to me? *You might be asking yourself how you are going to cope with earning a living and keeping the children . . .*

The word 'children' appeared especially black on the white paper.

You may also be thinking as you read this that I am being indelicate, unsubtle and interfering. But I thought I would take the risk.

Rose was inviting me to filter my grief through her. I had slept in her bed and now she was sleeping in mine. 'But it won't do, Rose,' I murmured, into the empty study. Above all, and above everything, I owed Nathan direct, undiluted grief. That I must grant him. And I would. I did.

'Welcome back.' Barry looked up from the stuffed Filofax. 'We've missed you.' He was wearing his leather blouson jacket, but he had added to the red Kabbalah wristband a couple of others in pastel colours.

He sounded as if he meant it. A lump wedged itself

in my throat, but I managed a weak wave in his direction as I disappeared into my office. In my absence, it had been swept and cleaned. Two polite mountains of paper sat on the desk.

'Hello.' Deb walked lightly into the room. 'How are you?'

'I hope I'm managing.'

'I'm so very sorry, Minty. It must be quite dreadful.'

I managed to smile. 'So dreadful that I need diversion. Please tell me what you've been doing.'

She needed no second invitation. Within five minutes, I had been acquainted with every shudder and sigh that made up her affair with Chris Sharp. I was reliably informed that he was the most talented man since Einstein, and fantastic in the sack. Chris had such ambitions for Paradox, and vision that stretched far into the future of the industry and the changes that were likely to take place. 'He says that people will compose their own television viewing programmes in the not too distant future . . .' Her voice dipped, swooped, grew dreamy as she released one detail after another. She said things like: 'To think I could so easily not have met him.' Or 'Do you think he's good-looking?' As I listened to the outpourings of the former cool-urban-hunter now girl-clearly-besotted, I was reminded that other things did exist.

'Is he nice to you, Deb?'

'Oh, sure. Sure. But he doesn't really want absolute commitment at the moment. And that's how we're playing it.' Deb reached over and flicked on my screen.

'He's organizing new software.' She fiddled with the keyboard. 'It might mean I have to find a new job because it's not sensible for us both to work for the same set-up.'

Alarm bells clanged. 'Hang on, Deb. Why should you leave? You like the job, and you've earned your place here.' But I could see that whatever I said would make no difference. 'Tell me about the projects.'

A suggestion of worry traced itself across her glowing features. 'That's a bit of a story. I'm afraid we had a clear-out after you went off. Chris and Barry have been talking hard about trends. Reality shows, property and things. Chris thinks we'll improve the margins that way. There's a couple of good ideas going through the pipeline at the moment.'

'And?'

'You'll have to talk to Barry, but I have a feeling . . .' She paused, then added, 'Chris feels we shouldn't be too cultural or earnest. It brings the strike rate down.' She giggled. 'Do you know what he's called the *Middle Age* proposal?'

'Tell me, Deb.'

'*Finished at Forty.*'

Later on, in the editorial meeting, we discussed strike rates, and I heard myself issuing comments that made enough sense to get me through. Not that either Chris or Barry paid me much attention: they were far too busy talking to each other.

'OK,' I said, and my voice sounded rusty and foreign. 'There's an article I read in *Harper's* about ballerinas.

232

Nora Pavane, one of them, is quite something, and a defender of the arts. I think we should grab her and ask her to participate in a series on dance.'

Chris reflected. 'Get her to front, even.'

'Yup,' said Barry. 'Sounds good.'

'I'll work on the treatment and think about the format,' I said. 'Ed Golightly at BBC2 might be interested. He's an arts editor, and I met him at a Vistemax do. I could set up the meeting.'

'Sounds good,' repeated Barry.

On the way home I sprinted into Theo's office. I wanted to talk over the financial and legal position and he had suggested that I call in.

He sat me down at his desk, and asked his assistant for tea, which arrived in a china pot. 'The next few months won't be easy,' he said. 'Probate will take a while and then I have to convene several meetings with the trustees to discuss the division. Meanwhile Vistemax are honouring the severance package.'

I let out a sigh of relief.

'And, of course, there's Nathan's pension. That will be sorted out.' He paused. 'There is the question that Rose might be due a portion.' With a steady hand, he poured me a second cup of tea. 'Whatever you receive won't be riches, but it will provide you with a base from which to operate. Add to that the money from your slice of the stocks and shares, and any earnings you may have, and I think you'll be all right, providing you're not extravagant. However, if you did lose your job, you wouldn't be destitute, and it will tide you over the worst.'

I stared at my tea. 'Theo, what was Nathan doing when he suggested Rose as a guardian? What was he thinking? He must have known how . . . difficult – impossible – that would be.'

'He made it clear that he wanted to put the boys' interest first. He said he had every faith that you would understand.'

'But I don't!' I cried. 'I don't. And to make it so public! He should have talked to me.'

Theo had witnessed many such exchanges in his office. Scenes in which outrage, betrayal, bitterness had burst through the dam of good behaviour and politeness. 'It's difficult to absorb, perhaps, at the moment. But things change. Why don't you drink your tea?'

Then he showed me the facts and figures of my new life.

'If you marry again, or live with someone else,' he said, as I rose to take my leave, 'you will be obliged to sell the house and the proceeds will be invested for the twins.'

He left me to reflect that, since Theo's hourly fees would make anyone's eyes water, this had been an expensive way to learn that celibacy paid.

I climbed on to a bus. At least I knew that now, I must be vigilant. Extra, extra vigilant. In the coming months, possibly years, I would require energy and the stamina to attack. At the moment, I was not sure I possessed either. What I did have was an overwhelming sense of panic. That would have to do. In fact, its blackness and sharpness would do very well.

*

Theo advised me to draw up a list of priorities, and a financial timetable. 'Be ruthless,' he said. 'Put together all the facts and figures to see the whole picture. It will make it easier for you.'

Fact. There was no one to fall back on.

Fact. I must get used to it.

Fact. A widow with two children was hampered as to what she could do to survive.

Fact. After cataclysm, the mind indulges in curious illusions. And they are fiction.

Once, early in the morning, I stumbled downstairs and Nathan was in the kitchen making breakfast. Coffee. Bacon. Toast. All those lovely aromas. He was in his dressing-gown, whistling under his breath. 'Hello,' I said, with a rush of pure delight. 'You're up early.' Without turning round, he reached back and pulled me close.

Then he was gone.

Yes, my mind skittered about. Concentration lapsed and I found it hard to read. Sleep was unpredictable, and I asked myself difficult questions. Would Nathan have known as he died what was happening to him? Had it been painful? I prayed not. But perhaps, if he had under-stood what was happening, he had been granted the chance during the final seconds to think, Thank you for a good life. I can't imagine what it must be like to die with the conclusion, I had an unsatisfactory/woeful/beastly life.

Did he manage to think about any of us?

The self-help manual *After Life*, which I was now

reading, said we cannot possibly comprehend Death. Anything we think we know is fantasy.

I want to know how the author knew that.

Sue Frost turned up at the house. At first I didn't recognize the figure in pink cut-off trousers and matching loafers – she looked older than the woman I had encountered in the supermarket. 'Surprise?' she said.

'Well, yes. But no.'

She held out a bunch of peonies and a couple of leaflets. 'For Nathan's sake I brought you these.'

Her eyes filled and so, to my distress, did mine. 'Thank you,' I managed.

'We'll miss him.' She was weeping openly now. 'We really loved him.'

The tears were rolling down my cheeks and I lashed out, 'But not enough to recognize me, which would have made him happy?'

The idea clearly took her by surprise. 'Yes. Well,' she wiped her cheeks with her sleeve, 'we all do things we regret. Anyway, the leaflets. I'm a counsellor, trained for these circumstances. In fact, I run the operation. If you like – if you feel you need help . . . If you need –'

'Closure?' I offered.

'– a listening ear, just ring this number.'

Scenes from our married life . . . summoned to help me counter the torture of sleeplessness.

. . . *'These are for the bride.' Nathan returned from his first day back at work after our honeymoon, and presented me with a bouquet of such beauty that I cried out with pleasure. 'This is to make up for no flowers at the wedding.'*

. . . 'Broccoli needs butter.' Nathan stared at the plate when I served him broccoli mixed with pine nuts and raisins. 'Why do we have to gussy-up vegetables?'

'Because,' I said, 'it's to make sticks-in-the-mud like you sit up a little. Things are changing, including broccoli.'

Nathan dropped his head into his hands and groaned. 'Nothing's sacred.'

. . . In the bedroom, I drew the bustier out of the elegant carrier-bag in which it was packed. From the bed, Nathan's eyes flicked over it. 'Put it on, Minty. I want to see you in it.'

I looked down at it: such a pretty, sexy thing. Into it I would insert a body altered by childbirth but pretend it wasn't.

'Minty!' Nathan was impatient. 'Put it on. It'll be like – it used to be.'

That was what Nathan wanted. He craved the heightened excitement of our affair, the novelty of his willing, inventive mistress.

I gave a tiny sigh and did as he asked. Thus accoutred, I joined my husband on the bed – but I was no longer willing or inventive for I carried a tally of the past, of routine and regret. No bustier would ever mask those.

'Oh, we're *absolutely fine*,' I heard myself say into the phone to Mrs Jenkins, who had rung up to ask if I needed extra help with the boys. Or 'That would be *such fun*' when Millie's mother rang up to invite us to a picnic on the common, giving the impression that the boys and I were thoroughly enjoying Nathan being dead.

I never found Nathan's diary although I searched his drawers and files. I went through the car, his pockets, the bookshelves. At the finish, I was forced to concede that I had lost the tussle between us. Nathan had decided to deny me the intimacies revealed on its pages and I grieved for that, too.

Yet there was a curious beauty to grief, a haunting, solitary beauty that was hard to describe and more than a little alarming. It was *almost* a pleasure.

Meanwhile I worked steadily through the letters in the study, determined to reply to them all.

When I got round to sorting out the piles of newspapers that had accumulated since Nathan's death, which I had never read, I came across an advertisement in one of the supplements for the Shiftaka exhibition that Gisela had taken me to see. I examined the painting. A series of free brushstrokes created a forest glade, a mixture of deciduous and pine. Imposed on the mesh of foliage were the lines of trunks and branches so rigid and black they added an air of menace to what should have been a tranquil vista. I showed this to Felix, who said, 'Ugh.'

'Why "ugh", Felix?'

'Because there are nasty things. Look, Mummy.'

The leaves on the trees were withered, and the outcrops on the trunks were clumps of insects, not natural growths. Printed at the bottom of the painting was the legend: 'Only beetles survive the nuclear winter . . .'

The following Saturday, I cooked sausages and mash for lunch, which the boys and I ate together. Afterwards they demanded to go into the garden and I retreated into Nathan's study. I gave it a good hard appraisal. When it came to his study, Nathan had a tendency to behave like a bear in its den. *Don't touch anything.* It was very much his room, masculine and utilitarian, cluttered with papers and now a little dusty. *Don't touch anything.*

But in getting through a situation such as this – my personal nuclear winter – I must dare to look over the parapet. 'Good girl,' I heard Paige say.

I put my shoulder to the desk and heaved it, panting with the effort, from its position. *Why did you leave us, Nathan? Why didn't you take more care? Yes, I am angry with you.* I shoved it over to the window and the chair followed. If I sat here, I could see the garden where the twins were chasing a squirrel.

Wrong, I thought, rubbing my shoulder. You're wrong, Rose. Anger makes you strong.

The study seemed bigger, and unfamiliar, a friendly area on which I would imprint what I wished. Moving the desk had let loose a snowstorm of papers: a directory of key Vistemax employees, which went straight into the bin, invitations, a timetable, and an out-of-date list of golfing fixtures at a club I had never heard of. They went into the bin too.

The doorbell rang. The silence in the house was so pleasant, rather reassuring, in fact, that I was tempted to ignore it. It rang a second time, and I went to see who it was.

Rose was on the doorstep, clasping a long brown-paper

package. She was wearing jeans and a short, tight jacket. She seemed strained and harassed. Instinctively I made to shut the door, but she placed a foot on the step and prevented me. 'Don't, Minty.'

'I'm not sure I can take this,' I said, a sour taste rising in my throat. 'But thank you for your letter.'

'You look awful.' She peered at me. 'Are you taking care of yourself? You should, you know. Have you seen the doctor?'

'There's no point, Rose. Go away, and don't come back. You've been very kind but we're not friends any more.'

'That's true.' She nodded reflectively. 'But you still need someone to check up on you.' She added, 'I know what it's like.'

'Don't you think that's what makes it impossible?'

'In normal circumstances, but these aren't. So . . . here I am.'

Several cars roared down the street, followed by a lumbering white van from which blared heavy rock music. Opposite, Mrs Austen glanced up from her pots. Fork in hand, she stared openly at us.

'Be kind, if only to a dog. Is that it?'

'That's it.'

The sourness turned into humiliation. 'Kindness to canines apart, there must be some other reason.'

She held out the package. 'I think this is meant for you. I've opened it. It's from Nathan.'

I examined the label. It was addressed to Minty Lloyd but the address was Rose's. 'The wrong wife.'

She smiled wryly. 'Maybe Nathan had fallen into the habit of thinking of us as a composite. He always was thrifty.'

I thrust the package back at her. 'Go away. Don't come back.'

Rose should have obeyed. Any reasonable person would have done so. A reasonable person would have seen where the line had been drawn, and that the old loyalties were finally dead.

But she was not prepared to give up. 'It's a plant for the garden. He must have ordered it months ago.'

'A plant? What on earth for? He rarely went into the garden.'

'Did he not tell you? He was thinking of redoing it. In fact, he was quite excited at the idea.' She pointed to the package. 'It deserves a chance, don't you think?'

'Why?'

'Lots of reasons. Not least that Nathan obviously wanted a rose.'

'It's a *rose*?'

'A white one.'

The urge to throw back my head and laugh hysterically at this extra twist of the knife was strong. 'I don't know anything about plants.'

'But I do.'

It was ridiculous. Nathan should have been more careful. But, then, in conflating his two wives, he was making a point. Or perhaps he had reached a fork in the road where he had been too tired to consult the map. 'You want to come in and plant this thing?'

'Well, yes. I don't feel we can waste it, under the circumstances.'

I thought of all the reasons why I didn't want Rose to come inside the house with this muddled gift from Nathan.

'I haven't much time.' She shifted the package to her other hand and checked her watch, a plain square Cartier that rested on a tanned wrist. 'So?'

Across the road, Mrs Austen was entranced by this drama on the doorstep. She put down her fork and wiped her hands on her blue and white apron. Any minute now she would cross the road and push herself on to Rose and me.

I stepped aside. 'You'd better come in.'

17

Rose walked into the hall and waited. Her gaze travelled over the unopened post on the table to the moraine of shoes and jackets at the foot of the stairs and the pile of ironing on the chair.

'Don't look at how untidy it is,' I said. 'It's been difficult.'

'Of course.' Up close, Rose had as dark a pair of shadows under her eyes as I did. 'Of course you won't have been able to cope.' She fixed on Nathan's coat, still on the peg. 'When Nathan left, it was the same. Stuff everywhere. No sense to the day. No shape.'

I bristled. 'Do we need to rake over old ground?'

'There isn't any point in pretending that what happened didn't.' Rose's shrug had changed. It was no longer weary and burdened, as it had been years ago, but light and sophisticated, an almost Gallic gesture.

I led her into the kitchen. She placed the package on the table. 'You've made it nice,' she said. 'Different, but nice.' Her eyes flicked towards the door. 'How are the boys? Are they in?'

Again I bristled. 'They're in the garden.'

Her eyes went past my left shoulder to the back door. 'I didn't catch more than a glimpse of them at the funeral. It . . . gave me quite a shock to see how like

Nathan they are. Is Felix the one with the slightly fairer hair?'

'No. That's Lucas.'

'They seemed big for five-year-olds.'

'They're six,' I said. 'They were six in March.'

'Sam was nothing like Nathan until he was eighteen or so. Then he turned into Nathan's clone. I wonder if they're going to be tall like their father.'

'I have no idea.'

If Rose imagined that she could spread her maternal wings over my children, she was wrong, wrong. *I could never fault her as a mother,' Nathan said. 'Never.'*

I gestured towards the kettle. 'Can I make you some coffee?'

'No, thank you.'

The shadows of four children fell over the ensuing hard, cold silence.

I broke it: 'The twins are not your business, Rose. I don't know what Nathan was doing when he made that extraordinary . . .' I dropped my voice '. . . that *senseless* request. Was he having a huge joke at our expense? If I die or end up paraplegic or mad, my children will be with *you*. What was he thinking of?'

She moved restlessly. 'Don't make too big a deal of it, Minty. It's optional and unlikely to happen.'

'Even so,' I said bitterly, 'I don't want you involved with them.'

'For goodness' sake!' she flashed at me. 'Do you think I want to be?' She checked herself. 'Sorry.'

'I've realized I didn't know Nathan at all.'

Rose sighed, and said, as if it was the most obvious thing in the world, 'That's what I thought when he left. It astonished me how little I knew about someone I'd lived with for so long. It happens all the time, and it's probably better that you can't pry into every nook and cranny of someone's mind.'

'Sometimes I wonder if Nathan was so bored that he dreamed up the guardian idea because it gave him something to think about.' I knew perfectly well that I was traducing him.

And Rose evidently agreed with that: 'If you think Nathan would have been so selfish . . .' She sent me a glance that suggested no bridge would ever span far or wide enough to connect us. 'He was only thinking about the twins.' She tapped the package and said, without much enthusiasm, 'Shall we get on with this?'

Smarting, I led her into the garden. But if I had been wrong to accuse Nathan of self-gratification, it did not mean that his motives had been entirely pure.

The twins had burrowed out of sight behind the shed. On our return from Cornwall, their heads filled with tales of pirates and rock fortresses, they had set up a camp, which, they had informed me, was very, very private.

'Where are they?' asked Rose.

I pointed to the shed. 'In their headquarters. I think it's the Jedi battle command.'

'Ah,' said Rose. She bent down and tugged at an elderly lavender bush. 'You didn't care for my garden. You never did.'

Rough, moss-infested grass. Shrubs that required pruning. Overgrown flowerbeds. Casual outrages, the result of Nathan's and my neglect. 'No. I never did.'

She straightened up, a sprig of lavender in her fingers. 'Funny, that. I imagined every blade of grass and leaf would be imprinted on my memory. But once you leave a place, you leave. Or, rather, it leaves you.'

I had devoted not inconsiderable time to imagining Rose's feelings on being banished from her garden. 'You mean you *forgot* about it?'

'No, never that.' She rolled the lavender between her fingers. 'It holds the early days . . . of us . . . of me.'

'Height, route and rest?' I asked. 'Did you build those in?'

'Height? Route?' Puzzled, she frowned. Then her brow cleared. 'You're talking about the plans I sent to Nathan. Did you like them? He asked me for some ideas and it sort of took off. I knew the garden inside out, after all.'

'Actually, he never mentioned them. I found them in a notebook.'

'Oh.' Rose flushed fiery red, and her lips tightened. 'If you like, I can send you what I suggested. I have a copy.'

'No.' I said. '*No.*'

After a moment, she added, 'I don't think Nathan liked it that I didn't mind doing the plans. I had an idea that he wanted me to say I'd have nothing to do with it. I think he was surprised that I didn't *mind.* Anyway, that was why he ordered the rose, don't you think?'

'Probably.' I flapped a hand at a damaged section of

fence. 'The boys. Playing ball. It ought to be mended, but I was never interested in it. Nathan isn't . . . I mean, Nathan wasn't. Occasionally, he had a fit of conscience and did a bit of digging. When I moved in here he said that it had been your thing, not his. I took the implication to be that it wasn't mine either.'

'Poor Minty,' said Rose, ultra-dry. 'What a lot you had to put up with.'

There was a shout from behind the shed, and Felix emerged red-faced and wailing, 'Mum! He hit me!' He flung himself against my knees.

'Shush,' I said. 'He didn't mean it.'

Felix wailed harder, and I shook him gently. 'Shush, Felix. Say hello to Mrs Lloyd.'

But Felix decided that he wanted a scene and upped the decibels. 'Don't show me up,' I whispered to him, at which Felix threw himself down on the lawn and kicked his legs in the air. He looked like an angry insect. Out of the corner of my eye, I caught sight of grinning Lucas waving a stick to which he had attached Felix's Blanky. I transferred my attention back to the insect, who was now roaring. I tapped his bottom. 'Stop it,' I said sternly, which had no effect.

Rose said, 'Oh dear,' in the amused way of an onlooker when they really wanted to say, 'Don't you have any control over your children?' The black rage, with which I was becoming familiar, swept over me. It was an ugly emotion and I manhandled the screaming Felix upright more roughly than I should have done. 'Don't you dare say *anything*, Rose.'

'Why would I? It's nothing to do with me.'

'You know perfectly well why you would.'

She hauled a pair of gardening gloves out of her handbag. 'Can I take a look in the shed?'

I bent over Felix. 'Why don't you show Mrs Lloyd the shed, and I'll talk to Lucas?' But Felix refused to co-operate and clung to my hand. As we passed the lilac tree, Rose paused and pulled a branch towards her for inspection. She exclaimed softly at its condition, then allowed it to snap back.

Weakened by neglect, the shed door shuddered when Rose opened it. The interior was festooned with spiders' webs. A garden fork was propped against the wall, its tines caked with earth. There was a rusty trowel, a spade and a stack of flowerpots. A packet of fertilizer stood in a corner, so old that it had hardened into a lump. I prodded it with my foot. 'Nathan always meant to take this to the council dump.'

While I cornered Lucas and ordered him to return Blanky, Rose ferreted around in the shed. She emerged with the fork and a trug with a splintered handle, into which she had teased a handful of the fertilizer. 'Now.' She catalogued the wandering lines of the lawn, the tangle of weeds and grass, the unpruned clematis. She shaded her eyes with a hand, and I knew she was peering into the past. 'If I'm truthful, I didn't *want* you to be a gardener, Minty. Certainly not in my garden.' Her eyes betrayed sudden amusement. 'But I needn't have worried.' She picked up the package. 'Where shall I plant this rose?'

'I don't want it.'

Her fingers curled round it protectively. 'But Nathan sent it. He must have been thinking of us both. It belongs here, and it matters where it's planted.'

'What's the point?' I gestured at the garden. 'It's not likely to flourish.'

Rose hacked off the wrapping package with the secateurs. 'I take it you'll be living here for the time being?'

'You know as well as I do that I have to be here. Anyway, the twins' school is very close.' I peered at her. 'I assume you've talked to Theo about the will?'

'Yes, I have.' She wasn't going to pursue the subject. 'If you're staying here you should think about the garden.'

Felix's little fingers clenched mine. 'Rose, I don't think it's your business.'

That silenced her. No doubt Rose was grateful for her little extra acquired immunity – she had had time to get used to being without Nathan. But I had not, and I was not under control. She did not challenge my rudeness but smiled at Felix, who had raised his head. His tears had ceased, and he was studying Rose with unabashed curiosity.

Rose crouched at his level. 'We haven't really said hello, Felix.' She held out her hand. 'I knew your daddy.'

Felix dropped my hand. 'Daddy . . .' he echoed, and favoured Rose with one of his devastating wide-eyed looks, which I knew could reduce its recipient to weak-kneed adoration. Rose's eyebrows flew up and, in that instant, she had been ravished.

She swallowed. 'He's so beautiful, and innocent,' she

murmured. Her eyes filled. 'And so like . . . him. But, then, what else would you expect?'

Felix moved closer to Rose. 'Why are you crying? Mummy, why's the lady crying?'

I gave him a little shove. 'Go and find Lucas, Felix. I think he's in your special camp.'

Felix required no further urging. He scampered round the shed and disappeared. Rose wiped her eyes on her sleeve, and sniffed.

'They're a little difficult at the moment. I'm feeling my way.'

She didn't answer. Hovering on the borderline between irritation and murderousness, I said, 'Just shove the damn thing in, Rose, and go away.'

'OK. I don't want to be here any more than you want me.' She began to pace up and down. 'Here,' she pronounced eventually. 'If I plant it here you'll be able to see it from the kitchen window.'

The fertilizer had leaked from the trug, and left a white trail over the lawn. Rose rubbed it in with her shoe and began to dig. Last night there had been drizzle, and the damp soil yielded easily to the fork.

I watched her. 'When did Nathan ask for help with the garden?'

'I can't remember.'

'Lots of little chats about it, then?'

'*A garden must have good bones,*' Rose would have said. Or something like it. And, no doubt, Nathan had hung on her words.

'Nathan and I kept in touch. Obviously.'

Did the exchange of gardening notes constitute adultery? Yes, in a way – in a far more telling way than the slip-slap of flesh on flesh, and Elbow Talk in the panting aftermath. Nathan had wanted Rose's opinion. He had wanted to help himself to her *thinking* and her *creating*. He had asked to be put back on the distribution list of Rose's intimacies. *'I suggest an olive tree here. The lavender there.'*

Rose sieved the stones that had worked their way to the surface and evened out the perimeter of the hole she had dug. Her body was toned, her waist defined. 'This is crazy,' I said, at last.

She continued to dig. 'No, it's not.'

'I really don't want it.'

Rose pulled herself upright and leant on the fork handle. 'You *should* want it.'

I closed my eyes. 'Were you seeing a lot of Nathan?'

Her head whipped round. 'I wasn't *seeing* Nathan.'

'Excuse me?'

The roots of the rose were dry and unpromising. Rose eased it into the hole, teased the roots apart and dribbled soil on to them. 'It really should have soaked for a while, but no matter.' She tamped down the soil with her foot. 'Perhaps you should know, Minty, that it's not possible to dismiss a marriage just like that. And, believe me, I wanted to.' She looked up. 'Hold this steady, will you?'

I obliged. Under my fingers the rose was thorny and unyielding. 'How stupid did you want me to feel, Rose? Because I felt very stupid when I realized how often Nathan contacted you.'

'Well, now you know what it's like.' Rose didn't sound

that interested. She slapped her gloved hands together, which made a dull, hollow sound. She began to say something, checked herself, and stepped back to survey her handiwork. 'I wonder what he was thinking when he ordered this one. It's a repeat flowerer.'

I swung round on my heel and walked back into the house. Behind me, I heard the rattle of the shed door, Rose's footsteps on the patio, then her 'Goodbye, twins. I hope to see you again.' *She is not having my children*, I thought, bleak and unfair and sorrowing.

Rose came into the kitchen and placed the wrapping on the table. 'I don't know where you put the rubbish.'

'Leave it.'

'Fine.' There was a short pause. 'I must go because I have an article to write. Deadlines.' The professional female was speaking to the professional female. You see and hear the exchange everywhere. Two women lunching: one or other taps her watch and murmurs, 'The meeting', or 'You should see the house,' or 'I want to sleep for a decade.' Rose and I used to talk to each other like that.

'Go, then,' I said.

She shook dirt from the gloves into the sink. 'About the children, Minty . . .'

'*Don't* bring them into it. We're doing fine. We're coping.' *Felix's little figure sitting at the foot of the stairs.* 'We're doing our best. I don't need help.'

Again, Rose glanced at her watch, and there was a degree of hesitancy. 'Keep watering the rose for a few days.'

'Rose, you are not involved. OK?'

She said softly, 'Don't take it out on Nathan.'

'Nathan is dead,' I hissed through my teeth. *'Dead.'*

Across the street Mrs Austen, who had given up hope of any further street theatre from number fourteen, was loading her car with plastic bags of rubbish. A lorry was depositing a builder's skip on the opposite side of the road.

Provoked beyond endurance, I cried, 'Did you plan this with Nathan in one of your cosy chats? Did he say to you, "Minty needs help. She's not up to looking after the twins"? Which was his way of telling you I wasn't up to scratch.'

'That's your interpretation, not mine,' Rose said quietly. 'I'm only their guardian if you're not around. It was a precaution, that's all.'

'I wish you'd vanish,' I said. 'But you won't.'

Rose swung round so abruptly that she dislodged a cup from the dresser, which fell to the floor. Neither of us moved to pick it up. It rolled away and came to rest by the table. 'I don't know what you spend your time imagining, Minty,' her voice was flat, 'but just *think* for a minute. I've tried to get rid of Nathan. After he went off with you . . . After you took him, I had to remake my life, and it was tough. I have no wish to be dragged back into his. Or yours. I don't want *anything* to do with your children.'

'Then go away.'

'But equally I have no intention of vanishing, as you put it, for your convenience. I will do as I wish, when I think fit.'

Angry, jangled and edging closer to despair, I lay awake for much of the night. When Rose had brought me to number seven and introduced me to Nathan, it had been a warm night. *'Perfect, Minty, for dinner in the garden. Do come.'* Before the introductions were completed, my disloyalty to her had already taken shape. It hadn't been difficult to effect. As the three of us discussed the nature of long-lived friendships, I looked at Nathan and widened my eyes a fraction. It was sufficient.

He said to me afterwards, 'I don't know what came over me, Minty. I've sometimes been tempted before, but I've never *done* anything.'

In the end, we had married thinking the other had wanted the opposite of what they really did. In a rush of blood to the brain, Nathan had abandoned Rose and their life in Lakey Street because he had developed a yen for something that was unpredictable, spontaneous and glamorous. He wanted to try another way of living before it was too late. 'Your flat is perfect,' he said, flinging himself on to the – necessarily – small double bed. 'We're free of all those tedious domestic complications.'

I didn't tell him that he wasn't seeing straight. That would have embarrassed him. No one wishes to be told that they're trying fruitlessly to turn the clock back.

'You do understand?' he asked.

I stroked his face. 'We're as free as birds.'

I didn't confess to entertaining an attractive mental picture of a woman moving around the kitchen at number seven or presiding over the dinner table, clean socks in the drawers, milk in the fridge, soap in the bathrooms, in a house where there was plenty of space. That woman was me.

The clock said 5.15 a.m. I ran my hand over my body, and felt my ribcage and hipbones outlined more sharply than before. My eyes stung, my head was thick and heavy. There was no more sleep to be had that night. I got out of bed, went downstairs and let myself out into the garden.

It was chilly and I shivered. A spot or two of rain fell on to my face as I picked my way over the lawn.

I should have been honest with Nathan and told him, 'We won't be free. It isn't like that.'

His death – his untimely, stupid death – deserved to be marked by more than small eruptions of anger between Rose and me. Nathan was owed a banquet, a cinematic farewell, a clash of cymbals. I owed him an august sorrow that would cleanse any spite, guilt and disappointment.

I knew this. I knew it very well. And yet I found myself staring down at the rose. I reached over and grasped it by the stem. A thorn drove itself into the base of my thumb and a pinprick of blood appeared. With a little gasp of pain, I pulled the rose from the earth.

18

Two months later, at three o'clock precisely, Barry, Chris and I got out of a taxi at BBC Television Centre in Wood Lane. 'Right,' said Barry, after he had paid the very large fare. 'Now to battle.'

I murmured, 'All for one and one for all.'

Barry laughed. 'Glad you haven't lost your sense of humour, Minty.'

Television Centre had been built in the 1950s and was a maze of studios, stacked scenery and coffee bars in odd corners. Ed Golightly's office was situated in a basement of E Block, opposite Scenery Block A. We were ushered through a half-empty production office and into a room that was furnished with a black leather sofa and chairs and overlooked the Hammersmith and City Line.

Ed was short, with red hair, to which he drew attention by constantly running his hand through it. He had the world-weary expression of a man who had devoted his life to the tough business of pushing arts programmes on to the air.

He was rifling through the Paradox dossier entitled *Pointe of Departure*, which I had prepared and sent to him two weeks earlier. He did not look up. 'Sit,' he said. Then, at last, 'Right.' He had the grace to add apologetically, 'I've only just got round to reading this.'

I heard Barry click his tongue against his teeth, but Chris said, 'Take your time, Ed.'

'Would you like me to run through it?' I offered. 'The idea and format is simple. A well-known ballerina will have a go at the tango, breakdancing, belly-dancing and rock-and-roll . . .'

Ed leant back in his chair. 'Any particular ballerina in mind?'

Barry took over. 'Nora Pavane. She's excited about the idea. Legs that do things you wouldn't believe.'

'Very bankable. Very personable. Can talk to anyone,' Chris said.

Ed grimaced. 'I have a problem – a big one. As arts editor, if I submit any idea to our controller with the word "dance" in the title, he'll utter profanities. Or laugh. That's the way it is. Now, if I said Nora had agreed to have live cosmetic surgery, no problem.'

'Do you have any budget at all?' Chris asked.

Ed was guarded. 'A little.'

At this point, I suggested, 'Why don't we get Nora to meet the controller? Is there a do coming up where we could arrange it? I'm sure if he met her he'd be charmed.'

Ed seemed marginally more galvanized by the project, and rifled through his diary. 'He's giving a lecture at the Royal Television Society.'

Barry cut in: 'Easy, then, Ed. I know the director of the RTS. He used to work for me on *The Late, Late*

Show. I'll email him and get an invite for Nora. She can sit next to the controller at the dinner afterwards.' He grinned at Chris and me. 'That's it, then, guys.'

On the way home, I picked up my winter coat from the cleaner's and a couple of bottles of fruit juice from the shop on the corner of Lakey Street. The wire coat-hanger cut into my fingers as I walked. The day had been warm and sunny. In Mrs Austen's window-box, a bright blue lobelia was blooming. It had been a successful day and I should have been feeling happy about it. Yet if anyone had asked me – if Nathan had been there to congratulate me on a successful pitch – I would have replied, 'You know, I don't care that much.'

Eve was washing up in the kitchen. 'The boys are outside,' she said. 'It is so nice.' She stacked the plates and said, 'I go now,' then went up to her room. Her radio snapped on.

I squinted out of the back door. The boys were running about in their pyjamas and did not notice me. I listened to my phone messages. Poppy's breathy voice filled the kitchen. Could I ring her office? She'd be there until late. Next up was Sue Frost. Had I decided about bereavement counselling? I ran myself a glass of water and drank it. If being married invaded one's privacy, it was even more the case being a widow. Everyone wanted to help themselves to a bit of my predicament. Mrs Jenkins was constantly advising me on how to handle the twins. Paige and Gisela offered contradictory advice. Mrs Austen had asked me point-blank if I had enough money to live on. Kate Winsom had insisted that I sign up for a course of colonic irrigation. 'It's so cleansing. At a time like this you can't afford to house toxins.' Others demanded to know how I was managing. Without waiting for an answer, they proceeded to tell me how they would manage. I had begun to feel like a large fish in an aquarium where visitors are parked below the water level so that they can enjoy uninterrupted views of the exposed underbellies. No one ever considered a shark's right to privacy. They should.

Obediently I rang Poppy. 'It's Minty.' Since the funeral, we had met only twice, each time with the twins, and our conversations had remained within the bounds of politeness.

'Thanks for ringing,' she said, more hesitant than usual. In the background I could hear the subdued whine of a printer. 'The thing is, Minty, I wanted to ask you how things were progressing with Dad's will.'

Was it odd that Poppy hadn't talked to Theo? 'We . . .' I emphasized it '. . . will have to be patient a little longer. Theo is still waiting for probate to be granted.'

She hesitated. 'So, we're no closer to sharing out the money?'

'Theo's doing his best.'

'It takes such a *long* time.' Poppy's urgent cry echoed down the phone. 'Can't we hurry it up?'

'Is there some problem about the money? Theo explained it quite carefully. Have you a complaint?'

'No, no, nothing like,' she countered hastily. 'I was just wondering, that's all. Theo did say that Sam and I were due our share, and I could . . . do with my mine. There are one or two things that I must . . . I would like to use it for.'

'Can't Richard tide you over?'

'No.' Her voice veered upwards. 'I mean, yes. I *will* ask Richard. He's always so generous. But I don't rely on my husband.' She gave a little laugh. 'Well, as little as possible. Did I tell you he's been promoted again? So have I, in a modest way.' The printer choked, interrupting her. 'Oh, God, I must go. I'm trying to print out a delivery note to go with a huge order for Christmas candles from Liberty's and the printer keeps jamming. Will you let me know as soon as possible?'

Through the open door, I saw Felix stick out his leg and Lucas go sprawling over it. I switched my gaze back to the kitchen. If Nathan was sitting at the table, he'd say, 'She's my daughter, and I must help.'

I took a deep breath. 'I'm worried you're in trouble, Poppy. Would you like to talk things over some time?'

'No!' Her panicky voice convinced me that I was right. 'It's none of your business.'

'Are you sure?'

Poppy turned hostile. 'I'm absolutely sure, thank you, Minty. Could we leave it now? Please?'

'I'll ask Theo to get in touch with you.'

I terminated the call and I went to say hello to the twins, who occupied me for the next couple of hours. But I was troubled by my conversation with Poppy.

Later, when I came downstairs, my eye lit on a vase of dying irises in the hall. I carried them into the kitchen and emptied out the water, which smelt disgusting. I dropped one of the flowers on to the floor and its pulpy stem left a stain on the tiles. I knelt down and scrubbed at it with a tissue, which disintegrated. I got to my feet to fetch the dustpan, and pain flickered in my knees. That made me smile. Nathan had married me because he thought I would make him young again. But instead I had grown older.

I scraped the rubbish into the bin and the lid banged shut.

A deep, unhealed loss held me in its tight grip.

I was woken by the sound of starlings on the stairs. I glanced at the clock – 5.30 a.m. Groaning, I got out of bed. 'Just what are you two doing?' I demanded. The twins were dressed and kitted up with their school rucksacks. 'And what are you carrying?'

'It's our food for the journey,' Felix explained.

'Turn round.' Felix did so, and I unzipped the rucksack. Inside I found an apple, a couple of chocolate biscuits and Blanky. The last was significant. Felix would never leave the house without Blanky. 'Did you pinch these from the tin?'

'It's for our journey,' Lucas repeated.

'What journey?'

Felix tugged at my hand. 'A special journey, Mummy.'

I sat down on the top stair. 'You were running away without telling me. I wouldn't have liked that, you know.'

This worried Felix. 'We're going to find Daddy,' he said.

To hide the rush of hot tears, I dropped my head into my hands. There were further starling rustles and a twin inserted himself at either side of me. I put out my arms and drew them close. 'What am I going to do with you?' They knew the question was rhetorical, and neither answered. 'I've told you both about Daddy. He's gone to another place where he will be perfectly at peace. But he can't ever come back.'

'Oh, yes he will,' said Lucas. 'When we dig him up.'

I ached for their misery. My sadness was now complete, and I searched desolately for the best words, the right thing to do. 'Well,' I said finally, 'why don't we think about it in bed?'

Fifteen minutes later, they were asleep, but not before I had extracted a promise from them that they would never, ever leave the house without telling me or Eve. I lay awake, borne aloft on a layer of biscuit crumbs – they had insisted in eating their provisions.

'Minty!' a voice called behind me, as I was dashing out of number seven on the way to work.

It was Martin. He was in his office suit, with a brief-case and a matching overnight bag in the softest leather, the kind top executives favour. 'I was hoping to catch you. I'm sorry I haven't been around, but I've been so busy. Paige tells me you're coping . . . but . . .' He placed a finger under my chin and tilted it up. 'Bit pale, thinner, but that's to be expected.'

I licked my dry lips. I had almost forgotten how to respond to human beings, let alone friends.

'I'm afraid I need to talk to you,' he said.

That shook me out of my torpor. 'Trouble?'

'Trouble,' he conceded. 'Have you got time?'

I glanced at my watch. 'I'm due at a meeting in an hour.' That would take up the morning. Lunchtime would be devoted to buying new school uniform for the twins. An afternoon meeting was scheduled with Ed Golightly at the BBC and everyone was crossing fingers for the green light. With luck and a following wind, I would make it home for the twins' bath. 'I have time.'

'Coffee, then?' Martin jerked a finger at the café on the corner.

We sat at a too-small table that lurched alarmingly if one or other of us leant on it. Martin blew into the cappuccino, and the resulting ruffle on the froth mirrored his frown. He looked baffled and angry. A dot of shaving cream nesting behind his left ear skewed his conformist, businesslike appearance.

'Martin, this looks bad.'

'It is.' He picked up his cup and put it down again. 'Paige and I have split up. Or, rather, she told me to go.'

'*What?* She hasn't said anything to me.'

Naturally that was neither here nor there to Martin. He raised his eyes and looked directly into mine. 'You know the expression "a blow in the solar plexus"? It doesn't describe the half of it.'

A picture of Nathan sitting in the blue chair, dead, swam into view. 'I have some idea.'

'Yes, of course you do. I was forgetting.' He frowned, and the hollows under his eyes deepened alarmingly. This was a man who was hoping to be mistaken, who was grappling with a mystery he suspected he had no hope of solving.

'How long had it been brewing?'

He shrugged and took refuge in flippancy. 'Who knows what goes on in my wife's mind?'

I searched for a clue to Paige's decision. Had Martin beaten her up? Demanded that she become a sex slave? I tried the obvious line. 'You can go a bit mad after having a baby. I did. You feel so unsettled and unsure.'

'*Paige?*' he said. 'Never.'

Yet his bewilderment and hurt were so profound that I could almost touch them. 'Paige feels I don't pay enough attention to the children but apparently I demand too much from her. She says she has enough children to look after. She needs to concentrate on them and I get in the way.'

Despite the sun warming my back, I felt cold. 'Martin, Paige *has* gone mad. Are you sure the doctor is keeping an eye on her?'

'As far as I know, but I've been away quite a lot.' He pushed aside his untouched coffee. 'It's a battlefield at home, but Paige is sane and well. I've no doubt of that. Each time she gives birth she becomes . . . well, stronger and more implacable. Like Clytemnestra or whoever that dreadful woman was who killed her husband for fun.'

'He'd just slaughtered her daughter.'

264

'Had he? Oh, well.' He reached down for the handle of his bag. 'It's perfectly correct that I don't devote every waking breath, or every sleeping one for that matter, to the children. I leave that to Paige.'

'What do you want me to do, Martin?' I asked gently. 'Although I'm not sure what I *could* do, except try to persuade Paige that's she wrong.'

Martin gazed down at the table. He was searching for something to cling to. 'Try to persuade her to do anything and you'll achieve the opposite. But could you keep an eye on her? She's not as strong as she thinks.' He got to his feet. 'Thank you for the coffee.' Large and baffled, he hovered above me. 'I know it's a lot to ask, Minty, at the moment, but if you could keep tabs on her? Sooner or later she'll come to her senses. Actually, I'm not sure I want to live with her at the moment anyway – she's so awful.' He yanked out the expanding handle of his suitcase with some force. 'She should never have left the bank. That's where her energies are best deployed. Children have ruined her.'

When I tackled Paige, she was unrepentant and not at all mad. 'Martin doesn't fit in with the children,' she said, as she hefted baby Charlie from one breast to the other. I noted the breast was looking less joyously abundant, and floppier than it had been. 'He's always coming home at the wrong time, and wanting a meal or his shirts washed.'

'Linda can do that, or some of it, surely?'

She thought about this for a while. There was an exultant expression in her eyes, which I didn't recognize. 'He prevents me concentrating on the children.'

I changed my mind. Paige was unhinged. 'Have you been to the doctor lately?'

'No need.' She addressed the fuzzy head of her sucking son. 'Mummy's fine, isn't she? We're doing just fine.'

'You should go,' I said.

There was a hum in the quiet, organized kitchen: dish-washer, washing-machine. Upstairs my twins were being entertained grudgingly by Jackson and Lara. It was only four o'clock on a Saturday afternoon but the table was already laid for the children's six o'clock supper, and the oven timer had been primed to spring into life at five thirty.

Oddly at sea, I twisted my hands in my lap. 'Obviously I can't occupy the high ground on broken marriages –'

'Obviously,' said Paige, rudely.

'But that's it, Paige. I can say something because I know.'

'Know what?'

'How to convince yourself that what you're doing is OK.'

Charlie thrust his head back and Paige's nipple popped out of his mouth. 'Oh, look!' she exclaimed. 'He's got a sore lip. Poor little boy.' She nuzzled his cheek with lingering tenderness. 'Mummy will make it better.'

I didn't often think about my mother and it's safe to say that, while she was alive, my mother didn't often think about me in a real, proper, motherly way. First, she was always too tired from trying to earn a living after my father abandoned us. Second, she didn't like me. Consequently, I lay many of life's ills at her door because, as the self-help manuals point out, it's your mother who sets the tone. When she was alive, I pretended she was dead. Then she was dead and, for a while, I pretended she wasn't.

'Listen to me.' Paige did not look up from Charlie. I got up and snatched poor Charlie out of her arms. He felt bulky and compact and smelt of half-digested milk. He protested at this sudden change, but I didn't care. 'You *will* listen to me. It's very easy to think yourself into rightness. "Yes," I used to say to myself. "Rose is so complacent. She doesn't care about Nathan in the way he needs. She deserves to lose him. A person as careless as Rose doesn't deserve a husband like Nathan." In the end, I felt it was almost my duty to take Nathan away.'

'And you succeeded. So?'

'You're missing the point, Paige. You can reason yourself in and out of anything. That's the trouble with reason. It's flexible.'

Paige stood up and held out her arms. 'Give me my baby,' she ordered. 'He needs changing.'

I clung to Charlie. 'You can't honestly think that the children will be better off without Martin?'

'Hark at who's talking.'

'Felix and Lucas are suffering terribly.'

Paige succeeded in prising Charlie away from me. 'I

appreciate your concern, Minty,' her face closed, 'but I'd rather you didn't interfere in this one.'

'Don't imagine because I've been away that I'm letting you out of my sight,' Gisela said. 'I want to know everything. You'll hate me for being a busybody, but you'll be grateful too.'

Gisela had been in the South of France for a month, and on her return she had phoned and arranged to take me out to lunch. The Vistemax car had picked me up from Paradox, a little perk that I made no effort to hide from Deb *et al.* Gisela was installed inside it. She was tanned and fit and kissed me warmly. I kissed her back – I'd missed her.

'I hope you're demanding answers from Theo,' she continued. 'Unless you're stroppy, lawyers let things drift.'

The car purred off in the direction of Kensington. I gave an edited rundown on the financial and legal situation, then asked, 'Did anyone help you, Gisela, when you were struggling with all the detail?'

She hesitated. 'Sometimes . . . Well, Marcus did. He's good on that sort of thing.'

'Actually, the detail isn't my main worry. It's the boys. They miss Nathan.'

She glanced down at her hands, folded elegantly in her lap. 'It's awful for you at the moment.'

'Sometimes their sadness is almost too much to bear. They wanted to go looking for him the other day. They'd packed a bag each.'

A variety of expressions chased across Gisela's smooth complexion. Then she said briskly, 'Bear it you must.' She opened her bag and produced her diary. 'Now I need *your* advice. Or, rather, I'd like to talk to you, so I'm going to offer you a bribe.'

'I suppose it's about Marcus.'

'In a way everything's always about Marcus. I've tried not to let it be, but that's proved impossible. He's sort of . . . always there.'

'Because you want him to be,' I pointed out.

'I suppose so.'

The car slowed for traffic-lights. The thought of the expensive food Gisela was about to buy for me made me feel a little nauseous. 'Gisela, I'm not that hungry. Appetite seems to have deserted me.'

'That's no surprise. Look at it this way. Many women would kill to be in that position. Actually, I want to whisk you off to Claire Manor for a couple of days' pampering. The treat's on me, so you'll have to listen to my problems and you might forget yours.'

I reached over and touched her elbow. 'You are lovely. It would be . . .' Then I heard myself say, 'But it's a bit soon for me to leave the twins. I don't think I could do it to them.'

Steel crept into Gisela's limpid, sympathetic gaze. 'Yes, you can, Minty.'

I tried another, perfectly truthful, tack: 'I can't afford it, Gisela.'

'I've already said I'm paying.'

'I can't take any more time off work, not one second.

269

Paradox are waiting for an excuse to offload me now that I'm a liability.'

'Is that true?'

I thought of Chris Sharp and his ambitions. 'I think so. Or, rather, I don't wish to give them an opportunity to prove it.'

'Of course. I see that absolutely. We'll go at a weekend.'

As the car slid to a halt in front of the restaurant, she turned to me. 'You're looking bad, Minty. Pale and sad. That isn't good for Paradox. You must give yourself two days off. It's the least you can do.' She took my hand and patted it. Deal?'

'I'll have to see if Eve can cover, and all that. I can't just say yes like . . .' Like the old days.

There was a tiny flicker of impatience. 'Well, I won't take no for an answer.'

That night when I got ready for bed, I forced myself to conduct a mirror session. The eyes and hair it reflected lacked lustre. Most of all, my eyes bothered me. They were lifeless.

19

I planned my assault on Barry carefully. The La Hacienda nightclub was two flights of steps underground and sparing on lights. Barry had taken Chris, Deb, Gabrielle, Syriol and me there to celebrate the green light for *Pointe of Departure*. Chris and Deb lounged on a sofa and Syriol was dancing solo in the gloom on a small square of dance-floor. Iggy Pop was deafening. Barry sucked at a bottle of Bacardi Breezer (half sugar).

I took a swig of tequila and the salt burnt my lips. 'Barry,' I shouted, 'can I leave early a week on Friday? There's no meeting or anything – I've checked.'

He removed the bottle from his mouth and shouted back, 'Why?'

I edged closer and put my lips to his ear, hoping he wouldn't get the wrong idea. 'Weekend away.'

'Must you?' he yelled.

I glanced round. The strobe light on the dance-floor had turned Syriol a peculiar colour. On an adjacent sofa, a couple were eating each other. Deb was gazing into Chris's eyes, but his were fixed on Syriol. The gloom and the noise were uncomfortable and I felt old.

'Yes, I must,' I said. 'But I'll be back first thing on Monday morning for the meeting with Ed.'

'Mind you are,' he said. 'We have to keep pushing to show that we mean business.'

Eve was also agreeable. She was briefed and bribed with double pay, the meals planned. I rang Paige and begged her to act as back-up. Still smarting from our previous conversation, she was not forthcoming. 'Only in an emergency,' she said. 'Jackson has maths coaching on Saturday mornings, and Lara has ballet all day. Sunday we're at my mother's.'

The edifice of care was thus constructed. No expedition to the moon could have been planned in more detail: meals, clothes, money. No contingencies could have been so closely considered.

I explained to the twins that I was going away for two days and two nights to a place where they made you pretty, and my promise to take them to see the dinosaurs at the Natural History Museum when I returned was written in blood.

But I was making a bad fist of it. Lucas jumped up and down on the spot. 'Don't leave me! Don't leave me!'

Patiently, I explained that Eve would look after them, and it was not for long. I listened to myself spell out – soothing and placatory – that I would be away Friday and Saturday and be back to kiss them goodnight on Sunday.

'But you're pretty already, Mummy.' Felix reached for Blanky.

He had succeeded in pricking my conscience and I said, more crossly than I intended, 'I need a little rest,

Felix. It's hard work looking after you two. Did you know that?'

Felix and Lucas took a simultaneous step back, exchanged some form of extra-terrestrial communication and, without a word, filed out of the room.

'Twins,' I called, 'please come back.'

They climbed the stairs, still ominously silent, and went into their bedroom. The door banged. An object was dragged across the floor and thumped against it. I went up to investigate. 'Felix, let me in! Lucas!' I rattled at the door. No answer.

I dropped to one knee, applied an eye to the keyhole and saw the back of the painted chair wedged against the door. 'Felix, Lucas . . .' I wished I sounded more certain, more like a parent in control.

For all the response I got, I might as well have been in outer space. The twins were out of sight but there were cautious flurries of movement. The carpet pile pressed into my knee and my toes cramped, as they always did in that position.

In that position I was a fool. In that position the twins had the upper hand.

As I got to my feet, a piece of paper shot under the door: 'Go away, Mumy' in green crayon.

I leant against the wall, and crumpled slowly, wearily, to a sitting position. The misspelt 'Mumy' was clear, accusatory and reproaching. It cut like a knife.

This was usually the moment when I demanded, 'Nathan, will you please sort this one out. The twins are naughty/revolting/obstinate/crying . . .' Looking

273

back, I had issued the challenge to him more often than I cared to admit now. And, imperfectly concealing his pleasure at my SOS for a firefighter, Nathan would slouch into the fray: 'You all need your heads knocking together. Just be firm.' He had been fond of saying 'Take no nonsense. Let them know who's leader of the pack.' Occasionally, I teased him for being pompous and – sometimes – I cried because I couldn't get the hang of family life. Here was the continuing conundrum. How on earth had an intelligent, capable woman like me got into such a muddle?

I looked up, fully expecting to hear Nathan's tread on the stairs, the hand on my shoulder, his voice in my ear. Then I heard myself murmur aloud, *'Nathan will never have really grey hair.'*

But all that lay in the past.

Go away, Mumy.

At Claire Manor, I resorted to a sleeping pill and woke in an unfamiliar bed artfully draped in muslin *à la Polonaise*. Across the room, the curtains fell expensively to the floor and the cushion on the chair sported antique-style tassels.

It was the kind of room that was featured in magazines. It exuded discreet affluence and comfort, an exemplar of the bargain struck between fantasy and reality. No one could, or would, ever live in it.

Luxuriously and beautifully run as it was, Claire Manor was not an innocent place. In fact, its *raison d'être* was knowingness. In the bathrooms there was a battery of potions and creams, which guests were invited to secrete in their luggage. If we used them, they wooed enticingly, dewy skin and renewed collagen were ours. They posed an interesting dilemma. There was no chance that they could deliver what they promised, but if the situation was left to Nature there was absolutely no chance of achieving them either. A selection of books ranged on a shelf – *The Insightful Soul, Ten Steps to a Beautiful Body, Yoga for the Spirit* and *Managing Ourselves* – added to the cool, considered conspiracy.

Across the corridor, which was covered with deep-pile carpet, Gisela occupied a room identical to mine – except that it was larger, had a complimentary fruit bowl and the bathroom was draped with more towels.

No child ever set foot in Claire Manor. None would be permitted to invade its pink, scented, draped and hushed interiors.

I stretched out to experiment with toe aerobics, and tried to recapture the uplift of spirits I had experienced when Gisela and I arrived in Reception. 'I can run amok,' I confided to Gisela. 'Eat pickled onions and order a BLT on Room Service at four in the morning.'

She had looked at me oddly. 'Minty, this is a health farm. May I remind you that your body is a temple?'

In the cold light of morning, groggy with the sleeping pill, an all-too-vivid mental picture took shape. I knew that Lucas and Felix would be sitting up in bed and saying to Eve, 'Mummy's gone too.'

As we ate dinner (mung beans and onion ragoût), Roger phoned Gisela twice for no good reason. Gisela listened, soothed, then apologized for the intrusion. 'Roger gets agitated when I go away. He hates it.' She poked at a bean. 'This is a man who has run a couple of large companies and made millions . . .'

'And?' I prompted when she fell silent.

Gisela grasped her water glass. 'That's what I want to talk to you about. But not tonight.'

The threat of the conversation-to-come loomed over me as the last vestiges of sleep fell away. There was a knock at the door and a girl in shell-pink uniform came in carrying a tray. She had thick fair hair pulled up into a ponytail and a stern expression. 'Your breakfast.' She placed a single cup of hot water with a slice of lemon beside the bed. 'It's a beautiful day,' she commented, as she pulled back the curtains and warm sunlight flooded in. 'You've had your programme explained to you.' She picked up the printout on the table and checked it. 'Do you know where to go for your first appointment?' She pressed a hand on my foot under the bedclothes. It was a professional touch, designed to reassure and give the illusion of expertise. 'Enjoy your day.'

'My body is a temple,' I muttered, and sipped the hot water. On the breakfast-satisfaction index, it had a long way to go.

At home, Felix would be staring glumly into his cereal bowl as he did every morning. Breakfast was not Felix's thing. 'Not hungry.' Lucas would have eaten his already, quickly and efficiently. They had grown cunning and wily, accomplices in deception. When he thought I wasn't looking, Felix slid his bowl to his brother. I watched for that. Nathan and I had discussed the prospect of Lucas becoming all-powerful over Felix. Nathan had scratched his head and said, without a trace of irony, 'It's the law of the jungle. They'll have to learn.'

'That's strange,' I had said. 'Usually I'm the toughie, and you're the softie.'

'Times change,' said Nathan.

They had. They had. Times had changed out of all recognition.

I picked up the phone and called Eve. 'Everything all right?'

She sounded hoarse and tired. 'I think.'

'You think?'

She coughed, a nasty sound. 'It is all right.'

Nine o'clock. Fitness class. I went through the motions. Squeeze pelvic floor (now they tell you). Control breathing. Contract sitting bones and concentrate on hip flexors. The language and the commands issuing from the lips of a slender instructor in grey sweats were familiar. Their aim was that unreachable perfection. That was how she made her living.

'Stretch.' 'Flex.' 'Bend.' Along the way to this moment, I had picked up another language, now more familiar than this one, which was full of commands like 'Wash behind your ears' and 'Just you get into the bath' and 'I'll have no more nonsense'. Its aim? To get me through the day intact, and to end up with a pair of fed and washed boys.

Ten thirty. I climbed naked into a contraption that

resembled an iron boot, and was encased in mud to my neck. It was not an entirely pleasurable sensation. An hour later, I was hosed down by another honey-blonde in a white uniform. She directed a stream of water on to my torso. I yelped. It was ice cold. The girl smiled encouragingly. 'You're doing very well, Mrs Lloyd.' Her gaze slid over my stomach and hips.

I grabbed a towel and wrapped it round me. Used as I was to nakedness at the gym, I had not until this moment appreciated how delightful and desirable modesty was.

After each procedure, the girls in charge – the white uniforms – wrote a report and slid it into the plastic folder that every client carried around.

One o'clock. Wearing dazzling white towelling dressing-gowns, Gisela and I met for lunch: French beans and walnuts in a lemon dressing. The dining room was sunny, with a view of an immaculate English garden in which delphiniums and poppies mingled with exot-ically shaped foliage.

'My report card?' Gisela seemed distracted. 'Oh, it's fine. Except they think my diet's unbalanced, which I assured them it was *not*.' She pulled herself together. 'Have you rung home? All under control?'

'Eve sounded a bit strange, but so far so good.'

The dressing on the beans had been made extra, extra tart and the inside of my mouth puckered at the first mouthful. I had never cared for lemons. A tall, tanned man at the adjacent table was gazing with unabashed horror at the plate of mung beans and tofu that had been placed in front of him. He looked across to me, and I found myself smiling in sympathy. He shook his head, and smiled back.

Gisela was not enjoying her meal. Unusually, she was jumpy and unsettled. I forced down a mouthful. 'I guess Marcus has issued an ultimatum.'

She leant back in her chair.

'He's called your bluff,' I went on. 'It's either Roger or him?'

Gisela picked up a spoon and attacked the small slice of paw-paw balanced on a piece of melon. 'It's very inconvenient of him to make a fuss at the moment.'

'Poor Marcus.'

The corners of Gisela's mouth went down. 'He knew the situation.'

That was irrefutable, and I pondered the rules of Gisela's life. Was Marcus a permanent lover or was he only permitted to be so between husbands? Was there a code of practice for this sort of thing? The melon on my plate was unripe and frigidly cold, and my teeth jumped as I bit into it. 'What are you going to do?'

She tensed. 'That's what I want to talk about.'

'I'm touched that you feel you can confide in me . . . and this is wonderful,' I gestured to the room, 'but I don't know that I can help.'

'I'm surprised.' Gisela was taken aback. 'You've been there. In your time you've been ruthless, and I wanted your clear head.'

I absorbed this in silence. After a moment, I said, 'But you knew that, one fine day, you'd arrive at this point.'

She sighed. 'I tried not to think about it because I knew that if I did I'd lose my nerve. Even I thought how peculiar and far-fetched the set-up was. Marcus accepted that I wasn't going to marry him until he began to make some money. He had other women too, and whenever I was free he wasn't, and vice versa. The timing was hopeless. But I always told him he was free to go, and he could have abandoned me years ago. It's only now that he's put his foot down. I never quite meant *not* to marry him. Things didn't work out quite right.'

'I don't hold any brief for Roger,' I said, 'but I suspect it would hurt him a lot if you left.'

Gisela bit her lip. 'Normally I don't have this problem. My husbands usually die, and that's quite different.'

'Quite different.' The conversation wasn't leaving a good taste in my mouth and I applied myself to the frozen melon.

Gisela had abandoned hers. 'I've realized something rather dispiriting. I'm no longer a risk-taker.' I was about to say that I considered her to be quite the reverse when she added, 'Marcus has been my life. If I say no to him I'm cutting him off for ever, and I can't bear to think of that. Being married to Roger is more complicated than it ever was with Nicholas or Richmond. They left me alone in a way that Roger doesn't.'

'Are you sure he has no idea about Marcus?'

Gisela dropped her eyes to the table. 'No.'

The big hand of the clock over the buffet table had inched on to the hour. 'Gisela, I've got an appointment with hot stones. We'll have to continue this conversation later.'

Gisela consulted her file. 'And I'm for the mud.'

She hurried off, and as I threaded my way through the tables, the tanned man said as I passed, 'I ate the tofu.'

'And lived?' I murmured.

'Just.'

Whoever dreamt up the hot-stones treatment had known a thing or two about the human psyche. The girl in the white coat explained that, during the Middle Ages, patients were cupped with heated glasses to draw out their bad humours and this was not a dissimilar process. Such a neat idea, and so suggestive. Bad temper, ill grace and melancholy could be dispersed with a hot glass or stone. So, too, could grief and regret – if you believed it.

I emerged with red patches imprinted on my skin and a pounding head – the toxins making their exit felt – and fell on to a massage couch.

An angel in white pressed confidently on my spine, a light, detached touch.

Behind my closed eyelids, the twins ran downstairs on a Saturday morning and into the kitchen. 'Daddy, what are we going to do today?'

And Nathan, biting into his toast, would say something along the lines of 'Well, I think I'll test you on your spelling.' Then, when the cry of outrage went up, 'No? what a surprise. I thought you boys loved spelling. I'd better think of something else. Let me see, what about doing some dusting for Mummy? No?' Five minutes or so later, the twins having unaccountably rejected homework, housework and gardening, Nathan pulled in his fish. 'Wait for it, yes, one of you is sending me a message. It says . . . I'm getting it . . . What *does* it say? Adventure playground and pizza? Am I right?'

Very often I had said, 'Oh, Nathan, just *tell* them.'

The masseur's fingers sought out the area of my sciatic nerve. That particular game had been played for the last time, and I was shaken by its loss. I would miss its absurdities, the crackle it imparted to a Saturday morning.

'You're very tense, Mrs Lloyd,' the girl remarked.

How many times a day did she repeat this mantra – so soothing in its understated sympathy? She was implying that those lying on her couch had the troubles of the world locked into their muscles and only she, the professional, could help.

She cupped my head and manipulated my neck. 'I think you're especially stressed. I can tell from the way the muscles have clenched.' The fingers dug and probed. 'They are very . . .' she paused for effect '. . . tight.'

It was like being given a medal. My fatigue was proof that I mattered in the outside world – all those burnt-out movers and shakers – and I merited a place on this couch. I needed her, and she required my depleted state as a reason for working. It was a tidy arrangement.

At the end of the session, she fussed over the removal of the towels. 'I'll leave you now.' She stood in the doorway. 'You must take care of yourself, Mrs Lloyd.' She meant every word, yet none of them.

'Thank you.'

I had just arranged myself satisfactorily beside the pool, which was a deep turquoise flanked by fake marble pillars, when I felt a presence. It was the man from the dining room.

'Hello.'

My response was polite, if not enthusiastic. 'Hi.'

'I could do with some company.' He smiled invitingly. 'I'm here on my own, and finding it tough.'

'Food killing you?'

He dropped into the seat beside me. 'Whoever invented tofu deserves to be taken to the vet and put down.'

I laughed. 'You can order the non-diet diet, you know.'

'I shall. Name's Alan Millett. I'm here because my family have thrown me out while they organize my birthday surprise. They don't know that I know.'

'But you went along with it?'

'Why not? It's giving Sally, Joey and Ben enormous pleasure. I agreed that I needed a bit of a break and allowed them to pack me off.'

The plastic envelope fell to the ground and I bent over to pick it up. I found myself looking up at Alan Millett in the way I'd looked at Nathan when Rose had taken me home to meet him. Alan Millett looked back at me. He had an open, honest face. It said, 'I am a family man, and I love my family but . . . hey, you know what?'

'You have interesting eyes,' he said. 'Has anyone ever told you so?'

Had my Pavlovian responses been blunted? Why did I not feel, This might be worth a punt? Why did I not instinctively arrange my features into invitation? I sat up straight. 'Yes. My husband.'

A woman at the other end of the pool stood up and peeled off her dressing-gown to reveal a bright red swimsuit. She stepped lightly, confidently down the pool steps and launched herself, with a muffled gasp, towards the centre.

Alan Millett tried again: 'Would you like a drink? I think there's pounded wheat-grass juice or something equally unspeakable.'

'You haven't taken to the culture.'

'Not in the slightest,' he said cheerfully.

'I'm with you, but please don't say anything. My friend has given me this as a present.'

'That's funny,' he said. 'I'd have thought you'd be all for it.'

I watched the swimmer for a moment, then asked, 'What's your birthday surprise?'

'A party with a marquee and all the works. They must have thought I was blind. Strange markings on the lawn. A stash of candles. And, most telling of all, my wife bought a pair of bathroom scales. That means she's trying to squeeze into a new dress.' He spoke affectionately.

'You'll enjoy it?'

'Sure. It's not every day you turn fifty. Why not

'celebrate?' He inclined slightly in my direction and raised an eyebrow. I knew that I had only to respond and opportunity would fall into my lap. Light, amusing and with no strings. 'I didn't catch your name,' he added.

'I didn't say, but it's Minty.'

'Unusual. And why are you here?'

'For all sorts of reasons.' I got to my feet and tied my dressing-gown cord tightly round my middle. 'Your family sounds very nice, and I hope your party's a success.'

I left him staring thoughtfully into the pool's blue depths.

As I dressed for dinner in the luxurious room, I found myself talking to Nathan. 'I was the target of a pick-up today.'

'And?'

'Not interested, Nathan. He was very nice, but it isn't the same.'

The answer to that was indistinct.

I was frightened that I was beginning not to remember Nathan with any precision. My memories of him were already blurring and changing shape. *Was that true? Was it really like that? Did he really say that to me?*

20

'Minty, you worried me last night.' Gisela was blunt. 'You looked terrible.'

Rule Five: apart from life or death situations, a friend's duty is to lie.

'It's the toxins,' I said. 'They won't be told.'

It was early on Sunday morning and we had escaped into the manicured manor grounds – ha-ha and borders, stone steps and an expanse of lawn – for fresh air before the day's work. It was going to be hot, but we had caught the moment when the air and plants were fresh. It felt good to be alive.

Gisela pressed the case: 'For obvious reasons, you're not at your best,' she lowered her voice sympathetically, 'but is anything in particular worrying you? You can tell me, you know.'

'It comes and goes,' I admitted. 'I panic.' Even to articulate the word caused the ever more efficient black feelings to take up residence in my chest. 'I panic that I can't carry what I've got to carry.'

Gisela, the adventurer and realist, understood perfectly. 'You've got enough money, I take it? The pay-out?' The insider who would be privy to the exact sum of the Vistemax severance package, courtesy of pillow talk, but could not admit it, she spoke with extreme delicacy.

'Let's put it this way, I need my job for the time being.'

She regarded me shrewdly. 'Sometimes we get what we want.'

'I didn't want Nathan *dead*.'

'I meant, you wanted a serious job. And at least you know what you have to do. There's a lot to be said for that.' She kidnapped my arm. 'No feeling sorry for yourself. Understand? It's the resort of the stupid. And don't think, Minty.'

Between not thinking and not feeling sorry for myself, there wouldn't be much space. But Gisela had a point: setting stern standards to curb internal wails was sensible and life-preserving.

She picked her way down the path, then ran alongside a herbaceous border and stopped by a plant blooming in a bright blue cloud. 'Marcus was right to say that enough was enough, but I wish he hadn't. Things were fine as they were.'

The bees were banqueting on this plant, and I bent down to thieve a sprig. Its smell was sharp and vaguely familiar and I tucked it into my pocket. 'Fine for you, perhaps, but Marcus clearly has another point of view.'

'That's what I mean about not thinking, Minty. It weakens one's position.'

It struck me then that Gisela and Roger made a perfect pair. Had he but known it Marcus, with his hopeless romantic notions about his *dame lointaine*, had lost out a long time ago. 'Marcus has had a rough deal.'

An unseen string jerked Gisela round to face me.

'What I can't make Marcus understand is that living with a person you love is not necessarily the best thing.'

I glanced back at the venerable, grey-stone manor, every window polished, every blade of grass trimmed. It was expensive, exclusive and out of reach for most. 'So that's it,' I said, tumbling to the whole picture at last. 'You don't want to lose all this. It's too risky. Poor Marcus.'

Lymphatic drainage consisted of someone passing their fingers over my face and neck with fluttering movements. It was not unpleasant. In fact, it was the opposite, and I felt myself slip into drowsiness.

The fingers fluttered and stroked . . . Birds wheeling south . . . The beating of a moth's wings at dusk . . . Little slaps of the sea on the shore.

I was trying not to think.

Little slaps of the sea . . . Like the sea at Priac Bay, which Rose had described so well that day – the day Nathan had died in her flat – and to which I had taken the boys.

It was a tiny bay, she had said. (She was right and the boys had loved it.) The coastal path ran along the cliff above it and there were always walkers tramping along. Correct. Thrift grew in clumps, sea grass and, at the right time of year, daisies. The sea can be many things, Rose said, but she loved it best when it was flat, you could peer down through its turquoise glimmer to hidden rocks and seaweed. From the coastguard's cottage you could look out over the rocks where, centuries ago, wreckers had plundered stricken vessels.

A path was cut into the cliff where the pack animals had waited as the looters scrambled up with their booty.

After a while, the fingers swept across my neck. 'You'll feel sleepy for the rest of the day,' the girl informed me. 'You must allow yourself to give into it.'

As I dressed, yesterday's headache stole back. I checked my watch. Eleven o'clock. The day stretched out in a beautifully solipsistic shape. It would be the last one like it for a long time.

I made my way out of the beauty suite – all pink swags and niches where potions were arranged in tiers to be worshipped – and my mobile rang. I answered it.

'Minty . . .' Eve sounded hoarse and frantic. 'I no well. I ill.'

I sat down on one of the chairs in the corridor – left, no doubt, to aid those weakened by the pursuit of beauty. 'What sort of ill, Eve?'

'I can't breathe.'

'Where are you?'

'In bed.'

'Where are the twins?'

'At Mrs Paige's.' I heard her choke, and the phone was tossed around. The choking sounded serious.

'Eve – Eve? Can you hear me?' A nasty silence. 'Listen, Eve, I'm coming home now.'

Gisela understood, and did not understand. 'I suppose you must go.' Her tone implied that she could not conceive why the au pair's illness could not be dealt with by someone else. 'It's only until tonight.'

'I know. I'm so sorry.' I was fully dressed, with my packed bag at my feet in Reception. There were two flower arrangements in pastel colours, a portrait of a girl on horseback in a tight green costume, and three receptionists with immaculate complexions. 'I can't thank you enough for your generosity, but I need to go back. If Eve is really ill, I must organize cover for work tomorrow.'

Gisela tensed impatiently. 'Oh, well.' She was cross because her present to me had been spoilt, and because she needed to talk to me further.

'Let me know about Marcus.'

She took a step back. 'Of course.'

I picked up my bag and heard myself say, 'You will think about Roger?' although why I should care about the man who sacked Nathan was a mystery.

She flung me a savage look. 'Don't worry about him. He gets exactly his side of the bargain.'

On the way back in the train, I stared out of the window at the speeding landscape and remembered the Nathan who, having left Rose, came to me alight with fervour. 'I've done it, Minty.' He kissed my arm all the way up its length. 'I've left Rose. And it's all going to be quite different.'

The discrepancy between his excited words and what we were alarmed me. This man had greying hair, a knee joint that ached and grown-up children: I fancied the Lexus, his credit card and the nice house.

But the curious thing was – the really, truly curious thing – I had believed Nathan.

*

Eve was curled into a foetal position in her bed. The window was closed so the room was stuffy and smelt of illness. There were a couple of glasses and a half-drunk mug of tea by the bed, with a packet of aspirin.

I saw immediately that the situation had progressed beyond aspirins. Within fifteen minutes, I had bundled Eve into the car and driven her to the nearest A&E unit.

Three unpleasant hours later, during which we had witnessed a drunken fight, a screaming girl put into handcuffs and a man covered with blood begging for help, a doctor announced, 'Pneumonia,' over the flushed, almost comatose Eve, with a veiled suggestion that it was my fault. He explained that Eve required a couple of days in hospital to stabilize her, then a period of careful nursing. Again, I caught a hint that it was up to me to make up for deficiencies in my duty of care.

I left the hospital, furious with him, with Eve, with myself, with everything.

Paige delivered the boys back to me. When I answered the door at number seven the twins, who hadn't been expecting me, let out a collective shriek and windmilled at high speed into my stomach. 'Careful, you two.'

'You smell funny,' said Lucas, sniffing my arm, which only that morning had been anointed by the hand-maidens at Claire Manor.

'Don't you like it? It has roses and thyme in it.'

'Dis-gus-ting.'

Paige brushed aside my profuse thanks and declined to come in. There was no mistaking the new coolness between us. 'How is everything?' I probed gingerly, but she wasn't having any of it.

'Before you ask, I can't help out tomorrow.'

'Oh.'

Paige shook her head. 'Can't be done. Linda has a day off, and I'm busy with the children. Sorry.' She softened. 'Why don't you try Kate Winsom or Mary Teight?'

She left with my thanks ringing in her ears. I hit the phone.

Kate Winsom's son was going to tea with another boy after school. 'I'm so sorry I can't help, particularly as . . .' She left me to conjecture the precise nature of her regret at my widowhood. Mary Teight had arranged to take her daughter to the doctor.

Millie's mother, Tessa, was contrite: 'Oh, Minty, I'm so sorry but Millie is staying with her father tomorrow. Why don't you ring an agency?'

'I would,' I pointed out, 'but today is Sunday.'

'Can't you take the day off?'

After Tessa my list of contacts ran out. I knew no one else – except Sue Frost, who didn't count because I didn't want unsolicited counselling on childcare. This state of affairs reinforced my sense of isolation.

While the twins ate chicken nuggets and chips, I paced up and down the kitchen, recalling Chris Sharp's hard, hazel gaze – which wouldn't soften if I rang up and said my childcare arrangements had crashed. From Barry's point of view that eventuality came under 'liability' and 'not on top of the job'.

Gisela rang to check that I'd made it back home and

to tell me about the marvellous facial I'd missed. 'They used mud imported from the Dead Sea. Have you sorted things out? What are you going to do?'

'I don't know,' I replied truthfully.

She tsk-tsked. 'It can't be that difficult, surely?'

There spoke the childless woman. 'Gisela, I'm sorry we didn't have time to talk things over further. Have you made your decision?'

'I don't know,' she said. 'I really don't know.'

'There's an awful lot of not knowing about,' I said.

The twins retreated to the floor and began to wrestle like puppies, my return having made them feel safe enough to lapse into boisterousness. Even so, now and then one or the other would bound up and touch base with my arm, knee or face.

I fought not to panic. I fought not to hate Nathan for leaving me in the lurch. I fought to reclaim the clear, hard sight of my former life that would urge me to ring up an agency first thing in the morning and employ *anyone* who was available.

The boys' noise level rose. 'Mum!' Lucas shrieked, and I found myself warding off a serious head-butt.

'You mustn't do that, Lucas, you might hurt someone.'

I wasn't sure I could dump them on a strange agency person.

'Mum,' said Lucas, 'Dad says . . .'

There was a sudden wrenching hush. I knelt down and drew my boys close. Their heads nestled into my shoulders, and their little bodies sank against mine. I murmured, 'Yes, Lukey. What did Dad say?'

A strange agency person might take against Lucas's head-butting or Felix's silences. An agency person might handle them roughly, or feed them eggs, which they hated. An agency person wouldn't understand that they ached for their father.

'Dad says . . .' echoed Felix, the eyelashes round his big eyes resembling wet feathers. I looked into their blue depths, which seemed to contain so much more knowledge than his years allowed. I turned to Lucas. 'What does Dad say?'

Lucas stared at me blankly. Then he shook his head. 'Dunno,' he muttered, and launched himself across me to hit Felix. There was a shriek as Felix was felled.

I allowed them to fight. Fighting gave them relief, the consolation of thumps, and I looked at the clock on the wall. Never had the numerals on it appeared so black and precisely etched. Sunday . . . Sunday . . . Time was running out.

My mind clicked into overdrive. One scenario in particular sounded a reveille to the black feelings.

'Sorry,' Barry would say, when I rang in to tell him I couldn't make the meeting on Monday. 'I'm not sure this arrangement is working.' I pictured him spreading his hands, the wristbands rippling. 'We need someone we can rely on, Minty. It doesn't look like you at the moment.'

The mark of a civilized man – the civilized woman not being included – is to be able to hold contrary propositions in the head at the same time. Nathan . . . was dead. His children lived.

An idea took shape. *Listen*, it insisted, as I dismissed it. I spread my hand and studied the fingers. *Think about it.*

The decibels ascended to a dangerous level and I set about prising the boys apart. Felix rolled over and bit my hand hard. I snatched it back. '*Don't* do that.' He stiffened and rolled away. I crouched beside him. 'Felix, you never, *never* bite people. Have you listened to Mummy? I'm trying to teach you something important.'

There are many ways in which to tackle survival. 'We will now discuss in a little more detail the struggle for existence,' Charles Darwin wrote in *The Origin of Species.*

Once, after we had been married for a little while, in the middle of making frantic love, Nathan halted. 'I have never desired anyone like I desire you, Minty,' he confessed, in a thrillingly passionate way. He did not say, 'I have never loved anyone like I love you,' as he had once before. I had noted the omission but concluded that desire would do fine.

It had and it hadn't. Desire was good and it got us through some bumpy times. The absence of mutual love was another matter – and I chose to ignore it.

Again, I picked up the phone and, with a tearful Felix clinging to my legs, dialled the innocent configuration of numbers. It was answered quickly.

'Is that Rose?'

'Minty.'

'I know I'm disturbing you . . .' The pause confirmed this diagnosis. 'I want to ask . . . I *have* to ask you a favour.' Rose wasn't going to help me and another long pause ensued. 'Please . . .' The word hurt, and I felt a flush creep up my cheeks.

'I'm not sure, Minty. What is it?'

'You have no reason to help me. Except for the boys. There's a problem.'

'Why me?'

'Because Nathan thought you should be involved. I'm doing what he . . . suggested.'

'The boys,' she cut in. 'Are they OK? Are they ill?'

Confession of my predicament punctured the angry boil. I found myself sobbing hysterically down the phone. 'I need someone to look after them tomorrow. I can't miss work, and Eve's ill in hospital. After tomorrow I can arrange cover.'

Sam delivered Rose to the doorstep of number seven at eight o'clock precisely. 'He was staying with me, and gave me a lift,' she said.

Sam hovered on the doorstep. 'Hello, Minty. I can't stop.'

'Congratulations again on the job,' I had the presence of mind to say.

He frowned. 'Bit of a poisoned chalice,' he said. 'I'm up here to sort out the final details.'

'Has Jilly decided to go with you?'

'I'm working on it.'

I remembered Poppy's request. 'Is there anything I can do?'

'Actually, no. We'll sort something out.' He smiled to take away the sting. 'Nice of you to offer.'

The ranks had been closed and I took the hint. I

didn't feel I could do or say any more – which constituted a tick for Failure and a cross for Endeavour. Sam said goodbye and I led Rose into the house.

She followed me into the kitchen, placed her handbag on the table. She was dressed in jeans, a skinny T-shirt and a black cardigan that made her arms appear even more slender than they were. 'I'm not sure what to say, Minty. I'm not sure why I'm here.' She had her back to me. 'But I think I'm doing this for Nathan.'

The boys were summoned from their bedroom, which they were in the process of dismantling. Lucas was wearing his green trousers, and Felix his blue socks. 'Boys. You remember Mrs Lloyd.'

'Rose.' She held out a hand. 'Hello, Lucas? Good, I guessed right this time. Hello, Felix.'

A burst of wind rattled the cat-flap. Clunk. It was, as always, an eerie sound. A shadow passed over Rose's face.

'That's the cat's door,' said Felix.

'Do you have a cat?' asked Rose.

'Mummy says no.'

The twins maintained their distance and confined themselves to scrutinizing her. They conveyed boredom, rejection and more than a little weariness. 'This is Sam and Poppy's mummy,' I explained. 'She's going to look after you today. You remember she knew Daddy.'

Felix hunched his shoulders. 'Why can't you look after us, Mummy?'

'Because I have to work. Otherwise the office will not be pleased with me.'

'He sounds *just* like Sam,' said Rose.

Again, the rattle of the cat-flap. It reminded me of the ordinariness of life, the inexorability of each day with its small routines. Rose had declared how wonderful and diverse she had discovered the world to be. For me it was different. The click-clack of the redundant cat-flap only anchored me to the shifting, echoing landscape of loss, calamity and grief through which I was journeying.

Rose busied herself with her bag. 'I imagine I was the last resort?'

'If I'm absolutely truthful, yes.'

That made her smile, and the atmosphere lightened. 'You must have hated ringing me.'

'Yes. And if you're truthful, you hated coming here.'

'Well, that's clear, then.' She produced a packet of coloured marker pens and two pads of paper from her bag. 'Felix and Lucas, shall we see who can draw the best cat? Then I'll take you to school.'

Felix had been busy working things out. 'You're Poppy's mummy? Like Mummy is our mummy?'

Rose nodded. 'Exactly the same.'

Lucas seized a pad and a green pen. Felix held back. 'These are my blue socks,' he informed Rose, and stuck out a leg. 'Daddy liked them.'

Rose looked steadily at the sock, and the small foot inside it, and tears spilt down her cheeks.

I turned away.

Before I left the house, I glanced into the kitchen. Rose was leaning against the table, one leg swinging, and the twins were drawing. Rose was saying, 'Did you know that your daddy loved swimming? Once he swam so far out to sea that we had to go and get the boat to rescue him.'

In a manner of speaking, I was gazing into the heart of my darkness, however brightly lit it was.

'Goodbye, boys,' I hitched my bag on to my shoulders. 'Be good.'

They barely glanced up. ''Bye, Mummy.'

At six o'clock on the dot I let myself noiselessly into the house. Rose was ensconced with a boy at each side on the sofa in the sitting room. She had her arms round them. 'Then your daddy got hold of the fishing-line and pulled. He pulled and pulled . . .'

So intent were all three that they did not hear me come in. Rose lifted a hand and absently stroked Felix's hair. He snuggled further into her.

'Do you know what was on that fishing-line?'

'The biggest fish.' Lucas held up his hands. 'As big as this?'

'No.'

'A dead man?' Felix's eyes widened in alarm.

'No.'

'A whale?'

'I'll tell you,' said Rose. 'It was a suitcase with "R. Pearson" painted on it. Inside it there were tins and tins of peas.'

I scuffed a foot on the carpet and Rose turned. Our eyes locked and her arms tightened round the twins. 'Look who's here!'

'Yes,' I said. 'It's your mummy.'

*

Rose stood in the hall with her bag over her shoulder. 'Goodbye, boys. See you soon.' She handed over the front-door key. 'They were no trouble.'

One thing was absolutely settled with regard to the situation between Rose and me. I was in the wrong, the black-hearted villain of the piece, and Rose was the person to whom wrong had been done, which left me – if one accepted the determinist argument – free to continue to err. 'Nathan loved you,' I said. 'He always did.'

Suddenly Rose laughed. 'Oh, my God, the tables *have* turned.' She choked a little. 'Don't you see how funny it is?' She held out a hand, a wooing gesture. 'Don't you?'

I could not bring myself to take her hand. 'I'll work on it.'

Rose sobered up, and her face now registered sadness and regret. 'I think Nathan did love me, despite everything.'

'But you,' I pushed it further, 'did you . . .'

Rose moved towards the door. 'I've done you a favour today, Minty. Let's leave it at that.' She placed a hand on the catch. 'For the record Nathan, having done it once, would never have left the twins. And he would never have regretted having them. Ever.'

'That wasn't my question.'

'But it's my answer,' she said gently. She tugged at the door latch.

'Here, let me,' I pulled the handle. 'The lock's tricky.'

'Oh, I know *that*,' said Rose. 'It always was.'

21

Before twenty-four hours had elapsed Poppy was on the phone. 'Minty, I don't think it's a good idea to use my mother as a fall-back nanny.'

As it happened, I agreed with her. 'Did Rose put it that way?'

'Not exactly, but she told me you rang up at the last minute and begged her to step in.' She added, 'I object.'

'I had to find someone to look after the boys.'

'You're their mother. Don't you understand how it would have *upset* her?'

I reminded myself that Poppy had no children so she didn't have the faintest idea. Poppy had not lain naked and trussed and given birth amid what resembled a cocktail party. She did not lie awake at night entertaining that special brand of parental imagining: *Lucas might run out into the road when a lorry just happens to be coming down it at full speed*. She didn't understand that adaptation was survival. Furthermore, Poppy had no idea how a pair of fair, tousled heads had a way of sneaking past every defence. 'Your mother could have said no.'

An impatient noise sped down the line. 'Don't you know by now that Mum puts up with everything?'

'I'm not sure I agree, Poppy.'

'She has some crazy idea that Dad would want her

to look out for them. I've told her she shouldn't stand for it. Richard says you should make your own arrangements.'

Despite my best intentions, I was stung by the last. Our occasional rueful exchanges had seemed to indicate that Richard and I understood each other. 'Did he really?'

'Um. Well, we both agree.'

It was a fair bet that Richard had said nothing of the sort. 'Poppy,' I said, 'I'm doing the best I can, but things are difficult at the moment, and the boys are more important than anything else.'

'And?'

'I was afraid I might lose my job if I didn't turn up.' Even to say the words caused sweat to break out on my top lip.

'Can't you negotiate? There's legislation for this kind of contingency.' Pause. 'I wouldn't stand for it, Minty.'

'I expect you would if you had to.' My knees were shaky now. 'There's theory and then there's practice.'

'Oh, for goodness' sake.'

I glanced round the kitchen. Without Eve, it was showing signs of neglect. There was dust on the windowsill, spilt coffee grounds by the rubbish bin and a couple of dirty saucepans waiting for attention beside the sink.

'By the way, two things, Poppy. I don't think it would do any good if I intervened in the Jilly-Sam situation. I got a polite brush-off from Sam.'

'I bet you didn't try hard enough.'

'Actually I did. I put feelers out, and it was clear that I wouldn't get anywhere. I'm afraid the ball's back in your court. You'll have to deal.'

'Hmm. You sound like Sam. All bossy and older sibling. And the second thing?'

'I've spoken to Theo. I'm afraid the money won't be forthcoming just yet. He couldn't say when it would be.'

'Oh, my God,' Poppy said. A note of desperation had crept into her voice. 'Are you absolutely sure?'

I didn't have time, or the inclination, to take on Poppy's woes. This was the girl who had dressed up in black for my wedding, called her father – and, by extension, me – an old goat and deliberately mucked up family Christmases. She and I didn't have a relationship where if one was in trouble the other said, 'Hang on, I'm coming at once.'

Against all reason, I said, 'Poppy. I suspect you've got yourself into trouble over the poker. Am I right?'

There was a choking sob. 'I can't tell *you*.'

'Actually, you can.'

It took a little more urging and probing but eventually Poppy confessed: 'Poker got a grip on me. I don't how – it's a mystery how quickly I became wrapped up in it. I lie awake at night, and ask myself, "How?" Then I borrowed money because I didn't win, and I can't afford to pay it back. I couldn't pay off my credit card, so I borrowed it from one of those firms that promise the world and forget to tell you that the interest is unbelievable. A career in candles isn't big beans – well, it's a career in candles. Need I say more? I can't tell Richard, who would be horrified, I can't tell Mum, and the bailiffs will come and I'll get credit blacklisted if I don't do something soon –'

At this point, I interrupted: 'Poppy, listen to me. Have you stopped playing? That's the first step.'

'Of course I have.' Poppy was a hopeless liar.

'I don't believe you.'

The situation was still too delicate for the direct approach and I had been clumsy: she turned savage. 'It's none of your business. I can deal with it. If you can just arrange for the money, it'll be sorted.'

A lifetime of self-help manuals came to my rescue. 'Why don't you go and talk to someone?' I lowered my voice. 'Poppy, I can find out who.'

There was more choking. 'I miss Dad. It's like having a hole in the head. *Why* did he have to die?' Silence, and then her bleak, disembodied voice at the other end of the line: 'I wish I was dead.'

I glanced at the clock. I had one hour precisely in hand, but I could put it to better use than pressing the jacket that was next on the list. 'Hang on, Poppy.' I felt the thrill of stepping into untrodden territory. 'I can come over.'

'No,' she said. 'Don't.'

Eve was lying in the furthest bed from the entrance to the ward, which, I imagined, gave her a modicum of peace. The traffic in and out was staggering – trolleys, visitors, doctors in white coats.

She was propped up on pillows and her colour matched the linen. 'Hallo, Minty.'

'Eve, are you feeling better?' I placed a basket of fruit on her bedside table and drew up a chair. She was too exhausted to talk much so I held her hand and stroked her fingers. The gesture seemed to please her for she smiled faintly and closed her eyes. After a while, I went in search of information.

The staff nurse was ensconced at the nurses' station. She was neat, careworn and so small she barely crowned the pile of paper in front of her. 'Who?' she asked. It took her a couple of minutes to sift through the notes and get a fix on Eve. Then she informed me that Eve could leave hospital the following day, but required dedicated nursing and would not be properly on her feet for at least six weeks. She outlined a programme of light meals, bedbaths and pill-taking. A chill trickled down my spine.

I tackled the live-in agency stand-in, who had arrived for the week, and gave a run-down of Eve's nursing care. The girl – Australian, blonde, smiling – shook her head and said politely, 'I'm afraid the agency rules say I can't do anything except look after the kids.'

The telephone odyssey began again. 'If you could pop in once,' I pleaded with Tessa/Kate/Paige, 'just to check up on Eve and make sure she's taken her pills and eaten something.'

Tessa said, 'If she's really ill, you'd better get in an agency nurse.'

'I already have an agency nanny, and she's costing the earth.'

Kate was more sympathetic and less helpful: 'You'd

305

better stay at home, Minty. How would you feel if something happened to Eve?'

Paige said, 'I'm not talking to you, Minty. Not only do you lecture me, but I've discovered you're on Martin's side.'

'How?'

'He let slip he recruited you over a coffee.'

'That was ages ago. Anyway, what should I have done? Ignored him?' There was a silence and I added desperately, 'Eve does need checking over, and the agency girl can't or won't.'

'OK.' Paige wasn't enthusiastic. 'I'll send Linda over. She can give Eve a meal.'

That was the best I could wrest from the situation. It was bad but not terminal, and I set about drawing up a list for Linda.

To begin with, Eve was very weak. Then she got better and stronger, but it was not straightforward. Some days she could get up for an hour or so. On others the lightest tasks were beyond her. Ignoring my dwindling cash reserves, I hired the agency nanny for another two weeks.

Paige was of the opinion that I should sack Eve. 'You've got to survive,' she argued. 'You can't afford a weak link. It's either you or her.'

Centuries' worth of social and ethical thinking that had crept snail-like towards compassion for, and nurture of, the weak flicked through my brain. 'As a matter of interest, is that what you feel Martin is? A weak link?'

Paige gave the impression that she was talking to a recalcitrant child. 'I haven't time to nurture a liability. You haven't time for a non-functional child-carer.'

Eve might have been ill, but she was no fool. She could scent what was blowing in the wind. 'Please don't lose me the job,' she begged, in genuine terror that I might cast her out into the streets. For ten seconds or so, the idea of buying her a one-way ticket to Romania jumped to the top of the list. I took her sickly face between my hands. 'Don't be silly, Eve. The boys need you and they're very fond of you. I need you, too, for them, so will you please concentrate on getting better?'

As I climbed the stairs to her room in the evenings, bearing a meal tray, I wondered what Nathan would make of me now.

At Paradox, I had taken to draping a jacket (which I changed every two days) over the back of my chair and leaving it there. This was to encourage anyone glancing into my office in the early morning or late evening to conclude that I was already/still at work. I typed out a list of so-called 'lunch' meetings in twenty-point, bold Garamond and stuck it on to the side of my computer screen. In fact, I was sacrificing a proportion of the family's weekly budget on taxis so that I could to race back to Lakey Street to feed Eve. It was a killing schedule, but I had a discovered a quirk in my psyche: I didn't mind putting myself out.

Barry and Chris had developed an unhealthy symbiosis. 'Chris thinks my thoughts and walks my walks,' Barry announced, during an ideas meeting that Chris had dominated.

Deb went pale and stared hard at the coffee machine. 'I'm looking for a new job,' she had told me earlier, without enthusiasm.

Chris had not looked at Deb. He gathered up his papers and waggled his fingers. 'See you later, guys.'

Barry followed him, leaving Deb and me at the conference table. She cocked an eyebrow. 'I feel I've fallen behind, Minty. And I can't put my finger on how it happened.'

At the weekend, I took the boys to Gisela's for tea. Since I had been there last, she had redecorated the drawing room in pale gold and cream, with Venetian mirrors and authentic tapestry cushions.

'Felix, no,' she said sharply, when Felix picked up one of the cushions. 'It's very old and valuable.' Her attention veered to Lucas, who had discovered that the Aubusson rug concealed an exciting stretch of parquet – perfect for sliding.

I called the twins to heel but they were restless, uneasy and disinclined to obey. This had been a pattern for the last few days and I was fighting to get to grips with it. Lucas happened to be standing close to Gisela when he sneezed fulsomely. I hastened to pass him a tissue, which, after he had used it, he offered to Gisela with his sweetest smile. Gisela recoiled. 'Why don't I ring for Angela, and she can give them tea in the kitchen?'

Roger put in a brief appearance on his way to a golfclub gathering. He advanced into the room in a hearty manner and kissed my cheek. 'So *good* to see you,' he murmured, one eye on his wife. 'I hope everything's under control.' He looked healthy and wealthy, but not particularly rested or happy.

I was tempted to punish him with a catalogue of what was not going well, but spared him. More than once over the past few weeks, as I reflected on what had happened to Nathan, I reassured myself that Roger, for all his power and success, was as likely to be done-to as often as he did-by. Soon or later, Roger's career would end.

After he had left, and Angela had brought in tea and chocolate cake and taken the boys away, Gisela asked after Paradox and the job. I put down my cup. 'I have a fight on my hands,' I told her, 'and I'm going to need every ounce of guile I possess.'

Gisela cut a minute slice of chocolate cake and arranged it on her plate. 'I appreciate how difficult it must be for you, Minty. I admire how you're handling everything.'

It was nice of her to mention it, but I wondered if she meant it. 'Have you heard from Marcus?'

At his name, she leapt to her feet. 'No, I haven't.'

I waited for more information, but Gisela had retreated into painful reflection. The scene on the tapestry cushion at my right elbow depicted hunters in the forest and a wounded white stag. The forest had been woven with a dreamy, mysterious quality, and its floor was carpeted with little animals and flowers. 'Are you angry, Gisela?'

'I am and I'm not.' Gisela took up a position by the long window and fingered the curtain tie-back. 'OK. I'll say this. In the end, I felt I had no choice. I'm married to Roger, and I can't break a vow as easily as Marcus suggests.'

This shone a new, fascinating light on the situation. 'Gisela, since when have you minded about marriage *vows*?'

She tossed her head. 'You've read me wrong, Minty. I always observed the contract. I did exactly what was expected and what I undertook to do. Marriage is a business, not some mystical revelation.' She fiddled some more with the tie-back. 'In the end, it wasn't a choice. That's what upset me . . . a little. I did not have it in me to consider the alternative, with Marcus, to what I have now, with Roger. I couldn't see it.'

'Ah.'

'Does that make me dead?'

I hazarded a shrewd guess. 'Is that what Marcus said?'

Gisela smiled bleakly. 'Something along those lines. But it's done.' She returned to her seat, and I watched her slip back into the hostess's skin, straightening her skirt and lifting the teapot. 'More?'

Gisela's pact with the devil had evidently not made her *that* happy. 'Are you sure?'

She put down the teapot. 'You know what they say about addicts? If you take away the addiction and the fuss around it, there's nothing left to fill the day.'

'Charity work?'

It was as bad a joke as Nathan would have made.

Gisela managed a wintry smile. 'Then I would be truly dead.' She pointed to the cushion. 'French. Eighteenth century. Note the superb vegetable dyes.'

'Noted.' I had half an ear listening for the twins and whether they were creating mayhem with Angela.

Gisela traced the outline of the wounded stag on the cushion with a finger on which gleamed an important diamond ring. 'I had become used to a set-up where everything on the surface appeared straightforward but wasn't, and only I knew about it. There was an edge to my life, like the hem on a garment. I could say to myself, "I'm married to Nicholas, or Richmond, or Roger, but I have the option to pack my bags."' She laughed. 'The trouble is, since I've told Marcus to go, I spend all my time thinking about him in a way I never did when he was on the scene.'

'Oh dear,' I said. 'That's bad. You've got guilt plus the grass-is-greener syndrome rolled into one.'

Gisela was startled. 'What do you mean?'

'It's a stubborn, pesky illness that won't go away.'

'How do you know?'

'I'm intimately acquainted with it,' I said.

In the car, Felix piped up, 'If we don't have a daddy, does that mean we're not a family?'

'No, Felix. You can be a family without a daddy.'

'And you really are a mummy.'

I stared at the snarled traffic. 'I really am a mummy.'

When we got back, Eve was in the kitchen. She looked a lot stronger, even if her clothes hung off her. 'I make supper,' she said, and when I tried to stop her she held up her hand. 'I do.'

I helped her to cut up cucumber and carrot sticks, and to heat up the shepherd's pie. She moved painfully slowly, but with determination. Afterwards she insisted on clearing up. She raised her normally indifferent eyes to mine and, in them, sparked gratitude. 'You are nice, Minty.'

During the bad nights, I had been getting rid of Nathan. It should have been a logical process – Nathan was no longer there to wear his shirts, socks, suits, shoes, ties, and they were easy to sort and pack. But their disposal defied logic. Sometimes I managed to clear a drawer; sometimes it was beyond me. It was a process that had to be secret because I didn't wish the boys to witness it and because . . . it hurt. So I accomplished it in fits and starts, stealthily, during those nights.

It was a quarter to two when I got out of bed and opened the doors to Nathan's wardrobe. Already light dust coated the contents. There were his ties, blue, red and green. A scarf was jammed on to the shelf and I picked it up. It was an expensive one, and I caught the faintest echo of his aftershave. The sensation of a sharp instrument striking through my breast made me gasp. I sank down on the bed, holding it between fingers from which the feeling had drained.

Nathan was dead.

After a while, I put it aside, took out his favourite

grey suit and laid it on the bed. Into the jacket I tucked his favourite blue office shirt. Round the collar went the tie, red silk. A pair of silk socks and polished shoes completed the ensemble.

There. This was the shell of Nathan. I could pretend he was there, leaning against the pillows, hands folded behind his head. *Minty, will you please pay attention . . .* Pillow punched. Shoes eased off and discarded. *Minty, what do you think?*

The bag for the hospice charity shop was on the floor. If I removed the tie from the shell and placed it in the bag, part of Nathan had gone. If I took out the shirt, as I now did, and folded it carefully, another bit of him had vanished. The shoes . . . the shoes? If I dropped them into the bag, it would be impossible for Nathan ever again to walk into number seven and run up the stairs – *where are my boys?*

And with the suit went the businessman who formulated strategies and said, *Our competitors are really strong. Let's give them a hard time.*

'When I married Nathan,' Rose had confided to me, at one of our lunches in the early days, 'I was broken-hearted from a love affair that had gone wrong. But Nathan was so anxious to make me happy, how could I resist? He was a rock, and Hal was unreliable sand. What more could I ask?'

I was not so convinced by Rose's capacity to sort out the rocks from the sand. This was a woman who, she also confided to me, used to slip into St Benedicta's church *en route* for home and light a candle under the

Madonna. If that was not building a house on sand, I didn't know what was.

'Hal could never be what I wanted,' Rose had added. 'We both knew it. But Nathan was.'

Downstairs, one of the twins cried out. I swept the suit into the bag and went to find out which one.

Felix had had a bad dream. 'Mummy, there was a big, big cat with big claws and he was trying to claw me . . .'

I drew his hot little body close and whispered, 'It's all right, Felix. Mummy's here. I've chased the bad cat away. Look, it's gone.'

It was not all right. Yet as I soothed my son with this lie I took a curious pleasure and pride in its construction. Until the boys were big and bold enough to know better, it was my business to shield them from the worst.

22

When I turned out the pocket of my black linen trousers, I discovered the sprig of the plant I'd picked at Claire Manor. It was brittle and withered, with only faint traces of the blue that had attracted me. Intrigued, I looked it up in one of Nathan's books. It was called *nepeta*, and its old nickname was 'Kattesminte'. It was so powerfully attractive to cats that infant seedlings had to be protected against them.

The phone rang as I was reading about catmint.

> If you set it, the cats will get it
> If you sow it, the cats won't know it.

'I know I'm not talking to you,' said Paige.

'OK,' I said. 'I'm not asking you how the baby is.'

'He's a bit of a screamer.' Her voice wavered. 'I've never been so exhausted.' For Paige to admit anything of the sort was serious. 'Three children, and I have to make them into human beings without turning myself into a monster.' Her voice veered up the scale. 'It's so tough that I sometimes wonder.'

It was almost unheard-of for Paige to have doubts. 'Paige, have you been in touch with Martin?'

'Tell you what, ask me about Lara's arabesques instead.'

'Paige. Have you been in touch with Martin?'

'Minty. Don't interfere. OK?'

I raised my eyes to the ceiling. 'How are Lara's arabesques?'

'Funnily enough, very good. She has an excellent line, but she's let down a bit by her feet. Pats of butter, unfortunately. But we'll get to work on them.'

I felt sorry for the ramshackle, terrorized Lara. From now on, her feet would not be her own. At the other end of the phone Paige sighed heavily, a sound pregnant with despair and uncertainty, and I weighed in. 'You've got to think again about Martin.'

'I *think* about him, Minty, all the time, and I'm very fond of him. Very. But I haven't time to be married. Not with three children. Not if I'm to do things properly.'

'Paige, have you eaten today?'

'Eaten? Not much. I'm far too busy. And before you ask, no, I'm not sleeping well. I know you think I've gone mad with post-natal depression and maybe I have, but at the best of times, Martin's a reluctant father. He doesn't enjoy it. He hates the house being full of children. Now, who's the one with a psychosis?'

'All the same he needs to be there.'

There was an ominous silence. 'Minty, I'm not sure about lectures from you.'

'Where is he living?'

'At his mother's. She's put him in the attic bedroom for the time being.'

*

316

I rang Martin and arranged to meet him the following afternoon at the bank. 'Minty, is this urgent? I have a big convention in Geneva and I'm travelling for the next couple of weeks. But if you really need to see me I can fit you in at two thirty.'

To his credit, Martin was on time, which didn't give me much opportunity to study the building's stunning glass atrium. He stepped out of a lift, kissed my cheek and steered me down the corridor. 'This had better be good.'

'You asked me to keep an eye on Paige.'

'Ah, my wife.' For all the lightness of tone, Martin was on the alert. He led me into the canteen, which was more like a banqueting hall, did the equivalent of clicking his fingers and, lo and behold, we were presented with freshly made espresso, hot milk and a *cantucci* biscuit each. Living with his mother was doing him no harm physically for, unlike his wife, he was immaculate, slim, and healthy-complexioned.

I could never resist *cantucci*. I dipped mine into the espresso and bit into it with the special pleasure reserved for the forbidden. 'Martin, you must go home.'

He frowned. '*She* threw me out. Remember?'

'*She*'s just had a baby. We've agreed you're half mad when you've had a baby. You stay half mad, I reckon, until they're adults. Paige is half mad anyway.' Martin snorted. 'She won't listen to me because I'm a sinner. Or, at least, she won't take my advice.' I stared longingly at Martin's *cantucci* and, obediently, he handed it over.

'The children, Martin. They'll be suffering from all this. They may not show it but they will.' I included my own in the generalization, which made the declaration even more impassioned. And if Felix and Lucas hurt, I hurt. 'Do you really hate them?'

'Is that what Paige says?' Martin frowned. 'I knew before they arrived it would be tricky, but even I was surprised by how impossible it became. I warned Paige that she was obsessed. But . . .' He gave me a steady look – the I-am-a-rock one in which Nathan had specialized. '. . . I would never have left of my own accord.'

I countered, 'Paige has had a baby. She's weak, her hormones are all over the place, and she's not thinking straight.'

To my acute distress, Martin's eyes filled. 'Ignore me,' he muttered. 'But could you stop right there?'

I made a rapid reconnaissance of the room. No one had noticed Martin's tears – had a beady-eyed rival taken it on board, it would have done him no good. A group of bankers in pinstriped suits plodded in. They were all as plump as pullets and spoke to each other in low, earnest tones. I jabbed a finger in their direction. 'Doesn't look that much fun working here.'

'It isn't.' He shaded his eyes with a hand. 'Nothing's much fun, these days.'

'You could put things right.'

Martin pulled himself together. 'As a matter of interest, Minty, why are you taking this view?' He meant, why should you, the wrecker, argue so strongly for the opposite?

I might have taken offence but I'd grown used to my label. 'I have two small boys,' I said.

He directed a countenance so full of woe at me that I was forced to look down at my coffee cup. 'Just walk back in, Martin. Tell Paige she's wrong and that you won't have a broken family. Tell her it's for the children's sake.'

'I didn't agree to be hauled out of an important briefing meeting so that you could tell me what's blindingly obvious.'

'Nevertheless.'

To my surprise he reached over and took my hands. 'It was well done, Minty.'

I let them rest in his. I knew perfectly well that whatever I said or advised would have little influence on him, but I had said and would continue to say it. 'On second thoughts, Martin, tell Paige it's for her sake too. *Do it.*'

I left him by the state-of-the-art elevators, which would whisk him back up to the nineteenth floor, and headed out of the door.

A postcard arrived in the post. 'Dear Minty. I enjoyed seeing the boys and I wondered . . .' there was a space between 'wondered' and 'if I could see them again? I would love to take them to the zoo or to the cinema perhaps. Rose.'

The card did not exude confidence. The writing was

hesitant and the wording suggested that Rose had written it against her better judgement. But in her sending and my receiving, an element shifted in the balance between us.

A week elapsed before I responded.

At Paradox, I chipped away at the final details for *Pointe of Departure* and toyed with the notion of developing a history of choreography but discarded it. Deb announced that she was off to work for Papillon and when I told her how sorry I was, she replied, 'Oh, I don't have time to hang around any more,' in a nonchalant manner that imperfectly hid her unhappiness. The mention of time got me thinking about the abandoned middle-age project, and I retrieved it from my 'reject' file.

I threw myself at administration. I wrote letters to the bank. I had several long conversations with Theo. I researched addiction counsellors. I paid bills. I rearranged the furniture in the sitting room and my bedroom, so that the house took on a different aspect. Nathan's study had been transformed into a cosy, feminine space. My papers were on the noticeboard: school rotas, work schedules . . . those lists.

My clothes occupied the total space available in the wardrobes and drawers and on the pegs. My bottles occupied the shelf in the bathroom. Upstairs in the attic a cardboard box contained Nathan's razor, a shaving brush made from badger hair, a hairbrush and a new comb still in its plastic wrapping. There they would wait until I gave them to Felix and Lucas.

I lay awake and counted the ghosts. I had been wrong. There *is* some kind of justice, for no one ever escapes anyone else. Nathan had never got away from Rose. Rose had never got away from Hal. Rose and I had never got away from each other.

After Rose had been sacked as books editor and I had taken over, I plotted how I would spice up the pages and transform them. *My* books pages would fizz with new ideas. Yet when Timon sacked me, he damned my efforts: 'Your pages were nothing new,' he wrote.

Rose told me that she had suffered torment and anguish over Hal, her first lover. But also moments of such sweetness and ecstasy that she carried them with her for always. I do not possess memories such as those. But Rose's were like fragrant sachets tucked into a drawer. I envied her.

My reply to Rose took me a long time to write, and the words were bottlenecked at the end of my pen. 'Would you like to come to sports day at the boys' school?'

It was agreed. Rose would come early to watch the opening events with Eve, and I would join them for those in which Felix and Lucas were competing – the sack race, egg-and-spoon, sprint, high jump. There was a dire form of advanced torture called the Parents' Race, which, Lucas informed me, I was expected to win.

Sports day minus twelve hours. Felix and Lucas dragged me into the garden after their supper. They wanted to practise running and the three-legged race. I protested that they would get indigestion but Felix pulled at my arm and said, 'Please.'

I found myself standing patiently – an adverb that had many nuances – with my watch in my hand as the boys pelted up and down the lawn until Lucas turned pale and said he felt sick.

Sports day minus five hours. The starlings were roosting outside the bedroom door again. It was five to six in the morning. Lucas snuck into the room, climbed on to the bed and nuzzled me. 'Mummy, you must come.'

'Why?' I squinted at him. He was in his dressing-gown.

'Come and see,' he persisted.

Somehow I got out of bed and stumbled into the boys' room. There, neatly laid out on his bed, was Felix's sports kit. T-shirt, navy blue shorts, white plimsolls and white socks. 'Have I got it right, Mummy?' he asked.

'Look at me,' Lucas said, and tore off his dressing-gown. He was wearing his – but the T-shirt was back to front. He mimed a couple of air punches and dropped to one knee. 'Ready, steady – go.'

'Come here, Lukey. You've got your T-shirt on wrong.'

Felix scrabbled under the bed and, with an air of triumph, produced my trainers, which he must have taken from my wardrobe, and laid them at my feet. 'That's for your race, Mummy.'

'Right.' I wrestled with Lucas and the T-shirt.

Felix was cataloguing his kit. 'There are my shorts. These are my shoes . . .'

'Very good, boys,' I said. 'Brilliant. Couldn't be better.' I sat down on Lucas's bed. 'Do you know how early it is?'

Felix had finished his inventory and was hopping about with his pyjama bottoms round his ankles. 'You will come, Mummy, won't you?'

I rubbed my eyes. *'Of course,'* I said.

At Paradox, I worked solidly through the morning and got ready to leave on time, armed with the file entitled *Statistical Analysis of Depression in Females, 40–65.* Then Syriol called, 'Visitor for you, Minty.'

A wan, appreciably thinner Poppy sat on one of the seats leafing through *Television Weekly.* At my approach, she threw aside the magazine and leapt to her feet. 'Hi. I'm sorry to do this to you, but have you any news from Theo?'

'No. It's taking a heck of time, but there's nothing I can do.'

'Oh, God, Minty.' She had tied her hair back savagely. It didn't suit her.

'Here,' I said. 'Sit down.'

'I keep thinking Dad would have so hated me for this. He was always so careful and taught me to be careful, and it's haunting me. I can't get this picture out of my head that he's thinking I've let him down.' She wrapped her skirt round her fingers, bandage-style. 'I hate to think he'd be disappointed in me.'

'You've got to talk to Richard, Poppy.'

She shook her head. 'I have to deal with it myself. It

was a mistake, and just because I'm married to Richard it doesn't mean he has to know *everything* about me.' She fingered her handbag strap. 'My poker debt is a private matter.'

'What about your mother? She'd understand.'

'You don't know Mum,' Poppy said miserably. 'She's not forgiving on some things. What I need is the money Dad left me. Then I can pay off my debt and I won't bother you again.'

'Theo's still wrestling with the Inland Revenue. There were a couple of problems that no one could iron out to do with the money your father inherited from your grandmother.' I was curious. 'Why did you do it, Poppy?'

She shrugged. 'It was exciting. I thought I could beat the system. All the usual excuses.' She observed a point on the wall. 'So boring and predictable.'

She was so agitated that I got up, went to the water-cooler and ran a mugful. I pressed it into her hands. 'You know, it's all perfectly manageable.'

Barry walked down the corridor and raised an eyebrow. I made a nondescript gesture, and he disappeared. I glanced at my watch. Time was leapfrogging and Lucas was due to run in the egg-and-spoon.

Poppy noticed the gesture. 'I'm sorry to bother you, Minty. I know you're busy.' The concession was so unexpected that I sat down beside her with a thump. 'I don't understand, Minty, why I was caught. Then I think I *wanted* to be caught by it . . . Oh, what the hell? What the hell?'

There was not much slack in my finances, but

sufficient to take a temporary knock. I reached into my handbag for my cheque book. 'Look, why don't I lend you some for the moment? It'll stave off the problem, and then you and I will go to see Theo. He's bound to confidentiality.'

Poppy raised her head. 'Would you do that?'

Her astonishment was almost offensive but, funnily enough, I understood. 'Yes.'

'OK. Thanks.' Tears streamed down Poppy's cheeks. 'I'm a mess . . . Minty. That's what I am. And what do I do about it?'

Egg-and-spoon race. Next up the sack race. Felix was in that one. I hauled my notebook out of my bag. 'Actually, Poppy, I've done some research on counselling.'

'Counselling!' She was dismissive.

I stared at her. 'Are you serious or not?'

Poppy didn't answer. I grabbed her wrist, hauled her out of Paradox, hailed the first taxi and told him to drive to an address in South Kensington. 'I'm taking you to a counsellor who's highly recommended. When we get there, Poppy, you're going to make an appointment and I'm going to watch you do it.'

By the time I arrived at the common, the races had been run, the rosettes pinned on to chests and the picnics were in full swing.

There was the usual mêlée of parents, mostly mothers, with one or two progressive, unemployed or browbeaten fathers. An area of the common had been roped off. It contained a table on which flapped a white cloth held down by several silver cups. Their status came under the heading 'reprieved': the cups were the relic of an earlier era and there had been much solemn debate among the staff as to whether competitive races should be allowed.

It was hot and sunny, and children in blue shorts and T-shirts ran about like ants on speed. It took me two seconds to locate Rose in the crowd. She was sitting on a tartan rug with Felix, an open cool bag between them, and her full pink skirt was the colour of a flower. Eve was with another group, chatting to a friend. A similar tableau was repeated *ad infinitum*: tartan rugs, open cool bags from which crisps, cold pizza, fruit juice, and wine – to save the adults' sanity – flowed.

Rose waved a cocktail sausage in the air, and said something to Felix, who laughed so hard that he fell back on the rug and kicked his legs in the air. He always threw himself backwards when I made a joke but I hadn't seen him laugh like that for a long time.

'Hello.' I collapsed on to the rug beside them.

Rose was cool. 'Hello, Minty. Lucas is over there.' She pointed to a knot clustered round the PE teacher. 'He did well.'

Felix thrust a sausage at me. 'Careful.' I bent to kiss him. He was hot and sweaty, and smelt of wine gums and orange juice, which was not particularly enticing but dearer to me than anything else I could think of. 'How did you do?' I whispered.

He pressed his mouth to my ear, and the roar of his

breath assaulted my eardrum. 'I came tenth, Mummy.'

Rose gazed into the middle distance. A couple of teams were conducting an impromptu tug-of-war. 'The boys kept asking where you were. Whatever it was, I hope it was worth it.'

'I do too,' I echoed fervently.

'Really, really worth it,' she repeated. 'Lucas was . . . a little tearful. He won the egg-and-spoon.'

I knew what Rose was thinking. Hell bent on pursuing my career, I was prepared to sacrifice my sons' happiness and welfare. 'Oh, come on, Rose, you know as well as I do what happens in the office. You told me that whenever Sam and Poppy had a carol service or sports day or whatever, there was a last-minute panic or hold-up at Vistemax, which made you late.'

Rose had always been fair. 'True.'

I squinted to where Lucas was at the centre of the PE-teacher huddle. 'What's going on?'

'A disputed second and third in the twenty-metre race.' The implication was that I should know what was going on. 'He was so hoping you'd turn up in time to see him run. They both were.' She paused and said quietly, 'But you were carrying on in your own sweet way, Minty.'

'Sometimes you sound like Nathan,' I remarked.

At that, she flinched and reflected for a moment. 'But Nathan would have asked what could be more important than supporting your sons at sports day.' She shaded her eyes, watching Lucas. 'At least, that was the sort of thing he said to me.'

'Rose, I didn't want to be late.'

Felix tilted back his head. 'Are you talking about my daddy?' He blinked his blue eyes. 'Did Daddy run in races?'

'I'm pretty sure he did, Felix.' There was a proprietorial note in Rose's voice – to which I objected. Lucas came running over, the windmill in full sail. He was grubby and happy. He brushed past without seeing me, and flung himself against Rose. 'I was very fast.'

'Yes, you were. Felix and I are hoarse from shouting.' She placed a finger on the rosette pinned to his shirt.

'Lukey,' I said, feeling the flame of jealousy, 'hello. Let me see your rosette.'

Rose looked up, and read my thoughts. She could almost have said, *But you took Nathan*. Instead, she raised her eyebrows and murmured to Lucas, 'Have you said hello to Mummy?'

I clasped Lucas to me. I don't know why I didn't defend myself and explain to Rose why I had been late. There was no reason for me to defend Poppy, except perhaps a curious loyalty.

Rose stacked the plastic picnic plates and mugs. She swept up the crisps packets and stowed them in the cool bag. 'Have you eaten? There's a sandwich left.'

'No, thank you.' My voice shook.

Rose's self-command was perfect. She dusted a shard of crisp from her finger. 'Now that you've turned up, I think perhaps I should go.' She picked up a canvas bag and hitched the handle over her shoulder.

A couple of yards away, a toddler was roaring for its

mother, a posse of children were playing tag, darting between the spread rugs, and one of the teachers was telling off a sullen girl with scraggy plaits. 'It's a long time since I've been at a sports day.' Rose pointed at the roaring toddler. 'Presumably it has a mother. By the way . . .' She hesitated. 'Minty, I don't know what you'd say to this, but Felix has been going on about a kitten. Would you allow me to get you one? I know a source.'

'No,' I said flatly. 'No kittens. No cats.'

'OK. It's just that it might help Felix –'

'Perhaps we shouldn't repeat this,' I said. 'It's too difficult. I'm sorry I ever involved you with the boys.'

'How silly, Minty.' Suddenly an angry red patch appeared on Rose's neck, and she was transformed from the cool creature of a moment ago to someone who was seriously angry. 'It can't do any harm and I'm interested in them. I like them.'

'Even so, Rose.'

'Nathan was right.'

'And what was he right about? What did you both conclude during your cosy chats?'

Rose stared at me, and her features hardened into acute dislike. 'Nothing.' She hitched the strap of her bag further up her shoulder and walked away.

23

I worked late into the night on the resurrected *Middle Age* idea. 'If we accept that time is an artificial construct,' I wrote in my notes, 'then what matters is experience. Experience is what tempers us and helps us to carry our mistakes. It also helps us to understand that death, which is waiting, informs life.'

Was that correct? Did I believe it? As a theory it sounded good, and convincing, and the people to whom it applied were the cream of the earth: the rounded, complete, mature personalities. It would be nice to think that I was among them.

I pushed aside the notes. The idea required further work because it was still gestating. It needed time to grow wings.

I rubbed my eyes and ran my fingers through my hair, which required cutting – goodness knew when that would be possible.

What had Nathan been right about?

What had he and Rose agreed about me?

I was on the switchback again.

I went to make some tea and, on the way, glanced up at the landing where the ironing-board was and where Rose, when she lived here, had placed her desk. She was still in this house, Nathan too.

I put the kettle on, unlocked the back door and went outside into the summer night.

What had Nathan and Rose decided between them?

I sat down on the bench and ran my fingernail along the table. There was lichen growing on it, and it needed scrubbing. I remembered Nathan sitting opposite me at this table. We had been married for three years and one day. Because it was such a warm evening, we were having supper outside, seafood pasta – I was eating the seafood without the pasta – and we had embarked on a negotiation as to where we should take a holiday.

'I want somewhere hot,' I said, as I always did so my pitch held no surprises.

He dug his fork into the pasta, twirled it expertly, then lifted it to his mouth. 'And I want to go Cornwall,' he said, as he always did.

'I've looked up a place on Rhodes. Nice villa by the sea. The boys would like it.'

'The boys are too young. When we took Sam and Poppy . . .' Nathan did not continue. He put down his fork and looked everywhere but at me.

That was the moment when a voice in me articulated clearly, 'Do you realize you've taken on enough history to fill a library?'

I got up, went inside and rattled in the cupboard for salt. I was ashamed and devastated by the revelation and also, curiously, calm because everything was now crystal-clear.

Nathan would never let go of his past life, *could* never let go.

He followed me into the kitchen. 'Minty, this has got to stop. I can't pretend I didn't have Poppy and Sam.'

'No,' I said.

Upstairs, one of the twins called. Nathan and I turned our heads in the direction of his cry. 'You or me?' asked Nathan.

On that at least we were united.

Now, in the kitchen, I ran hot water into the sink and plunged my chilled hands into it. Then I boiled the kettle and took a cup of camomile tea up to bed where I drank it. I switched off the light and lay down. After a while, I put out my arm and let it rest in the space that Nathan should have occupied.

Rose did not reply to the messages I left on her answerphone. I allowed two days to elapse. Then I took myself round to her flat after work.

She answered the door. She was dressed in a skirt I recognized from Prada, a leopard-print cardigan, and a necklace of large wooden beads. She looked wonderful, and not very surprised. 'I suspected you'd turn up sooner or later.'

She did not invite me in, so I summoned my best brand of gall. 'You didn't answer my calls. I've come to sort things out.'

Rose kept her hand on the door, and I said, 'Rose, if we get this over and done with, then it'll be over and done with.'

Eventually she stepped aside. 'Come in.'

The sitting room was a mass of flowers and smelt

gorgeous. 'I've just landed a one-off slot on a gardening series for television,' she explained. 'I'm doing small city gardens. People have been kind and sent flowers.'

'Who with?'

'The Activities Channel, but it's being made by Papillon. It probably won't get a large audience, but you have to grab these opportunities. Anyway, it'll be fun.'

'Papillon? That must be Deb.' I glanced at the label on a huge bunch of lilies, which read, 'Love from Hal'. 'How is Hal?' I asked.

'Fine. Busy.'

'I often wondered if you'd marry him.'

'As it happens, he has asked me.' Rose pointed to the blue chair. 'Sit down, Minty.'

I avoided the blue chair where Nathan had died and sat on the sofa. 'Why not marry him?'

'I like what I am. I'm fine as I am. I don't want change anything,' Rose replied, but her voice was not entirely steady. 'Hal's the sort of person who never leaves you, and he hasn't. So . . .' She fell silent. 'I don't know what to think. I may or may not. Probably not. I don't want the disruption. I've got used to thinking of myself as independent.' A flash of uncertainty and doubt. 'It's difficult at my age . . . so . . .' She switched the subject. 'Say whatever you want to say, then go. Let's not waste each other's time.'

My mouth and throat were dry, but I couldn't bring myself to ask her for a drink. 'I want to know about you and Nathan.'

'Nathan and I were married. We had two children. I

had a good job. Then I hired you and brought you home to meet him over spaghetti. You know the rest.'

'No,' I said. 'That's not what I am asking.'

Rose was keeping something back. The light played on her honey hair and creamy skin. In the past, Nathan had touched that hair and skin. They had belonged to him.

Thirsty, and burning with humiliation, I asked the question that had to be asked: 'Rose, did you take Nathan back as a lover?'

Rose shifted in the chair. Slender but not too slender, toned and groomed, she was a world away from the frazzled working mother I had first encountered in the Vistemax office. Yet she was vulnerable too. *It's difficult at my age.* And vulnerability had its own eroticism. Of course Nathan would have wanted her back.

She placed her hand on her chest in the region of the heart. 'It feels like a stone sitting on my chest, mourning Nathan. Like a gigantic attack of indigestion.'

'I know,' I said.

We could ask each other, Do you weep for him, like I do?
'*Do* you?'

'You're not answering the question.'

'That's because I'm not going to.'

I bit my lip. '*Tell* me, Rose. What was it you and Nathan decided?'

'He said you were ambitious.'

'So was he at my age. So were you. You had a fight with him about going back to work.'

334

The hand on her chest curled into a ball. 'It's irrelevant now. Old, old ground and I don't wish to go over it.'

'Old ground for you, perhaps.' I closed my eyes for a second. 'But Nathan didn't like it, and it was a source of friction.'

'For God's sake, Minty, what do you want?'

'I suppose . . .' I said miserably '. . . I want to tell you that he wasn't really happy with me. And that he regretted leaving you.' I hesitated, and then I forced out the words through gritted teeth. 'Did he come back into your bed?' Rose made a noise between a laugh and gasp, but I ploughed on: 'Nathan had been there so many times before . . .' Yes, he had shared the everyday language of small noises and touch with Rose. He had listened to her breathing in the night, heard her clean her teeth, fill the kettle . . . 'It wouldn't have been such a big step.' Rose held up a hand to stop me, but I ignored it. 'I could never share the long history you had with him. I could never compete. You were always there, ahead of me. Always.'

'Stop it, Minty.'

I had wit enough left to obey her.

Rose flashed a wry smile. 'I want never gets.' It was a saying we'd used often in the office. Once. Years ago. Timon, the editor, had always wanted more books, fewer books, different ones. *I want never gets.* Except, in that case, 'I want' usually did get. She continued, 'When Nathan first told me he was having an affair with you, I asked him why he'd told me. If someone's having an affair, they should be very clever and very secret. I still believe that.'

'Nevertheless I need to know.'

Rose's smile had vanished. She leant towards me to emphasize her point, and I smelt her jasmine scent. 'I don't have to tell you anything, Minty.' She spoke without malice, almost gently. 'You lost the right to my confidences long ago. I don't have to discuss anything with you and I certainly don't feel I have to help you sort things out.'

She got up and disappeared through the door, then returned with a bottle and glasses on a tray. 'You'd better have some of this. Hal brought it from Italy.'

As I accepted a glass, my blouse dug into the flesh under my arm. 'The boys ask after you quite a lot.'

Quick as lightning, I picked up the flash of delight that lit her face. 'The boys . . .' Her voice was soft, almost possessive. 'They are sweet.'

My instinct was to hiss, 'Keep off my sons.' Unreasonable, I knew. I looked down at my hands and struggled for mastery of myself. 'Old friendships and old loyalties. Do you remember? You talked about them at that supper when I first met Nathan. How hard it is to shake them off.'

She smiled grimly. 'Believe me, I could shake you off, Minty, with no trouble at all. It wouldn't take much.'

She meant it, and I flushed – not with anger but despair. As the woman who had pinched her husband, I was culpable, pitiable and all the other things that Rose cared to name. And yet all those years ago, I had witnessed her rush into the office, too-pink lipstick smudged, sweater ill-fitting, swearing that Nathan/the children had been difficult/demanding/cross, and I'd thought it was the other way round.

I drank my wine, and looked around the room. In its calm, ordered magnolia and cream, with the blue touches here and there, it reflected what Rose had become. And it was a room that had been arranged entirely to the satisfaction of its occupant. 'There are advantages to living alone,' I remarked.

She understood what I meant. 'Actually, yes.'

We exchanged a glance. *Funnily enough, we do understand each other.* Rose put down her glass and said, 'Nathan and I were married for a long time. We knew each other well. Just as . . . just as . . . you and I do. It was easy to pick up conversations.' She got up and walked over to the window. 'My life with Nathan was private until you came along. If our marriage had bad patches, and areas of blindness, it was ours and it worked, until you prised it apart. Then everyone took a good look, and it was open house.' She turned and stared at me, calm and steady. 'You'll admit that I don't owe you anything, Minty. No explanations. No loyalty.'

'Nathan came here because he wanted comfort, and conversation,' I cried. 'He didn't find them with me. Your bed would have been a natural progression.'

She leant her forehead against the curtain. 'Could be.' She sighed. 'Why don't you stop now and go away?'

'Because I'm angry with myself, Rose, but I'm also angry with Nathan.'

She swung round sharply on her heel. 'Didn't you once say to me that Nathan is dead – *dead*? Didn't you? In your so-matter-of-fact way?'

'Yes, I did.'

'Then leave him alone. Give him *some* peace.'

'You're right. I shouldn't be here.'

'Quite,' she said coldly. She poured a second glass of wine and hugged it to her chest. I made no move, and she said, 'Aren't you going? Go.'

What did the self-help manuals have to say on the subject of the second wife apologizing to the first? Those books that encouraged people to believe they could take a grip on their lives and make changes, that concocted dazzling fantasies of resolution, forgiveness and other castles in the air?

'I want to say sorry to you,' I admitted. 'I didn't realize what I'd done until I'd married Nathan and had the boys. Then it all seemed different, particularly when I grasped how disappointed Nathan was . . . at times. He used to look at me sometimes, and I could see how he hated what he'd done. It wasn't that he didn't care for me, but that he'd realized how much he cared for the things he'd discarded.'

Nathan had used Rose badly. I had used Rose badly. I already knew that the full import of one's transgressions don't really hit home until years after the event. The manuals don't mention that one. It was probably too complicated a subject for them to tackle.

'Poor Minty,' said Rose, and her irony cut me to the quick. She remained hunched over her wine, neither drinking it nor looking in my direction. 'You were welcome to him,' she admitted. 'He had hurt me so much. Sometimes I thought I'd die of the hurt. But you know the aphorism "This, too, will pass"? It's true, it does. Thank God. When he turned up here on the day he died, I didn't make him particularly welcome. Actually, I didn't want him here. I was busy. He could see that, and he was disappointed. But I didn't feel I had any reason to put myself out. I had spent so *long* shaking free, and Nathan's problems were not mine . . . I could no longer engage with him, not in the way he wanted . . . Actually, I blame myself for that.'

'It was a shame,' I managed. To be unwanted when you are dying must be terribly hard . . .

She gave a choking sound. 'For God's sake, he left me for you. Remember?' She turned an anguished face towards me. *'Remember?'*

'I think of it most of the time. Never more so than now.'

Rose made a visible effort. 'You have the twins to consider. Sam and Poppy suffered. You may think that they were too old, but they weren't and they did. I blame you and Nathan for that. There was nothing I could do to help them. You can't inflict your anger and mistakes on your children.' She twirled her glass between her fingers. 'I won't let you.'

A tiny pulse beat in Rose's temple and, no doubt, one did in mine. I fixed on the blank television screen in the corner of the room. 'I'm truly sorry about Poppy and Sam.' For good measure, I threw in, 'Poppy's taken it out on me. She's a fighter.'

Rose bent down and picked up a tiny mother-of-pearl button. 'That's Poppy for you. Sam's struggling a bit at the moment. I'm a little worried about him and Jilly . . . The job in America has thrown them both. They seemed so good for each other, but you never know. I want to be around to help, but I'm busy earning a living and getting on with my life and they have to sort themselves out.' Her voice was tender. 'Much . . . much as I love them.'

The tenderness excluded me. 'They're growing older, as I am, Rose, and more invisible.'

'Just as I felt, then.' She added, in a kinder voice, 'Grief saps the confidence, Minty. I can tell you that. But it can be fine in the end. Believe me.' She gestured at the room. 'When Nathan left, I felt I'd failed myself and the children, but I survived. It took blood and tears, but I did it.' She balanced the button on the palm of her hand. 'Nathan did what he wanted to do. I failed to see that he was changing. And why shouldn't he change? It was his right. But I didn't see it then. So, it wasn't all your fault, you know.' She was letting me off the hook, a little.

The wine had loosened my tongue. 'Roger and Gisela Gard came to dinner once. Believe it or not, I was playing office politics. One of the twins was naughty and Nathan dealt with it. I saw Roger watching him and I could almost hear him thinking, This is a man who's lost his stuffing and brimstone, and the thought flashed through my mind that it was better to be dead than a failure.' I put down my wine glass. 'The question is, did I wish Nathan's death on him, Rose? Did I?'

Rose swirled her wine round her glass. 'When Nathan left, I thought how much easier it would have been as a widow rather than a dumped wife. For a start, no one could have said it was my fault, unless I'd fed him hamburger and chips every night. If he'd died, the situation would have been easier to handle.'

'Yes.'

She put down her glass, and the gold ring gleamed. 'I still would have lost my job to you, wouldn't I?'

'Probably,' I conceded. 'I wanted it and I reckoned loyalty in the office was an old-fashioned concept.'

'And now?'

I thought of Chris Sharp. 'Much the same.' I looked down at the carpet. 'Was Nathan trying to humiliate me when he asked that you be made the boys' guardian?'

'Perhaps he was thinking of what was best for them.'

'Perhaps.'

Rose took my hand. The touch of her flesh on mine was unexpected. 'Minty, what you don't understand is . . . I had got away. Finally. At last. I had stopped dreaming about Nathan. I wasn't about to involve myself in his life again. I had cut him off.'

I allowed my hand to rest in hers and told her what festered in my mind. 'I never loved him, Rose, not truly. Not really truly. Not heart, soul, body and mind. He knew he was getting older and wanted different things, and I wasn't going to make it easy. If I'd loved him, I would have let him . . . oh, go to Cornwall, a million things.' My fingers pressed Rose's. 'I think he felt desperately alone.'

Rose took away her hand. 'I'm going to show you a letter, Minty.' She went to the desk in the corner, picked up a small Jiffy-bag, pulled out an envelope and handed it to me.

I spread out two closely written sheets of paper. 'My dearest Rose . . .' Didn't *'Dearest'* mean closest to my heart?

I have no right to ask what I am going to ask, but I have an idea it might be necessary. If you receive this letter, which I am lodging with Theo, then I will have judged correctly.

I am writing to ask you to remember that you were once good friends with Minty. If you are reading this, it means she is on her own with the twins. Of course, I have no idea how long that might be for. When I came over to see you in the flat, I asked you if you would be a guardian if anything should happen to me and to her, and the boys were still under age, and you said you would consider it. I can't think of anyone better to ask. It is a huge thing to lay on you, especially given our history, but I know you through and through, Rose, and there is no one I trust more . . .

For a moment, I could not continue. 'Oh, Nathan . . .'
'Are you OK?' asked Rose.
I nodded.

All I can say in mitigation for my actions towards you is that the complications of feelings and impulse take us to strange places. They certainly took me away from you, whom I loved, to Minty. But I loved Minty, too, and I want to say the following. There is so much in her to admire (you spotted it first when you became friends) and that still holds true. It has been difficult for her, and not as she expected. Thus, I ask you again, if she ever needs it and asks you for help with the boys, or even if she doesn't ask you, please will you do it?

I put down the letter, picked up my bag and got to my feet. 'Why didn't you tell me about this? I know I hurt you beyond words, but you *should* have told me.'

Rose's response was short and simple. 'Yes.'

'It would have made everything easier to bear.'

'Yes, I suppose it would. But I wasn't thinking about you, Minty.'

So Rose had taken her revenge on me with her silence, and I could have expected no better and no less.

My head swam, and I wanted very badly to go home. I managed to say, 'He knew I never loved him properly. Truly, properly.' I was weeping openly. 'It's in the letter.'

Rose folded it and put it on the desk. 'When he left me, I stopped loving Nathan the way *he* wanted. It was inevitable. There was no other way of surviving.'

We looked at each other. In that exchange lay the past we had shared, mourned and regretted. She picked up the Jiffy-bag. 'One more thing. He asked Theo to send this to me. I think it's a diary of sorts. I haven't read it, Minty. Or only a little bit. I couldn't. You should take it.' She placed the envelope in my hands and I peered inside. It was the missing notebook.

That, too, had gone to Rose.

The hardest thing of all to govern is the heart and I had finally understood that I couldn't blame Nathan for the struggle with his. If one's own nature and impulses are unfathomable, then to reach into other minds to make sense of the rage, passion and loyalties that lie within them is impossible. In our separate ways, Rose, Nathan and I had cheated each other and, in doing so, cheated ourselves.

'We must try harder, Rose, to make something out of this,' I said.

'Yes,' she said. 'Yes, we must.'

On my return to the house the boys, who had been watching for me at the window, ran out to greet me. I scooped them up, and hustled them inside. Then I closed the front door, leant against it and breathed deeply.

24

It was Friday, four weeks before Christmas. In the meeting room at Paradox I watched the clock inch past five thirty. Barry was in full flow and wasn't going to stop. What he had to say was interesting but I wished he had said it earlier in the day.

Chris propped his head in one hand. During a pause, he looked up. 'Are you in a hurry, Minty?'

'Not at all,' I replied coolly.

'We're coming to you in a minute, Minty,' Barry said.

In a feeble attempt to recognize the season, Syriol had draped a string of fairy-lights over the picture on the wall. It was by Shiftaka and I had persuaded Barry that it would be a good investment when he had decided to plough a proportion of Paradox's profits into an asset. (When I pointed out that his employees might be considered assets, Barry grinned and said he needed *fixed* assets.)

Shiftaka's painting depicted an abstract figure, half flesh, half skeleton, lying on a bed of glowing coals. The colours were violent reds, the blackest of blacks, and a white background that could only be described as dirty. The label read: *Kyoto RIP*. The jury's still out as to whether I consider Shiftaka a good painter or not, but I'm working hard on my 'uneducated' eye. Still, if

Barry *thinks* Shiftaka's cutting edge, it was a bargain.

When I had taken Barry to view it at Marcus's gallery, Marcus had been sitting at the desk, head bent over the laptop. At our entrance, he looked up and I was shocked: he appeared considerably older than I remembered. He took a second or two to place me and, when he did, there was an unmistakable flare of hope in his eyes, which was as quickly extinguished when it became obvious that I was not Gisela's envoy.

I had introduced the two men and explained that Barry was looking for an investment. Marcus swung into professional mode – easy of manner, patient, sizing up a potential client – and I thought how much nicer he was than Roger.

While Barry patrolled between the two rooms, Marcus turned to me and asked, in his unexpectedly deep voice, 'How's Gisela?'

'Fine, I think. I haven't seen much of her lately.'

He chose not to indulge in small-talk – another factor in his favour – and went straight to the point. 'She didn't seem to understand that I didn't want a wife. I wanted her. Not someone who stockpiles jam and checks the dinner menus. But when it came to a decision, I think she preferred it. Gisela has got used to being a professional wife.'

'I think you're right.'

Marcus's rightness, however, was of no help to him. 'What can she possibly gain with Roger? The dullness of such an existence . . . and I'm the one who loved her, not Roger.'

With regret, I noted the past tense. 'It's not dull, Marcus,' I pointed out. 'It's different.'

Barry had stopped prowling, and waved at *Kyoto RIP*. 'I'll take that one.' He pushed his face close to Marcus's. 'Now, you *are* sure I won't be throwing my money away?'

Marcus hadn't even blinked. 'Nothing is certain.'

So that was how Shiftaka had come to grace the walls at Paradox.

'Minty,' Barry had finally finished what he'd had to say, 'do you want to go ahead?'

I pulled my notes towards me. 'OK. Remember last year we discussed an idea for a programme on middle age? It didn't work. But this will. Three-part series on being a parent. *Baby Love*. The format? Each section to be an hour, featuring expert talking heads and personal experiences of parents. The programmes will ask: what are the stresses and strains of becoming a parent? Can you ever prepare for it? How does it affect a man and a woman physically and emotionally? What sort of impact do children have on marriages, friendships? How can it affect you if you become a step-parent to older children? How do you cope if you feel you're a failure as a parent? How do you *manage* as a lone parent?'

Good question. How do you manage as a lone parent?

Chris raised an eyebrow. Then he cleared his throat and made a note.

I continued: 'The trick will be to handle the material in a fresh, bold manner, and not be afraid to tackle the difficult aspects of being a parent. The programmes *have* to be honest and say things that most people only think. Children do change you. You don't always love them. Parents do fail. It is lonely.'

'Any up-side?' asked Chris.

'Oh, yes,' I replied. 'Plenty.' I thought of my beautiful sons and felt my spirit lift. 'But I'll leave that for the parents to describe. They'll do it best.' I picked up the treatment I had prepared and handed it to Barry. 'We want it fast, colourful, daring, and I think BBC1 should be the target.'

Chris frowned. Barry gazed thoughtfully at *Kyoto RIP*.

'Minty, thanks,' Barry said. 'Not quite convinced, but I'll think about it. We'll talk.'

'Think massive audience,' I urged. 'Trust me.'

Chris came into my office as I was shifting my papers into order. He closed the door and leant against it. 'I wanted to chew the cud about a few things, Minty.'

'Sure.' I clicked off my computer screen. As I did so, I noticed that my wedding ring was much looser and a vein running down my hand stood out in relief. Not a good sign. Film stars had hand lifts for less.

'You heard we got the Carlton deal for the documentary on the Pope?' He snapped his fingers. 'Should boost the quarterly figures.'

'Is that what you wanted to talk to me about? If so, can we do it tomorrow? I have to get home.'

Chris levered himself away from the door, and perched against my desk. Suddenly my small office was very cramped. The hazel eyes gleamed. 'You've had a tough year, Minty.'

His kindness was unexpected, and I was still having

trouble with kindness. It tended to reduce me. 'Yes. But I'm coming to terms with it and making my way.'

I needn't have wasted my energy: Chris's kindness was merely a vehicle for other considerations.

'Minty, it might be better if you were working for a bigger organization, which would have more slack for someone in your predicament. A very *real* predicament.'

There was no point in getting angry. If I was to survive at Paradox until such time as I wished to leave on my own terms, I could not be angry. 'Are you suggesting this or *telling* me?'

He smiled gently, and I could not decide whether it was genuine or not. 'Friend to friend, in this business it doesn't help to have additional pressures. A company as tight as Paradox needs to know it's functioning optimally with no unnecessary drag. You need to know, when a problem arises, that there's no problem in dealing with it, if you see what I mean.'

'Sweet of you, Chris,' I murmured.

In the old days, I would have deployed sex – which Nathan fell for. I would have opened my eyes, looked up from beneath the lids, and have made sure my cleavage was in the correct line of sight. I might have said, 'How nice of you to take an interest,' which would have introduced a faint chime of promise, sufficient to push Chris off the track. I'm not saying that I've come to despise such tactics, or would *never* use them again, only that sex took time and the boys would be waiting for me.

Instead I placed the last of my notes in my bag and

fastened it. 'Chris. Perhaps it would be better not to pursue this conversation. If you're trying to suggest that, as a working mother, I'm a liability, it could get you into trouble.'

No fool, he backed off at once. 'I was only thinking of you,' he said.

On the way home, I passed Paige's house. The front garden was ultra-smart because the gardener had recently completed the autumn spring-clean. 'You can't call it a *spring* clean,' I had pointed out to Paige, when I phoned her the previous day.

'I can call it what I like,' was her reply.

'Has Martin been to see you?'

Paige bristled. 'I *wish* you wouldn't interfere.'

'And?'

'He's here at the weekend. But I'm not taking him back, Minty. As I told you, I'm far too busy with the children to be married.'

The scene when I got through the door of number seven was much as I had pictured it. Eve had collapsed into a chair in the kitchen and a small riot was going on in the boys' bedroom. One of Eve's hands lay on the table, so white and thin that it alarmed me.

First, I tackled her. 'Look,' I said to the slumped figure, 'this is no good. It's been going on for months, and you haven't got properly better. You need to go home and see your family.'

She raised her face from her hands and I was startled by the light in her eyes. 'Go back?' She gulped a lungful of air – as if she was already breathing in the scents of river and mountains, of her home.

That decided it. 'You must go home for two weeks, see your family, rest, then come back.'

'I get coach.' Eve hauled herself to her feet, and her smile was pure joy. 'I telephone. Now.'

'No, it's a two-day journey both ways. You must fly.'

'The moneys.'

A stack of quick-fire calculations snapped through my brain. Eve needed a break. She needed her mother. Four days in a coach was not a rest. I needed Eve well and strong, as she herself wished to be. 'I'll pay your air fare, and you must go as soon as we can arrange it.'

As I went upstairs, preparing for riot duty, the rest of the calculation slotted into place. What with the hit my finances had taken with the loan to Poppy, Eve's air fare equalled a reduction in the Christmas-present list. It *definitely* put paid to the haircut, and the cost of her replacement would, no doubt, see off any strictly un-necessary seasonal frivolity. But that, I supposed, was what 'unnecessary' meant. You could do without it.

It was the day before Christmas Eve, the kind of day that paraded a weak sun as a joke. I eased the car into the parking slot and got out. It was very cold and I zipped up my fleece, powder blue, then turned up the collar. I could smell frosted leaf mould and the faintest whiff of frying fat coming from a van selling snacks parked further up.

I was relishing the moment of freedom, and allowing

my mind to drift, before I took up the slack in the reins and pulled them tight. Moments such as these kept me sane.

I was contemplating getting back into the warm car when a smart silver coupé drew up and parked in the space beside mine. One of the passenger doors flung open and Lucas tumbled out. 'Mum!'

He was followed closely by Felix. *'Mum!'*

Both were clutching picture books with an illustration of a dinosaur on the front. I knew this because Felix virtually pressed his into my face.

A figure emerged from the driver's seat in a tweed jacket, black trousers and boots. 'Hi,' said Rose.

She locked the car and, boys in tow, we moved off in the direction of the pond.

'Lucas didn't eat much lunch,' Rose reported. 'He was too excited. There was an exhibition about Tyrannosaurus Rex. The model ate model prey and snapped its jaws. Lucas was transfixed, and Felix . . . Well, I'm not sure he liked it much.'

'Was it crowded?'

'Was it *crowded*!'

We circumnavigated the pond once, and that was enough. It was scummy and the council's attempts to landscape it had only gone so far before the money had run out. It was too cold. By mutual consent, we retraced our steps to the cars. 'What are you up to?' I asked Rose.

'After Christmas I'm off to see Hal at the farm. I haven't seen him for weeks.' Her face registered anticipation and pleasure. 'After that Vietnam, I think. There's a piece I've got to do.'

We stood by the cars. 'Thank you so much for taking them today,' I said. 'I'm so grateful.' I fished out my car key, which had become attached to a piece of chewed bubble-gum, which I had confiscated recently from Lucas. Rose extracted her key from a brilliant green lizard-skin handbag and zapped the lock. 'Next time I'll take them to the zoo. When it gets warmer.'

We leant towards each other, and an awkward second elapsed as we clashed cheeks and exchanged the lightest of kisses.

'Thanks,' I said again.

'That's fine.' She kissed Felix and Lucas on the top of their heads. 'Be good boys, and remember what I told you.'

When the twins had been strapped into their seats, Rose and I drove off in opposite directions. Before she disappeared, Rose tooted her horn.

I drove back through the streets as people made their way home from work. It seemed that there were couples everywhere. Hand in hand. Talking. Sharing a bottle of water or chips. Some had their arms round each other. One man had his hand tucked into the pocket of his girlfriend's jacket. At the corner of Albert Bridge Road and Battersea Bridge Road, a couple was wrapped in each other's arms. As I drove past, I caught a glimpse of the girl's face. It was enraptured, alight, quivering with a new dawn.

My eyes smarted with tears.

I had not read a self-help manual in weeks. For one thing, I've hunted out the statistics. 'The most likely customer for a book on any given topic,' concluded one researcher, 'was someone who had bought a similar work within the past eighteen months.' This begged the question: if self-help manuals are so good at solving the problem, why would you need to buy another *on the same subject*?

'What did Rose tell you to remember?' I asked the boys eventually.

Lucas went, 'Roar, roar. That's the dinosaur eating the horse.'

'They weren't *horses*,' said Felix. 'Not then.'

'Boys, what did Rose ask you to remember?'

In the rear mirror, I watched Felix's brow wrinkle with effort. 'She said we looked more like Daddy every day,' he said.

I put out my tongue and licked my cheek where the tears continued to run. Rule Six is taken from something Rose said. *You must hold on, for this, too, will pass.*

Poppy had been a little sour about the family decision to hold Christmas lunch at number seven. 'Richard and I could almost be offended,' she pointed out, 'and our house is bigger.'

She had been mollified, however, when it was arranged that Jilly and Frieda would drive up from Bath, Sam would fly in from the States and they would stay with Poppy for a couple of days. Jilly was pregnant again and, in the latest bulletin, Sam announced that they had agreed she would remain in the UK until after the birth – 'We couldn't afford to have a baby in the States' – then join Sam in Austin.

The boys and I chose the Christmas tree from the trader at the corner of Lakey Street and brought it home with a selection of particularly nasty coloured baubles, and coloured lights with which they had fallen in love. It had been no use protesting that silver balls and white lights were prettier. They simply didn't see it. Any idea I might have cherished of a sophisticated, elegant tree disintegrated in the face of a determined pair of twins.

After all, and after everything, it was their tree.

We put it in the hall. Felix and Lucas did their best to hold it steady while I crawled underneath it to screw it into the stand. The three of us stood back to assess the effect. 'Mummy,' pronounced Felix, seriously, 'it's a bit crooked.' I bit my lip. This had been Nathan's job, and he had been expert in the fine-tuning. I saw 'Daddy' float through their minds, and I said, 'You're so picky, Felix,' but I crawled back under the pine-scented branches and thought, *You should see me now, Nathan.*

I planned everything down to the last detail. Presents: bath oil for the women, which I had employed Syriol to wrap – she was keen to earn a bit extra – and a good bottle of wine each for the men. Food: the turkey, ready-made gravy, cranberry sauce, bread sauce, vegetables and pudding were to be delivered by the supermarket. I reckoned I could manage to peel the Brussels sprouts and potatoes with the boys' help.

A big smile plastered across her wan face, Eve had

flown home on Christmas Eve with so much luggage – mostly sweaters and socks from M&S – that I was convinced she wouldn't get through check-in.

I had filled the stockings several days previously.

On Christmas Day, I had been up at dawn laying the table. Having thought long and hard about the *placements*, I decided that Sam should be at the head with his mother and Jilly on either side. Richard was at the other end of the table with me. Poppy had volunteered to sit between the twins so that she could keep an eye on them. 'You're to make decent conversation,' I had admonished them. 'What's decent?' asked Felix.

Sam arrived early, straight from the airport. He was tired, unshaven and foul-breathed. I sent him up to the spare bedroom where he could wash and brush up in peace. The rest arrived half an hour later.

There was confusion as to whether the presents should be opened before or after lunch, but I put my foot down and announced that lunch would burn if we delayed. Sam carved, and Richard poured the wine. Poppy had provided the candles, which were red, glittering and, to be honest, would not have been my first choice – and played cat's cradle with the twins while the food was served. With one arm round Frieda, Rose talked earnestly to Jilly.

No one paid me much attention, but that was fine, particularly as I was busy in the kitchen. That was how I wanted it. As we sat and ate, conversation flew back and forth across the table, little snippets of gossip, an old joke, a snatch of reminiscence. Only so much could be expected from six-year-olds, and before long the boys had decided they were jumping beans and Richard had to swap places to help Poppy control them.

When I emerged from the kitchen with two puddings burning merrily, there was a spatter of applause. I sat down, head spinning, speechless and not hungry. At that moment, Rose sent me a little smile.

We discussed jet-lag. 'I've been taking melatonin,' Sam rubbed his face, 'but it's not great.'

'You should try arnica. The pills, I mean,' Rose said.

'It might be better if you didn't quaff huge quantities of wine on board.' Poppy leant over to poke her brother. 'Eh?'

'Who are you to lecture us on behaviour?' Sam grinned all the same. 'I know where your secrets are buried.' For a second, Poppy's eyes were dark with terror. Under the table, I felt for her hand. After a moment Poppy's fingers tightened on mine. Sam continued: 'Who snitched the chocolate bunny from Gavin in the fifth form? That's what I want to know.'

After the pudding Sam got to his feet, wine glass in hand. 'We need a toast,' he said. 'Absent friends.'

'Dad . . .' cried one of the twins, and I swivelled round to see which.

There followed a heartbreaking, emotion-filled silence, which no one wanted to last. The twins wriggled, Frieda pulled a face, and the adults drank the toast. *Absent friends*.

At which point, Frieda threw herself back in her chair and overbalanced. 'Oh, for goodness' sake,' said Jilly,

'I told you not to do that.' Then she remembered it was Christmas and wiped the frown off her face. 'Come here, sweetheart. I'll kiss you better.'

Sam produced a digital camera. 'OK. Best smiles,' he ordered. 'Mum, can you move up a bit? Frieda, sit *still*. Lucas, can you get on to your mum's lap? Thank you.'

We held our poses, there were several clicks, and Sam fiddled with the camera. 'Have a look,' he said and passed it round.

Rose was in the middle of the group, with Jilly beside her. Richard's eyes were red. Lucas had moved at the crucial moment and, consequently, was a little blurred. Felix was pointing at something. Poppy was gazing at Richard. And me? I was positioned in the left-hand corner of the photo, looking tired, which was not surprising. 'It's quite good of you, Minty,' Poppy commented, and handed the camera back to Sam.

Rose sat herself down beside me. 'I've been thinking about the garden, as you asked. We could put the catmint by the fence. It would look good there, and leave space for the boys to play. What do you think?'

A candle guttered, and I leant forward to shield the flame. It was hot against my flesh and I flinched. 'Mum!' shrieked Felix. 'Mum! Can we have presents?'

The flame steadied, and I took my hand away.

A WRITING LIFE

Elizabeth Buchan

© Ian Philpott

BECOMING A WRITER

Looking back, I think I always wanted to be a writer without knowing it. A rather solitary child, I read voraciously for solace and to escape. I scribbled down notes about what I had read and what it had meant to me. As a small child, I loved stories of wild animals, and very often ended up sobbing when something terrible happened to them (which it usually did). I can also remember dimly the Famous Five and the sense of galloping excitement I got as I was precipitated into their adventures. Luckily, as a teenager, I was much more ambitious, and made myself read history and biography as well as fiction. It did not take long to learn from my reading of biography that I was incurably nosy about other people's lives. My responses – being enraptured, sometimes puzzled or shocked, or just plain swept away – to the treasure chest in the local library that I plundered on a daily basis was, I am sure, a subconscious preparation for a writing life.

In my late twenties, I began to realize that there was something niggling at the back of my mind, a desire that I could not quite pin down. At the time I was working at Penguin Books as a blurb writer, which turned out to be just the right nursery slope for the apprentice writer. Part of my job was to read through the Penguin list – from classics to cookery books, and political polemics to poetry. It was a free education for which they paid me. All the same, I sensed I was marking time.

But I also had small children and it was difficult enough to pack everything into the day. However, it was the stuffed day conundrum that provided the answer because I finally realized there was never going to be a right time to write. Thus, the only thing to do was to get on with it.

In general, I wanted to write the books I loved to read. I wanted to be educated and provoked; I wanted to be made to think and to be entertained in the widest possible sense and I wanted to laugh and, sometimes, to cry. If I could achieve some of those things in my own writing, I would be happy. Between that ambition and the blank page which now faced me, there was a considerable mountain to climb. Not least was the task of developing the writer's muscles – technical skill, confidence, stubbornness and the ability to concentrate. The learning curve was steep. Writing, in my case at least, proved hard work, but the process was full of surprises and never-ending interest.

MY LIFE AS A WRITER

The early days of writing were exacting. I got up very early in the morning to write one page before the children woke up and I went off to work. In the evenings, after the children were in bed, I wrote one more page. (Ten novels later, my working life is less penitential, and I look back and wonder how I did it but at the time it seemed the only way.) But I calculated that if I wrote one page, it would turn into two and two would turn into four, and so on. That tiny, daily progression was an optimistic and thrilling one, and made it worthwhile.

Where I write is very important to me. I have a little eyrie at the top of the house that used to be the baby's room until I pinched it. Up there, I'm surrounded by a haphazard pile of books and papers. I usually have about thirty to fifty reference books in easy reach for any one book that I'm writing and every so often I'll pick one out to check a fact or a date. From the window, I look down onto my terraced London garden and every twenty minutes or so (the limit of my concentration span) I look up and out at a motley garden theatre below – squirrels, foxes, jays all competing for territory, and I am constantly haring downstairs to rescue frogs from the jaws of my two cats.

Routine is very important to me too. Most days, I get up early, feed the cats, make my breakfast and take it to the spare room so I don't wake my husband. Breakfast in bed is my great luxury. The cats come up and settle either side of me and I read the newspaper. I'm usually in my office by about 8.30am where I work through until lunchtime. Often I get tempted out to lunch but if I'm in the last stages of a book I work through the day. To limber up for the day's writing, I will work through my most recently written chapter, tweaking sentences, and correcting words or phrases. This gets me back into the flow of the chapter before I start the proper writing.

I always write three drafts of each novel. I use the first to work out its structure or scaffolding – theme, plot and narrative. The second is for constructing the muscles, by which I mean the characters' motivations and psychology. By the time I reach the third draft, I really know the novel and I am writing from a position of strength which allows me to work in all sorts of subtleties, resonances and ironies that were not there in the first draft. I usually write from scratch so I rewrite a novel three times.

WHAT I WRITE ABOUT

Early on, I was amazed to discover that the subject chose me – the writer – rather than the other way around. I was wandering up and down the history shelves in the London Library when I picked out a volume about Paris during the Revolution that had been compiled by a contemporary a few years after the Revolution. Inside, there was a fold-out map of Paris surrounded by the *barrière*, the customs wall containing within it a population heaving with new ideas and resentments against a worn-out *ancien regime*. I fell in love with the subject on the spot. That was how I decided to write *Daughters of the Storm*.

Thus, I was pitchforked into the delicious and addictive process of research from which a couple of important considerations emerged. Rule number one: there is always another fascinating snippet to extract from the ether. Rule number two: you can have too much of a good thing. One of the things I had to learn was how to balance my research, and limit myself to using the one or two facts that would really propel the novel. My two early novels, *Daughters of the Storm* and *Light of the Moon*, were stuffed with research and, on re-reading them, I can see how easy it is to overburden the crucial elements such as character, plot and narrative with just one more of those fascinating titbits.

But the best research has always been inspired by other

writers, both good and bad. My childhood habit of analysing what I read has never left me, and sinking effortlessly into a novel by bold and invigorating writers such as Anne Tyler, Ian McEwan, Margaret Atwood or Antonia Byatt offers true insight and refreshment. On the other hand, you have to be careful not to be overwhelmed by feelings of admiration or to be daunted by how good they are. Always, I try to learn from them. For example: if I was dealing with the theme of jealousy, I might re-read *Anna Karenina* to see how Tolstoy handles Anna's disintegration.

For the early novels, I chose to hone in on the twin watersheds of revolution and war – terrific scenarios in their own right. The drama of those historical backdrops was also very convenient as I could throw my characters up against them, extracting passion, adventure and danger from the situations in which they found themselves. Then, as I went on, I became more interested in looking at the quieter aspects of our lives. Is it not true that the important moments of illumination or change in anyone's life very often happen when we are doing something as mundane as peeling potatoes or changing the sheets?

I very much like the notion of Jane Austen's 'square of ivory' onto which she painted her stories of one or two families which such brilliance. She was concerned with getting her heroines (in good moral shape) to the altar but, after that, she is silent. Contemporary novelists give themselves more leeway and, among other considerations, marriage is a fertile subject to write about.

The 'health' of marriage – and judging by the divorce figures this a little rocky at present – is an indication of what is going on with people and the society they live in. Until recently, it was considered one of the building blocks of society. It was sanctified by the church, and ratified by the state. Governments and experts talked about the family and made decisions and assumptions based on the old nuclear unit. That is all changing. There are many reasons for this and people will argue as to what they are and why.

In my own novels, I have written about wives who stayed with the absent and erring husband, and wives who have been abandoned. In an earlier novel, *Consider the Lily*, I wrote about an initially loveless marriage and how it was transformed into something that worked. In each of these situations, there were hugely interesting psychological and social aspects to fictionalize. For example, in *The Good Wife*, the wife decides to stay with her husband because she does not want to damage her daughter and she decides to take the risk. In *That Certain Age*, the contemporary heroine has to try and balance marriage and motherhood with her work. In *The Second Wife*, I compare two other marriages to Minty and Nathan's. Some might conclude that the bargain Gisela has struck with Roger to be questionable but the marriage works. More problematic is Paige and her marriage to Martin, but Paige is undergoing a type of transition as she pushes herself back on track from having three children after giving up a high-powered career.

My unwritten rule is never to base the characters on anyone I know or think I know. I may borrow certain characteristics – a passion for something, a particular way of talking, or an attitude – to drop the grit into the oyster around which the layers are then built. Beyond that, the characters are my own creation and, just as important, they have to be managed. The novel is an artefact and I am its author. To lose control of the

REVENGE OF THE MIDDLE-AGED WOMAN

After seven novels, the inspiration for *Revenge of the Middle-aged Woman* arrived when I stumbled across the aphorism: living well is the best revenge. That's all very well, I reflected, but how do you do it? Once again, a subject had chosen me. At the time, there was a lot in the press about divorce, younger wives and the reactions of deserted middle-aged women. Running through as a subtext was always a subtle denigration of, and a pessimism about, middle age, which seems surprising considering we all get there in the end. I decided to write a story that would take middle age as a theme, and to write about its grief, surprises and discoveries as truthfully as I could. I took the obvious situation: a forty-something woman left by her husband for a younger woman, and explored how she pulled herself together and instigated the healing process.

As I planned the novel, I became increasingly exhilarated by the subject because it seemed to me that the qualities and intelligence that a middle-aged woman brought to a situation like this were quite different and probably more substantial than those a younger woman would bring. Ultimately, I ended up with Rose, a woman who wouldn't have chosen her situation but who actually weathers it with, I hope, grace and humour.

THE SECOND WIFE

I had no idea I would write a sequel but the response to *Revenge of the Middle-aged Woman* had been extraordinary. I received letters from readers from all over the world telling me how they felt about the novel. Many of them asked me what happened next to Rose, Nathan and Minty. Hey presto, once again, a subject had chosen me. What happens when the mistress becomes the wife? And what sort of emotional drama does it engender – extreme hatred, unease, social comedy or, even, reconciliation of sorts?

In writing about Minty second time round, I had to contend with a number of problems. Pretty, glossy Minty was the villain in *Revenge of the Middle-aged Woman*, so I had to engender empathy for her without betraying what she was in the first book. Even office sex kittens grow up, and Minty embarks on her journey to maturity as she tackles a situation where Nathan, her husband, turns out to be both tired and disappointed and she herself is surprised and alarmed by what she has taken on. Like Rose before her, Minty has to search for resilience and humour in order to survive and, in the end, it is her response to motherhood that is her redeeming quality.

One of the themes of *The Second Wife* is that of feeling second-best, something that I think many of us experience at some time in our life. In Minty's case, she encounters the presence of the first wife everywhere she goes. In essence, Rose is everywhere in the house where Minty lives, from the attic to the cellar. Another theme which always preoccupies me is the bargains and accommodations which people make with each other. Minty and Rose's relationship is technically finished and yet ... and yet. I felt that the way to portray the relationship between the two women was perhaps not the obvious one. To sum it up: they are never quite done with one another; they cannot be. Given the drama and anguish all parties have experienced, how do they absorb the fact of each other in their respective lives? They can never again be good friends but they are linked by elements that are almost stronger – by memory and by the children.

And how does the husband fit into this? I like Nathan and I feel sorry that he made a mistake. Nevertheless, and this is not to be overly moralistic, he cannot escape the consequences of his passion for Minty. Instead of contemplating a liberated future at fifty-something as Rose is doing, he finds himself back at the beginning of a cycle with a new, young family. Writing about Nathan's feelings made me focus on the question of how we pace ourselves. After his experiences, I am pretty sure Nathan would argue that the timing of our decisions and actions is crucial to the success of our lives.

I was astonished when a reader pointed out how large a part death plays in my novels. That set me thinking and I concluded that, by writing novels that hope to have a degree of realism or emotional truth about them, I have to face the subject of death in some way. It is 'the other' again, the flipside of life. If novels deal with living, then death should be there too. In *The Second Wife*, I took my most intimate look at it as I recalled the memories of that time after the death of my father, which was a huge blow for our family. It was not an easy experience and I discovered the power of the tiny detail to affect me the most. For instance, sorting out my father's ties after his death was one of the most upsetting moments. They were so much a part of him and to discard them was to say the final goodbye.

As I plotted *The Second Wife*, I realized that having Nathan die would be a way of creating a flashpoint for Minty. If he was absent then the novel would not just be an examination of a stumbling marriage, but could also explore other things: bereavement, parenthood, how to absorb oneself into a family who does not want you and coping with children. How would Minty deal with her regrets, her guilt and her grief? How was she going to square up financially? How she was going to work? How would she keep her sense of humour? To do that, Nathan was sacrificed.

I did not do vast amounts of factual research for *The Second Wife*. I just watched what was going on around me, and the marital dramas in the book are a reflection of what goes on everywhere. I was lucky enough to talk to several second wives who were generous with their funny/sad anecdotes about occupying the lowest rung in a family's pecking order. They had experienced the icy chill of the back row in the church during the christening of the grandchild belonging to the other wife. They had been pointedly excluded from the group family photograph. They had endured abuse from the children of the first family, and also financial hardship. Some of the material makes for robust social comedy although I am quite sure it is not so funny if you are on the receiving end of it ...

MY NEXT NOVEL

The novel I am writing at the moment is different. Once again, I had no control over the subject. On a whim, I walked into the Victoria and Albert Museum and decided to look at a tiny exhibition of illuminated pages which, probably during the nineteenth century, had been cut out of a medieval Book of Hours and sold to collectors. I took one look at the exquisite, glowing miniatures and that was it! No argument. In precisely five minutes, the new novel was sorted and I returned home with it complete in my head.

The Book of Hours has taken me back to the broader canvas. It centres on a curator, Amy, who is searching for a lost Book of Hours. In their heyday, rich patrons commissioned them from the best artists and the beautifully painted pictures accompanied the prayers that were supposed to punctuate the days. They were highly prized objects and very often handed on from mother to daughter in an epoch when women rarely had control of their property or money. These books also exerted considerable religious power but, by the nineteenth century, they had become collectors' objects. In *The Book of Hours*, Amy's search is crucial to putting her life together after a tragedy. Equally, the making of the book was crucial to its painter who was searching for ways to make art better and deeper, and to the woman who commissioned it, as she longed to be free to live her life as she wished. As Amy edges closer to finding the lost Book of Hours, she discovers that Chiara d'Alessi had a strange and extraordinary story and, if Amy looks hard enough, she will find out what it was.

The Book of Hours is about an emotional, psychological and historical journey. It will have lots of detail about medieval life and painting, and also about the highly charged contemporary art world which seethes with ambitions and egos, and is driven by a combination of big money and a love of beauty.